Lifelong romance addic... Zealand. Writing feeds... happy endings and the e... You can follow her at jc... jcharroway, instagram.co... and twitter.com/jcharroway.

Cara Lockwood is the *USA TODAY* bestselling author of more than seventeen books, including *I Do (But I Don't)*, which was made into a Lifetime Original movie. She's written the Bard Academy series for young adults and has had her work translated into several languages around the world. Born and raised in Dallas, Cara now lives near Chicago with her two wonderful daughters. Find out more about her at caralockwood.com, 'friend' her on Facebook, facebook.com/authorcaralockwood, or follow her on Twitter, @caralockwood.

ONE NIGHT ONLY

JC HARROWAY

NO STRINGS

CARA LOCKWOOD

MILLS & BOON

First Published in Great Britain 2018
by Mills & Boon, an imprint of HarperCollins*Publishers*
1 London Bridge Street, London, SE1 9GF

One Night Only © 2018 JC Harroway

No Strings © 2018 Cara Lockwood

ISBN: 978-0-263-26645-0

MIX
Paper from
responsible sources
FSC® C007454

This book is produced from independently certified FSC™ paper
to ensure responsible forest management.
For more information visit www.harpercollins.co.uk/green.

Printed and bound in Spain
by CPI, Barcelona

ONE NIGHT ONLY

JC HARROWAY

MILLS & BOON

To E
for inspiring the fun, bubbly, caring Essie. x

CHAPTER ONE

IF THIS SETTING, so far from the wreckage he'd left behind in New York, couldn't provide ballast, nowhere could. Ash Jacob closed his eyes, sucked in a deep breath and focussed on the sun warming his back, the hypnotic chatter of English birdsong and the continuous distant hum of London traffic.

'Shit!'

The violent exclamation pulled him up short. So he wasn't the only one having a bad day. His vision hazed as the bright July sunlight hit his retinas once more, his surroundings sharpening into focus. He stretched one arm along the back of the park bench, the wooden slats of which dug into his fatigued muscles—a reminder that he'd spent twelve hours on a plane yesterday, largely bent like a pretzel despite his first-class seat.

'Bloody, buggering, shit.'

What a charming turn of phrase.

His mouth twitched and his mood lightened. She stood a short distance away from his secluded spot in St James's Park, her short, flowery dress revealing bare, shapely legs; golden hair streaked with enough russet to turn her long ponytail to fire in the right light; a small denim backpack slung over one shoulder, which made her appear younger than what he estimated as mid-twenties.

A student? A tourist? A fellow soul, far from home?

One delicate finger jabbed at the screen of her phone, as if she could poke it back to life by dogged persistence alone.

Intrigue and a flicker of lust made Ash sit up straighter. Her quirky English accent and endearing choice of expletives reminded him that New York was a long way away. And yes, the women in his exclusive, affluent circle had the kind of polish and poise that this beguiling stranger seemed, at first glance, to lack, but the effect of the jut of her pert breasts and the cut of her fine-boned features in profile on his jet-lagged libido equalled, if not surpassed, his usual level of interest in the opposite sex. An interest that circumstances had shaped into two simple rules: one—on his terms; and two—one night only.

He shifted on the hard seat, his jeans becoming skintight, at least around the groin. The beauty dropped the hand holding the offending device to her side and cast her wide eyes around their corner of the park.

Ash slammed his own stare closed again, pretending to enjoy the formerly relaxing ambience. He'd come to London to work on a joint business venture with his oldest friend, not to rescue an English damsel, no matter how long her legs or how curvaceous her ass. And more importantly, he'd come to get away from public drama and get his life back under control. Control that couldn't come soon enough.

'Um, excuse me...'

Damn.

She'd moved that delectable derrière of hers closer. There were few people around, mainly joggers and the odd parent pushing a stroller. She *must* be talking to him. Ash relaxed his eyelids and slowed his breathing. Perhaps if she thought he was asleep, she'd leave him alone. Find someone else to rectify her technology issues.

Her footfalls scuffed the gravel of the path.

There was an embarrassed tinkle of laughter.

Right in front of him now.

Close enough for her scent to tickle his nose— light, floral and mixed with the unmistakable smell of sunscreen.

His libido roared anew. Man, would he love to see those curves and that milky skin clad in a bikini and sprawled on a lounger at his holiday place in the Hamptons.

The sexy intruder delicately cleared her throat.

The sweet sound rolled over his out-of-sync senses. Physically, she embodied the epitome of his type. Under other circumstances, he'd turn on the charm, get to know her enough to assess if her persuasion for no-strings sex aligned with his, and pass a satisfactory afternoon between her thighs.

But the last thing he needed right now was an encounter with a woman *that* beautiful, especially one who awoke his interest to the degree currently rendering him momentarily trapped on the park bench by his tight jeans.

He'd been played in the past—the old, female-inflicted wound recently reopened in the most humiliating and public way being the main reason for his rather hasty departure from New York.

For now, women were categorically off the agenda.

And really, who talked to complete strangers in a city centre park? His appearance today could only be described as dressed down compared to his usual attire of bespoke tailored suits. He'd wanted an escape from the cloying, air-conditioned hotel he'd booked for his first couple of nights in London until the Jacob Holdings apartment had been spring-cleaned. Some fresh air. Green spaces. Anything that helped to reprogram his brain from its current gut-churning cycle of guilt and bile-inducing self-loathing.

So he'd thrown on a T-shirt and his comfortable jeans, both the worse for wear having spent forty-eight hours in a suitcase, forgone shaving off the three days' worth of scruff and headed outdoors. The casual look was a visual cue that his move to London represented a major change from the norm; a shift from everything he'd lived, breathed and strived for these past ten years: his role in the family business, which was fraught with dysfunctional politics in the hands of his ruthless, manipulative and, as he'd bitterly discovered in the most degrading way, cheating father.

'Excuse me, are you…okay?'

Ash surrendered to the soothing voice with a sigh that dragged his mind back from the edge of a dark abyss. She wasn't going to give up. Perhaps she was lost. He didn't know London that well, but he'd spent enough time here over the years to have a vague sense of direction. Better to hear what she wanted and send her gorgeous ass on its way.

He opened his eyes, forcing his face to exhibit a tight, inquisitive smile instead of the frustration that put his teeth on edge at having the embodiment of feminine temptation literally thrown into his path.

'Of course. Just enjoying the sun.'

Her answering beam had two opposing effects on his overwrought body: the fullness of her pouty lips direct-messaged his groin with a slug of not wholly unwelcome blood-pounding heat, and her open, friendly stare twitched his shoulders up several notches until his muscles cramped. Were all English women this naive? This trusting? For a man who trusted no one, she was a complete mystery.

'Oh, good. I don't suppose I could ask for a favour…?' She waggled her dead phone in front of his face. 'My phone just died.'

'Okay… Are you lost?'

Give her some damn directions and watch her groan-worthy legs walk away.

But then his view would be far less appealing.

Another megawatt smile warmed his insides and made him think of childhood trips to Coney Island.

'No. I wondered if you could take a picture for

me.' She pointed at the view of the London Eye in the distance. 'On your phone…and perhaps…send it to me?' Her voice wavered and she curled some escaped strands of hair at her nape around her index finger.

His expression must have been comical. Had he woken up in some parallel universe or was her friendliness some sort of ancient British ritual? Did he care if it meant a few more seconds surreptitiously eyeing her glorious body and fantasising about her naked under him?

Ash shifted, discreetly readjusting himself in his pants as he allowed his gaze to properly take in every inch of porcelain beauty. Up close, she was stunning. Flawless creamy skin, enormous sky-blue eyes and a charming dusting of copper freckles across her slightly upturned nose. And on first impressions— the embodiment of a sunny disposition.

And if she wanted a photo, she was clearly a tourist. Perhaps this was her last day in London?

Another point to his libido.

As if matching his interest, she flicked her stare over him from head to toe, skimming over his creased tee and well-worn jeans and flooding his body with heat to rival the summer sun. Was she flirting?

'Sure,' he said.

Why not? He could surely oblige her with a photo and perhaps anything else she might want. He lifted one eyebrow as her eyes returned to his face. Bright spots of red appeared on her high cheekbones as she straightened the charming little head tilt she'd employed while checking him out. Yes, perhaps she was exactly what he needed… A little help with his current hard-on predicament. She seemed to share his physical interest. Perhaps that would cure his mind-numbing restlessness and get his usual focus back on track.

The tension snapped with her tinkling laughter. Ash grinned back. At least she owned her flagrant sexual curiosity in him—how refreshing. He reassessed her age—perhaps she wasn't as sweet as she looked. She flicked her ponytail, sunny smile back in place.

He shifted on the bench, fishing his phone from his back pocket. The angle of the sun meant her dress was practically see-through from his position. Should he tell her? Or just enjoy her shapely silhouette? Imagine those long legs wrapped around his waist…

No.

His mind zapped to ancient history come back to haunt him. His recent discovery of the lengths his ex had gone to in order to deceive him, and the depth of that lie, only confirmed his stand on the opposite sex. He was done with women, unless they, like him, wanted one thing only and understood the rules.

The weathered wooden rungs of the bench creaked as she sat next to him. 'You're American, aren't you?'

He nodded and then looked away from her open, earnest face. At least this woman couldn't be interested in the prestige and power of his family name or his considerable personal fortune, dressed the way he was. She couldn't know his family owned half of Manhattan and a sizeable chunk of London. She couldn't guess he'd come to London to distance himself from his 'real estate tycoon' reputation—as well as from the ruthless deception by one family member in particular. Not unless she read the society pages of the *New York Times*.

He tasted bile. How could his father do that to him? To his own son? Making a mockery of the years of professional loyalty Ash had given the family business? Fuck—did he have 'trusting schmuck' stamped across his forehead?

The sexy stranger didn't seem aware of his inner turmoil. She turned her body to face him so her bare knees bumped his denim-clad thigh, eyes alight. 'London is an amazing city, isn't it? Have you seen Buckingham Palace? It's just over there.' She pointed over her shoulder, warming to her change of subject and speaking with dizzying speed in her excitement about the tourist attractions the city had to offer.

'And do you know about the Seven Noses of Soho? I'm scouting them out today. Fun fact…' She pointed towards the small lake in the park. 'Did you know the pelicans were a gift from a Russian ambassador to King Charles the second in 1664?'

She talked so quickly, her charming accent distorting the English until she might as well have been speaking Mandarin. Noses? Pelicans? Perhaps the impotence coiled inside him was steadily infecting and destroying his brain cells. Perhaps he was more jet-lagged than he'd assumed. Perhaps testosterone had fried his usual laser-sharp mind.

'So, you wanted a picture?' He unlocked his phone and leaned forward, preparing to stand. Do a good deed for the beautiful English rose so he could get on with trying to cobble his shit back together. He could no longer pretend that his sole motivation for coming to London was for a new business opportunity. Other factors had made him flee across the Atlantic—his guilt at forcing his mother to face her sham of a marriage, and the shameful publicity that had followed his bust-up with his father. Belonging to a high-profile family had its distinct downsides.

But he'd left all that behind.

Focus on the here and now.

London, the rich culture and vibrancy of the city, provided abundant distractions, though none quite as appealing as the distraction warming the sliver of space between her body and his and momentarily taking his mind from his troubles.

'How long have you been here?' Another head tilt, her tongue peeking out to swipe her lower lip.

A silent groan rattled his skull.

So not fair.

'A day or two.' How could he ignore such delicious temptation right in front of him? Surely he'd read her signals correctly. The perfect diversion sat before him looking at him as if he were a tasty snack—what could be more temporary than two travellers making a connection and enjoying one lost night in London?

No need to confess his real identity—one of New York's top corporate attorneys, a real estate mogul and heir to the Jacob fortune. Not that he wanted to publicise any association with his bastard father right now. Hal Jacob's ruthless streak had long made Ash wince. But even he hadn't seen the train wreck approaching, hadn't anticipated the far-reaching, closer-to-home consequences.

He scrubbed his hand over his face, forcing his dark thoughts to take a sharp left turn, and focussed on the enticing, quirky and sexy woman in front of him. She smelled fantastic. Just the thing to settle the out-of-control spiralling of his thoughts,

Yes, she was a little greener than most of the women who passed briefly through his life, but just as striking. Practically the polar opposite of the sophisticated women he usually invited into his bed, her bubbly personality was as intoxicating as a breath of fresh and fragrant summer air. The flicker of interest in his groin built, stirring his limbs with urgent energy.

Ash covertly checked her ring finger—bare.

But in his experience, women who looked like her—peaches and cream complexion, whimsical ponytail—wanted more than he was willing to offer. Wanted a relationship. And he never went there, no matter how appealing the inducement.

Not since his ex-fiancée…

Ash stood in an attempt to banish the jitters in his legs. He'd take her damn snap and put an end to this weird Transatlantic lesson in charming, but eccentric, cultural differences. Remove himself far from temptation.

He stepped into the centre of the path and raised his phone to the distant iconic view of one of London's most popular tourist attractions. With a click he'd completed his obligation, his intentions still wavering between polite dismissal and revealing some of his cards in case he'd been wrong about her and she shared his philosophies on casual sex.

'Have you taken the ride?' She appeared at his side, her eyes focussed on the giant wheel, its half-glass pods glinting in the sun.

'Not yet.' He held out his phone for her inspection, his mind flitting to a different kind of ride as she leaned close to stare at the screen and the tips of her silky hair glided over his wrist.

Fuck! No amount of English fresh air was going to shift this…urge. And, away from the negotiation table, Ash was never more in control than in the bedroom.

Yes, a little summer loving would both banish his restlessness and put his head straight. Hopefully, the control he demanded in the bedroom would re-infect the rest of him and shunt him back onto an even keel in time for the first day of his new business venture tomorrow.

The captivating stranger smiled, and his heart rate accelerated again.

'Thanks so much. You're a lifesaver.' She rattled off her number and he typed in the digits, sending the photo via text.

'My name's Essie, by the way.' She held out her hand—delicate; smooth-skinned; short nails painted purple.

He shook it, the brief slide of palm-to-palm grating in its formality after the mild flirtatious banter bouncing between them.

'Ash.'

She grinned as if he'd confessed his name began with HRH and he'd come to invite her back to the palace for afternoon tea.

'So, Ash the American tourist...' She had her photo, but she wasn't leaving. In fact, she was twirling that hair again, her eyes glinting with an unmistakable interest—one matched in him. No, his instincts were spot on.

'So, Essie, English fun facts expert...'

Another laugh that shot straight to his balls. 'Wanna grab lunch?' she said. 'I don't know this part of London well, but there's a cute deli not far from here and I have tons more facts about the city...' Her pretty blue eyes gleamed.

Heat soared in his chest. She *was* coming on to him in a subtle, fetching way he found way more enticing than the overt advances of his usual hook-ups. Absolutely, he'd be up for a no-strings one-time with this beautiful stranger. And as a tourist, he needn't spin his usual spiel about *having a good time*, *keeping things casual*, *hooking up* and other euphemisms that let the women he bedded know exactly where they stood. Where *he* stood.

She'd leave London to go back to whatever charming part of the UK she came from and, as far as she'd know, he'd go back to America.

He held out his arm, indicating she take the path ahead of them before tucking both his hands in the front pockets of his jeans. She smiled, swung her hair over her shoulder and set off at his side. For a few beats they walked in silence, the warm summer air heavy with possibility and an insistent flicker of sexual chemistry.

Something stirred in his gut—that delicious coil of excitement that the anonymity of meeting a stranger in a foreign place brought. Today he could be anyone. There were endless possibilities to re-invent himself and shake off the recently acquired shackles that held him down as if his feet were en-tombed in concrete.

Not Ash the duped, who'd not only been cheated on but also lied to by the two people in his life who should have had his back. *Yeah, fuck that guy.* He was Ash the American tourist, killing time with the interesting, beautiful breath of fresh air that was Essie.

'So...' he flashed his first genuine smile her way, enjoying the telling pink flush of her cheeks '...tell me about these noses.'

Essie Newbold laughed and bumped shoulders with the sexy American she'd spent the afternoon and eve-ning with. Well, she would have bumped shoulders with him if he weren't so tall—instead, her shoul-der bumped his arm. But the effect was the same.

Contact.

Those delicious little trembles of static electricity zinged to all her highly attuned erogenous zones as they'd been doing all day, every time their arms had brushed as they'd hunted the Seven Noses of Soho or when they were squeezed together, chest to chest, on the standing-room-only Tube. She'd never been more grateful for the crowding of London's underground.

Instead of allowing the momentum of her flirty little shoulder bump to ping her away from him, Ash scooped his arm around her waist and grinned down at her.

Her head swam.

She was really going to do this—sleep with the dreamy man she'd met in the park this morning? Her first one-night stand.

Essie slipped her hand into the back pocket of his jeans, her fingers pressing into his tightly toned backside. Where had her uncharacteristic bravery come from? The desire for something more than the dribs and drabs she'd tolerated from her no-good ex?

Her ex's idea of foreplay had been a mandatory squeeze of the boob. And to her shame, she'd accepted such lazy, shoddy attention.

All the more reason to explore a one-night stand with the drool-worthy, confident American. She'd gain some much-needed experience in the one-night-stand stakes, and hopefully score herself the kind of orgasm that only existed in her world as a mythical will-o'-the-wisp, and afterwards they'd move on having both had a good time. Unless Ash was a serial killer, it was a win-win situation. She absorbed the foreign, heady thrill of his big warm body next to hers. Not that it was cold—her shivers originated purely from anticipation.

The best kind of shivers.

She sucked in a stuttering breath—she'd never felt more reckless. And, if she was honest, she also felt a little embarrassed. There was no law that stated that, before her twenty-fifth birthday, she should have experienced at least one night of no-strings sex, but, as she touted herself as something of a relationship expert, didn't she owe it to the readers of her relationship psychology blog to experience what all the fuss was about?

Ash's hand looped around her shoulder. She reached up and clasped his fingers. They grinned at each other, Essie's belly jolting in time with her excitable pulse.

No serious scientist could rely solely on academic theory. She could finally verify her years of extensive research with some cold, hard, scientific data.

Surely he must be able to hear the blood whooshing through her head?

Because in practical terms, what did she really know about relationships, especially the functional kind?

Her face fell at the momentary wobble. Her one serious boyfriend during uni had left her practically swearing off the opposite sex for good on the grounds she clearly couldn't spot a decent relationship candidate if he was stark naked in front of her wearing a *pick me, I'm a safer than houses bet* hat.

A trait she'd inherited from her mother perhaps… The woman had, after all, procreated with Essie's lying, cheating, deserting father and spent many years playing second fiddle to his actual wife, his *real* family.

Not that Essie had known all that back then. She'd simply been a girl who desperately missed her beloved father while he'd worked overseas for long stretches of time. Clearly she and her mother shared a desperate-for-love vibe that usually sent men running.

But Ash wasn't running.

And she wasn't looking for a relationship. Just sex. She'd gleaned from Ash's subtext that, like her, he was only interested in a one-night thing. She shoved the buzzkill thoughts from her mind, focussing on the specimen of manly perfection beside her. Exotic Ash. A gentleman. Funny, intelligent and interested in what she had to say.

So different from her ex, and she'd wasted two years in that flawed relationship.

Her throat tightened.

Perhaps she was ready for a change. It was, after all, the eve of a brand-new chapter of her life—her new job working for her until-recently estranged half-brother began tomorrow. Or perhaps it was just charming, sophisticated, sexy-as-sin Ash with his crinkle-eyed smile, his quick wit and his tales of

New York that earned him a place at the top of Essie's bucket list.

Nothing at all to do with his muscular physique and his dark good looks, which were enough to attract smiles and stares everywhere they'd gone today. And she instinctively knew, as if it were stamped on her overworked ovaries, that Ash would be phenomenal between the sheets. High-calibre screaming orgasms—another experience sadly lacking from her rather pathetic repertoire.

But she could still back out of this. Thank Ash for his company and bid his sexy American butt farewell. Her insides twisted while her indecision ping-ponged inside her skull, releasing an uncharacteristic verbal catharsis.

'I've never done this before.' She nibbled her lip, ignored the heat almost suffocating her and raised her eyes to Ash's.

Now he'd think her some sort of ingénue when really she'd simply tolerated mediocre for far too long.

He turned to face her, drawing her closer with the arm banded around her waist while his glittering blue stare danced over her features. 'Okay…'

No judgment. Only the heat she'd seen in his eyes most of the afternoon.

The sizzle and spark over lunch at the funky deli had turned into flirting around Piccadilly Circus and Trafalgar Square, where Essie had provided a 'how to' tutorial on travelling the Tube. Flirting had turned to inhibition-lowering drinking at a typical Victorian Soho pub, where Ash had insisted they sample pints of tepid real ale, which was strong enough to make Essie both giggly and bold. Which was probably how they'd come to their current location—on the pavement outside his hotel, with his arms around her and her lips tingling to kiss him.

Still she wavered, caught between lust and caution.

She wanted to slap herself. Her doubts, her desperation to get it right where her parents had got it so wrong, hadn't helped her avoid heartache. She'd just had one bad experience...

Ash didn't have to be the perfect man—he could be perfect for now, this one night. Then she'd never see him again. And she could try out her sexually sophisticated legs.

Ash smiled, his blue eyes sparkling with promise and his yummy mouth stretching in a sexy, lopsided way.

Full lips so close.

Warm breath laced with hops.

Shrugging off the last reservation, Essie stood on tiptoes and kissed him, right there in the street where people walked around them. For a second he seemed frozen, his stubble chafing her chin and his lips slightly parted as she feathered the lightest of kisses on his beautiful mouth. And then his hand found the small of her back, pressing her close as he took control, angling his head and orchestrating the slide and thrust of lips and tongues, a thrilling concerto that left her head light and her legs weak.

Wow. The easy-going, considerate gentleman

she'd spent the day with had a demanding side. She wanted more. The street snog was so good, her stomach clenched like the final seconds of a free fall, and her heart ricocheted against her ribs.

Ash groaned and pulled back from her kiss, his erection a hard length against her belly. He looked down as if trying to dissect her inner secrets from her irises. 'Not that I'm bothered…' he pushed back a stray wisp of hair from her face '…but I'm intrigued. Why not?'

Essie captured her lip with her teeth, her insecurities rising like bile. What did she want this sexy tourist to know about her poor track record with the opposite sex? Despite her psychology degree and her PhD in human relationships, her own love life, and most of her non-romantic personal relationships, relied heavily on the theory she pored over for her studies and for her beloved blog, one she'd started as an undergraduate as a way to purge her own feelings of abandonment and constant rejection at the hands of her father.

Ash wanted her; the evidence was crystal clear. Why burst the bubble? Yes, she normally avoided picking up hunky strangers in parks. But once he'd cracked his first genuine smile, Ash had relaxed into a fun, smart and entertaining guy. She hadn't confessed she lived in South East London and was soon to graduate from her PhD. She'd merely gone along with his wrong assumption—that she, like him, was a tourist. It added to the mystique, the risqué recklessness currently pounding through her blood and fanning her libido to a blaze.

But they'd never see each other again after tonight. Who better to take off her training wheels with than a sexy stranger, a temporary tourist, soon to be on a plane to a whole other continent?

While Ash fingered the end of her ponytail, waiting, Essie shrugged. 'My male role model growing up was an unreliable, lying shit. It kind of put me off men.' Oversimplified, but true. She'd spent years trying to fit her subpar relationship with her ex into a perfect mould, desperate to have the opposite of her parents' dysfunctional union and determined to flex her psychology muscles and prove she could practise what she preached. But when she'd finally conceded that the emotionally abusive relationship she'd pinned all her hopes on was over, she'd given up on her own happily-ever-after and shelved finding love, preferring instead to focus on helping others with their relationships through her blog.

'I'm a man.'

Wasn't he just? She nodded, stopping short of rolling her eyes back at the solid hard bulk of him pressed against her. 'You are.'

She knew enough about human interactions to know there was more to Ash than the charming backpacker, despite appearances. For a start, he was older than the typical traveller, she guessed early thirties. Although casually dressed in slightly rumpled clothing, he carried himself with that air of command, confidence and authority that was such a turn-on—

she practically had drool on her chin. That he was bothering to explore the reasons behind her hesitancy instead of ramming his tongue down her throat or hurrying her inside faster than he could say 'God Save the Queen' was another astounding point in his favour.

But the less she knew about him, the easier it would be to walk away. When she left in the morning, she'd feel satisfied no boundaries had been crossed, no misunderstandings had been created and no feelings had had time to develop.

Mustering every ounce of confidence and female allure, she gripped his biceps and pressed her body closer. 'Are we on the same page?' Her limbs twitched while she waited for his confirmation. What if she'd read him all wrong? What if, like her ex, Ash thought her too clingy? Surely he could appreciate the merits of this—they'd never see each other again.

Ash dipped his head, pressing his mouth to hers once more. 'Totally.' The word buzzed over her tingling lips and then the tip of his tongue dipped inside. With a surge of lust Essie embraced the kiss, scooping her arms around his neck with renewed enthusiasm.

Please let her be right about his sexual talents.

When she pulled back, breathless, she registered her surroundings. They'd come to a stop outside a rather upmarket hotel in St James's. She looked up at Ash, her eyes round.

'Is this where you're staying?' She'd guessed

that he was more than he'd seemed in the park, but wealthy…?

He shrugged, a playful twitch on his lips.

Yes, Ash had offered to pay for her sandwich at lunch, but after she'd insisted on paying for herself, he'd accepted they'd be going Dutch for the rest of the day. He hadn't flashed money around—a definite turn-off for Essie, who had what her flatmate called *money issues*.

He released his grip on her waist and Essie missed his touch instantly. 'I know the owner. I'm only here tonight.' He placed his index finger under her chin and tilted her face up to his. 'Changed your mind? It's okay if you have.'

So considerate.

Her body was still fully on board with spending the night with this ruggedly handsome stranger. And did it matter if he had rich, hotel-owning friends? She wouldn't know him long enough to confess her monetary hang-ups, ones that originated with her absent father, who used affluent bribes and constant gifts as a substitute for investing quality time in his only daughter's life.

A shudder snaked down her spine.

One of the reasons she'd taken a job working for her half-brother, which began tomorrow, was to start earning some money. Finally, after five years of full-time study, she'd actually be able to support herself rather than take more student loans. Because she'd rather be in debt for the rest of her life than take one penny from her scheming father. She'd never once cashed one of the regular cheques he sent towards her tuition fees. It felt like hush money, and by accepting it she would be condoning what he'd done, to her, to her mother, to his wife and to Ben. She'd rather live on a park bench.

Ash, perhaps interpreting her silence as a change of heart, stepped back half a pace, ending the delicious contact between them and leaving Essie more bereft than the dark turn of her thoughts had done.

'I'm happy to walk you home…or put you in a cab.' He shrugged as if it was no big deal but his stare darkened as he looked down at her, waiting. A stare of longing, one that matched the well of sizzling heat rising up inside her.

Don't spoil what promises to be the best night of your life with your hang-ups.

Essie moved closer, her fingers finding the belt loop of his jeans. She tugged, bringing his chest into contact with hers, scraping her nipples to exquisite, nerve-tingling awareness.

No way would she back out now.

'Are you sure?'

Yes, yes, yes…

At her silent nod, he took her hand, laced his fingers through hers and led her inside the glass and chrome rotating door of the swanky hotel.

Essie hurried after him, his longer strides swiftly guiding her across the elegant foyer that she was too turned on to appreciate. Her last thought—how nice it must be to know someone who owned such a well-appointed and convenient establishment—fled the minute the lift door closed and Ash pinned her against one wall with the stealth and predatory instincts of a jungle cat.

Essie surrendered to the reckless impulses, so foreign but urgently addictive. She climbed him, her own instincts set free as her hands tugged his hair and her mouth found his while her legs encircled his thighs and she clung to him for dear life.

Every taut inch of him was hard. She knew, under his slouchy clothes, he'd be sleek and toned and bulging in all the right places. They broke apart long enough to hurry from the lift to his room, although she was so turned on that Essie was certain she'd floated.

He took a key card from his pocket, swiped it through the reader and stood back so she could enter first. Essie turned to welcome him as he followed her inside, her pent-up libido and the fizz of adrenaline in her blood making her embarrassingly eager. She gave him no time to activate the lights or even wait until the door had fully closed before she leapt at him, the air leaving her in a whoosh as he caught her around the waist and hauled her up to his equally insatiable mouth.

The chemistry between them practically melted her body to his as if they'd been welded together.

The kissing, unlike anything she'd known, was so voracious she whimpered out her pleasure. With dizzying speed, Ash deposited her on the bed, whipped off her underwear and produced a condom.

Essie panted while he tore at his fly and covered

himself, a look of desperate concentration on his face, barely visible in the gloom. This was wild, audacious and thrilling. But then Ash's mouth was back on hers, his fingers stroking her nipple to a peak through her clothing while he pushed slowly inside her, and she lost herself to what she was certain would turn out to be the single best sexual experience of her life to date.

She wasn't wrong. Ash pulled his mouth from hers, yanked his T-shirt over his head and reared back. With her hips gripped in his large hands and her stare locked with the white-hot one he bore down on her, Ash pounded into her again and again.

He was a god—ripped torso, a smattering of dark hair trailing down to his magnificent manhood, which she couldn't see, but which was currently rendering her a speechless bag of raging female hormones. When he scooped her hips with one arm, not losing his rhythm, and slipped his free hand between them and located her clit, her world fractured and a broken cry left her throat as she came, shortly followed by Ash.

Yep—best sex ever.

Go, Essie.

CHAPTER TWO

ESSIE EXITED THE Piccadilly Circus Tube station into glaring sunlight and joined the mass of people heading towards the start of their work week. Stifling a yawn with the back of her hand, she dragged her sunglasses from the top of her head and scoped out another coffee fix. Of course, if she'd had more than three hours' sleep last night, she wouldn't need another dose of caffeine. But she always worked on her blog first thing in the morning when the words flowed freely and the ideas were fresh, and this morning, the morning after the best sex of her life, had been no different.

Ash had kept her up into the early hours with his impressive stamina. After a second round of high calibre, sheet-clawing sex, another life-redefining orgasm, she'd sneaked out of his hotel room, like a sexually enlightened Cinderella, in the early hours while Prince Charming had slept.

She sniggered, scuffing the toe of her Converse on the tiled floor. Yes, it hadn't been her proudest moment—leaving without so much as a 'nice to meet you, thanks for the orgasms'—but that had been the unspoken deal, right? The casual sex secret code. One of the pros. No awkward swapping of numbers, no obsessively checking her phone for his call and no stalking him on social media to confirm his single status.

Of course, in practical terms, she was no expert. But she'd been right—what had occurred with Ash last night far surpassed the commonplace.

Good thing he was leaving the country soon. Sex that good should come with a health warning.

Hazard! You are ten times more likely to develop feelings for this man. Avoid sexual contact at all costs. Danger! Disappointment ahead.

And she'd had enough of that to last a lifetime.

Essie accepted her coffee from the barista, wincing as she set off at a quicker pace into Soho—starting her new job for her brother on a few hours of sleep was not her wisest move.

She sipped her latte and checked her phone for directions, cursing at the time displayed as she hurried along unfamiliar streets to meet Ben at the basement-style club and cocktail bar he'd recently purchased and had just completed renovating.

Of course, she wouldn't have needed the map if she'd scouted the route to her new job yesterday as she'd planned. But the sun had been shining and she'd disembarked the Tube a few stations early to indulge in a pleasant walk in the park. Meeting a sexy stranger hadn't been part of the plan. But she couldn't tell Ben why she'd got…sidetracked.

Essie quickened her pace, holding her coffee out in front of her. Of all the days to be late. And for Ben, too. Her older half-brother, seven years her senior, had taken a chance, offering her a job at his new club. Yes, she'd done some bar work throughout uni, but she'd never held a managerial position. All the same, she had assured him she was capable— she had a PhD, for goodness' sake, well almost, the conferment ceremony only a few weeks away—and she was determined to make the best of the chance to work for her brother.

This was more than a job. Working with him would hopefully lead to a closer relationship than the cordial but unemotional one they currently shared. Not that she blamed Ben for the distance—she had been equally hesitant. Their father had kept *her* existence a secret from his only son, too. They both had some making up for lost time to do.

That was why Essie had grasped at his request to help out, when his current manager had quit unexpectedly, with both eager hands. If she had a career plan, bar work would have no place in it, but the job comprised predominantly night shifts, which protected her dedicated blog-writing time during the day. And until she decided if she was cut out for a stuffy academic position, it provided a perfect stopgap. And the pay Ben had offered was great.

Essie rounded the corner, dodging a steady stream of smartly dressed office workers and frantic stallholders setting up their fresh produce and delicious-smelling street food for Soho's famous, three-hundred-year-old Berwick Street Market.

She stepped off the kerb to dodge a fruit and veg vendor carrying a precarious tower of produce-laden boxes six high, narrowly avoiding a delivery van that screeched to a halt. The coffee sloshed inside the takeaway cup with a violent lurch. A spout of scalding liquid jettisoned from the sip hole in the plastic lid and sprayed the front of Essie's favourite dress, deliberately chosen for her first day at work.

She cursed while a trail of coffee dripped down her cleavage and soaked into her bra. Her eyes stung as she dabbed at the brown stain with her fingers and stepped back onto the pavement, pushing her way back into the hustle of the commuter crowds.

She breathed through her disappointment over the dress, her face forcing a bright smile. Ben wouldn't care how she dressed. Only that she turned up, offered him as much help as she could and became someone he could rely on. And if she hurried, perhaps she could beat Ben and his business partner there and she could clean up before making a good impression.

This part of Soho housed an array of trendy bars, eclectic restaurants and small, elegant hotels. The innocuous, black-painted street frontage of The Yard— sandwiched between a designer menswear store and an Italian deli—meant Essie almost walked straight past. If it hadn't been for a van parked on half of the pavement and the sign writer blocking the other half with his ladder while he worked on the shiny new nameplate, she might have missed her destination completely.

Essie followed the harassed sign writer's directions to the narrow alleyway between the deli and the club that led to the rear entrance of The Yard. Yanking open the ancient, squeaky door, she entered the cool gloom of the darkened interior.

'Ben?'

She made her way along a maze of dimly lit corridors, following the sounds of activity, her insides a flurry of twisting energy, one she couldn't blame on the barely tasted coffee.

The bar area swarmed with electricians rigging reams and reams of neon lights into every available nook and cranny. The sharp chemical tang of new paint filled the air and a very harassed-looking Ben paced near the front entrance door with his mobile phone glued to the side of his head. When he saw Essie, he visibly sagged and quickly ended his call.

'I am *so* glad to see you.' He gripped her elbows and kissed her cheek, a gesture that felt far from natural. She forced her breathing to deepen so she didn't pass out from excitement.

Baby steps.

Although they'd known of each other's existence for some years, their sibling relationship held a new and fragile quality. Recalling the first time Ben had made contact still held the power to suffocate her with emotions; the date, time and what she'd been wearing when his call had come in engraved on her memory as if it were yesterday.

Twelve months ago, he'd relocated full-time to London, which had taken their contact from the occasional awkward video call to an actual face-to-face meeting. From that moment Essie had been secretly and cautiously smitten, because all they'd really shared to date was a genetic bond with their devious and unscrupulous father, a string of hesitant emails and a few quick, stilted coffee dates. If they were going to have a lasting relationship in the future, using this opportunity to get to know each other better was crucial.

Essie shrugged off her doubts by rummaging in her backpack for her notebook and a pen. She was here to lighten Ben's burden. To show him who *she* was. To build on their sibling status, having been denied that opportunity all their lives by their father.

She bit down hard on her lip—she wouldn't spoil her first day by thinking of Frank Newbold. She flipped open the notebook, pen poised, a picture, she hoped, of cool, unfrazzled competence. The coffee stain notwithstanding.

'Tell me what you need. You look stressed.' And so much like their father, a man whose face she could no longer bear to look at.

Ben scrubbed his fingers through his already messy hair.

'The shit's hit the fan with one of my New York clubs…' He winced.

As well as renovating The Yard in Soho, Ben owned and managed a string of clubs in New York, where he'd grown up.

'You don't need to hear my work woes.' His wince turned into a hesitant smile. 'But I am going to have to leave you to things here—I have to fly to the States tonight and sort shit out.'

Essie rolled her shoulders back. That he would trust her with his shiny new cocktail bar and night-club gave her shivers that bubbled up at the back of her throat, threatening to close off her windpipe.

'Of course.' She swallowed, eager for another of his grateful smiles. 'That's why I'm here.' She could pull a pint from her years of working the uni bar, and the rest she'd learn on the job while her own ca-reer path loitered in an uncertain slump. Her moti-vations were more about personal bridge-building than flexing her managerial muscles in the hospi-tality industry. But looking at the furrows in Ben's brow and the dark circles around his tired eyes, she knew she'd walk a path of hot coals to help, even if it took her away from developing her relationship blog full-time, one of the ideas she'd considered now that she'd finished her PhD.

A small frown settled between his brows. 'Are you sure you can spare the time? Shouldn't you be job-hunting or schmoozing professors?'

Essie snorted a nervous laugh. Now that she'd finished her PhD, an academic position held far less appeal than it should. She'd considered a university teaching post but was way too intimidated to believe she had anything useful to teach others. She'd love to focus full-time on promoting her blog to wider audi-ences, but part of her secretly baulked at dedicating all her energy to making it a success—the 'lost little girl' part of her who missed her dad and couldn't understand why he spent so much time away. After all, what did she know about healthy human relationships? Everyone would see through her, know she was a fraud.

'I'll be fine until you can replace me with someone better qualified.' She had plenty of time to build her own career, whatever that looked like. She only had one brother. And, for now, he needed her.

He cracked a wide smile. 'Great.'

Essie flicked through her notebook to hide the attack of rapid blinking. She'd be the best bloody bar manager he'd ever seen. He wouldn't be able to resist falling deeply in sibling love with her.

'So, to recap on our previous conversation…' She tapped the pen on the page, tempted to push it behind her ear to inspire greater confidence. Perhaps she should have bought a clipboard. 'My predecessor has already hired waitstaff, bulk ordered the beverages and organised a cleaning crew…'

Ben nodded. 'All you have to do is be around to supervise things here.' He squeezed her arm. 'You are awesome.'

Warm treacle flooded her veins but she shrugged off his praise with a small shake of her head. She wished she'd recorded the moment so she could play it back to herself in the privacy of her flat later or every time her bones rattled with insecurities.

'The decorators have finished downstairs in the basement, and the interior designer will be here in—'

he checked his Rolex '—thirty minutes. Can you make sure they install the leather seats in the VIP area and remind them we decided on the black privacy curtains for the booths instead of the white?'

Essie nodded, scribbling a quick note as they walked. Ben ushered her out of the path of a man in paint-speckled overalls hefting a ladder on one shoulder and offered a tight, apologetic smile.

'Oh, and can you remind the electricians before they leave to install the string lights upstairs on the roof garden?' He sighed. 'Sorry. It's a lot.'

Essie shook her head. 'Not at all. I have a list.' She brandished her notebook with a reassuring grin.

A small nod. 'Have you…had any contact from… Frank?' Ben shot Essie a cautious look, tinged with the usual flash of guilt. He felt somehow responsible for their father's actions, but they'd both been victims of the lies.

She shook her head. The last thing she wanted to discuss was their father and the endless sob story he'd made of her young life. How he'd decimated her childhood adoration of him, a daughter-father rite of passage, through cowardly evasion and cruel deceit. Essie had learned early on, by the amount of time he'd spent in London, that she'd ranked pretty low on her father's list of priorities. But to discover, on her fifteenth birthday, that her whole life, her very existence, had been a lie, that she hadn't mattered enough, that she had a half-brother…

She swallowed back the familiar burn in her throat and shoved her father from her mind. Today was the start of something new, something positive—she wouldn't let him tarnish it the way he'd managed to tarnish every other significant moment in her life. Birthdays, school awards ceremonies, her first prom night—he'd been conspicuously absent.

Ben led the way to a door beside the bar. 'Come and meet my buddy.'

Her mouth twitched with a small, indulgent smile. Despite growing up in Manhattan, his mother's hometown, he'd lived in London for a year. His accent and his choice of slang wavered wildly between the two, something else about her big brother Essie found endlessly endearing.

How could this amazing man be related to Frank? Not that she was the best judge of character. She'd idolised their father growing up, but he'd used his frequent business travel to successfully navigate his deceptions and conduct two separate lives on two separate continents; conceal two separate families.

Essie tossed her coffee cup in a black bag and ducked through the door Ben held open for her.

'Although he's supposed to be a silent partner, he's up to speed with everything so, between the two of you, you should have most things covered. I'll be back in a few days—plenty of time for us to put the finishing touches to the launch party.'

'I promise, your club is in good hands.'

They'd chosen the perfect trendy and glamorous location—this part of London was always buzzing with young, beautiful people. And now she'd seen the club's interior, which was tasteful, chic and oozing sophistication, that she could participate in her brother's venture filled her with pride and renewed hope. And something less tangible…a small bud, blooming open, affording a glimpse of the full beauty to come.

Belonging.

Something she'd craved for as long as she could remember.

As the door from the bar closed behind them the noise levels dropped as if they'd entered a vacuum. Ben grinned at her impressed expression.

'State-of-the-art soundproofing. Costs a bloody fortune but worth it.' He took a left turn, pointing out the salient landmarks as he strode ahead.

'Kitchen here and staff break room. Staff toilets on the right.' Another left turn. 'You can use this office.' He paused outside a room where the furniture had been sited but still wore its protective Bubble Wrap clothing. He flashed his handsome, lopsided smile and Essie nodded, eyeing the sparse space.

They'd arrived at the last room. Ben rapped lightly on the door.

'Come in,' a voice said.

If she hadn't been so dazzled by the warmth and camaraderie of her brother's welcome and the affectionate bonding moment of him sharing his shiny new club with her, she might have clued on sooner. But she followed him into the room, blind to everything but Ben and blissfully oblivious to the impending catastrophic confrontation.

And came face-to-face with Ash.

The smile she held on her face morphed into a

frozen grimace. Her cheeks twitched with the effort of keeping it there, like a painted-on clown smirk.

She scoured her gaze over his height and breadth, seeking confirmation. But, no, it was definitely him.

The verification came, a breath-stealing blow to the solar plexus.

'Essie, this is Ash Jacob, my oldest friend and now business partner. Ash, my little sister, Essie Newbold.'

Essie wanted to run a lap of honour at hearing Ben's description of her, but her stiff skeleton could barely manage a small chin tilt in Ash's general direction as her neck muscles seized like a rusty gate.

Confident, commanding Ash stood, smoothing down his graphite tie as he rounded the sleek, modern desk and strode into her personal space with his hand outstretched in greeting as if he had not a care in the world. Saliva pooled in her mouth, her throat too tight to allow it passage. Her mind ping-ponged inside her skull, playing catch-up.

His gorgeous face, now clean-shaven to reveal a chiselled jaw and sinful creases that bracketed his full mouth, was relaxed, a small, polite smile on his lips as if he welcomed a total stranger, not the woman he'd come inside last night with a yell she heard every time she closed her eyes.

The memory of his now absent stubble scraping across her nipples gave her an acute pang of longing to see the relaxed, playful Ash of last night. Tourist Ash. Not this tie-wearing, professional version with distant, accusatory eyes and a tense jaw. But for the embers flickering in his navy stare, she'd almost have believed she'd concocted last night's torrid one-night stand. But her hips and thighs still bore the ghostly imprints of his fingertips as he'd held her tight and drilled into her with fierce determination.

'Nice to meet you.' The rich, dark rumble of his voice scraped her eardrums. Her coffee soured in her stomach. How could he maintain such a poker face? Why didn't he suffer the same jaw-dropping disbelief currently rendering *her* speechless? And why, oh, why out of all the men in the universe had she chosen her half-brother's best friend and business partner for her first one-night stand?

Ash's warm hand enclosed hers, reminding her of last night's touches. Touches that should have been more intimate but paled against this simple handshake, because this time all pretence was stripped away.

Ash Jacob was The Yard's co-investor.

Ben's silent business partner.

Ben's billionaire friend from uni. A man she'd wrongly assumed was a tourist and picked up in St James's Park. A man she'd had sex with, twice, whose bed she'd only left mere hours ago. A man to whom she'd confessed her pathetic lack of sexual experience, and thought she'd never see again.

Molten heat engulfed Essie's throat. She swallowed it down with a sour chaser of you've-only-got-yourself-to-blame. But her stomach rebelled the dose of self-inflicted medicine.

Pulling herself up, she levelled her best cold stare

on his sinful good looks and returned his handshake with an overly firm one of her own, ignoring the delicious glide of his callused palm.

Social pleasantries complete, she yanked her hand from his as if he were a live wire, connected to the mains.

He'd lied to her.

Deceived her.

Pried into her sordid hang-ups about her crappy father figure.

Why had she told him such personal information? Why hadn't she asked more about him? She really was a one-night-stand rookie. Her burning eyes darted away, but not before his image branded her retinas.

She'd wanted to experience the casual sex hype, desperate to lend an air of real experience and authority to the relationship advice she touted on her blog. All because, despite her qualifications, despite years of academic research, despite actually having had a long-term relationship, she feared herself an imposter.

Of course, the fact she'd been starved of earth-shattering orgasms during that relationship and that Ash was…easy on the eye had helped…

She snatched another scan of his sublime body. Unlike the relaxed, slightly crumpled hottie she'd met yesterday, today Ash wore a crisp white shirt with the sleeves rolled up to the elbows and sharply tailored suit trousers that complemented the silver-grey tie and highlighted the intense blue of his eyes.

Gorgeous. Mouth-watering. A duplicitous scumbag...

As hot as he'd looked dressed down in jeans and a T-shirt, he wore this sharp, professional outfit like a second skin, as he wore the power that oozed from him. As he lived and breathed the air of command and authority that immaculate tailoring afforded. Her breath caught. She could have slapped her own forehead. Another piece of the puzzle slotted home— Ben's new business partner was a top New York attorney...like a character from that TV show, only a hundred times hotter and a thousand times more untouchable.

But she *had* touched.

The seconds stretched.

Awkward seconds. Seconds absent of the expected social niceties. To compensate, Essie blurted the first inane thing to pop into her head.

'So you're Ben's business partner?' *Duh...*

Ash nodded. Slow. Easy. His stare glittering. As if he recognised the turmoil rendering her tongue-tied. And not one hint of regret or embarrassment. Unlike her, who was practically molten with shame.

'Guilty as charged.' His voice carried a bite that had been missing from the deep, hypnotic rumble of the easy-going sightseer. As if he was used to being in control?

And lawyer humour... Really?

'Ben has been talking about you all morning,' he said. 'Of course, he mentioned a while ago he'd recently united with his half-sister, but I'd failed to pay attention to your very pretty name.' His eyes flicked down the front of her dress. To the coffee stain...

Perfect.

Essie fought the temptation to fold her arms across her chest and keep on folding herself into a tiny origami Essie. Had Ash told Ben about last night? About how she'd thrown herself at him? How she'd blurted out her inexperience and then eagerly climbed his ripped body? Had he laughed at her? And why was *he* pissed? She'd been the one deceived, duped. Dazzled by his confident charm and his promise of a string-free night to remember. It wasn't as if she'd stalked him here for a repeat performance...

And how much of her sad little tale, her pathetic past, did he know? Had Ben told him all about her sorry past? Had Ash linked the woman confessing her daddy issues before fleeing his bed with Ben's sister?

As if he'd heard her thoughts, he said, 'Imagine my surprise when I heard Ben's sister was to be our new bar manager.'

The trembles turned into jolts. Surely Ben would have said something if he knew. She tensed her muscles to hold herself still. It wouldn't do to show a man like Ash, the real Ash, any weakness. Last night, she'd have run a mile from this powerful, controlled man. She *should* run now. Leave with what was left of her self-esteem intact before Ben clued on and her embarrassment became full-blown.

But leaving her brother in the lurch...? When he needed her help more than ever? Not an option. Not if they were to have a chance at a deep and lasting sibling relationship.

Ben snorted, flicking Ash a friendly but distracted grin.

'Leave it, Jacob. Essie's been a lifesaver, stepping in at the last minute.' Ben rounded the desk and flopped down into the chair Ash had vacated, leaving the two of them alone on the other side of the impressive block of wood.

Essie levelled her stare on Ash. She narrowed her eyes but kept her voice free of the sarcasm fighting to break free. 'Tell me, have you been in London long? Had a chance to do a little sightseeing perhaps?'

For Ben's sake, she kept the acid from her tone, but Ash shrugged, seemingly indifferent, and Ben looked too engrossed in the screen of his phone to have even heard the vague barb.

Ash moved to an informal seating area in one corner of the office, which was decked out like something from an exclusive gentlemen's club. He held out his arm to offer her a seat and then, when she declined, sank down into the leather, all the while assessing her with his narrowed stare.

'I have managed a tour of the more…exciting highlights the city has to offer.' He quirked a brow, his mouth twisted. He reclined, one arm stretched out along the back of the sofa, thighs spread in that confident, manly way that screamed, *Look at my junk! Oh, wait, you've already experienced it.*

Heat slammed through her, pulsing between her legs with every lurid memory of him inside her last night: his hips slamming into her; his gruff voice commanding her pleasure; his uncompromising control brooking no arguments, even though she'd been one hundred per cent complicit.

Her cheeks warmed. She'd fully embraced the *wham-bam, thank you, ma'am*. She dragged her gaze from his crotch, pressing her lips together so she couldn't lick them. This morning, one night had been enough.

But now, with him looking at her as if he wanted a repeat performance, her body hummed with need, in traitorous, clit-throbbing agreement.

One night *hadn't* been enough.

Not of this man, who she suspected would be twice the lover of relaxed, tourist Ash. Was that even possible? No. She didn't want to know.

'So you have managerial experience? Hospitality experience?' Ash flicked his eyes over her from head to toe as if they were alone, his tone grating and transforming her buzz of arousal to one of irritation. It was the way he asked, as if he already knew the answer and found her…lacking.

Another lawyer trait? Or pure, unadulterated arsehole?

Essie changed her mind. Selecting the chair opposite him, she faced him, forcing her body into as relaxed a demeanour as he displayed. She was, after all, an expert at body language.

'I'm a graduate.' She lifted her chin. 'I've just completed a PhD and I have lots of hospitality experience.' So she didn't have a Harvard law degree, but she wasn't an imbecile. She could work a till and wipe down tables. 'Would you like to see my CV?' She pursed her lips in a tight, sickly smile.

'What's with the third degree?' Ben joined them, taking the second armchair. He shot Ash a curious glare and then turned to Essie. 'Forgive my friend. He's not long arrived from New York. He's not used to your English customs and manners yet.'

Ben turned back to a smiling, completely unfazed Ash.

'Look, it sucks balls that I have to leave today, but I expect you to look out for my sister, Jacob. Employ a dash of that charm that gets you endlessly laid.' Ben's grin dropped. A frown lodged between his brows. 'But keep your hands off my sister.'

A titter of hysterical laughter clogged Essie's throat while her cheeks flamed. She'd already sampled his friend's goods. She lifted her chin, her stare honed on Ash. She might not be able to control her flush response, but she could certainly control her misguided libido.

'I can manage anything your friend can dish out, Ben. Don't worry.'

Both men looked at her as if inspecting her for the first time. Their faces were unreadable and likely concealed very different thoughts. Essie examined her fingernails and tried to keep her feet still.

Although certain she lacked the sophistication of the New York babes Ash probably usually bedded, Essie wasn't a pushover. And this job was about her and Ben. Not her and Ash. So she'd let some personal baggage escape last night, been indiscreet about her track record—that ended right here, right now. Arrogant Ash had seen all he was going to see of unguarded, easy-going Essie.

She returned Ash's stare, the standoff a game of wills.

'Good,' said Ben. 'Because Ash here has a bit of a reputation with the ladies…if you know what I mean.' He winked at Essie, who tried to catalogue the sparse contents of her fridge to stop another telltale blush giving her away.

'Don't worry.' Ash's lip curled. 'Little sisters aren't my type.'

Essie concealed her indrawn gasp with a nervous chuckle. Was he daring her? Goading her to out them to a clueless Ben? White-hot fire replaced her blood—she'd been his type less than twelve hours ago when he hadn't even bothered to fully strip either of them before he'd lowered her to the bed and pushed his delicious dick inside her.

No.

Not delicious. Wrong. Forbidden. And probably as devious as the rest of him.

She cringed, her fatigue-weakened body veering towards kissing the smirk from Ash Jacob's handsome face one minute and coming clean to Ben the next.

Day one on the job, and already locking horns with the co-owner, who now knew more about her than most people…as well as sneaking round behind her brother's back?

Well, from now on she'd be the consummate professional and just get the job done. She couldn't risk disappointing Ben or she'd be back to square one.

Alone.

Rejected.

No relationship with her father to speak of, and no relationship with Ben.

Her whole life, she'd felt somehow responsible for the choices her father had made, as if she were the reason he'd stayed away. And now she was responsible for the mess she'd made of this, too.

But she refused to play into Ash's sexy hands. Her sister status meant more to her than point scoring over Ash. She could ignore him at work, pretend she'd never met him, try to forget how he'd expertly shunted her into not one, but the two best orgasms of her life. She could pretend just looking at him radiating the kind of self-assurance born of supreme confidence wasn't a real fucking turn-on…

Ben's phone chirruped a text alert and he pulled it from his pocket with a sigh.

'My car's here. I have to go.' He stood, and Essie and Ash followed. He stooped to kiss Essie's cheek again and turned to shake hands and shoulder bump with Ash.

'Play nice.' Ben levelled an index finger at his friend, who shrugged, his expression all laid-back charm and cocksure nonchalance.

Ben turned back to Essie.

'And if you need me, email.'

Essie nodded, more than half tempted to fling herself at her brother's Oxford-clad feet, wrap her arms

around his knees and beg him to stay. To mediate
between her and Ash. To stop Essie from orchestrating a rerun of last night's recklessness. To see that
underneath the stained dress and the bad decisions,
she was a worthy sister.

But instead she stood and watched him leave
while her stomach flopped to her coffee-speckled
shoes.

*Get a grip. You're a grown-ass woman. Soon to
be Dr Essie Newbold, psychologist and relationship guru. Not some insecure sad sack ruled by her
hormones.*

She straightened her spine and prepared to follow Ben's lead and leave the room that shrank the
minute she and Ash were alone, compressing the
available oxygen.

'Well, you failed to mention this last night…'

She yanked her stare back to Ash.

Every minute hair on her body stood to attention.
Ben seemed to have taken the sun with him, too, because the room's temperature plummeted as Essie
and Ash faced off.

'Me?' Was he for real? 'What about you?' Playing the charming tourist and allowing her to believe
he'd be leaving town in a few days. Laughing at her
London anecdotes and listening intently when she'd
offered top tips for surviving the capital, when all
the time he probably knew the city better than her.
If she'd known last night that he owned a sizeable
chunk of St James's, she might have put two and
two together and kept her knees and her mouth shut.

And now she and Mr Moneybags had to survive an intolerable working relationship, where every time they crossed paths she'd blush beet red at her folly.

Her phone vibrated in her bag, a reminder it was time to publish the blog post she'd drafted that morning. Oh, the irony. She'd waxed lyrical about casual sex, clutching her shiny new members' badge to the one-night-stand club. Now the pieces of that newfound air of authority lay scattered around her two left feet.

Perhaps she could quickly pen an alternative piece: *How to work with people you want to...jump.*

No.

Not jump. Ignore.

Ash stepped close, his big manly body producing enough heat to scorch her bare arms, lobster red. Flicks of blue flame danced in his eyes.

'I didn't conceal anything. I just didn't mention anything personal.'

The unspoken hovered in the air... *Unlike you.*

Essie wanted to curl in on herself, but she held her head high. Being eager to take off her casual sex training wheels was nothing to be ashamed of.

'If you made wrong assumptions, that's your problem,' he bit out. 'And what was with the *"My phone died. Please take a photo for me..."* Why were you playing the tourist? You live here.'

She'd wanted the photo for a future blog post, the wheel symbolic of the spectrum of human emotions and the sun catching the Eye a reflection of hope—a new day. But she couldn't tell him that, couldn't tell him about the blog. Not when her reckless, mind-blowing one night with him was the focus of today's post. When she published it later, this new element of fucked-upness, would give the subject matter even more credence—a cautionary tale of how people concealed what they really were to get what they wanted. To get laid.

The perils of casual sex...

'You're the one who lied. Ash the tourist? From what Ben told me, you own half of London.' *Typical.* She'd inherited her bad taste in men from her mother...

She bit the inside of her cheek, scalding heat flooding her body. Her mum was a good person who'd raised Essie virtually single-handedly. No, she only had herself to blame for her foolhardy behaviour last night and its humiliating consequences this morning.

Where were all the honest, dependable, upfront men? And why was she a magnet for the opposite type? The ones who evaded the truth, like Ash. The ones who claimed they wanted a relationship but took more than they gave, like her ex. The ones who made promises and then broke them and threw money at the situation so they avoided dealing with real life, like her unreliable, phoney father...

Ash's stare raked over her features. 'So?' He lifted his chin, looking down his nose with a lazy smirk on his face. 'You didn't seem to care who I was last night. In fact, all you seemed concerned about was marking your one-night-stand card—or was that part of the act, too?' He inched into her personal space, invading until the breadth of his chest eclipsed her field of vision.

Essie placed the flat of her hand between his well-developed pecs, ignoring the burn of his body heat and the clean male scent wafting up from his expensive shirt.

'I'm not the only one who made wrong assumptions. And I rocked your world last night, counsellor.' Her fingers wanted to curl, to dig, to tug. But she forced them to stay flat. Time to put some boundaries in place. No matter how fantastic their brief, steamy interlude, the after shame currently making her hot and twitchy rendered the high worthless. Another important post–casual sex lesson she could impart to her readers.

His mouth kicked up on one side, and he snorted a soft gust of air.

'Funny, I thought I'd rocked *your* world?'

Her internal muscles clenched at the memories of his spectacular manhood. She laughed, stepping away from toe-tingling temptation and heading for the door with a shake of her head. There was no chance of damaging this man's ego, but she didn't trust her voice to emerge without the breathiness that made her light-headed.

'No?' His hurled question stopped her in her tracks. 'We could rectify that situation, right now.' He flicked his stare to the uncluttered slab of a desk, his sinful mouth twisted, but his eyes hot.

Challenging?

Essie imagined herself spread there with Ash, determined to prove something, between her thighs. Thighs that loved the idea if the tremble between them was any indication. She instinctively knew that sex with hot lawyer Ash would be twice as intense as sex with hot tourist Ash. No mean feat.

Tempting.

Lying made sense, serving a dual purpose of bringing him down a peg or two and fortifying her own wobbly defences.

'There won't be anything more between us. I'm here for Ben, my *brother*. And, as you'll remember from last night, I don't trust your type.'

His cocky, lopsided smirk lifted her shoulders until they threatened to dislocate.

'You're right, there won't be.' He closed the distance between them, his dismissive stare dipping down the length of her body. 'Ben is my friend, this is my business and I don't trust anyone.'

'Good. So we agree on one thing.' That didn't mean she couldn't toy with him as he toyed with her. Make him crave a repeat performance. One he'd never get to experience. It was childish and vengeful and filled her with white-hot shame. But she longed to cut the arrogant jerk down to size. To claw back some of the dignity her poor choice and shabby vetting had decimated.

He nodded. 'It seems so. I made it clear yesterday—one shot is all you get from me.'

Her back teeth ached as she ground them together. 'What a gent you are. Ladies must be lined up around

the block.' She forced his spicy scent from her nose
with a short snort.

He raised his dark brows. 'I've never had any
complaints. And you didn't walk away unsatisfied.'

She wanted to deny his prowess. To tell him he'd
been a lousy lay, but that was one lie too far. Instead she stepped closer, fighting the urge to rub
her body against his like a cat. 'As you're so…expe-
rienced in the casual sex department, I'm sure you
know this.' She looked up at him from beneath her
lashes. 'There's a world of difference between mind-
less fucking and the ultimate connection found during a real, honest human interaction.'

She dropped her head back with a prolonged sigh,
feigning a look of utter ecstasy while she ran her fingertips slowly down the length of her exposed throat.
She released a breathy moan, her hand coming to rest
at the top of her cleavage.

And then she snapped her head up and dropped
her arm to her side. Her expression returned to one
of mild scorn while power blazed through her nervous system at the sight of lust glittering in his eyes
and the tent in the front of his trousers.

'If you've never experienced the latter—' a shrug
'—I feel sorry for you.' She smiled her brightest
beam. 'Have a good day.'

She turned on her heel and left his office with her
burning back ramrod-straight and her belly quivering
in time to the soundtrack of *When Harry Met Sally*.

CHAPTER THREE

Essie spent the rest of the day holed up in Ben's office answering phone calls, sending emails and hiding from Ash. For all her bravado, her encounter had left her shaken to the core. Not because his confirmation there would be no more sex in their future left her reliving their one night together, over and over until her erogenous zones ached and clamoured for a rerun, but because, burning with righteous indignation, she'd rashly clicked *publish* on that morning's blog post, retitling it *The OMG Pros and One-Night Cons of Casual Sex*, while still reeling from their verbal and sexually charged spat. And now her tongue-in-cheek cautionary tale of her first one-night stand winged its way through cyberspace to land in the inboxes of the thousands-strong audience her relationship blog attracted.

Stupid.

Reckless.

But providing a belly-warming kick of satisfaction. Her small, naughty smile turned into a lip nibble. Thinking about her blog should have brought her

a sense of pride. Her usual posts were heavily theoretical and science based, calling on the latest psychological research on relationships, love and the
complexities of all forms of human interaction.

But crammed full of shame, betrayal and an overwhelming head spin of good sex hormones, she'd
thrown caution to the wind and edited her earlier
draft with personal details of her explosive but reckless night with Ash, detailing a pared-down version
of the sheet-clawing sexploits and their disastrous
morning-after fallout as reasons for prudence.

She'd kept it totally anonymous, only referring
to Ash as *Illegally Hot*, but she shouldn't have mentioned him at all. She was a professional with a serious academic reputation to consider, not some
kiss-and-tell reality blogger.

Her belly twisted even as her breathing accelerated, a sickening swirl of opposing emotions. The
added personal anecdotes afforded her writing an
air of authority she'd never before believed she possessed. As if, overnight, she'd become a true expert,
at least on her chosen topic.

Heady stuff.

She grinned, dragging her lip back under her teeth
as the first comment came in, lighting up her phone
with a ping.

Well, BatS*#tCrazy liked it. They'd even asked
where they could find *Illegally Hot*…

Bugger—it was too late now for regrets.

She slammed her laptop shut with screen-cracking

force. Ash didn't strike her as an avid pop psychology reader—he'd never know.

As the triumphant head rush dwindled, the lip-gnawing insecurity returned, full-blown. She'd begun her blog, *Relationships and Other Science Experiments*, as a first-year psychology undergraduate. Still struggling with the knowledge of her father's betrayal, emotionally and geographically isolated from a half-brother she'd never met and angry with her father's desertion and the lies he'd spun to cover it up, she'd taken to putting her own complex and often overwhelming feelings and thoughts into a sort of online diary. Shortly after, she'd made the mistake of falling in what she'd assumed was love. Two tumultuous years later, the ex she'd pinned all her happily-ever-afters on had left her with her self-esteem in tatters, and her heart seriously doubtful that honest, dependable men—let alone love—actually existed.

Around the same time, she'd fallen in academic love with social psychology and her fascination with the intricacies of human relationships began, guiding both her writing and her choice of PhD study.

Initially, she'd been amazed to acquire a handful of keen followers who had warmed to her quirky, often humorous take on the complexities of interpersonal dealings. No subject was taboo. From the rude man on the Tube to the day-to-day social minefield of undergraduate life, she tackled the full gamut of complex interactions humans faced and presented the science behind them.

And now she had a whole heap more fodder for

her writing in the guise of her sexy but arrogant boss, her one night of orgasmic bliss and the awkward, self-inflicted quagmire her temporary job had become.

Essie reopened her laptop, determined to end the day leaving no stone unturned when it came to her responsibilities towards Ben. With tomorrow's to-do list stuck on a virtual sticky note on her desktop, she performed one last check of her emails before heading home.

There was one from Ben's interior designer and another from his PA, asking for her bank account details for payroll. But it was the one from her brother, entitled *A Favour*, that she pounced upon.

Essie
I left some documents in the safe for Ash to sign. I can't get hold of him—suspect he's still jet-lagged and has fallen asleep. Can you please take them around to him and then scan the signatures through to the bank before six p.m.?

PS A spare set of keys to Ash's apartment is also in the safe, in case he's out of it and doesn't hear you knock.

A combination number and address accompanied the request.

Essie dropped her head into her hands, tempted to headbutt the laptop screen and pretend she hadn't read the urgent missive. The last thing she wanted was any further interaction with Ash after last night's reckless abandon and today's humiliating reunion.

Didn't billionaires have teams of lackeys traipsing after them, doffing their caps and facilitating their masters' every whim? Why her?

But Ben would be in the air by now en route to New York. There was no escape. If she kept her head, kept her focus on the goal and not the infuriating, sexy-as-fuck Ash…her mission couldn't fail.

Get in. *Don't have sex with him.*

Acquire a signature. *Don't have sex with him.*

Get out. *Don't have sex with him.*

Simple.

Ash closed his eyes, braced his palms flat on the tile and let the steaming water pound down on his head. Perhaps it would rattle some fucking sense into his brain.

Stupid. Impulsive. Fantastic sex.

He curled one hand into a fist, knuckles bloodless.

He'd moved to London to claw back control of the wrong turn his life had taken, not to embroil himself in another personal shit storm of epic proportions. While he licked his wounds and disentangled his suddenly public personal life, he'd hoped to forge a new path away from Jacob Holdings. A fresh start. Something of his own, untainted by his father.

Sleeping with the intriguing and exotic stranger he'd met in the park had been beyond reckless. He should have vetted her beyond her flirtatious smiles, her sexy laugh and her astounding body. But he'd

been charmed by her bubbly, ingenuous personality, so unlike the somewhat cynical sophisticates he
normally bedded.

Cynical like him.

And she'd upped the intrigue factor with her hesitant confession of her relative inexperience.

Fuck.

Ash dumped a palmful of shampoo onto his head.
But knowing exactly who she was only threw up
more questions. If Essie lived in London, why the
hell did she need a picture of one of its iconic landmarks? If she had a degree and a PhD, why was bar
work so appealing? And what was the deal with her
and Ben?

He scrubbed at his scalp, nails punishing. Now,
not only did he have to work with her—fucking eye-
ball-scalding torture right there—but he also had to
watch her prance her sexy ass around his club covered in those flirty little dresses she liked to wear,
all the while keeping his libido under control and his
hands to his damned self.

Screwed.

He rinsed his hair, welcoming the sting as the
suds ran into his eyes.

Not that he'd known it at the time, but sleeping
with Essie had broken one of his life's cardinal, cast-
iron, unbreakable rules: Never screw a mate's sister—the golden bro code every decent male lived by.

And he was decent. He didn't use people. He
didn't cheat. And he considered the consequences
of his actions.

Usually.

Unlike his no-good, lying, asshole father.

His other rule—never more than one night—well, he hadn't broken that…yet. Although he'd been sorely tempted in his office earlier.

It was sure as shit going to test every single ounce of the rigid control he not only prided himself on but needed like oxygen in order to resist temptation. The minute she'd walked into his office behind Ben he'd wanted her again so badly he'd had to think of his whisker-chinned, sixth-grade music teacher Miss Lemmon to stave off his boner.

When he'd awoken at four that morning to find her gone, part of him had sagged back on the pillows with relief. He'd done his job. Shown her a good time—actually, a fucking fantastic time.

Yes, she'd understood the unspoken rules, sneaking out of his hotel room in the middle of the night. No number on the nightstand. No scribbled note demanding he call her. No hijacking his cell phone. But the sense of relief had done little to comfort him. A part of him, the part left restless by betrayal and humiliation, the part he'd hoped to leave behind in New York, had coiled like colic in his gut until he'd arisen before the dawn, taken a frigid shower and numbed his mind with several hours of legal work.

Despite walking away from Jacob Holdings, he still had unfinished deals for the family business, one in particular that, as shareholder, he had a personal interest in. No matter how much he might want to throw his father under the bus in retribution, he had his sisters' future inheritance to protect and his mother's share when her divorce from the old bastard was finalised. At least he could atone for causing the split by recommending a hotshot divorce attorney to get his mother a fair slice of the pie. But even drafting a complex and lengthy contract hadn't dragged his mind away from the fascinating Essie.

He sighed, succumbing to the inevitable. Every muscle clenched and his cock thickened. He gave it a couple of lazy tugs as the memory of Essie's whimpers and her cries echoed inside his head…

Ash slammed his eyes open and slapped the tile beside the showerhead. Here he was thinking about the other ways he'd like to fuck her, when there wasn't going to be a next time. There should never have been a first time.

He'd been done with women even before he'd set foot on English soil. Plus she was Ben's sister and now his club's temporary manager. An employee. And, more importantly, someone he couldn't trust.

Perhaps he could fire her? Employ a replacement manager before Ben returned from his trip and say it hadn't worked out with Essie. But Ben, quite rightly, wouldn't tolerate the slight. And if it came out that Ash had fucked his little sister and then fired her for humiliating him, their longstanding friendship wouldn't survive. And right now, Ash needed his friend—the only friend he could be certain hadn't known what his fiancée had really been up to all those years ago.

Her dumping him practically at the altar had left

him struggling to trust the opposite sex, but his father's recent revelations and the public backlash had thrown Ash into a tailspin until he no longer knew which way was up and who he could rely upon not to snigger behind his back.

Of course, Ben didn't know the latest twist, the one that had prompted Ash's departure from New York. How the third wheel in his past relationship—the work colleague she'd claimed to have cheated with—had been nothing but a ruse. A decoy to stave off the marriage his ex had no longer wanted and conceal what had really been happening. Ash closed his eyes against his own reflection in the glass. Some things were so shameful they couldn't be shared, no matter how good the friend.

He completed his shower routine with a bitter taste in his mouth. A taste that morphed into the sweetest honey when Essie slipped back into his mind. With her blue eyes blazing and indignation thickening her accent and giving her extra height... he'd wanted to kiss her pinched-with-disapproval mouth and haul her spectacular ass out of his club at the same time.

She'd duped him. And no one duped him any more. He made sure of that in his professional sphere; his uncompromising reputation had become legendary.

And personally...? Fuck, there he was a mess. But he'd get there if it killed him. He'd claw back control, starting with his libido and the temptation threatening to derail him in the shape of Essie Newbold.

Now he had to spend the next two months both avoiding her and checking up on her so she had no opportunity to hoodwink him again. Not to mention hiding the fact he'd fucked her from his best friend, all the while fighting the urge to repeat the mistake.

Hi, Ben, how was New York? You know how I never date? Yeah, you understand why... Well, just FYI, I fucked your shiny new sister and I wouldn't mind having another crack at it, no strings. Hope you don't mind...

For a man who loved the law, loved truth and valued honesty and loyalty, he had certainly waded in some pretty murky waters recently. And it messed with his already reeling head.

He'd thought a satisfying night with the bubbly, curvaceous redhead would soothe his battered pride and redress the balance. But all it had done was land him deeper in the shit and reaffirm his stance on trusting no one.

Slamming out of the fogged-up cubicle, Ash threw a towel over his head and scrubbed at his hair. Looping that one around his damp shoulders, he quickly towelled his legs dry and then wrapped the second towel around his waist.

Just as he'd finished cleaning his teeth, he heard the noise and froze, every sense on high alert.

Someone was inside his apartment.

His SW1 penthouse apartment equipped with state-of-the-art security.

'Um, hello...?' A female voice.

Tossing the towel from around his neck, he strode

from his en-suite bathroom, expecting perhaps to find the building manager or the cleaner he'd hired to ready the place for his arrival.

He came to a halt just inside his bedroom.

Essie stood in the doorway, her cheeks flushed as if she'd been running and her mouth hanging open as her stare took a slow, sensual meander over his naked torso. Her hot eyes settled on his groin.

He'd been hard most of the day, thinking about her and their night together. Hard in the shower, tempted to bang one out just to attain a measure of relief from the memory of her tight warmth gripping him. And now here she was. Wide eyes touching every inch of his bare skin, and the hard again parts of him behind the towel.

Her chest lifted and fell with shallow pants, which pushed her luscious, pert breasts in his direction. Having taken her time leisurely touring his body, she met his stare again.

He lifted one brow, lips twitching, tempted to fling off the towel so she could really go to town.

'You wanted something?' Had she come for a do-over? Fuck—that was refreshing.

It wasn't his usual style, but damn if he wasn't seriously considering bending the rules and bending her over. Just to clarify that it had been as ball-emptying as he remembered.

No. He didn't do second times. Clearly his libido was on New York time.

She stuttered back to life. 'I... I... Ben needs you to sign these forms for the bank. He couldn't get hold of you.' A pretty pink flush stained her chest above the neckline of her dress, which still bore this morning's coffee stain. It did nothing to diminish her allure. If anything, it heightened her attractiveness, a sign she was human, clumsy and lacked the vanity to rush home and change.

'I was in the gym and then the shower. How did you get in?' He took the folder from her and tossed it onto the bed. Perhaps he should offer her the use of his washer and dryer…get another glimpse of that phenomenal body.

Wishful thinking, asshole.

The phone in her hand buzzed, and she glanced at it, distracted.

He dropped his towel as if he were alone and strode to the dresser, selecting a fresh pair of black cotton boxers. If she chose to waltz into his home uninvited…

'For goodness' sake—do you have to?'

He shot her a look, the underwear he'd been about to don still dangling from his hand. Why should he be alone in this fierce, futile and, frankly, damned inconvenient attraction? Time to play with her a little.

'Hey, you saunter into my home, uninvited. If you don't want to find a guy naked, I suggest you call or knock first.'

He tugged the boxers on, noting with a slug of satisfaction the way her stare clung to his nakedness until the last second. Or perhaps she was gloating at his steely length, ready for action. But he was only human. She was a beautiful woman with a knockout body—but that didn't mean he'd act on his unconscious reaction to her. Or his conscious thoughts of splaying her over his bed and fucking her out of his system for good.

Her cheeks flamed.

Another buzz of the phone.

Someone was desperate to get hold of her.

'Got a hot date?'

She scowled a death stare at him, dropped the phone into her bag and then fisted her hands on her hips as if she couldn't quite believe his audacity.

Believe away, darling.

'None of your business.' She tossed her head with a haughty lift of her chin, the long swathe of russet hair gliding over her shoulders. How would that gorgeous hair look spread over her naked back as he took her from behind; the tips brushing her rosy nipples as he pinned her to the wall and sank to his knees in front of her; spread out over his stark white bed sheets as he pummelled her up the mattress?

'So first you accuse me of being a liar, and now you break into my home just to give me attitude?' He could live with the latter, but having his integrity questioned pricked at the crude stitches holding him together.

She glared but had the good grace to blush. 'Look. I… I'm sorry about calling you a liar. You didn't actually lie to me. I just… I was gobsmacked to see you again.'

'Apology accepted. And that made two of us.' Ash

moved to his walk-in closet, still visualising all the ways he'd like to make her come.

'But, I didn't break in,' she called after him. 'Ben told me where to find your spare key. And I *did* knock.'

'Ah, yes. Ben. A bit awkward, isn't it?' He selected a black T-shirt and poked his head around the door as he tugged it on, furious that his urge to touch her again was not only still present but seemed to intensify despite the stained dress, reminders of her name-calling and his own rigid rules. Well, if he had to suffer, he wanted answers. 'Tell me, what is a graduate with a PhD doing working behind a bar?' She was too smart for this job to be a career move, unless her degree was in hospitality management.

She bristled, her hip jutted to one side in a move that accentuated her curves and the shapely length of her bare legs. Legs he'd like to sink between… face first.

'I… I'm considering my career options. Ben was left in the lurch, and us working together is a good opportunity to get to know each other better.'

So she had a mission that involved spending time with Ben? Damned inconvenient for him and his raging inner battle, but equally intriguing, forcing her deeper into the crevices of his mind where she'd taken up residence since yesterday. He needed an eviction notice.

Another buzz from her bag. Why didn't she silence the damn thing?

'Why don't you answer that?'

She shook her head. 'It's just some…notifications.'

She breathed a long sigh. 'Look, we're all grown-ups.' She looked at him while she twisted a few strands of her hair the way she had yesterday. Perhaps, like him, her head was saying one thing while her body had ideas on a refresher.

But Ash didn't do regret over relationships any more—been there, done that. Look where he'd ended up after yesterday's lapse in judgment. And he was damned determined not to give in to the unfathomable desire currently dragging at him. A desire to have a second dip in the water.

'It was just a one-night thing. As I told you, unlike you, I'm no expert. But isn't it best to just…move on? Forget it ever happened?'

Was she convincing herself?

And she was right. His head had moved on pretty quickly—he'd trained himself well. But his libido, and his dick in particular, were as keen as mustard. It must be those damn flirty dresses that clung to her gorgeous tits like a second skin. Or her warm cinnamon scent infecting his bedroom. Or that pouty bottom lip her teeth kept tugging on…

'I'm sure it makes sense to you, too. After all, we have to work together.'

He emerged from the closet tugging up his jeans and buttoning the fly, trapping his still-eager dick behind a row of studs. If only he could trap his erotic musings as easily.

'Do we? Couldn't you resign? Tell Ben you've changed your mind?' Yes—remove temptation. She and Ben could get to know each other on their own time. His own sisters drove him crazy sometimes—how much time did they really need to spend together?

There was a small gasp as if he'd suggested abandoning kittens at the roadside. 'I'm not letting Ben down like that.'

'Surely he won't care.'

For a second she paled as if he'd struck a deep, throbbing nerve. 'Why would you say that? What has Ben said?'

Until today he'd never given much thought to Ben's news a year or so back that he had a half-sister in London. Their friendship had stretched over the years as careers took hold, their recent contact limited to a snatched beer after work or a trip to the gym. What was the nature of Ben's relationship with Essie? How close were they and why had she been out of the picture growing up?

One thing was certain: she didn't know Ben well enough to be confident in his reaction to her quitting. Interesting… He shrugged. 'I just mean I can replace you within the hour. No disruption to service.'

Fire shone from her stare. 'Oh, I just bet you could. Well, I'm not disposable and I'm not that easily substituted.' She stalked nearer, shunting his body temperature dangerously high with her teasing scent—summer, cinnamon and all woman. 'I'm not an inconvenience to be sidelined, quietly slinking away as if I don't exist.'

Whoa, where was all that coming from? He had clearly done more than touch a nerve—he'd sawed one in half and poured salt on the cut ends.

Her eyes danced over his crotch and then lifted. 'Couldn't you move back to New York?'

Not until the gossip-feeding frenzy had died down and his personal life was no longer entertainment news, but he wasn't sharing that shit. And why? So that she didn't have to feel embarrassed about over-sharing with her one-night stand? He parried with a step of his own. 'But then what would you stare at?'

'What do you mean?'

'You're practically drooling, sweetheart. I know I was a little wiped out last night, so if you want another crack at it...' He tilted his head towards the massive bed, which dominated the room like an elephant, every muscle tensed in anticipation of finally getting what he craved.

She closed the distance between them, eyes glazed and mouth open as if lust oozed from every pore.

'I'm perfectly capable of separating a meaningless fuck from the work that needs to be done at the club.' Her stare lingered on his mouth.

Was she waiting?

For the pithy reply banked up on his tongue, or another taste? His mind fogged as her proximity, her scent, her heat flooded his blood with the testosterone that had dogged him all day, just knowing she worked in the same building. Close enough to hear her throaty chuckle while she spoke to contractors and the soft humming that accompanied her fingers clacking on her keyboard.

'*My* club.' Time to remind Miss Compartmentalised who steered the ship. 'But are you capable of the work? Ben and I need someone honest, dependable, committed.' Ash ignored the flare that turned her irises to molten metal. He ignored the urgency of his own needs beating at his body until his muscles screamed with inertia. 'Tell me, who are you today?'

Her hands fisted on her hips, a move that tightened the fabric across her full breasts outlining her erect nipples…begging for his tongue?

'What does that mean?'

'Yesterday a ditsy student tourist, today a competent professional in charge of *my* club? I don't take well to being deceived.' He battled for his legendary control, which he relied on as armour to protect himself. 'I don't trust you. So until I know my club is in safe hands, you and I will be working very closely together. Got that?'

Her stare narrowed but her eyes gleamed with something close to the incandescent flare burning through his veins. Perhaps that was the answer: to fuck this inexplicable chemistry out of their systems; to quench the fire. He'd said it wouldn't happen again, but that was before she'd stormed into his bedroom. Before all her talk about meaningless fucks and moving on. Before she'd drooled over his deliberate nudity and was still mentally stripping him with her hungry, slumberous stare.

Her mouth hung open while said stare burned the flesh from his features. 'I'd never do anything to damage Ben's business—you're just paranoid.' She dropped her bag and fisted her hands on her hips once more.

He inched closer, chest puffed. 'You've got that right. It works well for me these days.'

Her eyes blazed. 'I'm here to help my brother open *his* club. No matter how much you want me gone.' Her breath hitched. 'Unless I hear it from Ben that my services are no longer required, I'm staying, so you'd better get used to the idea.'

She jutted her chin forward, bringing her mouth only centimetres from his, her breath fanning his face. She looked halfway to orgasm already—panting, flushed, her mouth saying one thing while her body strained in his direction.

Don't touch her.

Back away.

Too late...

In less than a heartbeat she'd pushed her hands into his still-damp hair and dragged his face down. But he'd been on the move himself. He scooped her around the waist and hauled her from the floor. Their mouths clashed and she gave a cry close to a victory wail as she parted her lips under the surge and slide of his ferocious kiss.

All reason fled. Their tongues touched, the thrust and parry of wildness a perfectly matched duel. Her body moulded to his as if they'd been forged side by side. Her passion seemed to enflame the lust that had been simmering in him since she'd swanned into his office this morning—his knees almost buckled. He wasn't alone.

Who was this woman he couldn't resist? Her wilful determination turned him on as much as it pissed him off and her demanding sexuality was…magnificent. His first impressions about her had been dead wrong. Essie fully embraced her sexuality—another fascinating aspect to her complex personality.

Like electricity and water, they sparked off each other. Her hands twisted his hair until he growled. Her greedy mouth sucked on his lips as if she wanted to consume him whole and her thighs clung to his waist as he hoisted her higher to press his steely length against her warm, wet centre, delivering the friction they both seemed to crave.

If he hadn't been staring her down, eye-to-eye, while they consumed each other, his eyes would have rolled back in his head. Her fantastic body aligned with his, her wet heat seeped through the denim covering his thigh as she ground herself there and her nipples poked through the two layers of clothing separating her chest from his.

A fresh surge of blood turned his dick to granite. Yes.

One more time to banish this tigress masquerading as a pussycat from his system and restore his control over the explosive situation. He didn't need to trust her. He just had to fuck her. Just sex. Great sex. One last astounding time.

With one arm now curled around his neck like a vice, her free hand snaked between their bodies to rub him through his jeans before fumbling for the buttons of his fly. She writhed in his arms, all sexy little whimpers and catches of her breath. Fuck, she was a hellcat. Challenging, uninhibited, eager. He'd been doomed from the minute he'd opened his eyes to the sight of her yesterday in the sun-dappled park.

He spread his feet, cementing his balance so he could do a little exploring of his own. Cupping her ass in one hand, Ash delved beneath the hem of her dress with the other. His fingers skimmed her thigh, zeroing in on her to find the source of the warm patch on his jeans—her soaked panties. With their working mouths and challenging stares still locked, he slipped his fingers beyond the cotton and lace.

She was fiery hot and slick against his fingers, and when he swiped forward and located her clit she broke free from the kiss with a moan. Her sultry glare—half *fuck you*, half *fuck me*—dared him. Spurred him on. Not that he required the encouragement.

In two strides, he'd deposited her ass on the edge of his dresser, which, like the rest of his home, was sleek, minimal and uncluttered. She spread her thighs, welcoming him into the cradle of space she created with a tug of his shirt.

While his fingers resumed the slip and slide against her, his other hand sought her pebbled nipple, strumming through the layers of fabric. But that wasn't enough for her. She released her grip on his shoulders long enough to unbutton the top few buttons of her dress and yank both it and her bra down, exposing one pale, creamy shoulder and a perfect, pink-tipped breast.

Fuck.

He groaned.

Perfection.

He dived to get his mouth on her. *Just one more taste.* Then he'd stop this madness.

But Essie was having none of that. One hand returned to his hair, her grip punishing and directive while the other drove him wild by rubbing his erection through his clothes. Her pert flesh filled his mouth and he sucked hard, drawing her in deeper and guided by her continued twisting and tugging on his hair and her repeated 'yes'es. Her hips shunted against his hand, as if she was as desperate for her release as he was.

Just one more time. Until he worked this baffling urge from his off-kilter system. This time he'd walk away sated, equilibrium restored. Cured.

Pinning her to the furniture with his hips, he pushed two fingers inside her and feathered his thumb over her clit. His mouth returned to hers while his fingers strummed the damp nipple his mouth left behind.

True to the Essie of last night, she clawed his shoulders, her moans growing in frequency and volume.

'Tell me when you're close,' he mumbled against her lips, reluctant to break away from her breathy and frantic kisses.

She nodded, her eyes heavy and her hair a wild tumble around her flushed face. His clothing was practically cutting off his blood supply to his groin. But he couldn't move, couldn't have stopped now if he'd had a gun to his head.

He left her breast long enough to scoop one arm around her hips and shunt her ass to the edge of the dresser, changing the angle of her hips.

She cried out and tore her mouth from his. 'Yes, now... I'm...'

He dived on her exposed nipple once more, laving and lapping like a starving man as his fingers plundered her slickness and his thumb circled her swollen clit.

She detonated, her whole body taut as her orgasm jolted her forward. If he hadn't been there to block her fall the force of it would have tumbled her from the edge of the furniture. Ash kept up the sucking and circling until he'd wrung every spasm from her magnificent, trembling body. Until she pushed at his shoulders instead of clawing at them.

Her head fell forward, resting on his chest. 'Oh, wow...'

The scent of her hair made his eyes roll back. Thank fuck she couldn't see. He recited the most boring legal jargon he could think of to stop himself from burying his nose there and taking a deep, decadent inhalation. He'd fall asleep surrounded by her honeyed scent, just as he had last night...

Fuck.

His blood turned to liquid nitrogen.

What the hell was he doing?

He couldn't trust this woman.

He couldn't trust anyone.

His body turned rigid as reality dawned.

This had disaster written all over it. This business

venture was his fresh start—a place no one knew him or his fucked-up family. A place of anonymity to regroup and wrestle back control. Why was he so fascinated in her? Why couldn't he stay away?

He stepped back, tugging his hand from Essie's underwear and avoiding her confused stare. He lowered her to the floor, steadying her by the elbows while she found her balance and righted her debauched clothing.

Too late for gentlemanly heroics now. Not that he claimed to be either. Not any more. That was a fool's game.

He sucked back a swallow that reminded him of all the reasons his head had been right about this ill-advised encounter after all. He'd tasted betrayal— a different kind, but it sucked all the same. He was done with trusting the wrong person.

The humiliating scene at the Jacob Holdings offices flashed into his head. On discovering his father had been cheating on his mother, he'd lashed out at the man he'd worked alongside for ten years. He'd expected his old man to bristle, maybe tell him to mind his own business, but he hadn't expected the vile mouthful of home truths he'd received in return.

Fire snaked along his frozen blood vessels, reminding him of the subsequent damage he'd inflicted, especially on the mother he'd been trying to protect.

He turned away, adjusting his rapidly diminishing hard-on, which recoiled at both the bitter memories of his fight with Hal and the reality that he barely knew this woman he couldn't seem to leave alone.

'What? We're done?'

He turned back and offered a single, decisive nod. End it now. With his sanity and dignity intact, his fresh start still tenable and his principles only slightly grubby.

For the longest beat she stared, her expression neutral but her eyes stormy. Wordlessly she skirted him as if he were a shark and walked to his bed. She collected the file he'd tossed there earlier and returned to stand in front of him.

'So, counsellor—' she blatantly eyed the bulge in his jeans '—the defence rests?'

His fingers curled into fists to stop himself from kissing her sassy mouth once more. Pissed at him and flushed from her orgasm, she was even more breathtaking.

He ground his jaw clenched. 'I think it's best.' He'd never needed his attorney poker face more.

She barked a humourless snort. 'Don't worry. I may not be an expert at casual sex, but I am an expert at surviving rejection.'

What the fuck...?

She pressed the file to his chest, holding it there until his hand replaced hers.

'This needs to be scanned by six.' She slid one last look down his torso to his still-hard dick. 'Have a good evening.'

And she left.

CHAPTER FOUR

'EVERYTHING'S FINE,' Essie said to Ben. His partner wanted to replace her as if she were…an inconvenience. She'd thrown herself at a man who'd had the sense to resist. And she had no idea where Ben's head stood and was too scared to ask. Sure, everything was fine.

Essie hunched over the desk and rubbed at a nonexistent scratch. Perhaps that was why her joy at his call was diluted. Fear that Ben, too, would agree with Ash and fire her, then disappear from her life as quickly as he'd appeared.

'Are you sure?' said Ben.

She pressed the phone to her face and hoped her brother couldn't hear the blood pounding through her head. She shouldn't be wallowing—she had work to do. 'Of course. The decorators finished up today and I'm meeting your head barman soon.' Ben trusted her with his club, and she wouldn't allow her frenzied attraction to Ash to make waves or damage his business venture.

No. She and Ash were done.

But the years of self-doubt had infected her fresh start with Ben. Every childhood disappointment, every time her father let her down and every cruel taunt from her overcritical ex rattled in her brain until nausea threatened.

Perhaps Ash was right. She should walk away.

No. She wanted a future as part of Ben's life. And their father had already robbed her of a past with her only sibling.

'How are things in New York?' Had he seen their father? Had Frank Newbold asked about her? She shouldn't care, but that little girl part of her, the part that had idolised him, had flown into his outstretched arms every time he'd come home, still craved his attention, even when she'd declared herself done with his toxic brand of parenthood.

'Someone's putting their hand in the cash register.'

Essie gasped. 'Oh, no, Ben. That's terrible.' A slab of guilt settled on her shoulders. Ben needed drama at The Yard as much as she needed another brush-off from Ash.

'I'll sort it out, don't worry. Did the bank get their signature in time?'

Essie's face heated with the reminder of what she'd done last night.

'Yes.' Despite all the reasons not to, despite Ash's obvious ability to resist, she yearned for the full-on repeat performance Ash had denied her yesterday.

He'd wanted her—the physical evidence, thick and hard behind his fly, had been irrefutable. She'd never have guessed a sexually charged man like Ash

possessed so much command over his body. Or her
so little.

The trust between her and Ash was non-existent.
He seemed to think she was some sort of industrial
spy out to ruin his investment and she couldn't be
sure he wouldn't sack her at any moment, regardless of her relationship to Ben. But she wanted him
anyway. Physically. Another new experience for her.

She'd trusted her ex with a blind faith that left her
curled into a tight ball. She'd been so desperate to
make just one relationship work that she'd ignored
the warning signs—the criticisms, the bullying, the
control. When he'd finally grown bored and left her
on the grounds that she was too clingy, and she'd
seen clearly for the first time how dysfunctional the
relationship had been, she'd vowed never again to
give someone that kind of power.

And she certainly wouldn't give it to Ash.

But, she'd known the minute he'd stepped from
his en-suite bathroom, droplets of water dotting his
sculpted torso with only the towel and his scowl as
a barrier, she'd intended to make good on her plan
to seduce him then walk away. A plan that had put
the control of their rampant sexual attraction firmly
in her hands.

But that chemistry between them had become a
magnetised force field drawing her in, and her plan
had backfired. She'd seduced him all right, but she'd
bungled it. Failed to put a stop to the wild kissing
and grinding that had scored her another orgasm,

but scored Ash another point on his 'ability to resist her' scale.

'Are you and Ash getting to know each other?' Ben's voice pulled her back from thoughts of Ash's naked body, every inch of him hard and straining...

No.

Ash was getting to know how easily he could turn her on to the point of spontaneous combustion. How eagerly she surrendered to their physical need that flared to life like a science experiment gone wrong. How her traitorous body succumbed to the pleasure he crafted so effortlessly.

The only positive outcome, aside from the fantastic sex, was that her blog post on one-night stands had been quoted on one of the UK's top online women's magazines and reposted over and over on social media. It seemed people loved *Illegally Hot*. The spike in followers and comments had, only this morning, spurred Essie into publishing another article featuring the panty-melting *Illegally Hot*, entitled *Dares, Disasters and Don't Go Theres*—those relationships we knew were bad for us, but we craved them anyway—drawing on last night's disappointing disaster. As if purging her thoughts, her fears, her doubts in cyberspace would cure her of her irresistible and seemingly one-sided attraction to Ash Jacob.

It was wrong, but she couldn't deny the buzz that the soar of popularity delivered. She'd always considered her blog as something of a hobby, but, with her PhD complete, perhaps the boost in credibility was just what she needed to take herself more seriously as a writer. She could even start running some pay-per-click ads…invite experts in the field to guest blog… She scribbled down some ideas while she zoned back to answering her brother's question. 'Not really.' Apart from Ash's bedroom skills and his considerable control, she knew zilch. A fact her analytical brain tolerated poorly.

'What's his deal? He seems a little…uptight.'

Plus he hated her, wanted to fire her and didn't trust her.

'Has he upset you?' The fact that Ben had protective instincts towards her left her gooey inside. But the only thing she needed protection from was her own reckless libido. The goo turned to brittle concrete.

'No, of course not.' Another lie. Because she *was* upset. Upset that she'd buckled to her searing attraction to the infuriating man, who displayed enough warning signs to send her running. And furious that she couldn't be certain, given half a chance, she wouldn't do it all over again.

'He…he said he doesn't trust people.' What was that about? Just her? Women in general? The entire world?

'He is a bit closed off…' A small sigh.

Closed off? A massive understatement. She'd need a pickaxe to excavate Ash's psyche.

No. Focus on the sex. Control that.

What was she thinking?

No more sex.

Her voice squeezed past strangled vocal cords.

'How are you two friends? You're such a lovely, warm person.' Ben and Ash had known each other a long time. Essie's stomach clenched. She'd gate-crashed a long-standing friendship with her ill-judged fling. But it was over now.

Ben chuckled and then went silent. 'He wasn't al-ways so...uncompromising. It's not my story to tell, but let's just say he was badly hurt by an ex.'

Something they shared in common.

'It's left him with trust issues that make him a bit cynical.'

Cynical. Controlled to the point of snapping.

Of course a broken love affair would be to blame. Essie knew both first-hand and professionally that only relationships had the emotional power to wreak such long-lasting havoc. The psychologist in her longed to probe Ash's secrets in light of this new clue, her resolve to ignore him stretched paper thin.

The least she could do, for Ben's sake, was try to give the exasperating man the benefit of the doubt professionally while giving him a wide berth per-sonally. Ben deserved better than returning from his business trip to find his partner and his manager at each other's throats.

Perhaps, with a little subtle digging, she could help him deal with whatever held him back. Because if she knew anything, she knew Ash Jacob was on the run from something. Not a crime...more like a battered heart. She knew the signs—she'd spent years seeing them in the mirror. And she preferred to divert attention to other people's dysfunctional relationships than focus on her own.

The idea that Ash might be pining for a lost love left a bad taste in her mouth, one without an explanation. A change of subject. 'I'll have to speak to you some other time. Josh your star barman is due any minute.'

With her hollow assurances echoing in her head, and her mind racing with Ben's cryptic confession, she ended the call to her brother just as a text came in.

Josh had arrived.

Essie rushed to the rear entrance to welcome the twenty-one-year-old classics student. They headed to the bar and were halfway through introductions when Ash joined them without being invited.

Essie froze mid-sentence. Her body zinged from relaxed to nerve-tingling awareness.

Josh was handsome in that trendy, glasses-and-beard kind of way. But the mere presence of Ash in the space—his imposing height, intense, bright blue stare and commanding demeanour—shunted the room temperature to stifling. She couldn't even waft out the pheromones before they had chance to hijack her brain again and enslave her until she started clawing at his sublime suit.

Before she could question his presence, Ash stuck out his hand and introduced himself to Josh. 'I'm Ash Jacob, co-owner.' He flicked a curt nod at Essie and took a seat at the bar. 'Carry on.'

Carry on? Carry on? How was she supposed to

do that when the mere sight of him decked out like the sort of lawyer she'd never be able to afford fried all her neuronal impulses not directly relayed to her lady parts and robbed her saliva-making capabilities?

And sitting in on Josh's orientation? He hadn't issued an idle threat or exaggerated last night. He didn't trust her. He intended to watch her every move in case she put a foot wrong and committed some sackable offence. She bristled. As if she'd *ever* do anything to jeopardise her brother's enterprise. Did he think she'd put her hand in the till or help herself to the vodka?

Jerk.

All her good intentions to make peace with him, to help him, fled. She'd prove to him that, not only was she one hundred per cent invested in this club, but she could employ similar levels of self-restraint to the ones he'd shown.

She was dreaming if she believed they could be friends—the sexual-attraction barrier loomed in the way like an immovable boulder worthy of Stonehenge. But that didn't mean she had to act on her… urge. Again.

She led Josh behind the bar, seeking inspiration or at least a distraction from the persistent throb between her legs. How could Ash Jacob's brand of sex be so addictive? She'd only had one little taste…one and a half. He was orgasm nicotine and her poor brain's pleasure centres had taken a massive hit. No wonder she was reeling…

'Ben said you have lots of past experience so feel

free to set up the bar area as works best for you.' The words squeaked past her constricted throat and she bent to slide a box of spirits out of the way.

Josh chatted away, filling the stilted silence with his relevant work experience and his ideas for making the bar space work.

She barely heard a word. Too aware of Ash scraping his keen eyes over her while his mouth formed a mildly amused smirk.

But, oh, what talent that mouth possessed. He should forget about law—his oral skills were seriously wasted in the boardroom. She'd never been so thoroughly kissed, nibbled, licked… Her nipples chafed against her bra and her legs grew restless, desperate to rub together to ease the ache at their juncture.

Sensing a pause in Josh's speech, Essie forced her mind away from Mr Jacob, orgasm whisperer.

'What about cocktails? Could you create a house cocktail, something unique, associated only with us?' She'd made that last bit up on the spur of the moment. She seen it done at other clubs, and it matched the philosophy Ben had for The Yard.

Josh answered and Essie busied her hands with straightening a perfectly aligned row of shot glasses as a substitute for drooling over Ash, who'd narrowed his eyes and begun idly rubbing his lower lip with his thumb and forefinger while he listened and observed.

Forget drooling—she was half tempted to see Josh promptly on his way and ride Ash right where he sat. Or drop to her knees, release him from his so-

phisticated trousers and swallow him whole. Wipe
that smug, self-satisfied grin off his face. Show him
she could rile him up as easily, effectively and thoroughly as he did her.

No. They'd been there, done that. The sex was
over. She'd humiliated herself enough.

Time to focus on her job and on Ben.

That was the relationship that required her energy.
A rewarding sibling bond, family, longevity. Something she'd craved her whole life. After all, she'd put
her beloved blog, her future career on partial hiatus
just to work alongside her brother. And who knew
how long he'd stay in London? If he moved back to
New York, the opportunity to build family ties, to be
a part of each other's daily lives, would be severely
compromised.

Her stomach pinched as if she'd sucked one of the
lemons sitting on the gleaming bar in a glass bowl.
'Well, I'll leave you to set up and familiarise yourself with everything.'

Josh smiled and started unpacking the box of spirits.

Essie rounded the bar and Ash swivelled on his
bar stool, the creak of leather drawing her attention
to him spreading his thighs wider.

Man-spreading?

Staking his claim as the dominant male in the
room?

When she looked up from his crotch, he held her
gaze, one eyebrow raised in challenge as if he knew

the flighty zigzagging of her earlier thoughts and their X-rated bent.

This was impossible. How was she expected to get anything done when he hovered nearby, watching her every move, tying her into sexually frustrated knots with just a quirk of his brow and some male posturing to which her qualifications and knowledge of body language should render her immune?

She turned a sickly sweet smile on Ash. 'Mr Jacob, do you have any questions for Josh?'

'No.' Ash rose to his feet. 'But I will speak with you in my office when you're ready.'

After Ash stalked through the staff door, Essie hovered in the bar area straightening chairs to gain a moment's reprieve from the hormonal maelstrom Ash induced.

With a deep breath she followed him, finding him behind his desk. She left the door open. Her, Ash, enclosed spaces…not happening.

'What the hell was that?' she snapped.

He shrugged, rising slowly from the chair and stalking to a halt mere inches in front of her face.

'What's the problem? I told you, until I'm certain my shiny new business is in safe hands, I'm all over you.'

Essie's eyes mentally rolled back with the fantasy his words concocted. Him sweaty. Her writhing. More life-redefining orgasms.

Yes, please.

'I can't do my job with you…hovering. And surely you're too busy…preparing briefs or something?' Her unfortunate choice of words forced a rage of heat up her neck—he'd looked astounding yesterday, both in and out of his tight-fitting briefs as he'd strutted around his bedroom, a supreme specimen of rugged maleness. Every inch of him lean and ripped—all smooth golden skin with a dusky sprinkling of dark hair as near to black as the silky mop on his head. No inhibitions and no need for any.

And even though he'd only been partially aroused then, as he'd donned his underwear and jeans, the sight of him had still left her mouth pooling with saliva and her clit throbbing. *Astounding.*

What was wrong with her? She never obsessed over men, physically or emotionally. Well, not since her ex. Essie Newbold, psychologist, would-be relationship expert—at least on paper—was now far too well informed to fall victim to the games played in the name of those relationships. Ash could do all the male posturing he liked—she simply suffered from a bad case of lust. She could control those...urges. Writing about it helped.

'Actually, I have some instructions for you.' His grin widened, eyes turning feral.

She practically choked. 'You...what...?' Her knees wobbled while she imagined the kind of instructions she'd like to hear coming from his mouth.

Strip. Spread your thighs. Bend over...

Stop.

He lifted that one brow. Mocking. Testing. 'You do work here.'

'Yes, but—'

'Good. I want you to go home now and pack an overnight bag. Where do you live?'

Was he for real?

Where the hell was he sending her?

Had he decided to winkle her out from under his nose by stealth? Send her on some fool's errand and insinuate a replacement in her stead behind her back?

'I live in New Cross.' At his blank expression she added, 'South London. Where am I going?' Perhaps he'd decided to work her to death so she would quit. Did he expect her to pull an all-nighter? The Yard wasn't even open yet.

'You're coming with me to Paris. Do you have someone who can pack a bag for you? We leave at six.'

Paris?

With him.

No way.

'I… I have a flatmate. But I'm not going to Paris with you.' The words had barely escaped her mouth when the throb returned between her legs. Twice as ferocious.

Him.

Her.

Alone in the city of love.

Whoa there. Don't get carried away—this is real life, not some fluffy shit you made up for your blog. He's done with you physically and he doesn't trust you. Oh…and you've used his sexual prowess to validate your online relationship advice.

Her face flamed. Why *had* she done that?

He smiled, the feline kind of smile that told her he saw too much.

'Worried you won't be able to control yourself?' He closed in. His eyes dipped to her mouth.

Huh, right... The air trapped in Essie's lungs. He was so close, a cloud of heat rose from him, carrying the scent of whatever he'd used in the shower that morning to Essie's nose.

And then he leaned down so his breath tickled her ear and sent tiny muscular spasms skittering down her exposed neck to reawaken her nipples. 'Now who's flattering themselves?' He reared back, his expression hard, serious, uncompromising. All business.

Bastard.

'We have work to do. Didn't Ben mention it?'

She shook her head, her feeble body swaying as the adrenaline dissipated.

'There's a club we wanted to check out. The best in France. Perhaps the best in Europe.'

He slung his hands casually into his trouser pockets so the fabric stretched taut across his groin. Essie dragged her eyes away, desperate now to get away from him so she could regroup and fortify her defences with Ash-proof razor wire and hormone repellent spray.

'I didn't get where I am today by being second best. The Yard is going to be number one. So we're going to go see what the competition is up to.' He tapped the desk with two fingers and then levelled them at her.

'Call your roommate. My driver will collect your bag in—' he checked his watch '—thirty minutes.'

Essie's weak body veered from nuclear meltdown to hypothermia. Her mind conjured excuses...*no passport...an ingrown toenail...an allergy to France*.

How would she survive a trip to Paris with Mr Rigid Control? There would be no way to escape the temptation of him for the hours of travelling time, trapped in a moving vehicle with only his astounding profile, catnip scent and magnetic sex appeal for distraction. Her poor ovaries would shrivel from exhaustion.

She lifted her chin. 'Will I be paid overtime?' She might as well make him suffer financially if he wouldn't be suffering from blue balls, although she doubted her meagre salary would hurt Mr Moneybags too much.

'Of course.'

'Separate hotel rooms?' She might be unable to refuse his reasonable, Ben-sanctioned request, but at least she would be able to escape the lure of lust when the work was over.

His mouth twitched.

'If you like, but surely that horse has bolted...' He shrugged.

Arsehole.

And why was he looking at her as if he remembered every detail of her naked? He'd turned away from her last night, put an end to the mad ride she'd have willingly enjoyed until the end. Perhaps despite his control he was still interested. That would certainly explain the way he looked at her. Her breasts throbbed and her clit tingled.

But where did that leave her and her tattered and grubby good intentions? Perhaps she should even the score; take back control of the physical attraction that showed no signs of abating, for either of them; remind him what he'd turned down. She narrowed her eyes. If she had to survive the extreme sexual frustration of being in his company she should definitely play him at his own game.

Her phone, set to send a notification every time someone commented on her blog, vibrated in her pocket, a timely reminder. *Aren't you already playing him? Writing about him?* Illegally Hot *is a real person.*

She swallowed and forced her thoughts back to ways of avoiding a repeat of yesterday's humiliating rejection. So he'd resisted once. So he wanted to pretend this insane chemistry would disappear. Time to up the ante. Bring out the big guns. Her mind scrabbled through the contents of her underwear drawer for the sexiest lingerie she owned—a treat to herself when she'd graduated with her first-class psychology degree. Some women loved shoes. Essie loved frilly knickers.

At least her roommate, Sarah, would be home cramming for exams today—she'd buy her flatmate something gorgeous from Paris to say thanks. A small smile tugged her mouth. Why should she suffer alone? The least she could do was take him down with her.

'Fine. And I insist on separate rooms.' She moved to the door, halting at his sexy drawl.

'Oh, and, Essie. Don't forget your passport.' With a wink that made a strangled gasp catch in her dry throat, he closed the door behind her.

The car probably cost more than her rented flat in South London—soft leather seats, sleek, shiny bodywork and chauffer driven. It even had a privacy screen. Not that they'd need that. The minute Ash held open the door for her and ushered her inside, he pulled out his phone and began tapping away.

Essie normally enjoyed silence—you could learn a lot about someone by people-watching. Their tells, their habits, their unconscious body language. But all she'd learned about Ash, apart from that the man never looked anything less than seriously fuckable, was that she wanted to know more.

Ben had told her Ash was from New York royalty, his family dating back to a wave of nineteenth-century immigrants. He'd worked for Jacob Holdings, his family-owned real estate business, since leaving college. He'd been to Harvard, and his net worth made her light-headed. But why had he moved to London? Who had broken his heart? And why couldn't he be less attractive so she wasn't incapacitated by the urge to jump him?

'Forgive me.' He looked up from his phone, his deep voice interrupting her train of thought. 'The time zones are messing with my schedule. I had some

New York deadlines to meet.' He pocketed the device and gave her his full, panty-melting attention.

Essie shivered, hot then cold, sliding her own phone into her pocket. She almost preferred being ignored.

The device buzzed immediately, halting whatever Ash had been about to say.

'That goes off a lot. Do you have a bet on? Tracking the stock market?' Playful glints sparked in his eyes, but she couldn't enjoy the banter for the slosh of stomach acid burning inside her. Her fans loved *Illegally Hot* and wanted more of him. She knew the feeling.

If only they could see him, edible in his crisp suit, his hair dishevelled and a scruffy smattering of facial hair reminding her how it felt to be kissed by that beautiful mouth.

'Something like that.' She shrugged, her cheeks hot. She should never have started the *Illegally Hot* posts. She changed the subject before she confessed.

'So, this club we're scouting—is there a dress code?' She only owned one little black dress, one she had asked Sarah to pack into her overnight bag. She'd seen plenty of photos of him with hot dates— gorgeous, sophisticated women: models, actresses, heiresses. Compared to the women he usually associated with, she'd definitely be the country mouse.

Except this wasn't a date. It didn't matter what she wore. She should have brought a bin bag, just so her libido stayed in check.

Ash turned and slid his gaze along the length of

her body until she squirmed and heat flooded her panties. 'Whatever you wear will be fine.' A shrug. 'I know the owner.'

So it wasn't a date. That didn't mean she couldn't enjoy tormenting him while she suffered right alongside. Regardless of his impressive willpower, he looked at her as if she might as well be naked. His eyes wanted her even if the rest of him could resist.

'You can change on board. We'll be going straight to the club when we land.'

So they were still on the clock? Shame. Now she had him in a chatty mood, she'd like to unearth one or two juicy personal details to fill in the blanks. Like why he'd walked away from his New York life, his family business and what must be an extremely lucrative legal career. And why someone of his social standing, exceptional hotness and phenomenal bedroom skills was still single? No halitosis, in possession of a full head of luxuriant hair, and he wasn't a pervert.

'It's not my area of expertise, but Josh seems competent enough—would you agree?' He rubbed at his bottom lip, drawing her eyes there.

She'd probably agree to anything for the intense stare he settled on her and what it did to her pulse. How was she going to survive this trip when every nerve in her body vibrated, desperate to have him lose that control he wore like a second skin? Lose it with her.

'He does. It's not my area of expertise, either, although I can pull a pint.' Her cheeks warmed. She'd pulled him, too. In a park. She stuttered on, changing the veer of her thoughts. 'The DJ called to speak to Ben—know anything about techno house?'

Ash rubbed his jaw as if his scruff irritated him, and Essie's fingers twitched. That stubble had been amazing scraping across her sensitive nipple last night. How would it feel on her inner thighs?

Oh, no...don't go there.

Her experiences of oral sex were sadly unfulfilling. Her ex had claimed he didn't care for it, although he loved it when she returned the favour. She cringed at her younger self. Of course her ex had lacked skills in the foreplay and stamina departments, too—probably why she was struggling to resist the phenomenal Ash. She knew instinctively he would excel at oral sex—she'd kissed him after all, felt his mouth at her breasts... She discreetly blew at the wisps of hair clinging to her heated forehead. Another dangerous temptation to add to the growing list.

He smiled, the genuine, lopsided version that had landed her in this mess in the first place. 'No, not much. You?'

Essie shook her head. She loved to dance, but her clubbing days were few and far between. Long years of research-laden academic study had put paid to partying and wild nights out. And she hadn't been interested in the hook-up side of clubbing after she'd had her fingers burned with her ex.

'Perhaps we can leave that to Ben, on his return.' He leaned back in the seat and looked out of the window at the passing city, the route to London City

Airport taking them parallel to the river. 'So, tell me about you and Ben. You didn't grow up together?' He turned a shrewd stare her way.

Great. So he wanted to make conversation and he'd chosen the one subject that made her skin raw and her scalp prickle. Her relationship with her brother was still so fragile, and brought all her insecurities to the surface like a rash.

Ben and Ash were friends. But Ash had barely heard of her… Was Ben ashamed of the connection with his illegitimate half-sister? Or perhaps she was so low down on his list of priorities… Been there, done that.

She shook her heavy head. 'We share a father, but I grew up here and, as you know, Ben in New York.'

It shouldn't matter that Ben hadn't discussed her with his oldest friend enough for Ash to remember her name. Yes, Ben had been the one to reach out after he'd discovered the truth about Frank New-bold's other life. But perhaps he now regretted the impulse. Did he consider her a cling-on? An inconvenience? Something else to be managed or swept under the carpet?

Could she really blame Ben for being ashamed to broadcast the existence of a sibling he knew little about, his father's sordid secret? The shame she'd felt growing up with Frank's constant absences and see-through excuses rose to the surface, boiling hot. Could she criticise Ben when her own father hadn't found her lovable enough for him to stick around?

She choked down familiar fears. 'What about you

and Ben? He said you've been friends since grade school.'

Ash nodded, glancing away. 'He's a good friend.'

Well, that seemed to be the end of that.

'You don't give much away, do you?' The trust issues Ben talked about?

'Try me.' He lifted one brow, daring her.

So tempting. But she didn't want to scare him into brooding silence once more. Something easy. 'Do you have a sister?'

He nodded. 'I have two—twins. Younger. Both a pain in my ass.' He smiled, flashing the grooves around his mouth.

'What about girlfriends? Anyone pining for you back in New York?' Her throat grew hot and achy. Why had she asked that?

'No.' He shrugged. 'I don't do girlfriends.'

'Not ever?'

He shook his head, a slow measured action that gave his stare plenty of time to scrape over her heated face. 'Not for years.'

So the ex hadn't just hurt him, she'd ruined him. He really was as closed off as she'd suspected. She took pity on the grey tinge to his handsome face. 'Human interpersonal relationships are…complex.' Hers included. All she knew about the opposite sex, beyond the theory she'd got from books and lectures, she'd learned from the behaviour of her selfish, largely absent father and her cruel, manipulative ex. She swallowed down the familiar lump threatening to make her feel two inches tall and changed the subject.

'Fun fact—did you know that having an older sibling can positively improve your mental health?'

He frowned as if she'd spoken in Russian.

She nodded, warming to her favourite subject. 'It…it's been scientifically proven. Ben and I have only connected recently, but…' She shrugged. She hoped it was true. Hoped what she found with Ben would positively impact both their lives for years to come.

His eyes narrowed slightly, as if he were seeing her for the first time. 'So Frank Newbold and your mother had an affair?' His lips formed a grim line, judgment hovering in his stare.

Essie squirmed as the acid in her throat burned its way through her internal organs. She bristled, lashing out instead of curling in on herself. 'Not exactly. Not every relationship is sordid—sometimes people are duped, lied to, manipulated.' The excuses kept on coming, as if she'd waited too long to purge. 'My mother didn't know about Ben and his mother until after I was born. Frank spun her the usual bullshit about having a rocky marriage and leaving his wife when the time was right…' Essie herself hadn't known until her fifteenth birthday. 'By then I was Daddy's little girl and Mum couldn't bear to break my heart with the truth that he'd probably never fully commit to us. I guess she always held out hope that one day we'd be a proper family.' Her throat burned so badly now she was surprised she could speak at all.

'So you didn't know about Ben?'

She sighed and shook her head. 'I was fifteen when I found out.' He stayed silent so she continued. 'My father was overseas, and I was angry that, yet again, he wouldn't be home for my birthday.' The burn invaded her eye sockets. Why tell him this? Speaking the words aloud wouldn't lessen the impact of the events. 'I stayed awake until the middle of the night, crept downstairs and called him at work. He wasn't at the office, but I was given another number I assumed was a hotel. A woman, Ben's mum as it turned out, answered the phone and I said I was his daughter. I'm not sure who was more shocked.'

A disbelieving frown. '*That's* how you discovered you had a brother?' Ash stopped just short of allowing his jaw to drop open.

She nodded, her face flaming. Not a pretty story, and one it seemed, despite his friendship with Ben, he'd never heard. She wasn't surprised. Why would Ben want to advertise such a sordid tale?

Ash's skin took on a green hue, his mouth now a fully blown grim line. Was he that appalled by her tawdry past? How dared he be so…judgmental?

The question stuck in her throat. She ripped it out, needing confirmation. 'Ben…never talked about me?'

He sighed. 'Not much. A mention here and there. But I…was busy…with work stuff at the time.' He grew pensive and turned to look out of the car window again. 'Perhaps if I'd known more about you, we might have avoided this...situation.' He spoke quietly, almost to himself. But the words stung just the same.

So now she was a situation? She wasn't the only one to blame for where they found themselves. 'So you usually screen all the women you sleep with, do you?' That must take up all his spare time, if the reputation Ben hinted at and the pictorial evidence was accurate.

He turned an inscrutable expression on her, but his eyes blazed. 'No. You didn't screen me, either, *your* first one-night stand. Perhaps we should both be a little more selective in future.'

She jutted her chin forward, humiliation making her irrational. 'What, next time you find an obliging stranger in the park?' She couldn't look at him, but she couldn't look away.

'Hey, you came on to me—all I did was make the mistake of sitting in a public place.' He leaned in, hard shards of metal in his stare.

What was wrong with him, making conversation one minute, lashing out the next?

What was wrong with her, digging for answers and then shooting the messenger?

'Well, all *I* did was make the mistake of sleeping with some sort of... Jekyll and Hyde character.' Could his signals be any more mixed? Just like the justifications and excuses currently spinning through her head and making her seasick.

They'd hissed the last few comments to each

other, their faces drawing nearer and nearer as they made their respective points. Now, only a couple of centimetres separated them.

His warm breath caressed Essie's parted lips.

Her pants forced her breasts closer and closer to his chest with each breath.

His bold stare dipped to her mouth.

Her fingers curled into the leather upholstery.

She leaned in…

'Sir, we're here,' said the driver.

Essie flopped back, spent. This couldn't go on. They'd never survive sharing a workplace sexually sparking off each other like this, and the minute Ben came back from New York, he'd see straight through them and their barely contained animosity. Perhaps Ash would get his way—perhaps Ben would fire her.

Drastic circumstances called for drastic measures.

Damn, what was a girl to do?

CHAPTER FIVE

'YOU HAVE GOT to be kidding me...' Essie spun on him the minute they boarded the cute little Learjet he'd hired to take them to Paris. Her baby blues flashed and she popped out one hip as she glared in slack-jawed astonishment.

'What do you mean?' He was used to impressing women with his wealth. He'd never experienced whatever snit had worked its way beneath her creamy skin.

She scanned the sumptuous interior, which was starkly white, from the plush carpeting to the soft leather seating.

'All this?' She spread her arms wide to encompass the luxury, her nose wrinkled as if he'd offered her a ride to Paris inside a dumpster. 'Ever heard of global warming? Carbon footprints? Scheduled flights? The Eurostar?'

Was she for real?

He swept past her, loosening his tie and shrugging off his jacket to drape it over one of the wide white leather seats that offended her so much.

'I'll plant a damn forest. Sit down.' Damn, she riled him up. Bubbly and playful one minute, vulnerable and hesitant the next and then hissing and wild when he overstepped some line he couldn't see. His cock stirred for the hundredth time that day. This torture had to end. One way or another.

After she'd left his apartment last night, his balls had been so blue he'd returned to his en-suite, switched the water to arctic and banged one out. Then he'd put out some feelers among his fellow legal professionals in the UK to see if anyone was looking to take on a new partner. As soon as Ben returned, he'd distance himself from the day-to-day running of The Yard. His commitment was always supposed to have been financial, with a spot of legal work thrown in pro bono.

When he'd walked into the bar this morning to see her smiling at Josh, he'd been so desperate to quench his constant need for her, his testosterone-addled mind had considered selling his stake in The Yard just to rid himself of her sunny smile and tinkling laugh, both of which he'd grown to crave as much as burying himself inside her again. What was it about her? And where could he get a shot to render himself immune?

But the more he discovered, unearthing the conundrum that was Essie Newbold as an archaeologist scraped away a layer of ancient dirt, the more he wanted to know. Who was this woman who intrigued him so much?

He had some answers—no wonder working for

Ben, despite being overqualified, was so important to her. The need to connect with her brother shone from the vulnerable look in her eyes when she talked about him. And she wasn't secure in their relationship, a fact confirmed by the brittle tetchiness at Ash's clumsy comments.

What the hell had Frank Newbold done to her? Was that what she'd meant when she'd said she was an expert at rejection?

Well, they had an hour—plenty of time to fill in a few more blanks. He waited until she'd settled in the chair opposite his before he selected two glasses from the bar and an ice-cold bottle of white wine and then sat opposite. A small table separated them but it might as well have been a spider's web for all the protection it afforded. And he needed as many obstacles as he could get—the struggle to keep his hands off her grew more urgent every second he spent in her exasperating, but highly addictive, company.

He poured them both a glass while the two-man crew readied the plane for take-off. If he didn't occupy his hands and his mouth somehow, he was going to splay her open and drop to his knees on the plush carpet and taste something other than her sassy mouth.

Carbon footprints...

The car journey alone had been an exercise in extreme gratification avoidance—he deserved a damned medal. He'd never had to work so hard to keep his hands to himself and his dick in his pants. And the novelty had grown pretty thin. An hour's travel time to Paris… An hour of looking but not touching. Fuck, he was more of a mess now than when he'd left New York with his bags packed full of betrayal and indignation and paps nipping at his heels. But the conversation helped—he wanted to know what made her tick almost as much as he wanted to kiss her again and then lay her over this table at thirty thousand feet.

Fuck.

When Ben had suggested Essie accompany him to Paris, he'd baulked at the idea. But Ben's proposal had made sense. After all, she was their temporary manager. This was the best way to iron out prospective teething problems before the doors opened. They'd only have one shot at making a first impression on the city.

Professionally, everything he touched became a success—The Yard would be no different. He wouldn't allow the failure that dominated his personal life to taint his work. And returning to Jacob Holdings with his tail between his legs after the public row between him and his father in their open-plan office area…not an option. The man was lucky Ash hadn't laid him out.

Ash took a slug of wine, wishing it were Scotch. He needed a distraction from the destructive thoughts and the dangerous urge to lose himself between Essie's magnificent thighs.

'What is your area of expertise?' He picked up the earlier conversational thread. He imagined her doctorate wouldn't be in bar work.

His question startled her—good. If he was to be off balance in her company... 'You said it's not bar work' He licked the wine from his lip and her eyes flared.

Yes.

Those pools of intelligence drew him in—she wanted him, too.

'I have a psychology degree and I've just completed a PhD.'

He frowned. Psychology? Well, that made sense. She was smart. She cared about people. And she could probably spot his bullshit a mile away. His collar tightened a fraction.

And then a fraction more. 'Why did you move from New York?' She jutted her chin in his direction.

Bingo.

He wasn't touching that one. Another millimetre tighter... New York was full of ghosts, full of reminders of his blindness and his failures and his guilt. And full of gossip on the state of his family and his past love life.

While she waited for his answer, Essie took a sip of wine. Her lips caressed the rim of the glass and she hummed her appreciation—blessedly distracting sound that shot straight to his aching balls.

At his prolonged silence she placed the glass on the table and narrowed her eyes. 'So it's okay to pry about my cheating father, my messed-up family, but you can't answer a simple question? Interesting.' She flicked her eyebrows up, her blue stare way too perceptive.

Fuck, the last thing he needed was her probing his head. He threw her a bone. 'Would it appease you to know I have a cheating father, too?' She stared, open-mouthed. 'That my sister, Harley, grew up knowing our father had cheated on our mother with an old family friend but only recently confided in the rest of us?'

Ash had been defending Harley and his mother when he'd confronted Hal at the office that day. But all the arrogant Hal Jacob had heard was criticism— something the megalomaniac couldn't tolerate.

Essie's eyes widened as she waited for more. But sharing his sob story wouldn't change the outcome. She wasn't the only one with a crappy father figure.

Discovering his father had cheated on his mother and made Harley complicit in keeping the secret had turned his stomach. But it had been the blows to come that had nailed the coffin lid shut for good on his relationship with a man he'd worked for his whole adult life. A man who was supposed to love him.

Essie leaned forward, placing her hand flat on the table between them as if offering the support of her touch, something he wanted but didn't dare accept. 'Does your mother know? Is that why you don't trust people?'

Ash forced himself to take a slow swallow of wine. Her questions left him raw, reeling, the truth too shameful to speak aloud.

Half the truth. 'She knows.' Ash had been the one to tell her of Hal's final revelation, thrown at his son in a fit of extreme spite during that fateful argument—that Ash's fiancée's affair with one of his co-workers had been a ruse, one big cover-up, to hide the fact that the man she'd been screwing was him, his own father.

'It's okay.' She levelled sombre eyes on him, full of compassion. 'I understand. When someone betrays our trust, we just want to protect ourselves.'

Yes, Ash had battled betrayal. His fiancée had chosen the father over the son. Perhaps she'd hoped Hal would leave his wife. But his father's involvement had shown Ash's whole life to be one big lie. He swallowed the razor blades stuck in his throat.

'Are your parents still together?' Essie's gentle probing continued.

He should change the subject. She'd winkled out the truth as easily as if she'd stripped him naked. But he surprised himself by answering honestly, albeit a truncated version of the final shit storm that had had him walking away from his New York life.

'No.' He couldn't add his part. He hadn't thought the consequences through yet. The public row had been photographed by some Jacob Holdings employee, who'd passed the photos to the gossip rags. Ash had needed to ensure his mother wasn't the last to know.

He fought the urge to shrink down into the leather. His mother hadn't known about the second affair with Ash's fiancée.

He looked away. Intelligent, compassionate Essie saw too much. And the inside of his soul, the hot pool of guilt simmering there, wasn't pretty.

He grabbed a lifeline, any lifeline would do. 'Tell me about your PhD.'

Essie stared him down. She saw through his pathetic deflection technique—had probably learned about the tactic on day one of her psychology degree.

So his personal life had spiralled out of control. He focussed on the chemistry dogging his every interaction with this woman, present even in this quiet, albeit stilted conversation that dragged him too close to the edge of a cliff, but also offered deeper insights into the woman occupying all his thoughts and fantasies.

Was he seriously considering another tumble?

Another shot at distraction with the fascinating Essie?

She released a small sigh through those plump, rosy lips of hers, letting him off the hook. Lips he'd like to see wrapped around his... He discreetly adjusted himself under the table. The abrupt change of tack helped restore his equilibrium.

'I have a PhD in Human Relationships. Just finished it actually.'

Another choking sensation, as if his collar had now shrunk two sizes.

He gaped. Fucking perfect. The one woman who had threatened his one-night rule since he'd created it was some sort of...happily-ever-after guru. Totally understandable after her short-changed parenting from Frank. But Ash wasn't a happily-ever-after guy.

She didn't seem to notice the meltdown passing through his body.

She twirled the stem of her glass while she continued. 'My study looked at the social interactions in modern families in the Western model and compared them to those in other cultures—cultures with multi-generational family bonds, where people live in close proximity to extended family.'

Well, that sounded better—more science, less agony aunt. Ash released some air past his strangulated throat.

'So you're a…' he could barely utter the words '…relationship expert?' Next thing she'd be telling him she wrote one of those advice columns. What the actual fuck had he gotten himself into? And why was he more intrigued than ever? Even this revelation wasn't enough to dampen his need for her, a torture that surely rivalled anything on offer at the London Dungeon.

Instead of the glare he'd expected, she tossed her head back while she laughed a dirty laugh. His body reacted with futile predictability. He'd had first-hand knowledge of the silky soft taste of that neck—the way she moaned louder when he tongued that spot just below her ear.

Her hand clutched her chest. 'Oh…your face.' She grinned and took another sip of wine.

At least her mocking him had snapped all that confessional tension. Thank fuck.

'Don't worry. I'm not trying to trap you into marriage, counsellor.'

'What do you mean?' Was he *that* transparent? Could she see the sweat beading on his top lip? Hear his balls screaming while they ran for the hills? See how close he was to spiralling out of control?

'You have that deer-in-the-headlights look.' Her lip curled. 'Trust me—I know that look well. My father, Ben's father, perfected something similar every time I asked him if he'd make it to my school plays or my birthday parties. Every Christmas that look came out, as predictable as Christmas carols or the Queen's speech.'

She blinked and stared at her wine glass. Ash wished he'd just gone down on her instead of starting a conversation—at least he might have put a smile on her beautiful face.

'He had this look—a sideways glance, a shifty, non-committal murmur…and I knew my celebrations would be a single-parent affair. That I didn't matter to him enough.' Her glassy eyes took on a faraway look. If she cried, he'd be doomed.

But she sniffed and tilted her defiant chin up once more. 'Sorry…it's a bit early for wine.'

What the fuck…? So not only had Frank Newbold strung along two families, kept two women dangling, but he'd also done some serious damage to his daughter's self-esteem. Smart, emotionally intelligent Essie had been constantly let down, left waiting and wondering, probably questioning her worth. Ash sobered. 'I… I'm sorry.'

He'd met her father many times. He hadn't seemed like the piece of work she described, but then, he'd kept his mistress and his daughter a secret from everyone for more than fifteen years.

No wonder Ben hadn't said much on the topic—how did his friend feel about the revelations?

But what did Ash know about fathers? He was clearly an appalling judge of character where his own was concerned. He hadn't been able to see what was happening right under his nose, with the two people who should have loved him most.

So Essie was as messed up as him. Beautiful, intelligent, funny and caring—but probably none of those things in her own eyes.

With a slug of wine, she seemed to compose herself. 'Sorry. You probably got more than you bargained for with that question.'

True. But just meeting her had been a not unwelcome tornado, ripping through his already weather-beaten soul. He wanted to pry further; to offer her words of consolation; to tell her she did matter. That she was all those things and much, much more. Tell her that he understood what it was like to have a shitty, selfish parent. But that would involve opening up his own pain for inspection.

Nope. Not an option.

His hand twitched, seconds from reaching for hers. But if he touched her now, he wouldn't stop until he'd slaked every need burning inside him.

Show some control, man.

She stood, all amusement leached from her pale face after her personal confession. She looked as sick as he felt.

'Look.' She braced her hands on the table so her

delectable chest filled his vision, a distraction he in-dulged in for a dizzying split second.

'I understand you have…issues. Who doesn't? But, this—' she waved her hand between them, as if the constant crackle of sexual tension were a living breathing, visible thing '—isn't going away. I'm not letting my brother down because *you* can't separate sex from business.'

He sputtered, almost choking on his wine. Could she separate the two? A small smile tugged his mouth. It had been a very long time since anyone had surprised him as much as she had. Damn. An-other magnificent point in her favour. And bringing talk back to the reason they couldn't stop looking at each other with lusty eyes—genius. Why hadn't he thought of that?

'So, I think we should find a way to work this from our systems.' Reaching for her wine, she took another slug. 'Now, please show me where I can change into something more appropriate for clubbing.'

Change…? No way.

He swept his eyes over her perfectly adequate, flesh-covering outfit. If she emerged in another of those flirty dresses that showcased her phenomenal body…

Doomed.

Again, her long legs featured in an X-rated fan-tasy—naked, draped over his shoulders, the heels of her shoes digging into his back… If he were to break his one-time rule to quench the insatiable fire, it would just be sex, until the flames dwindled.

With a resigned sigh, he directed her towards the restroom at the rear of the plane. He couldn't argue with her logic, though. Where their intense, combustive attraction was concerned, they were all out of options.

'Jacob, good to see you, man.' His old friend Lucas slapped him on the back with a shoulder bump and slid his delighted smile over Ash's shoulder to take in Essie. Ash had been right to fear her change of outfit.

She'd emerged from the plane's bathroom wearing a wisp of black silk that hugged her breasts and hips like a second skin and completely bared her back. A pair of skyscraper heels completed the visual suffering. She'd even scooped her swathe of golden hair up into some sort of relaxed up-do so the gorgeous translucent skin of her neck, shoulders and back paraded for his greedy eyes.

She'd sat opposite him for the remainder of the flight engrossed in her ever-present phone while he'd indulged in his lurid imaginings.

Further conversation was off the table, not because he wasn't curious to know more about her past—which not only held her in its grip, but seemed to have guided her choice of career—but because he feared she'd turn the spotlight on him. Pick apart his freshly opened wound with her insightful, analytical psychologist's mind.

He'd tried to get some work done, but the words on his screen had blurred in and out of focus. His mind had reeled from her scent and every time she'd shifted in her seat and he'd caught a glimpse of another sliver of skin, he'd had to dig his short nails into the leather of the arm rests to stop himself from peeling her out of the dress that had become an implement of torture.

Lucas, already endowed with that effortless French charm, looked at Essie as if he possessed X-ray vision and could clearly see the delights the dress barely concealed. Well, fuck that. For as long as it took to extinguish this all-consuming need— one surely brought on by something in the English water—Ash would be the only one sampling anything Essie had to offer.

While he'd tied himself in knots, fucking around with trust and rules and control, the answer had been staring him in the face all this time. He was never more composed than when in the bedroom. She'd said she could separate sex from their professional relationship. Time to test the theory. A win-win situation.

Ash placed his hand in the small of her back, wincing when she turned a sharp glance his way, presumably with the shock. He didn't need to explain his actions—he was done fighting this forest fire of need—and she'd suggested he take the driving seat. Time to buckle up, Ms Newbold.

'Lucas, this is Essie Newbold, my manager. I've told her all about La Voute, so thanks for the tour.' Now he wished he'd simply brought her to the club anonymously, because all he wanted to do was get her away from Lucas and onto the packed dance floor so he could legitimately put his hands on her some more and draw her close enough to feel those nipples.

Lucas laughed, took Essie's hand and pressed it to his lips.

Smooth bastard.

He held out his arm and directed them to the bar. 'The best way to enjoy La Voute is to experience it.'

The barman had clearly been pre-warned, because, on seeing the boss, he brought over a tray of luminous shots that glowed in the neon lighting as if radioactive.

'The house speciality. Enjoy.' Lucas handed one to Essie and, without taking his eyes from her, swallowed the second. 'I've reserved you a VIP booth upstairs.' Lucas replaced his empty shot glass on the tray and nodded to the barman. 'Make yourselves at home, drink whatever you want and, if you have any questions, you know where to find me.' He shook Ash's hand, which rolled into a fist when he turned to Essie and kissed both of her cheeks.

Ash forced a smile, a move that almost cracked his jaw, the tension in his facial muscles was so pronounced. He downed the shot and jerked his chin at the barman to indicate another round, getting himself back under control. He never succumbed to such puerile emotions as jealousy. What was she doing to him? Perhaps the extreme self-denial had infected his common sense.

'This is fantastic.' Essie's eyes sparkled as she

bobbed in time to the music. She'd stood on tiptoes to yell in his ear but she hadn't touched him.

Ash nodded, his eyes dancing over the unselfconscious sway of her body to the beat.

'You asked Josh to create a house cocktail. I liked that. What else do you want to do to The Yard?'

Her wary eyes warmed at his simple compliment. 'I love that graffiti art over there.' She pointed to a wall of exposed brick decorated with vibrant tagging. 'We could do that in the basement, get an artist in. Use neon paint so it glows in the UV light.'

He nodded and bent closer, although he'd heard her just fine. His own lips were only millimetres from her ear so her delectable scent curled around him like an aphrodisiac cloud.

'He's right.' He flicked his head in the direction Lucas had disappeared. 'Clubs like this have the X-factor. We should immerse ourselves, while we're here.' He handed her the second shot and tossed back his own with a grin of challenge. 'Let's dance.'

She eyed him while she slowly pressed the rim of the shot glass to her plump bottom lip, holding it suspended there for what seemed like an age, taking his stare captive. At the last second, the tip of her pink tongue poked out and dipped into the blue opaque drink. And then she tossed it, slammed the glass bottom up on the bar and turned for the dance floor with a sassy sway of her hips.

He groaned, adding *seriously fucking sexy* to her growing list of attributes. Ash followed, walking with his hard-on torture. He took Essie's elbow to keep them together as they weaved through the crowds. The crush of bodies moving under the strobe lights hemmed them in on all sides, forcing them to dance in the bubble of close personal space that suited his intentions just fine.

Essie's eyes widened as he palmed her hips and tugged her close. So he'd made an abrupt about-face? Better to switch tactics and settle than go into negotiations with a weak case. And it seemed this captivating woman weakened his body, his mind and his resolve.

He kept his hands and his stare on her, sliding his grip from her swaying hips to her slim waist as they moved in unison to the thumping beat. Her hands reached for his forearms, fingertips just shy of gripping. She closed her eyes, tilted her head back and lost herself to the music, as completely and perfectly as she lost herself to her pleasure.

His hands snaked to the small of her back and he hauled her tight up against him, the small gasp she made and the excitement in the eyes she snapped open spurring him on. His erection pressed into her soft belly. She knew the effect she had on him, one he hadn't been able to conceal since day one.

She gripped his shoulders, her bottom lip trapped between her teeth as she swayed against him, all sensual movements and lust-drunk eyes. They danced for half a track, heated stares locked, bodies bumping and hands lingering like the most exquisite form of tactile torture.

Fuck this. Fuck the club. If he didn't get inside

her soon, he'd need another cold shower. And he was done with pale imitation. He held the real thing here in his arms. If she'd been a property acquisition, he'd have already closed the deal.

Ash bent close, his lips caressing her delicate ear. The cascade of fine tremors down her neck slammed steel through his spine. But before he could utter one word of his argument, she turned her head so her lips grazed his.

Her stare lifted to his and then dipped back to his mouth.

His fingertips pressed into her waist. 'You suggested we work this out. We'll do it in my bed.'

She leaned back, eyebrows lifted.

'We will?'

He shrugged. 'Or yours, or the couch or wherever. As long as it involves me inside you.' He lifted a tendril of hair from her neck and wrapped it around his index finger.

'I thought you only did one night?'

He could no more explain his about-turn than he could walk away. It was an astounding turn of events for a man used to making verbal arguments and teasing out favourable deals for a living.

He gripped her bare shoulder, his fingers gliding over her shoulder blade.

'I'm making an exception. And there's something of an experience gap to rectify, so I'm told.' His thumb caressed the dip above her collarbone, setting off more tiny shivers.

She pursed her lips, as if giving the matter some

serious thought. Fuck, if he'd had any issue with his ego he'd be snivelling at her pretty feet by now. But he hadn't become one of New York's top attorneys by misjudging the opposition's intentions. She wanted this as badly as he did. He hadn't changed his stance on relationships, but they could still have a good time.

'Tell me what I need to hear,' he whispered.

'Just sex.' She wavered, her lip trapped under her teeth for a moment.

He nodded, her confirmation music to his ears. 'I agree.' He pressed his thumb to her bottom lip, tugging it free from her bite. The only thought in his mind—how quickly he could replace her teeth with his—drowned out all else.

Essie stepped closer until the length of her body pressed to his, her nipples grazing his chest, the heat between her legs scorching his thigh.

He tilted her chin up, his eyes dancing with hers. 'I'm not the guy for you if it's a relationship you're after.' He couldn't reiterate that enough, especially considering her past and her profession. Now more than ever he wasn't relationship material.

She dipped her chin, capturing his thumb with her pouty lips and sucking on the pad. She tongued his digit and then released him with a pop.

'I'm not interested in a relationship. And if I were, you'd be the last man I'd consider.'

Ash bit back a groan and rubbed his erection into the soft mound of her belly.

'So we agree. You chalk up a few more...notches

on your casual sex bedpost. We fuck this out of our systems. Then we walk away.'

She lifted onto her tiptoes and he bent lower to meet her halfway. Her lips feathered his neck as she whispered, 'We keep it fun—when the fun stops, we stop.'

She peeled back, challenge blazing in her mesmeric stare.

'I can do fun.' Only this time he'd take his time, savour every sexy inch of her, glut himself until he was spent and sated and his head straightened out.

A single nod. 'What about the tour of the club?'

'I've seen enough.' His fingers curled over her hips, the silky fabric of her dress bunching in his grip. The way his body coiled to the point of bursting, he could tear the damn dress in two.

He'd never brokered a more fulfilling merger and, as with the best deals, everyone would get what they wanted. He rolled his shoulders and followed her from the dance floor.

As if it had been painted in luminous orange paint across the ground, he was about to cross a line he'd long ago vowed out of bounds. But damn if he didn't want to throw on a pair of sneakers and sprint over, hell for leather.

CHAPTER SIX

Essie paused at the foot of the stairs leading to the VIP booths, dragging Ash to an abrupt halt. His brow dipped and he faced her, clasping both her hands between them.

'Second thoughts?' He cupped her cheek, pushing back wild wisps of hair from her hot face.

It's just sex. Fun.

She fought the wave of trembles that doused her from head to toe and shook her head, and then tilted it in the direction of the bouncer guarding the upper balcony.

'Lucas said we had a VIP booth.' She caught her lip between her teeth. Her breath stalled as she waited for Ash to get on the same page. Every inch of her craved him. Slickness coated her inner thighs, her core clenched in anticipation and her nipples chafed against her dress with every rapid breath she took. She'd never make it back to the hotel before flinging herself on him and demanding what he'd held out on for so long.

'I've never experienced sex in a public place...

That could be…fun.' She tilted her head, her fluttering heart knocking against her ribs. They'd either consummate this new agreement in the back of the limo Ash had hired to drive them to and from the club tonight, or they'd do it here, in the privacy of the VIP area of this chic, sophisticated club. She held her breath. When had she become such a risk-taking exhibitionist? What was he doing to her, this sexy but closed-off man, who at first glance seemed to have it all?

Ash's eyes scorched her. 'You want me to fuck you here? Upstairs?'

She nibbled the inside of her cheek, her flush hopefully hidden by the alternating dim and flash of neon lights. He'd suggested she broaden her horizons, something that worked for her out-of-control libido. What better way to build on the success of her first one-night stand? Keep things playful and risqué. Embrace the heady sense of power she earned from their no-strings encounters. If she focussed on the sex, she wouldn't think about anything else. Her doubts, her past, her bad decisions.

She nodded, her belly twisting with delicious spasms.

Ash's stare bored into hers while he clearly mulled over her suggestion. This bold, uninhibited demand was so unlike her. But this was what he did to her, what he brought out in her. And what she hoped like hell he'd embrace. She'd been turned on all day, all week. It was his fault—time to atone.

Because right now she barely recognised the wanton woman he drew out. Hormones raged through her. She pressed her thighs together to ease the persistent thrum of her clit.

Ash scooped his arm around her shoulders, nodded briefly to the bouncer manning the foot of the stairs and escorted a tingling-from-head-to-toe Essie to the upper balcony.

Essie tottered alongside his determined strides, grateful he, too, saw the merits and timeliness of her risqué plan.

At the top of the stairs, he swooped on her, hauling her up with an arm around her waist and his hot and greedy mouth, demanding an uninhibited kiss. Essie clung, losing herself to the thrusting power of his tongue sliding over hers and his strong arms banded around her back, connecting them from shoulder to thigh. Her head spun. This was happening.

Ash released her. 'You sure about this?'

She nodded, too turned on for speech. And too enthralled for doubts.

He strode ahead, tugging her behind. Now they'd established the ground rules, he was all action. Thank goodness. She didn't want to have to resort to begging and pawing at him. So tacky.

The balcony overlooked the writhing mass of bodies on the dance floor below. To the left was a row of discreet curtained-off booths, each lined with low, banquette-style sofas and featuring an LED illuminated coffee table. Ash led the way to the last booth in the row, the one closest to what Essie guessed was a door leading to a fire escape.

Adrenaline slammed through her, shunting energy to every part of her body until her pulse thrummed right down to her fingertips. Her senses heightened, her skin buzzing under the glide of fabric, the music vibrating through the floor and into her bones and her vision eclipsed by the virile, determined man in front of her.

Ash tugged her by the hand and flicked the gossamer curtains closed behind them. If someone came close enough, they'd see through the filmy barrier. But the angle from the ground floor provided sufficient privacy to keep Essie invested in her reckless, spur-of-the-moment idea.

He kept hold of her hand, his body close, taut with energy.

'You're astounding, do you know that?' He scanned her features with heated eyes.

She shook her head, her throat hot. If he didn't touch her soon, or allow her to touch him, she'd disintegrate into a million pieces.

He flared his nostrils, sucking in a breath, and then said, 'Take your underwear off.' A husky command. He held up his hand, palm flat, waiting for her offering. If that was his lawyer voice…he probably sealed every deal he touched.

Essie's blood turned to melted wax. Ignoring the liquidity of her limbs, she tilted her head, eyebrows arched. Who knew she housed such a perverse streak? He couldn't get his way all the time, even when his demands benefited her.

'You're a long way from Kansas, counsellor.' But

she obliged, because this daring tryst had been her idea. No time for coyness now, not when she was finally getting what she'd craved since the day after she'd met him, when she'd foolishly raised the stakes with her secret scribblings about *Illegally Hot*. Time to be all in, or get the hell out of Dodge.

She braced herself steady with one hand on Ash's forearm, while she shimmied her panties down her thighs and then stepped out of them, one foot at a time.

Holding his self-satisfied stare, she dropped her damp thong in the centre of his palm, with as seductive a smile as she could manage. Why deny the effect he had on her? That he'd agreed to this told her he was equally affected.

Whatever else they were, physically they worked.

Ash glanced at the lace and then grinned, tucking it inside the back pocket of his jeans. With one tug he brought their chests and thighs and mouths back together.

'You—' he cupped her face and slanted his mouth over hers, eyes open, bold stare pinning her immobile '—have been driving me out of my mind for days.' He took her hand and pressed it to the steely length of him, guiding her to stroke him through his jeans, his hand over hers.

'I could say the same about you.' He was rock hard. She squeezed her thighs together, seeking a modicum of relief.

'With the exception of this rather unorthodox and public time, we'll be taking this slow. I intend to get my fill of you. To taste every part of you, over and over until neither of us can walk.'

'Another new experience. I can't wait.' Essie clung to him, her eyes just shy of rolling back. 'I thought you'd never break.' She looped her arms around his neck and tugged his mouth down to hers once more as she pushed him backwards towards the low upholstered seats lining the booth.

Through kisses, she fumbled with the button fly on his jeans until she'd freed his thick erection behind. He hissed, his hand covering hers to still her frantic fingers.

'This time, it's your rodeo.' He cupped her breast through the fine silk of her halter dress, his thumb stroking the nipple to a hard peak. 'Next time, and the multiple times after that, will be my way. Understood?'

She nodded, ready to promise anything to get what she wanted—him, inside her, losing his phenomenal control.

Ash fished a condom from his pocket with a wry twist of his mouth.

'I was a Boy Scout.' He handed the foil square to Essie and sat back on the banquette, his arms stretched along the back and his stare flitting between her bare legs, her pebbled nipples and her face.

Essie's mouth filled with saliva. He was hers to play with. Sprawled out beneath her, hard, ready and willing.

Forcing herself to sidle slowly with a seductive sway of her hips, rather than bound onto his lap with

embarrassing eagerness as was her natural inclina-
tion, she sauntered close until her thighs slotted between his, which were spread wide, the prod of his
manhood rising above his open fly.

Essie placed the condom on the seat next to him
and lifted her dress above her knees. When his gaze
left hers to follow the path of the hem, she slowed the
progress down, enjoying the way air gusted from his
nose with every rise and fall of his broad, sculpted
chest.

As payback for torturing her with his impressive
stamina, she stopped just short of showing him everything, instinct telling her Ash was a man who
always got what he wanted in the end. She might
as well draw out the anticipation. Keep him on his
toes. Drip-feed him, until he snapped and took what
he wanted.

With her thighs bracketing his, she straddled his
lap, rising up on her knees to force his head back
on the cushion so she could kiss him the way she'd
longed to since this morning.

She traced his lips with hers and then repeated
her path with the tip of her tongue. She cupped his
face and angled his head so she could deepen the
kiss—a tangle and slide of tongues that left them
both panting for air.

He groaned and his arms left the back of the sofa,
one banding around her waist to hold her close and
the other sliding up her thigh until his fingers delved
between her spread legs.

He hissed. 'Fuck, you're soaking.' His fingers

probed her entrance from behind while his mouth settled hot and demanding over one taut nipple.

'Yes. It's your fault.' A whimper caught in her throat as he sucked hard through the silky fabric and then scraped with his teeth.

She released her hold on his hair to untie the straps of her dress, which were knotted behind her neck. She wanted him skin to skin. To feel his sexy day-old stubble scrape her nerve endings alive.

He obliged. With an impatient tug, he followed her lead and pulled the top of her dress down until both her aching, heavy breasts spilled free.

He cupped one, his hot stare tracing her while his thumb tortured the nipple again and again with rough swipes. 'So pretty.' Then he swooped, his mouth covering the glowing bud with long sucks and flutters from his talented tongue.

Essie dropped her head back, too strung out to hold in the moan of delight his fingers inside her and his mouth laving her breast unleashed.

He pulled back. 'You're going to have to stay quiet. We don't want visitors.'

Stay quiet? Was he aware how good he made her feel? She didn't give a damn if the whole of Paris rocked up with popcorn and opera glasses. But she didn't want him to stop, so she bit down on her bottom lip and focussed on the silvery wallpaper behind his head to battle the strong sensations he was thrusting upon her willing, eager body.

Essie cradled his head as he leaned in for another

taste, but this time fiery jolts of electricity slashed from her nipple to her core.

Enough.

She tugged at the hem of his T-shirt and collapsed forward so her face was buried in his divine-smelling neck. After two or three impatient tugs on his shirt hem, Ash released her flesh and between them they removed his shirt with hurried jerks.

Ash tossed it aside while Essie just stared at him up close.

Despite the time he spent behind a desk or in a boardroom, he somehow maintained the ripped physique now laid out for her. She spread her fingers wide as her hands glided over the smooth tanned skin of his torso and tangled in the thatch of dark hair covering his pecs.

His fingers clutched the fabric at her hips, releasing and then gripping again while she took her time exploring him. She kissed a path down his neck, the stubble scraping at her sensitive lips.

A strip of black hair ran from below his navel and disappeared into his boxers, which were tented with his ready erection. As if she had been jump-started, she flew into action. She grabbed the condom and tore into it. Ash, equally eager, shimmied his jeans and boxers lower down his hips, releasing his cock, which bobbed on his hard, grooved belly.

Essie licked her lips. She wanted to taste every inch of him. But the clock was ticking. And if she didn't get him inside her soon, she'd burst from sexual frustration.

He grinned. 'Later.' His voice was so low, he sounded like a stranger. In many ways, all the important ways, he was. But just like the first time, she wanted him anyway.

'Don't worry.' He grinned. 'I want to eat you, too.'

She'd been right about the oral skills—she couldn't wait. She rolled the condom over the hard length of him, her movements hindered by the inferno burning her up from inside and his constant fondling of her breasts and rolling of her nipples between his fingers and thumbs.

And then she rose up over him, gripping him between her legs and angling him back towards her entrance. Ash shuffled his hips under her and she braced one hand on his shoulder while between them they guided him inside.

She sank, stretched and filled to perfection so a cry escaped. Ash covered her mouth with one hand, a reminder of their public location. Although the expression on his face—his bunched jaw, his flared nostrils, his hooded eyes—told her he, too, struggled to contain the intense bite of pleasure.

This was what she'd craved since she'd walked into his office that fateful morning. His surrender to this flammable chemistry that rendered her helpless. She wasn't alone—confirmation was etched into the harsh planes of his taut features.

With his hand still clamped over her mouth, Essie began to move, rocking back and forth on his lap. The angle rubbed her in the perfect spot and she picked up the pace, bouncing on his lap with renewed energy, delivering what they both craved.

Ash settled back and gripped her hips, allowing her to dictate the angle and depth of penetration. But he didn't lay idle for long. One hand cupped her breast, tweaking and pulling her nipple until lightning snaked across her belly. The other hand delved between their bodies until the pad of his thumb settled over her neglected clit, strumming and circling.

'Yes,' she half hissed, half whispered. No way could she stay completely silent, not when he lay sprawled beneath her looking sexier than any sight she'd ever seen. And not when he filled and stroked her with sublime perfection.

When he started thrusting up from below, each blow accompanied by a harsh grunt while his big hands held her hips firm to hit the same spot over and over again, she lost all strength in her upper body and collapsed forward. Her hands clasped his sweat-slicked chest and her hair formed partial curtains before her face.

'Damn, you're tight. You clutch me just right.'

She whimpered, his verbal encouragement, his deep thrusts and his thumb back on her clit working a unique brand of magic over her body.

She gasped, flinging her wild hair back over her shoulders, her neck arched.

'That's it, ride me.' He panted out, his gruff commands low but no less insistent. 'I'm going to make you come so hard.'

With one last swipe of her clit and three rapid-fire

thrusts of his hips, she climaxed, her whole body tense as she fluttered and clenched around him. Her cries bounced off the walls, but they were both past caring.

He sat up, buried his face between her breasts and clutched her to him with breaking force as he convulsed and groaned out his own climax.

Essie swallowed past her dry throat, gripping his shoulders while the spasms petered out and her heart slowed.

The sheen of cooling sweat stuck their clammy chests together. Essie caught her breath at last. 'Well, that was fun.' She buried her nose in his hair, stifling a giggle.

He kissed her breastbone, between her breasts.

'Hell, yeah, it was.'

She cracked up, taking him along with her.

CHAPTER SEVEN

ASH WOKE TO the melodic sound of distant church bells.

He opened his eyes to find the hotel suite, which was situated in Paris's Eighth *arrondissement*, bathed in filtered sunlight and his body wrapped around a soft, warm, sleeping Essie. His morning wood nestled between the cheeks of her spectacular ass. He ground his hips, the bite of pleasure damping down the flare of panic that waking up spooning a woman had created.

He never spooned. He rarely spent the night with someone, usually leaving after the business end of the evening was over.

He held himself rigid until the wave passed, its grip on his chest lessening until he could once again breathe.

They'd agreed.

Just sex.

Fun sex.

Astounding sex.

And, seemingly to test him to the hilt, she wanted to experience new and adventurous sex. Would he even survive? She'd been incandescent last night. First agreeing to his renegotiated terms of engagement and then stating her own, which aligned with his so beautifully that he had discovered breaking his cardinal rule was easy. For the right woman. The right…inducement.

And then she'd blown him away by suggesting they fuck in the very upmarket club that they'd come to vet. Who knew studious, bubbly, relationship expert Essie concealed such a libidinous inner vixen?

Lucky him.

He'd gladly expose her to previously untried experiences—a tough job that he relished. This was the perfect solution. Keeping things fun and playful clearly delineated the boundaries, gave him back the control he needed like oxygen. And provided an out clause—because this would end. Sooner or later the fun would dry up. And they could walk away. No feelings hurt. A good time had by all.

He breathed deeply, preparing himself, just as he did in negotiations—take control, brainstorm all possible outcomes and, if all else fails, railroad the opposition. With that strategy in mind, Ash shelved the niggling seed of doubt and gingerly untangled his limbs from hers without waking her.

By the time they'd returned to the hotel in the early hours of this morning, they'd been beat. They'd shared a quick shower and collapsed into bed.

And now he wanted his breakfast.

Sinking beneath the sheet with slow stealth, he manoeuvred himself between her thighs. Essie slept like the dead, so she didn't wake until he'd opened her up and wedged his shoulders between her shapely legs.

She stirred, her head lifting from the pillow to level sleepy eyes on him. Eyes full of dawning realisation.

Fresh lust pounded through him, his dick burrowing into the mattress. 'Morning. Ever experienced wake-up oral?'

She shook her head, bleary eyes rounded.

'Do you mind?' His voice was gruff, from the sight of her rumpled and vulnerable, her hair a wild tangle around her face, and from the vision of her open and glistening before him.

Her eyes were tinged with growing excitement. She shook her head but continued to stare. Waiting.

Ash touched the tip of his tongue to his top lip, catching the flare of heat in her eyes and the way her breasts rose and fell with her shallow pants. Her scent enveloped him. He shifted her thighs until she was splayed to his satisfaction.

Perfect, pink and pouty. The strip of fiery hair neatly trimmed framed the most exquisite sight he'd ever seen. One certainly worth waiting for. Who needed the works of art housed at the Louvre, when they had a naked Essie in their bed?

'Are you going to watch?' A surge of blood flooded his groin and she dropped her head back onto the pillow with a hoarse groan.

'I don't think I'll be able to.'

He tutted. 'Your choice. But I will. I recommend the experience.'

She looked at him again, her cheeks flushed pink. 'I… I've never come this way before.'

Heat bloomed in his belly. Man, he loved a challenge. 'You will for me.' Leaning forward, he opened her lips with his thumbs and touched the tip of his tongue to her clit. She jerked. Her thighs slammed against his head and her hands flew to his hair to hold him in place. Not that he was leaving. Not until he'd gorged himself and left her begging him to stop. Until he'd ruined her and set the bar sky-high.

He'd warned her last night and he never made idle threats. They weren't leaving this hotel room until neither of them could walk.

Sucking the tiny bud between his lips, he flattened his tongue and laved at her, over and over. He watched her every reaction: the way she fisted his hair in her hands; the way, despite her proclamation, she lifted her head from the pillows every few seconds to stare at the action occurring between her thighs; and the way she urged him closer by lifting her legs over his shoulders and digging her heels into his back, demanding more.

She swelled in his mouth, her breaths now coming hard and fast.

'Yes…oh…yes. You're so good at that—' Her breath caught on a keen wail. He winced as she twisted his hair, drawing back for a second to part her and slide two fingers inside her tight, velvety heat.

'Having fun?' He scraped his teeth along one

inner thigh, delighting in the trembles that snaked across her flat belly.

'Yes. Yes. Don't stop.'

'I have no intention of stopping. Best breakfast ever.' He dived back in, this time matching the rhythmic laves of his tongue over her swollen clit to the plunging of his fingers, which he angled forward to rub her walls.

When she released his head so he could pluck and roll her rosy nipples, her neck strained as she held her head up to watch his every move and he knew she was close. He gave her everything, sucking and humming and plunging until she cried out, her voice a broken, thready cry that spoke directly to his pulsing dick.

He drew out the torture while she continued to clench around his fingers and then she pushed him away and collapsed back on the mattress.

'Oh, wow.' She laughed. 'That was definitely fun.'

He clambered up the bed to lie beside her. 'Glad I could oblige.' He pushed the wisps of hair back from her flushed face. 'Your exes were no good at that?' Responsive, sensual Essie had been cheated.

She turned to face him, propped on one elbow. 'Ex. Singular. He didn't like it.' Her cheeks darkened and Ash wished he'd kept his mouth shut.

What a douche. Some men didn't know what they had in front of them. Her finger snaked through his chest hair in slow, pensive circles.

'Of course, he didn't like the way I dressed or

laughed or the friends I kept, either.' Her brittle laugh failed to lighten the mood.

So on top of her shitty father figure, her only boyfriend had been a controlling, insecure bully? Ash swallowed, half tempted to further ruin their morning by demanding the asshole's address and investigating how well he liked Ash's fist in his face. 'Did he…lay a hand on you.'

She shook her head and looked away, her colour now a blaze across her cheeks.

'There are other ways, verbal and emotional, to diminish someone. I put up with it for longer than I'm proud of.'

His chest turned to a block of concrete. 'It's okay.' He trapped her hand under his, stilling her fingers. 'Sometimes it's hard to see what's right under our noses.' Insightful, analytical Essie, so in tune with others' needs, would hate that she'd tolerated a bad relationship for herself, just as he hated his own blindness and misguided trust.

'Fun fact,' he said, grinning when she levelled sceptical narrowed eyes on him. 'That guy wasn't worthy of the tip of this finger.' He lifted her pinkie to his mouth and pressed a kiss to the tip. 'Let alone the rest of you.'

Couldn't she see that? Didn't she understand any man would be fucking lucky to have her? He would have…once.

Essie broke the dark direction of his thoughts with an energetic kiss, tugging on his neck and then climbing on top of him and sitting astride his thighs.

She sat back and looked down at him, her beautiful face soft with desire and doubt.

He gripped her waist, questions banked up in his tight throat.

'We have to go back to London today.' Her words gave him pause as if she'd added, 'Back to reality.'

And Ben would return from New York. Would that alter their new arrangement? 'I know. Still time for a few more experiences though...' He could feed the desire and banish the doubt. Just fun.

She smiled, her hand encircling him and pumping with lazy strokes and the perfect amount of pressure.

'Have you ever been to Paris before?' he asked. The urge to offer more than new sexual experiences lifted the hairs on his arms. He wished they could stay a week. Wished he could wow her, wine her and dine her, as she deserved. Wished he could show her everything the French capital had to offer by day and indulge in her by night. All in the name of fun, of course.

Her thumb grazed the sensitive spot beneath his crown. He cupped her pert breast, his thumb tracing the dark tip. She shook her head, her mouth parting on a gasp and his balls rose up.

'We don't have enough time to see everything, but I've planned some sightseeing, if you'd like a whistle-stop tour.' Anything to put that sparkle back in her eyes.

She glanced at the window and the view beyond. 'Well, I can see the Eiffel Tower from here.' Her thumb traced the head of his cock, spreading the bead of moisture her stroking had released. Then her eyes lit up. 'Can we get real croissants?' She bit her lip, which he'd come to learn was her vulnerability tell, and a damned sexy sight.

He nodded, warmth from his gut spreading to his chest at her simple request. No Learjets or Tiffany baubles for this woman.

'Great.' She stopped rubbing him and jumped from the bed.

He recoiled, every muscle in his body taut and pulsing with energy to drag her back and bury himself between those thighs.

'Time for a shower, then, because I'm starving.' Instead of heading to the en-suite, she twisted her hair while her stare lingered on his still-raring-to-go groin. 'I've never experienced breakfast in the shower…'

Within seconds he'd hustled her into the bathroom and turned on the spray. She laughed and dragged him inside the glass cubicle, which was big enough for two.

Her mouth met his, her smile stretched wide. 'I wanted to do this last night. I'm sorry I was so tired.' And then she dropped to her knees on the tiles and gripped the base of his straining cock.

His eyes wanted to roll closed, so good was the sight of her on her knees. But he forced them open. He spread his thighs as the water pounded his back and cascaded over his shoulders. Essie smiled a sultry smile up at him, pressed her tongue to the base of his shaft and licked a path to the engorged tip. He braced one hand on the glass, terrified his jerking legs would give out before the fun was over.

Her warm mouth engulfed him, stretching her pink lips around his head. He grunted, an animal sound he was certain he'd never made before, and then he cupped her face, tangling his fingers in her wild, wet hair. An anchor.

She sucked hard and swirled the tip of her tongue over the sensitive crown, lingering on the spot that left him growling out her name and clamping his jaw so tight he worried for his enamel.

The minx had the audacity to smile around him, her mouth full, and then she bobbed her head, her eyes locked with his, full of challenge while she moaned and mumbled. He surrendered. He was always going to lose this fight. The sight of her on her knees with his cock in her mouth one he'd remember for ever. She worked him higher until every muscle screamed.

She was fantastic. Why had he battled so hard to fight this attraction? His balls tightened and boiled and fire flickered at the base of his spine.

'Essie...' The warning clear, no doubt by the look of twisted agony on his face.

Humming encouragement against him, she nodded her head, giving her permission. The flames licked along his shaft, lightning striking the tip at the moment he erupted on her tongue with a harsh yell and a slap of his hand on the tile.

She swallowed him down, releasing him with a pop and satisfied grin. He hauled her to her feet and crushed her close while she gripped his ass cheeks in both hands.

He pulled back, smacking kisses on her swollen, grinning lips.

'Best.'

Kiss.

'Fun.'

Kiss.

'Ever.'

Essie pointed her phone at the majestic gothic spires of Notre Dame and snapped some pictures. The private pleasure cruise Ash had booked took them down the Seine from the Eiffel Tower to the Pont de Sully and back. A perfect way to see so many of the city's iconic landmarks and to fully appreciate Paris's endless stunning architecture.

After they'd dressed, they'd spilled out of the hotel and found a charming Parisian café where they'd sat on the pavement at a gingham-covered table for two and feasted on warm crumbly croissants that melted in the mouth. This new experiences game they were playing left her floating on air. She'd even forgone posting on her blog for that day and switched off her phone in reverence to her first orally delivered orgasm and her first visit to the French capital.

Ash approached with two flutes of what was probably real champagne—she was too scared to ask, because today had already had enough of a fairy-tale quality to leave her both swooning and restless.

Because she'd woken up in Paris next to a gor-

geous man, any woman's dream, who lived a life-
style she couldn't comprehend—one perhaps, had
her parents been married, had she and Ben grown up
together, she might have glimpsed. But that wasn't
her reality.

Her reality had been the role of odd kid out—not
quite like many other kids from single-parent families but not quite like the whole families, either. Her
reality had been years of loneliness, confusion and
pining for an absent father. Yes, he'd sent endless
gifts and she'd never gone hungry, but her reality
had been an illusion. Just as her and Ash cruising the
Seine drinking champagne was an illusion.

'You look sad—Paris not what you expected?'
He sat next to her.

She shook her head. 'It's beautiful.' Her lip took
a severe nibbling while she tried to marshal her conflicted thoughts. 'Your parents' divorce… Was it
while you were growing up?'

Ash sniffed as if the warm summer air offended
him. 'They're in the process of it right now, actually. Turns out my mother could tolerate one affair,
but not two. Why?'

She took the glass of champagne he offered and
sipped. 'Just imagining what your childhood was
like.'

He looked away. 'Pretty normal, I guess.' He
shrugged and slid his arm along the back of the seat.

'Did you come here with your family?' She picked
at the scab, imagining fun-packed but rowdy Jacob
holidays. All five of them together.

He nodded, eyes wary.

Essie's glazed-over stare found the view again. 'I only remember one holiday with Mum and my father. I was ten.' The memories rushed in like a tidal wave, stealing the last of her high. 'I'd begged and begged to accompany him on one of his business trips to New York, promised I'd be so good he wouldn't know I was there. He appeased me with a trip to Chester Zoo.' She picked at a sliver of peeling paint from the seat. 'I didn't mind—it was the best trip ever. He bought me a stuffed elephant, we got our faces painted and he taught me to play chess back at the hotel.'

Ash's hand slid to her back, his palm warm between her shoulder blades, the rhythmic sweep of his thumb strangely unbearable.

'So you didn't see much of Frank?'

She shook her head, her face hot. Why had she even confided such a deeply personal moment with the power to shrivel her insides? The memory of what she'd done to that beloved stuffed elephant five years later when she'd finally discovered her father's deception still brought heat to her face.

'When I discovered the truth, that he'd lied to me and to Mum and his real family…' She met Ash's stare, shame and defiance warring inside. 'I… I built a bonfire in the back garden. It didn't end well for the elephant.'

Ash pulled her close and pressed his mouth to the top of her head, the gesture more than that of fuck buddy. But she wasn't naive enough to see Ash's display of romantic, even comforting, touches as anything but good manners and an attempt to keep their insatiable chemistry on the fun track where it belonged.

She sipped the frigid wine, pushing dark, dangerous thoughts away, and focussed on the view to stop the dangerous slide towards obsessing. It wasn't just the fact that Ash was way out of her league. He possessed a quick wit and was sexy personified. He had a dry sense of humour and regularly called her out on her more outrageous bullshit. A very addictive combination for a girl sadly lacking in healthy, long-lasting relationships, either in her own life, or displayed by her parental role models. A girl who'd spent two years in a dysfunctional, emotionally abusive relationship because she was so desperate to be the opposite of her parents.

She'd promised Ash she didn't want more than sex.

But if she ever changed her mind, ever considered herself capable of maintaining the kind of trust and commitment she frequently wrote about from a theoretical point of view, Ash represented exactly the kind of man she'd want.

Pity it was never going to happen. Not because he couldn't be sweet and romantic as he'd just proved, as well as an astounding lover. But because he'd meant what he'd said.

The ex Ben mentioned had clearly hurt him badly enough that he'd sworn off anything beyond casual for good. Those closest had the most power to cause lifelong pain.

She shuddered. She'd certainly never been back to a zoo.

'Oh, look.' She latched onto a distraction and pointed at a couple on the walkway lining the river-banks. A bride and groom, having their picture taken.

Ash followed the direction she indicated, and they stared for several stilted, silent seconds. Essie squirmed, covering the awkward moment with a blast of verbal diarrhoea to put him at ease.

'Ah, the city of love… Oh, fun fact. Did you know that falling in love has the same effect on your brain as snorting cocaine?' She wasn't fishing for a pro-posal, but she wasn't carved from stone like the gar-goyles atop Notre Dame. Just because love hadn't worked out for her parents, for her, perhaps for Ash, didn't mean others couldn't find it.

Ash looked away from the beaming couple, his stare skittering anywhere but on Essie.

'Did you know the divorce rate in the Western world averages fifty per cent?' He curled his lip and sipped his wine.

She gaped. She wasn't wholly surprised—if more men were like her father and her ex…and his fa-ther… His cynicism was more than a hardened law-yer thing—it must be the woman…

The set of Ash's mouth told her now wasn't the right time to pry. Time to drag the conversation back to fun town. 'I didn't. But you're ruining the ambi-ence, counsellor.'

He shrugged, a smile on his face, but his shoulders didn't drop to pre-shrug levels.

She rolled her eyes. 'Don't worry. I'm not hinting.' She nudged him with her elbow, trying to lighten the mood. 'From a scientific standpoint, I find it fascinating that something as nebulous as—' she made air quotes '—"love" is powerful enough to induce such a rush of euphoria on a neurological level.'

He stared for long silent seconds.

Essie brazened it out, but inside she wanted to roll into a ball and protect her soft parts.

'Do you really believe all that relationship babble?'

She bristled. Had he just ridiculed the basis of her entire research doctorate? The foundation of her precious and increasingly popular blog? The very doctrine she hoped to live the rest of her happy and contented life by, next time she was brave enough to dip a toe back into relationship waters? At least next time she met someone, she'd also have a sexual standard to measure them against, thanks to Ash.

For the first time in her life, she knew what all the fuss was about.

'I don't need to believe it. Just because we've never experienced it—it's science.'

'It's bullshit.' He flushed and then winced. 'It may be science, but science isn't for everyone. It isn't for me.'

Essie's heart rate accelerated. He was opening up. Had her earlier confessional mood infected him?

'Without changing my plea, I meant what I said

last night—just fun—why the hefty dose of cynicism?' She glugged more champagne in case this
conversation blew up in her face. The psychologist
in her couldn't help but pry. And the woman who'd
had fantastic sex with him was pretty interested, too.

She couldn't look too closely at why, preferring
to believe her interest was a side effect of the spectacular orgasms, professional curiosity or her constant need to help her fellow man.

With his eyes shielded behind sunglasses, she
had no non-verbal cues to help—Ash sat as still as
a statue.

'I had a fiancée. Years ago. I thought myself in
love, the kind you think exists, scientifically.'

Essie's throat tightened until she expected to hear
choking sounds when she breathed. She clamped her
lips shut, desperate for him to continue. To learn
more about this closed-off man who had so much to
offer and what had shaped him.

'Right up to the week before the wedding, when
I discovered she was cheating on me.'

Essie stared, mouth agape.

Who would cheat on Ash?

A splash of icy champagne spilled on her dress,
soaking through the fabric. She looked down, busy-
ing herself with wiping at the spill with the hem of
her dress, to both gather her own scattered thoughts
and give Ash some time to recover from his shocking confession.

But what did she say to a temporary lover on discovering he had indeed had his heart broken, some-

thing that had tainted all his future relationships? She knew what psychologist Essie would say. She even had an idea how relationship blogger Essie would handle it. But the woman who'd spent the night in his bed and was already struggling with the boundaries she'd agreed to Essie? She was all over the place.

'Have you…had anyone serious since then?'

He shook his head, confirming her theories. 'Casual works best for me.'

While part of her was happy that she and Ash were on the same page in their personal reasons for avoiding relationships at this stage in their lives, his confirmation came with an unpleasant hollowness in her stomach.

He'd really meant what he'd said.

'I'm sorry you were hurt. Your ex sounds a couple of sandwiches short of a picnic, if you ask me.' Humour seemed the safest option to claw back the light-hearted, Parisian vibe they'd had earlier. But it didn't banish the gnawing inside, or the restlessness of earlier. Or the urge to comfort Ash. But he'd hate that. She sat on her free hand.

Ash shrugged. 'I'm well over it. As I said, it was years ago.' He didn't appear over it. In fact, a greenish hue tinged his skin. 'I just think that whatever that emotion is—that drug-like high—it passes pretty quickly, and then what do you have?'

She had plenty of answers, but none she thought he'd want to hear. And perhaps he was right. What did she really know? Everything she'd learned about men came from her ex, a pathetic excuse for a man who'd needed to put her down to make himself feel like a man, and her waste-of-space father—a man who was only in her life thirty per cent of the time and never at the important moments. If she'd grown up with Ben, at least she'd have had a stable male role model, an older brother to fight her corner, vet her boyfriends and tell her she was worthy. But Frank had robbed her of that, too.

'Love didn't work out for you and the lazy, critical, controlling jerk-off...' He toyed with a strand of her hair, his stare searching.

'No.' As far as romantic relationships went, she'd proved her judgment was seriously lacking. She'd accepted meagre scraps, just like her mother. 'But that was my fault. People treat you the way you allow yourself to be treated, right?' Yes, she knew the theory down to the last detail, but putting it into practice for yourself... That was another matter.

Ash nodded in agreement, his stare fixed on the horizon.

'But, you're right. I haven't found it, yet. But I do know that as humans we're destined to strive for a meaningful connection, an interaction with other humans. We can't avoid it. It's evolutionary. A survival tactic.'

'Is that why your relationship with Ben is so important?'

Essie shrugged, feigning indifference while her insides shrivelled. 'You don't have to be a psychologist to see I have daddy issues. I grew up thinking I was an only child. I loved my father, idolised him as a little girl, but his betrayal ruined our relationship.' She shrugged, playing down the impact of her rolling stomach. 'I feel cheated—Ben's a great guy, as you know.'

Ash nodded.

And Ash? Another great guy who'd been hurt in the past, who she'd objectified on her blog in order to feel validated. Well, that ended today. No more *Illegally Hot*. And no more crazy ideas about Ash being anything more than a temporary fling.

Several beats passed.

'Hungry?' said Ash.

Essie nodded, despite her swirling stomach.

'Let's go to Montmartre for lunch. They have a street market today.'

And just like that they successfully hurdled the invisible barrier—with good, old-fashioned denial.

CHAPTER EIGHT

THE FOLLOWING SATURDAY night Ash emerged from The Yard's offices to find the bar awash with smart, glamorous opening-night customers. Cocktails and good times flowed. Essie and Josh had organised a happy hour to bring in office workers, and the online social media buzz she'd created had ensured it was standing room only. Their brand-new cocktail menu was inscribed in elegant script on the oversized contemporary chalkboard behind the bar. Every glass sparkled. The bar's state-of-the-art lighting created pockets of ambience, certain nooks and crannies of the chic space becoming intimate, dimly lit corners.

But instead of the satisfaction he'd anticipated, his body was strung taut, every muscle twitchy. Ash scanned the bar for Essie. He knew she wore the same slinky black dress she'd had on at La Voute a week ago, because just before they'd opened The Yard's door for the first time, she'd strode into his office with that slightly feral gleam in her eyes, locked the door behind her and perched her delectable derrière on his desk.

When she'd slowly bared her thighs, revealing that she'd removed her underwear, he'd been powerless to resist what had followed—him fucking her on his desk, a new experience she'd requested with a cheeky, 'For luck…?'

The restlessness dissipated as he recalled the past week of fantastic sex. They'd spent practically every spare minute screwing—starting with the flight back from Paris to London, where she'd ridden him in one of the wide leather seats at thirty-thousand feet, successfully earning herself a mile-high experience, and continuing at work, at his apartment and anywhere else they could get away with. The intense, couldn't-keep-their-hands-off-each-other phase was lasting well beyond the arbitrary time limit he'd set. Any day now, he expected the bubble to burst, the novelty to wear off, the fun to end and his life to return to normality.

But the desire was far from abating and Ash found himself in new territory.

Perhaps the out-of-body feelings rattling him were a symptom of having allowed the insatiable, enthusiastic Essie too much time in the driving seat? Time to wrestle back some of the control, dictate the…fun, suggest the next experience. His mind whirred with endless pornographic possibilities. Yes, that was just the right tactic to steer things back on track.

He spotted her at the far end of the bar and discreetly adjusted himself. She still carried the radiant glow her earlier orgasm had delivered to her translucent skin. She'd retamed her hair, twisting it into some messy topknot that left only a few wisps tickling her elegant neck. Just knowing that the halter dress she wore prevented her wearing a bra, and that her perfect tits were bare under the scrap of silk, flooded his groin with fresh heat. Heat that should have dissipated after their quick but thoroughly satisfying desk session. But no. It was as if the more he had, the more he knew about her, the more he wanted.

A very dangerous combination.

Ash set off towards the object of his disgruntlement, weaving his way through the throng. She chatted with Josh, who smiled at her and touched her arm. Essie laughed at something he said as she leaned close to speak over the general din of a hundred conversations and the vibratingly loud music.

Ash pressed his lips together and swallowed down the taste of acid. 'Fucking fantastic…'

A thump to his shoulder pitched him off balance.

'Go easy on her, man,' said Ben, who'd sneaked up behind him. Ben grinned at his friend and then looked at Essie, an indulgent smile playing on his mouth.

Ash slapped Ben's shoulder in greeting, his own shoulders cramping with the tension of lusting after Ben's sister. Add to that the very foreign stabbing pain under his ribs as he watched Josh and Essie together… He needed a lie-down and it was only eight thirty.

'She can't help helping people—it's who she is.'

Ben stared at the couple chatting as if he was as enamoured as Ash, although likely in a different way.

He nodded as he flicked his gaze back to where she conversed with Josh. He could just imagine the kind of help the hipster barman wanted.

He'd developed quite an insight into Essie's magnificent, multifaceted personality. She was so different—different from him, a cynical, cut-throat lawyer with a reputation of being just like his ruthless old man; from most people he knew—out for themselves, inward-looking, selfish; and from any other woman of his experience, which was probably why he struggled to put a stop to their sex spree.

She was too good for him. Too good for her spineless ex and her careless father, too.

She laughed with Josh, her head tilting towards him in that way that made a person feel she was truly listening.

Fuck. He would hurt her when this ended. Yes, she'd said what he'd wanted to hear, but his instincts about her had been correct—Essie was a relationship kind of girl. She'd just lost her confidence at the hands of the worthless men in her life.

Ben loosened his tie. 'Josh is having boyfriend trouble,' he said. 'Essie can't resist a distress signal.'

Ash grinned, his head now so light it practically lifted off his shoulders.

Josh was gay.

As soon as he'd registered the relief pouring through him, it morphed into something else, something not unlike the itch of head-to-toe poison oak.

What place did jealousy have in his orderly, controlled life? What place did any feelings have where
Essie was concerned? She wasn't his—because that
was the way he wanted it. Insisted on it. Made crystal
clear from the outset. Why, then, did his insistence
sound entirely self-directed?

'Hey, can you grab her? I have something I want
to say to both of you.' Ben tilted his head to indicate the cordoned-off stairs leading to the basement
dance club, which was quiet for now, but would soon
be heaving with partygoers, if their ticket sales were
any indication.

'Sure.'

Ash resumed his way across the bar to Essie, the
idea of ending things tonight forming in his mind.
Halfway there, she spotted him and he rebelled
against the idea with a violent mind spew.

Whatever she'd been saying to Josh stalled on her
lips, which hung a little open as she levelled her wide
stare on an approaching Ash. Fire licked his balls.
He'd come inside her not two hours ago. And already
he wanted her again. She could do that to him with
her open smile or her ready, but dirty, laugh. Even
her irritating fun facts lent her an irresistible and refreshing air you couldn't help but adore.

He skirted around her and bent low from behind
to speak in her ear—it was a club after all, the noise
levels rendering that perfectly acceptable.

'Ben wants to see us downstairs.' A satisfying
trill of shivers passed down her neck. Oh, yes, she
battled the same hunger raging in him. Thank fuck

he wasn't alone. Because that hunger was the only thing keeping him on an even keel.

Just sex—his rule.

Just fun—her rule.

He swallowed the panic and pressed his mouth to her ear. 'And I want to see you naked and splayed open for me,' he whispered. That would give her something to ruin those lacy thongs she wore, probably for his torment.

She tilted her hips and pressed her ass up against his groin, at the same time as leaning forward across the bar to tell Josh she'd talk to him later.

Not if he had anything to do with it—she'd be too busy coming around the cock she'd just flicked back to life with her sassy stunt. She knew exactly what she was doing, but payback would be fun.

He put his hand in the small of her back where the dress dipped low and led her downstairs. Her skin burned his palm. Her feminine scent buffeted his senses. And if he slid his hand a couple of inches south he could cup those rounded ass cheeks and ascertain if she'd donned the panties again after the desk session...

At the last minute, he inwardly bit out a curse and dropped his hand from her skin, seconds before they entered the VIP booth where Ben waited.

He'd opened the good stuff—Cristal. Three tall contemporary flutes sat on the table next to a small gift-wrapped package. Ash bit the inside of his cheek. He'd thought about giving Essie an opening-night gift, but he'd talked himself out of it, too terrified by the impulse and too worried it would blur the rigid lines he'd demarcated.

Ben kissed his sister's cheek and poured the bubbles with a flourish. Ash struggled to share his friend's enthusiasm. When they were all seated with a glass in hand, Ben raised his for a toast.

'I just wanted to thank you both for all your hard work these last two weeks, and for holding the fort while I was away. We wouldn't be here, opening night, without you two…so cheers. To The Yard.'

Ash and Essie joined the salutation, their eyes meeting briefly. Ash saw in her expression what he guessed was mirrored in his own—a flash of guilt. Fuck.

What with the new and dangerous emotions ensnaring him, and considering the potential mess when this ended for him, for Essie, for his friendship with Ben…he should be a man. End it tonight, on a high.

We opened the club…what say you we call this quits and part as friends?

The mouthful of wine soured. He made a fist under the table.

'And, Essie…' Ben collected the gift and handed it to her '… I want you to have this. Thanks for stepping in when I needed you.' Ben stared, earnest, while Essie looked at him as if he'd just saved her, single-handed, from a burning building. And fuck if Ash didn't want to see her level that look in his direction, equilibrium be damned.

'As a kid, I always wanted a sibling.' Ben swallowed, visibly moved. 'I'm just glad it's you.'

She took the package, her lower lip trembling. As she fumbled with the bow and the paper, an unseen force made Ash reach discreetly beneath the table to touch her knee in silent support. This developing bond with her brother fed her soul, healing the cracks her father had created with his callous selfishness. Her old man and that douche of an ex had really done a number on her self-esteem. But Ash had underestimated the depth of her longing to be a part of Ben's life. To have more of a family. To belong. She deserved those things.

Ash had grown up surrounded by his family. Until recently he'd worked alongside them, every day. His sisters were still, and always would be, a massive part of his life. What must it have been like to never know when your parent was going to drop by? To wonder if this time, this birthday would be different? To feel unworthy of their time and attention, something that was a fundamental part of the parental role in Ash's opinion. He knew all about shitty fathers... But at least he'd grown up knowing he'd mattered to both parents.

He gripped her knee tighter. The next time he saw Frank Newbold...

Essie flashed him a brief, grateful smile and then she tore through the last of the paper and looked on in wonder. Ash forced his fingers to relax. She wasn't his business. They were just having fun.

It was a framed snap of Essie and Ben outside The

Yard, their arms around each other and their grins, so alike, wide and beaming.

Essie's eyes filled and she threw her arms around her brother's neck.

Ash stilled, his breath trapped, a voyeur, an outsider on the growing sibling connection between these two. But he couldn't look away, or leave. A sick part of him forced himself to see what his selfish, indulgent actions put at risk. The siblings stood for a proper hug. Essie turned her face, which was pressed to Ben's chest.

Part of him had genuinely believed their chemistry would have petered out by now. That the insistent itch would have dissipated. But if anything, the need only intensified. Because now he knew Essie. He understood her quirky sense of humour. He could laugh at her strange English phrases and the way she'd translate them for his transatlantic education, and he reciprocated her enthusiastic desire for him, which seemed equally insatiable and only built in intensity with every day that passed.

Despite knowing the cost of deceit and betrayal— especially from a family member, one you should be able to trust with your life—the damage they wreaked. Despite knowing her past left her craving this relationship with Ben. Despite breaking his rules to have her only once, his resolve was steadfast. He couldn't, wouldn't offer her more than what they had right now. But was he ready to give her up?

He couldn't be what she needed. He owed it to

her, to his friend, to let her go now, before the toll of his selfishness grew.

His blood stilled as if turned to concrete. Before he could make an excuse and leave on some pretext or other, he heard familiar voices. He turned around in time to see his sister, Harley, and the others arrive. *Perfect timing.* He'd forgotten they were coming to The Yard's opening night, he'd been so busy losing himself in Essie.

Harley flew at him with a squeal of excitement. He lifted her into a bear hug. She'd arrived from the States today with her fiancé, Jack, who split his time between Europe and New York.

Ash gripped his sister tighter than usual, earning him a searching stare when he released her to the ground. At least his sister hadn't blamed him for his part in their parents' split. She, too, had had her fingers burnt with Hal.

'You look amazing.' He kissed her cheeks, forcing his fingers to relax on her shoulders, and then shook hands with Jack and, behind them, Jack's friend Alex and his fiancée, Libby. Ash made introductions and the group settled around the table as a waiter brought more glasses and a second bottle of Cristal.

Essie, Libby and Harley quickly fell into animated and excitable conversation and the other men started a debate about some upcoming English soccer game Ash had no clue about. He sipped his drink, a sense of unease capturing him as he watched the interactions around the table, as if from a distance. He'd done enough emotional wrangling for one night.

Damn, enough for a whole year. But the unwanted
thoughts pushed their way into his head anyway.

Fraud.

Outsider.

Pretender.

He almost snorted champagne out of his nose.
He'd long ago sworn off wanting what his sister
and Jack's friend had. So why now did the hair at
the back of his neck react to every look the couples
shared, every touch, every unspoken communication? Because he knew he was short-changing Essie,
like the men of her past.

He focussed on Essie, whose cheeks had pinked
up nicely with the alcohol. She participated fully in
the conversation with the other two women, who,
Ash understood, had become close friends in recent
months. But her gaze slid often to him, secret, non-
verbal cues passing between them with every flick
of her expressive eyes.

She was happy.

Ash's unease lessened. Perhaps he was overthink-
ing this. She'd never hinted she wanted more than
sex. Great, addictive sex. He should go with the flow
tonight. Enjoy his and Ben's and Essie's success.
Enjoy his sister's company and that of new friends.

The next time she looked up, he smiled back at
Essie, his spirit lightening. During a brief lull in the
chatter, Harley cleared her throat.

'So, we have something to ask you.' She glanced
around the group, her eyes finishing on Jack.

Ash's shoulders tensed to the point of cramping

as chills raced down his spine. Harley looked far too happy.

'We're getting married. Monday,' she said with a flourish and giggle.

The blow winded him. Married? They'd only just reconnected.

'What? Since when?' Ash reeled, his stomach tight.

Harley nodded, barely containing her joy. 'It's all arranged—we just planned it in the car on the way here.' She leaned over to kiss Jack while the others offered congratulations and indulgent grins.

Of course. Because that was how most people planned the most important commitment of their lives—spur of the moment. He hated to be the voice of doom, but they'd only been engaged a few months... And they had history.

More importantly, had she learned nothing from his experience? From their father's appalling behaviour, towards their mother, Harley herself and most recently towards Ash? All done in the name of so-called love.

Yes, he'd jumped in too soon, his engagement to Maggie impulsive, flushed with the enthusiasm of first love. And look where that had led. To heartbreak, and humiliation. To the ultimate betrayal. Its effects long-lasting, shaping him, controlling him, affecting his precious equilibrium even to this day. Affecting his ability to be open to someone new in his life.

He'd thought himself over it years ago, but now,

years later, its effects still carried power. Because the lies outlasted all else. Discovering Hal had been the real partner in Maggie's betrayal and that he had concealed it from Ash, from everyone, long after the affair ended, had sealed the fate on both his working relationship with his father and his personal one. Ash's whole life as he'd known it had, in an instant, become untenable. His stomach rolled. He couldn't bear to look at his father, let alone work with the man.

'What about New York? Mum and Hannah?' No way would Harley marry without her twin sister present. And was Hal flying in for the ceremony? He couldn't be in the same room as him. Not yet. The betrayal was still too raw.

And what about divorce and infidelity and lies? He hadn't exaggerated when he'd informed Essie of the reality of divorce statistics. And he'd seen enough professionally—inevitable prenups, prolonged bitter wrangling over assets, the financial and emotional toll of a commitment that seemed like a good idea at the time but didn't last. Not to mention his personal prejudices…

'Mum and Hannah are flying in tomorrow. We don't want a big fuss, just a simple service. Alex said we can have the ceremony at his estate in Oxfordshire—this is what we want.' She clutched Jack's hand, some freaky silent communication passing between them. 'We'll celebrate with extended families separately.'

Ash could understand. There was no way their father and Jack's parents could attend the same event, not after they'd recently discovered the reason for the long rift between the former friends was another historic affair between Hal and Jack's mother. What a selfish bastard his father had turned out to be. He'd always known he was arrogant and uncompromising, but he hadn't realised he was such a shitty human being. Once a cheater, always a cheater.

Surely these were all perfect reasons for Harley and Jack to employ caution. To get to know each other better. To allow their relationship to stand the test of time before marriage. Why the hell did they have to marry at all? Why not just live together?

It warmed him that Harley, who'd struggled growing up because of her dyslexia, was happy. But could he stand to watch her go through the devastation a wrong choice now would bring? Jack seemed crazy about her, but you never really knew what lurked inside someone. Everyone had their ugliness.

As Harley turned to Ben and Essie, including them in the invitation to Oxfordshire, Ash battled his helplessness. It seemed, unless he could talk her out of this, he'd have a ringside seat. The least he could do was offer her some legal advice for when the shit splattered through the blades of the fan.

CHAPTER NINE

ASH TOYED WITH the ends of her hair, which still clung to his damp chest and the day's worth of stubble on his chin. Even at three a.m., after two rounds of opening-night celebratory sex, the oblivion of sleep evaded him.

Essie's head grew heavy. Had she succumbed to exhaustion? Should he slide out from under her and pound out the continued restlessness in the gym?

'Just tell me, Ash.' Her sleepy voice whispered over his skin, a soft caress that offered both release and a rising of his hackles. His body stilled but she stayed immobile and he was pinned beneath her sprawled, languid body.

'The problem shared, problem halved thing is true, you know.' She lifted her head and levelled warm, compassionate eyes on him. 'I won't judge you. I won't even comment. I'll just listen.' She settled her head back on his chest, but not before she brushed her lips over his skin with a small sigh.

Seconds stretched while he balanced on the edge, wishing he could be as brave and open as she was.

He could deny he had anything to confess.

He could huff and puff his way out of it.

He could even feign sleep.

But he wouldn't insult her intelligence.

With a sigh that lifted and then dropped her head, he drew his fingers back through her hair. The silky slide of the strands carried a hypnotic cadence he craved. Or perhaps it was just Essie.

'I think she's rushing into marriage.'

Coward.

True to her word, Essie remained quiet. Only her heartbeat, steady but fast enough, beating against his, indicated she was still awake.

'I've made no secret how I feel about it.'

She nodded, the slide of her skin and hair over his chest a soothing kind of torture, because it drew him out, a security blanket, lulling him to deeper confessions, ones at his very centre.

'You're probably thinking I have a right to feel the way I do. I told you about my fiancée, my parents splitting recently, my insider knowledge of the divorce courts from law school.'

He was making a meal of this. Was it better to say the words outright, to rip off the bandage with a vicious tear, that would bleed him out quicker, but shorten the sting? Or keep them in and protect himself.

'I discovered my father had cheated. More than the affair my mother knew about.' Essie stopped breathing and her pulse thrummed against his skin. 'I was the one who had to deliver that news. I didn't want her to hear it from someone who didn't care about her.'

Her head lifted, tugging her hair from between his fingers, her face wreathed in understanding.

'That must have been horrible for you.' She sat up, crossing her legs and drawing the duvet into her lap to cover her nakedness. 'How did *you* find out?'

Ash nodded, the urge to flee the room and the shameful scrutiny strong. If he'd detected one hint of pity in her expression he'd already have hit the shower, but Essie's brow pinched in confusion.

'From the horse's mouth—my father told me. We'd…had a disagreement. He didn't like the way I'd dared to call him out on his bullshit so he lashed out, like he derived pleasure from inflicting the knowledge on me. The coward knew I'd tell her.'

He linked his hands behind his head as he shrugged it off.

'Some people are cowards. I understand your fears for Harley.'

'I just worry that she'll be hurt. As it is, she's marrying without her father present and our mother…' He sucked in a breath, and rose to sit on the side of the bed. 'She didn't know about that particular affair until I informed her.'

He swallowed bile. 'It turned out to be the last straw for her.' He stood and made his way to the door of the en-suite. 'So, you understand my trepidation about this…happy occasion?'

Essie's teeth worried at her lip, her eyes scraping him raw.

Tell her. Tell her everything.

He backed away. She had the sense to give him space.

He stepped under the steamy blast of the shower, welcoming the pound of the water as a replacement for the waves of self-directed emotion. He was a coward, too. Holding back, convincing himself he was happy. That he was justified in his mistrust.

And he still carried the full burden of guilt and self-loathing, not the half measure Essie had promised.

She joined him, as he'd known she would. She'd kept her promise, but offered silent comfort, just by her presence. Her touch, tentative at first, as if she was uncertain of her reception, grew bolder. She reached for the body wash and tipped a measure into her palm before sliding soap-slicked palms over his chest, abdomen and shoulders. When she moved behind him to soap his back, she pressed her mouth between his shoulder blades.

'I'm sorry that happened to you. Do you want me to go home?'

He turned to face her, scooping his arm around her waist and hauling her up so his mouth covered hers. 'No.'

Within seconds their lazy kisses grew torrid. Her slippery skin slid against his as she writhed and moaned in his arms, her hands clutching at him. Her fingers twisted in his wet hair and she angled his head and twisted her mouth away. 'I want you.'

He'd recovered sufficiently to be fully on board.

Slamming off the water, he scooped Essie up and lifted her from the shower. In two strides, he'd deposited her on the bed, still sopping wet, and fell to his knees between her spread thighs.

His mouth covered her, a hint of soap and whole lot of delicious Essie. He worked her higher, her moans and gasps telling him when the time was right. With a curse, he tore his mouth from her and quickly covered himself with a condom.

When he pushed inside her, she gripped his face, her blue stare burning into him in unspoken unity.

They climaxed together, eyes locked, cries mingling and the blurred and broken lines of fun scattered all around them.

Getting out of London, especially for the romance of an impromptu wedding at one of the UK's most lavish private estates, complete with a boutique winery and hotel, carried a surreal quality akin to flying to Paris, just to go clubbing. Essie, giggly with excitement, relaxed back into the leather upholstery of Ash's Mercedes, and tried not to drool at the confident, manly way he handled the luxury car.

It was the same confident, manly way he handled everything, especially when commanding her pleasure with skilled, devastating proficiency.

Ash was quiet, a fact she wanted to attribute to him driving on unfamiliar roads, but she couldn't deceive herself after his late-night revelations. What should have been a joyous family occasion had huge potential to become a trigger. Hers wasn't the only dysfunctional family in the world.

Essie shifted in the seat, restless.

That Ash had opened up to her on Saturday night enclosed her in a warm cocoon. She longed to reassure him about today. That his own pain at being left by his fiancée would pass. That his mother surely didn't blame him for stepping up. That his sister had her own life to live with a man who wasn't Hal Jacob.

Perhaps he regretted opening up to her. Many men struggled to talk about their feelings. She'd bide her time. He had enough going on with his family drama.

She'd spent all of Sunday, after a late start, where she'd crawled home from Ash's apartment to catch up on mundane life things like laundry and bill-paying and checking on her flatmate. Of course, she also had to catch up on her latest blog post, entitled *Love is in the air—is it catching?* It was wedding season, after all. She glanced over at Ash, prickles of guilt dousing her high.

Her blog continued to attract new followers and the ads she'd incorporated on her website, featuring well-respected books on relationships, had high click-through rates. People couldn't get enough of *Illegally Hot*, if the comments were any indication. But she hadn't mentioned him in the last few posts. His pain was real—not entertainment fodder.

In the beginning, writing about her overwhelming attraction to Ash and his extreme bedroom skills had helped control the impact he'd had on her life. Helped her to rationalise that she was simply, for the first time, party to a healthy, equal-terms relationship based on spectacular sex. But now… She shuddered. Every social media mention, every new follower, every demand for more of *Illegally Hot* carried with it a hundred tiny barbs to her conscience.

Perhaps she should confess. Explain why she'd done such a reckless and thoughtless thing.

No. She'd never actually used any identifiers— he'd never know he was *Illegally Hot*. He'd never read the blog. And this wouldn't last for ever—Ash would move on and she would chalk up this experience and believe in herself and what she had to say.

Because she was no longer Essie the downtrodden, the ignored, the inconvenient. She was part of something wonderful, respectful and mutually satisfying. And with a man as incredible as Ash.

And her relationship with Ben was also looking up. Essie hugged the memory of his thoughtful present to her chest. She'd all but sobbed over him on Saturday night.

I always wanted a sibling… I'm just glad it's you.

That he would make such a heartfelt declaration went a long way to healing the past hurts and humiliations inflicted by their father. Ben respected her. He was starting to value her as a part of his life, as her inclusion in today's nuptials proved.

Ash exited the A40 to Oxford and headed into the green and gold countryside. The sun glinted off fields of barley, filling Essie with a momentary sense of the contentment she'd craved her whole adult life. She was spending time with her brother and his friends, welcomed into his social circle.

An equal.

Valued.

Important.

'What do you think of our English countryside?' So Ash wouldn't want to talk about Saturday night, or the wedding today, but they could still converse.

'Very pretty.'

'Don't you miss New York?' Of course she understood why working with his father at the family firm would be awkward, but why set up shop in London, why move away from your entire life?

He shrugged, non-committal. 'The Jacobs are never absent from the business pages or the gossip columns for long.' He concentrated on the road, his mouth a grim line. But Essie was more concerned about the growing constriction to her chest.

'My…confrontation with my father happened in the open-plan offices of Jacob Holdings. Someone snapped a photo. The next thing I know, the whole humiliating business is splashed online, as if our sordid, fucked-up family drama is entertainment.'

Her lungs seized. He'd left New York to get away from his personal life and that of his parents' divorce being played out like a soap opera on the internet?

He jerked his chin. 'It was my fault. I hurt my mother. I should have spoken to Hal in private. When he confessed his…affair, I acted hot, without thinking, and I caused her pain. Humiliation.'

'It wasn't your fault.' Her voice croaked past her scratchy throat.

He shook his head, nostrils flared. 'It's one thing to be betrayed by someone who's supposed to love you. It's another entirely to watch that devastation play out publicly, everyone judging, commenting, whispering.' His lip curled.

Essie's head spun. How could she tell him she'd used the amazing, no-strings sex between them as fodder for her blog? Poor, affection-starved, sex-starved Essie had cast aside her principles for a taste of success—the heady feeling of being taken seriously.

They'd travelled deep into the Oxfordshire countryside by now. Essie stared at the hedgerows without seeing the beauty, her mind churning in time with her stomach. Why had she been so impetuous? So irresponsible? Not only had she treated the man she'd come to know and to care for like a…like an object, she had no doubt Ash could slap her with a lawsuit that would blow her beloved blog and any future career as a clinical psychologist out of existence.

Should she tell him now about *Illegally Hot*?

He'd hate her. He'd call things off.

What if her poorly timed confession ruined the wedding? Harley deserved her big day. And his mother was flying in…

Hello, my name's Essie. I shagged your son and then used the experience to flavour my online career…

What if she lost Ben and Ash in one fell swoop? She'd only have herself to blame.

As the silent miles passed, Ash lost to his thoughts, Essie to hers, she made a vow. A reckoning of her own making was heading her way. All she had to do was choose the right moment to explain to this amazing man why she'd done what she'd done.

Piece of wedding cake.

CHAPTER TEN

H E DESERVED A damned medal. He'd spent the entire
afternoon and evening with a fake smile plastered
on his face, walked his sister down the aisle and kept
his opinions to himself, when all he wanted to do
was drag Harley aside and beg her to reconsider her
rash decision. He couldn't deny the ceremony, under
a rose-clad arbour, had been touching. And Harley
looked so happy—even he'd had a lump in his throat,
especially when he'd glanced sideways at a stunning
Essie and seen her pretty eyes shining with emotion.

And he was man enough to accept that his feelings
were about *him*. His issues. Nothing to do with Harley and Jack, who'd had the wedding they'd wanted
today—intimate, full of laughter and in exquisite
surroundings.

But he couldn't shake his demons.

His mother, too, looked beautiful, but her face was
drawn and pale. She'd lost weight in the weeks since
he'd left New York. It couldn't be easy for her being
here alone at her daughter's wedding, her brave face
fooling no one. And he'd left her behind to deal with

the fallout of her rotten marriage. To deal with the
public speculation. To deal with his shame.

Ash looked out across the gently sloping vine-
yards from the terrace where he'd detoured after a
trip to bathroom. He sucked in air that felt too thin
and willed his stray emotions back under control.

This whole fucking wedding thing had unsettled
him anew. Not because he was still hung up on the
ex not worth his consideration, but because Essie's
gentle probing over the last few days and his cathar-
tic confessions had thrown up comparisons, ones between him then and him now, and the evidence was
growing increasingly hard to bury.

He'd struggled to answer Essie's questions about
love, because the truth was he could hand on heart
admit that he probably hadn't loved his fiancée. Not
the way he should have. The way Essie described
with her fun facts and scientific evidence. No wonder his ex had looked elsewhere.

And it wasn't the loss of that imagined love that
had hurt so much. It wasn't even the lies, the deception. What hurt the most was that he'd handed
over control of his happiness to those unworthy of
it. He'd held himself back for so long after Maggie,
believing the worst, something he never wanted to
experience again.

All he'd done was live a half-life in between and
then hurt others in his frustration with himself, his
mother in particular.

Perhaps he was incapable of the kind of love
Essie described. A chip off the old block. As ruth-

less, selfish and incapable of a meaningful, honest relationship as Hal Jacob. Genetics must count for something. But would he ever know if he refused to even consider the possibility?

Essie.

She was so open, so honest and so giving. Way too good for him with his issues and his rigid rules and his impenetrable guard.

Ash spun towards the festivities. He'd left her alone for too long. Not that he could claim her as his date, but, between him and Ben, they'd managed to keep both of their single sisters occupied on the dance floor all evening.

He re-entered the conservatory, his stare scanning for her. Her ready touch was the only thing to ease his restlessness. Her bright smile. And her dirty laugh. Even her fun facts.

The way she looked up at him. The way she embraced their chemistry with her cheeky sense of humour and her quirky logic. The way she commanded her femininity with grace and steely determination, and a massive heart.

He found her talking with Ben at the edge of the makeshift dance floor. The happy couple and Alex and Libby slow danced under the twinkle of a thousand lights.

Ben saw Ash approach and lifted his chin in greeting before kissing Essie's cheek and heading towards the hotel's main foyer.

Her porcelain skin glowed pale under the lights

and her eyes peeled back his layers, leaving him raw and more conflicted than ever.

'Are you okay?' She stepped closer, her stare flicking to the dance floor before settling back on his.

Ash threw caution to the wind and curved his hand over her hip. He hated that he couldn't touch her when he wanted to. Hated that he'd left it to Harley to introduce her to his mother as 'Ben's sister'. Hated that the past he couldn't let go, his hang-ups, had placed a filter across her pretty eyes.

'I'm fine. Are you having fun?'

She nodded. Her hand brushed his, fingers lingering for a second. 'You don't look fine.'

He couldn't fool her. 'I'm just worried about my mother—she's lost a little weight. I feel responsible.'

Ash guided her to a chair and took the one opposite. Her small frown and worry-etched eyes slayed him. He shouldn't have said anything. Should have allowed her to enjoy the festivities while he attended his pity party, solo.

He clasped both her hands in his while his mind raced with all the ways he'd been an idiot.

'Have you talked it through with her? I'm sure she doesn't hold you responsible.'

'She doesn't, but being the messenger of doom sucks whichever way you look at it. I can never take it back, or undo the pain.'

'But you were right. Better she heard it from you than someone else.' She paled and looked away. 'I feel guilty…about Ben.' Her teeth pulled at her lip.

'Don't look at me like that.' She stared at her lap, where her hands clenched.

He spoke softly, too uncertain of his own thoughts, motivations and emotions. 'How am I looking at you?' How did he feel about her revelation?

'Like you expect my brother to march you to the nearest church with a shotgun aimed between your shoulder blades.' She was too perceptive. Saw him way too clearly.

'I—'

Had their secret-keeping days come to an end? A natural conclusion? Her limpid eyes lanced him, and he wanted to wrap her in his arms, to carry her out of here and kiss her until she looked at him as she'd done on Saturday night after their shower.

'Why don't we talk about it when we're back in London?' It was about time he manned up. Came clean with Ben. It was his responsibility. He hadn't been able to keep his hands off her, despite his damned pathetic rules. Perhaps if he ended things now, he could go to Ben in all honesty and say, 'It happened, but it's over.'

His guts twisted with eye-watering force.

The thought of going back to being friends with Essie, or even acquaintances, left him more impotent and off balance than when he'd sweated his way down the aisle this afternoon with his sister on his arm and a hundred different divorce scenarios in his head.

But Essie deserved a full relationship with her brother. He wouldn't stand in the way.

She looked over his shoulder to where Harley, Hannah and Jack were huddled around Hannah's phone laughing, probably at some atrocious selfie. 'You have a great family. Aside from my mum, Ben's all I have.'

Ash's chest grew tighter and tighter. Telling Ben about them would shift things between him and Essie far outside the realms of fun. But if he was honest he'd lost his precious control of this attraction days ago.

Fight for her.

Where the fuck had that come from?

She looked wearier than he'd ever seen her. He'd underestimated the toll this had all taken on her, or he'd seen it but ignored it because he was selfish and wanted her still. He cupped her cheek. 'Why don't you head upstairs? Take a bath? Things are pretty much over here. Just some mushy shit going on over there.' He jerked his head back in the direction of his sappy sisters, who were a bit tipsy and had sandwiched Jack between them on the dance floor for one last slow dance.

She nodded, her eyes glassy as she stared at their entwined fingers in her lap. And then she shook it off, her expression brightening as she watched the twin sandwich on display. 'Fun fact—did you know that simply holding hands with the person you love can alleviate pain and fear and reduce stress? It's the oxytocin the brain releases.'

He nodded, his throat so damned tight he had to loosen his collar. 'I'll tell the happy couple.'

She stood, glancing over at the dance floor. 'I think they know.' She smiled down at him, the saddest smile he'd ever seen, before she turned to leave.

He halted her retreat. 'Don't worry about Ben.'

She shook her head. 'Don't worry about your mum.'

She left him floundering at the centre of the monumental mess he'd made.

Ash tapped gently on the door to Essie's hotel room, his eyes scanning the corridor. He had no explanation for why he stood at her door at one a.m., for any of the wedding party who might spot him. He just knew a team of wild horses couldn't keep him away.

If this was to be their last night before he confronted Ben tomorrow, he just had to kiss her one last time. Hold her once more. See the rapture on her face as they shared one last intimacy. Somehow, between the fun facts and the fun sex, she'd worked her way under his skin. All of her—her beauty, her vulnerabilities, her thirst for new experiences.

The door flew open and there she stood, dressed in a baggy, oversized T-shirt that hung from one shoulder, her long, pale legs leading to the views of nirvana he knew were underneath. He had no right to touch her—he never had—but he wanted her anyway. With the same ferocity of need he'd experienced since the day they'd met.

How had he ever imagined himself immune to her? He was a fool and it was too late for a vaccine.

'Invite me in.' He tried to temper the gruffness

from his voice, but he craved her so badly he could hardly draw breath. Perhaps it was the promise of one last time. But however he looked at it, he couldn't stay away. And he suspected it was simply Essie herself that drove his uncontrollable need. A need he'd have to quash soon.

Unless you keep her.

Fuck. She wasn't a possession. And she deserved way more than a commitment-phobic, cynical asshole like him. She deserved her happily-ever-after—the whole cake, not just the crumbs. Her scientific love. And he was the last man qualified to give her that.

But he could give her the only thing he'd ever given her.

A fun time. A new experience.

Why did it sound so empty? Hollow? Pathetic?

She held the door open and he stepped inside. As soon as she'd shut it behind him, she turned to face him. 'I need to talk to—'

Ash pressed his fingers over her soft lips. 'I know what you need. What we both need.' He'd made his decision to talk to Ben. The mess he'd made of his personal life was old news and he'd be damned if he spent what little remaining time he had left with her trawling through his issues.

He might not be the man for her long term, but he could show her how rare and precious she was, and what she did to him and, hopefully, when they parted, she would feel her own worth and have nothing to regret.

She nodded, her breathtaking face lifted to his as he dragged her close with one arm banded around her waist and slanted his mouth over hers. Her soft lips parted under his with a sigh. As always, she embraced what they shared, never once pressing him for labels, or more than he could offer.

Did anyone deserve a woman as amazing as Essie?

Ash bunched the hem of her shirt in his fists and lifted it over her head, breaking from their kiss for the split second it took to dispense with the garment and slide his stare over her magnificent nakedness. He scooped his arms around her waist, hoisting her from her feet and stumbling backwards towards the bed so she sprawled over him, covering him from chest to thigh in a tumble of naked limbs and a cloud of Essie-scented hair.

Ash filled his lungs and his hands with her, memorising every nuance of this unique woman. With every passing beat, her kisses grew more desperate, the breathy moans in her throat more frantic and her fingers more insistent. And her ardour matched his.

Ash rolled them so she lay under him, her writhing body urging him on. She tugged at his shirt and he helped her, yanking it up from behind his head and tossing it aside.

Skin to warm skin.

Ash gripped one of her thighs, pushing her open to slot his hips in between. He captured one pink-tipped nipple, laving and lapping until she bucked in his arms and tugged at his hair, the wild, demand-

ing side of her never far from the surface. His kisses
followed the bumps of her ribs, the dip of her navel
and the hollows beneath her hip bones.

He slid to the floor, tugging her ass to the edge of
the bed until he was satisfied with her position. He
spread her open, his gaze devouring every perfect
pink inch of her.

Just one more taste.

He pressed a kiss to each thigh and then he leaned
in to touch the tip of his tongue to her clit.

She sucked in a gasp, her hands fisting the bed-
spread. 'Ash…'

He pulled back, a rock the size of the Isle of Wight
lodged in his chest. 'Say it again. Say my name.'
Some base part of him needed to hear her call out
for him, to know that he wasn't alone with his unrest.
To know that she saw him and only him.

She nodded and he dived once more for the slick
haven between her thighs. 'Ash…' She resumed her
chant, his name over and over again, while he licked
and flicked and suckled.

Every time she spoke his name, his fingers clung
to her thighs with a fraction more force, as if he
wanted to stamp his presence all over her from head
to toe, leaving no doubt. He pushed the crazy idea
aside, focussing on the catches in her throat as he
forced her higher and higher.

She wasn't his.

'Yes… Ash… I'm close.' Her thighs juddered
against his face and he ceased his efforts. He wanted
to be inside her when she came, her muscles grip-

ping him like a fist as she wailed his name for the
last time.

She cried out, but when he tore into his fly, shoving his pants down with impatient jerks and pulling
a condom from the pocket, she helped him, pushing
at the denim and sliding her hands up and down the
backs of his thighs.

Ash gripped the foil between his teeth and then
covered himself. He shucked the jeans with a kick.
Gripping her hips, he tilted her ass from the bed and
plunged inside her with one thrust. Her body welcomed him, warm and tight and as close to perfect
as he'd ever experienced.

He held himself still, allowing her to grow ac-
customed to him inside her and allowing him time
to breathe around the block of concrete where his
lungs should be. Ash held her stare while their chests
heaved in unison, the patter of her heartbeat strong
and rapid against his chest.

'Ash…' She sighed, her fingers dancing over his
back, his shoulders and across his chest. He gipped
one wandering hand, his fingers interlocking with
hers while he pressed it to the mattress, and then followed suit with the other hand.

Her touching him with tender fingertips, while
looking at him the way she was…it was too much.
Too close to something he'd forsaken for good. Too
raw a reminder that, one day, some other lucky bastard would be gifted this woman's love.

He rocked into her, his thrusts growing in speed
and power as if he was chasing down his demons.

Every time he slammed home a tiny gasp left her throat. It was a sound he'd remember his whole life. Her wide eyes clung to him as if begging. Only, he was the one who should be on his knees. Worshipping.

Her breasts jiggled, desperate for his tongue, but he'd reached the point of no return, reached his limit. He released one of her hands to scoop her thigh higher until it curved over his hip. Holding it there, he sank lower, the last inch into her tight heat.

'Yes… Ash…that's—' She never finished the sentence. Her orgasm struck, her head stretched back as she gasped a prolonged wail and clamped down on him so hard, he almost closed his eyes in ecstasy. But then he'd have missed her riding out her climax with her beautiful stare on him, her swollen mouth slack as her moans petered into pants.

His head swam as oxygen deprivation sucked him under.

'Ash.' She cupped his face, pressing her mouth to his.

He collapsed forward as fire raced along his spine and down the length of his cock. He buried his face in her neck as he ground his hips through the last of the spasms. He wasn't gentle. His facial hair would mark her, but he needed a minute to flounder in private from the purging flood of emotions he daredn't name. A minute to swallow the incredible high she'd often told him existed. He crushed her beneath him while he reeled, spent, panting and completely mindfucked.

Essie ran her fingers through his hair, her soft lips pressing kisses to his temples, his ear, the side of his neck. The see-sawing of his chest dwindled away until he struggled to suck even one molecule of air past his tight throat. His scalp prickled and the sheen of sweat on his skin turned icy cold.

He shifted, gently withdrew from her languid embrace and shuffled to the en-suite to dispose of the condom. He couldn't bring himself to look in the mirror while he washed his hands. He knew what he'd see. A stupid fuck who'd broken his number one rule in life and was now paying the ultimate price. The only thing he'd had to avoid and he'd gone and done it anyway.

His best friend's sister. A wonderful woman he couldn't have and didn't deserve. A woman professionally obsessed with relationships and romantic love—two things he sucked at and had spent years forsaking. A woman who deserved a man to love her one hundred and ten per cent. To be all in. To worship her and leave her in no doubt that she was his number one priority.

No way could fucked-up Ash be that man.

Keeping his gaze averted, he returned to the bedroom to find Essie wrapped in a white sheet, her face peaceful in sleep.

Indulging in one last, ill-advised move, he slipped into the bed beside her and fell asleep with her perfectly slotted into his arms.

CHAPTER ELEVEN

THE INSISTENT VIBRATION of a phone alert woke him. Ash opened his eyes to find the bed empty beside him and the sound of the shower from the en-suite bathroom. His body stirred fully awake at the idea of joining a wet Essie.

As he slid from the bed, Essie's phone vibrated again. He flipped it over and placed it on the night-stand, pausing when the screen lit up to reveal the string of notifications, which had sent the device into an early-morning frenzy.

You have fifty-three comments

What the...?

Ash's stomach pitched. Since his own brush with the gossip columns and the subsequent social media roasting around the story of one of New York's most influential families crumbling in the most sordid way, he'd deleted his own accounts.

Was Essie victim to a similar backlash? No, why

would she be a target? Unless it was something to do with him…

Perhaps the gossip rags had caught wind of Harley's rushed, closed-door wedding. Perhaps they'd somehow acquired the limited guest list and sought a comment or a photo from Essie.

His scalp prickled even as he swiped his thumb over the screen.

It wasn't locked.

Every nerve in his body fired as he snooped— as soon as he'd verified that the messy, dirty Jacob drama hadn't spread to include Essie, he'd stop reading.

It took several beats for Ash to understand the content displayed on her phone. A blog.

Relationships and Other Science Experiments

So this was her little secret. Not quite an agony aunt. His mouth twitched at her sense of humour and her conversational writing style. He read on for a few lines, the latest post unsurprisingly one about the inexhaustible romance of weddings and the hidden tangle of complex relationships at play when extended families met, often for the first time in years.

One phrase, repeated in the comments at the bottom of the post, leapt from the screen and smacked him between the eyes. *Illegally Hot.*

Whatever it referred to, Essie's fans wanted more.

He shouldn't pry. No good ever came from snooping. But some unseen demon controlled his fingers, which scrolled the screen in search of earlier posts.

A familiar photo—the view of the London Eye taken from St James's Park. The photo he'd taken for her the day they'd met.

With each line he read, wave after wave of heat flooded his body until his fists clenched and his jaw ached.

She'd written about their one-night stand. About their shock meeting the next day. About some arrogant asshole who'd rocked her world, but had the emotional intelligence of a rock.

He was paraphrasing, but one thing was glaringly obvious. *He* was *Illegally Hot*. And Essie had used him as tawdry inspiration fodder for her online musings. Exposing his hang-ups in a public forum…for humour…for entertainment… To humiliate him? To laugh behind his back?

No wonder the damned phone was never far from her hand. And every ping, every muted vibration represented someone new reading about or commenting on his sex life…

Ash tossed the phone on the nightstand, his stomach rigid as he sucked in a breath laced with razor blades. She'd put their relationship on the internet. For anyone to see? And kept it from him? All this time? While he'd agonised over the rights and wrongs of his attraction to her. All these weeks she'd made a fool of him…been laughing at him… Did everyone know? The Yard's staff? Ben?

His gut ached as if he'd taken a knee to the balls. He needed to get out of here.

Essie appeared in that moment, her open smile sliding from her face as she took in his posture. He stood, silently tugging on his boxers and his shirt—he was exposed enough.

'*Illegally Hot?* Did you come up with that all by yourself?'

Wrapped in a towel, her hair wet, she hovered, breathtaking but paralysed, on the threshold. His vision tunnelled as he clamped his jaw shut and turned away from her to find his jeans.

She gasped, paling. 'Ash, I'm sorry, I—'

'You're fucking sorry? Is that all you have? Not quite your usual level of eloquence. Or is that reserved for your tacky sexploits?'

She moved towards him, a small anguished squeak leaving her throat. His outstretched hand stopped her dead in her tracks. If she touched him now, he might actually hurl, so tightly knotted were his intestines.

'Is everything entertainment to you? People's emotions? Their challenges? Their…pain.' What a fool he'd been. Again. He'd told her about his fiancée, his parents, his guilt over his mother… Would he read all about it online soon? Another science experiment?

How had he, only hours ago, imagined himself developing feelings for her? He didn't know her at all. Not this manipulative, deceptive version she'd hidden so successfully behind the bubbly, ingenuous, emotionally damaged exterior.

'I never meant to hurt you.'

Fuck, that sentiment sucked. 'So said every selfish person who ever acted in their own interest and only considered the consequences when they were found out.' Ash yanked on his jeans and scooped his own phone and the key to his room from the desk.

'Don't go. I can explain.'

'I don't give a fuck about your explanation. You used me. Not for one second did you consider my feelings before you published that crap—' he pointed at the nightstand and the offending device '—for anyone to read.'

'Ash…' She stepped closer, sucking the oxygen from the enclosed space until Ash's lungs recoiled. 'It was meant to be funny… I didn't name you.'

He snorted, expecting to see plumes of fire coming from his nostrils. 'Do you know why my family drama, my parents' split, was such salacious gossip, the kind you find funny?' He loomed over her, his chest working hard to oxygenate his blood before his head exploded. 'The juicy little details? The irresistible intrusion into our personal lives…all in the name of fair-game entertainment for the masses?'

Essie had the good grace to pale almost white and stay silent, a tiny shake of her head her only answer.

'The woman at the centre of the row between Hal and me, the final intolerable insult to my mother, the woman he confessed to fucking in front of my entire workplace, was *my* ex-fiancée.'

Her jaw dropped, and she swayed unsteadily on her feet, but it gave him no satisfaction.

Ash marched to the door, turning to cast one final look at the woman he'd almost trusted. Almost…

No.

'Forgive me if I have no intention of becoming a public laughing stock again.'

The door slammed behind him with a whoosh of air, blocking Essie's startled image from view.

Ash slapped his hand over the stop button on the treadmill in his apartment's fully equipped gym and wiped sweat from his eyes with a towel. He'd arrived home from Oxfordshire three hours ago, but he hadn't been able to quench the fire burning inside him any other way. Even now, after a solid hour of relentless pounding, when his noodle-like legs threatened to give out at any stage, the flames still licked at him—burning, taunting and mocking. Because he craved her still, when the taste of her betrayal should have turned his stomach for good.

Stupid fuck.

How could he have been so dumb? So taken in by her seeming ingenuousness and English-rose charm? When all the time she wielded a poisonous pen…or a noxious keyboard.

Of course he'd been right not to trust her. He'd been here before. Twice. Once with the lies his fiancée had told to keep her true affair with his father a secret, and once when Hal had finally tossed out the truth in a fit of malice for anyone at Jacob Holdings to hear.

Only this time, the pain slashed deeper, the wound gaping open. He'd thought she was different. He'd thought he'd learned his lesson and done everything in his power to protect himself.

Well, there was one more thing he could do. This time, he wasn't going down without a fight. He was done. Done with humiliation, done with being the last to know. Ash stumbled from the treadmill and eyed his phone where he'd switched it to silent. His fingers curled into his palm.

He wouldn't check.

How close he'd come to…feeling emotions that left him wanting to build barricades to protect himself! He needed fortifications more than ever, to protect himself from the feelings he'd realised last night were as foreign as the adopted country he'd chosen. Because whatever he'd felt for his ex, it paled in comparison to the unstoppable wave building in him now. He should never have let things go so far—caring for her hadn't been part of the plan.

A yell from his living room sucked him to his senses.

Ben stood framed in the doorway, his face slightly haggard with questions burning in his eyes. Ash had known this reckoning was coming, and yet he still recoiled. Telling your friend you'd slept with his sister was one thing. Telling him you'd allowed yourself to be duped, humiliated by not just one woman, but two…

Ash stalked to the kitchen with Ben trailing. He held out his arm, offering Ben a seat, and retrieved two bottles of beer from the fridge. 'What did she tell you?'

Is she okay?

No.

There'd be no asking about Essie, thinking about Essie and certainly no going to Essie.

'That it happened. That it was over.' Ben collapsed onto a bar stool, and accepted the beer Ash handed him. 'What did you do to her?'

Ash deserved the accusation in his friend's stare. He should never have slept with her after the first time. He had no defence. Never a good position for an attorney. But she wasn't blameless here. 'I met her the day before you left for New York. I didn't know who she was the first time.'

Fuck, that sounded all wrong.

Ben stared for long challenging seconds. 'I know Maggie hurt you and that you only do casual.' Ben gripped the bottle, his knuckles white. 'So why would you lead Essie on like that?'

Fuck, he didn't want to do this now, but there was no escape. 'We were just fooling around. She said she wanted the same thing. I should have told you.'

Ben paled even more, his lips thin and white. 'And now? You're done and she clearly wanted more because she's broken-hearted.' Ben speared his fingers through his hair. 'I offered her the job so I could get to know her, to make amends for the shit our father pulled. She's sweet and kind and fun. She's so desperate for approval…'

Ash nodded. It couldn't have been easy for Ben to find out he had a sister, either. A massive adjustment. 'I didn't know about your father, I'm sorry.'

Ben swallowed, his face twisted as he shook his head. 'Fuck… She's been treated so fucking shabbily by men, men who are supposed to care about her and love her and protect her, part of her believes she's unworthy of a decent relationship.' Ben took a swig of beer, wiping his mouth with the back of his hand. 'Please tell me you didn't take advantage of that.'

Had he? Had he unknowingly taken her fears and insecurities and used them for his own ends? He'd known Essie had a poor relationship with her and Ben's father, something Ash could relate to. Did she crave what she'd never had? Did she want it with him?

It didn't matter. It was too late. Over.

'If I did it was unintentional.' Ash ground his teeth together, willing truth into them—he'd told her his position from the start. But as he'd learned more about her, a part of him had known he would hurt her. He just hadn't guessed she'd hurt him in return.

Ben ignored his plea, as if lost to his own turmoil over his sister. 'He was never there for her. He kept me and his wife a secret from her until she discovered his lies by accident. Fuck. She deserves better than him.'

Acid flooded the back of Ash's throat. 'I agree. But she's not blameless in this.' He should leave it alone. Accept all the responsibility. But those fingers of mistrust still burrowed into his brain.

Ben stared. 'What does that mean?'

'Did you know about her blog?' The heat returned, scalding, diminishing.

Ben frowned. 'Not until today, but what does that have to do with anything?'

The words trapped in his throat, covered in barbed wire. 'She's…been writing about us. About me.'

'So? She mentioned something… What's the big deal?'

'Aside from the fact I don't enjoy reading about my private life, my sex life on the internet…?'

Ben shrugged, eyes darting.

Ash took a seat at the kitchen bench, next to Ben. 'Did you…catch up on any gossip while you were in New York?'

'What the…? You know that's not my style. What does this have to do with Essie?'

Damn, the words stuck deep down in his gullet. 'Remember when… Maggie…called off the wedding?'

Ben nodded, one hand scraping over his haggard face.

Ash gulped beer, the cool liquid soothing his parched throat. 'Turned out the affair was a cover. Some scapegoat schmuck. She was really fucking Hal.'

Ben sputtered. 'Bullshit.'

Ash stared straight ahead. He couldn't witness whatever expression his friend wore for fear the humiliation would burrow into him so deep, he'd need a lobotomy to excise it. 'It's true. I didn't know it at the time, but Hal took great pleasure in informing me in front of a whole office of Jacob Holdings staff.'

Several beats passed. The occasional swallow of beer the only sound. 'Word spread. Before I knew it, the gossip rags were speculating on the demise of my parents' marriage, whether my playboy reputation would be damaged or enhanced and how destructive it would be to Jacob Holdings stock.' He faced his friend. 'That's why I came to London. I couldn't go back to work for Hal. I had paps chasing me down the street and, having created the mess, I had to rush to tell my mother before she heard of it at the gym or the grocery store.'

Ben shook his head, shock rendering him slack-jawed. 'I didn't know.'

Ash snorted. 'You and me both.'

'Does Essie know?'

Ash nodded.

They sat in silence. Then Ben said, 'She's sorry for what she did. Perhaps if you talked to her…'

Ash shook his head. He would. But not tonight.

'I think she's in love with you.'

No.

Ash couldn't deny they'd had chemistry from the start. And yes, she'd slipped under his guard, blind-sided him with her honest and refreshing outlook on the world, her ethereal beauty and her bubbly personality. But not love.

Ben glanced at his watch. 'I have to be at the club.'

Ash jutted his chin in silence. Where did these events leave him and Ben? Would he survive bumping into Essie down the track? She'd always be a part of Ben's life, quite rightly.

At the door, Ben turned. 'Ash. I'm sorry, man.'

Ash nodded. 'Me, too.'

And then he was alone again with only his restlessness for company.

Essie stacked the last chair into place and stretched out her aching back muscles. The basement club had been booked out for a private function that night—a fashion show and corporate party. The removal crew would arrive first thing to dismantle the temporary runway and extra seating.

The last place she'd wanted to be tonight was here with her happy face plastered on and the requisite nothing-is-too-much-trouble attitude, but she'd promised Ben she'd lock up the club, and in reality she'd rather have been here with the noise and the bodies than home alone with her self-recriminations.

Riding back to London earlier with Ben, she'd found hiding her desolation from her brother impossible. He'd coaxed the whole tale from her, his bunched jaw the only sign of any judgment. To his credit, he'd been supportive and understanding, something she didn't deserve for her role in hurting Ash, her own guilt a sharp blade slicing deep.

Flicking off the lights, she made her way upstairs, her tired feet encased in lead.

Her stomach clenched at the memory of Ash's

face. She hated what she'd done to him. How much she'd devastated him through her thoughtlessness. She'd convinced herself he couldn't be identified, so he couldn't be hurt. But in light of his shocking confession about his father and his ex…

She'd betrayed his trust.

Humiliated him.

All because she'd been overwhelmed by their chemistry, in awe of the amazing sex and flushed with the heady power of holding her own in a relationship for the first time. And then later…

She only had herself to reprimand. If she'd been honest with him from the start, if she'd owned her feelings, said, 'This is who I am, take it or leave it,' instead of shoving them back inside for fear of his judgment or disapproval or indifference… He'd been honest with her from day one. He'd never once claimed to want anything beyond sex. She'd just misinterpreted his looks and his touches. She'd seen something, felt something that wasn't there. At least not for Ash.

She'd known the score going in and learned a long time ago that even when people said one thing, they usually did something else. Something that suited *them*.

But somewhere along the way, perhaps dazzled by the private jets and Paris and the glamorous clubs, she'd fooled herself into believing, just this once, she could have more. Have the real deal. An equal relationship where she was valued, cherished, respected. For once she'd ignored the loud and clear warning bells and imagined she could have someone for herself, someone who not just barely tolerated her, but actually wanted her in their life. Not an inconvenience, but as necessary as oxygen.

So the last time they'd been together in Oxfordshire had, at least for her, been way more intimate than all the previous occasions combined. She'd convinced herself they could be making love, not just banging each other. That didn't mean Ash had felt the same. She understood his anger, but could he run away so quickly if he shared one iota of her feelings?

Gnawing at her lip, she swung through the staff-only door. Yet again, she'd learned the hard way that relationships were fine in theory, the black-and-white science irrefutable, but disastrous in reality. She was an expert in one, but definitely a novice at the other. Nothing had changed. Only, this lesson carried a permanency that rolled her stomach and left her empty.

Bereft.

She slammed to a halt, her small gasp catching in her throat.

Ash stood in her office.

He wore running gear, his shirt dark with sweat as if he'd sprinted all the way with his backside on fire.

Perhaps sensing her behind him, he lifted his stare from a white envelope on her otherwise clear desk.

Essie's knees threatened to give way.

He was here.

To see her?

'Ash—'

'I came to deliver this. I… I assumed everyone

had gone home.' He looked away and another part of Essie cracked and crumbled.

'I'm sorry. Please let me explain.' The words tumbled out in a rush.

Ash collected the envelope from the desk and Essie spotted her name. He lanced her with a cold stare. 'Will your apology change the outcome? The facts?'

'No, but… Please…'

At his silence she ploughed on, certain he'd never forgive her, but desperate to have him understand. 'I didn't think I'd see you again after that first night. And then the next day you were my boss.' She lifted her gaze to his. 'I'd never had a one-night stand before. I…it made a good cautionary tale. Careful who you sleep with—it might turn out to be your boss.' Her voice trailed away with the ice of his stare.

She should have told him sooner. She'd been about to the night of the wedding. And then he'd looked at her as if he'd wanted more than sex and she'd succumbed, desperate to know if his feelings in any way matched hers.

'Yes, I can see that. Very entertaining.' He tapped the letter against his palm, his face an expressionless mask. His damp T-shirt clung to his ripped chest. If she hadn't needed every spare lick of saliva to lubricate her tight throat, she'd have drooled down her front.

'Ash, it wasn't like that. I never named you or wrote anything identifiable. And I didn't know about your…past—I would never hurt you like that. Only you know I was writing about us, well...just the incredible sex. I finally saw what all the fuss was about.'

Her excuses sounded all wrong. Her writing was exposition, scientific theory and a dash of poetic licence.

'I'm sure you didn't mean to be discovered. But lies grow. They twist and mutate and sprout claws. I could identify myself.' He thrust the envelope at her. 'I have a professional reputation. We fucked. That's it.'

Essie winced as if he'd slapped her.

'I don't want my sexual prowess to become a topic of public speculation. I'll be a laughing stock. I won't tolerate that again.'

'Ash. I understand you're angry with me.' She was furious with herself.

He pointed at the envelope trembling in her hand. 'Consider yourself severed. You can kiss your precious blog goodbye. Perhaps you'll be forced to sell out, practise what you preach, pedal your psychobabble for actual paying customers. You're about to find out the hard way, you can't hide behind theory for ever.'

'You...you're suing me? But—'

He stalked closer, pinning her with his steely glare.

Breathing became harder. His cold eyes flicked south to her mouth and then back again, the ice thawing. Or perhaps it was just her imagination. Just wishful thinking.

She pressed her back to the door, her palms flat to stop herself reaching for him. If he recoiled from her touch, backed away, she wouldn't survive.

This time her voice emerged a whisper. 'I'm sorry. Please let me explain.'

He was so close now his warm breath tickled her lips.

'My father was never there. Growing up, I would try to remember things I wanted to tell him, little things. I started writing them down until the next time he came home. And then later when I knew the truth, I used my blog to process my feelings. Writing about you was a lapse, a mistake—one I won't make again.'

If she took a deep breath, her nipples would brush his chest. But she couldn't even draw in enough air to stop her head spinning.

He'd listened patiently but now he snarled. 'Well, some of us don't have that luxury—we have to deal, internalise, without publicly splurging every one of our feelings. Do you think you're the only person with a shitty father figure?'

'Of course not. I—'

'Oh, spare me your pity.' The pain in his eyes stole the last of her oxygen.

If she hadn't been leaning against the door, her legs would have given way. How could someone do that to their own son? She'd thought Frank was bad enough. No wonder Ash had fled from his life in search of a fresh start. And all she'd done was confirm his beliefs that he was right not to trust anyone.

'I understand that. But I was blindsided by our chemistry. I'd never experienced anything like it. For the first time in my life, I had some power in a relationship. It was heady, wonderful, but overwhelming. For the first time, I didn't feel worthless, and then when people liked what I wrote… I got professional validation, too. I messed up with the blog. I should have told you. I was trying to tell you the night of Harley's wedding.'

He placed one hand on the door above her shoulder and leaned close. At first she was certain he planned to kiss her, the heat in his eyes, the small catch of his breath, the way the tip of his tongue touched his top lip for a split second.

But then he must have changed his mind. He made eye contact and Essie shivered.

'I was right not to trust you.'

He wasn't listening. He'd shut down already. She'd done the damage and missed the opportunity to make it right.

He backed off as suddenly as if they'd been interrupted in an illicit, forbidden kiss. Essie's bones rattled from the icy chills of his frosty brush-off. That he could deliver such a blow without a flicker of emotion told her he'd be a formidable opponent in the courtroom. Something she hoped she'd never have to witness or experience, despite the legal document clutched in her hand.

'Ash, I humiliated you in a moment of stupid impulsiveness and I regret it.'

It was the now or never moment. Mustering every

shred of her courage, she pressed herself back against the opened door to gain another sliver of space from his derision. 'But I kept the secret from you because I… I started to realise… I love you, and I didn't want anything to ruin that.'

Silence.

His cold stare remained unchanged.

Essie hovered for long, torturous, doubt-filled seconds. When he didn't move, didn't speak, she stumbled away, blindly barging through the exit and out into the night.

Much later, alone in a deserted Tube carriage, she looked down at the envelope still crumpled in her hand.

A bubble of hysterical laughter burst through her numbness.

How would she ever afford legal representation to fight him?

And why would she bother?

She loved him and she'd hurt him. It was time to face the consequences.

CHAPTER TWELVE

ESSIE'S TWENTY-FIFTH BIRTHDAY arrived with a predictability that left her gunning for a fight. At first, the card on the mat, addressed with an airmail sticker and recognisable handwriting, sent familiar chills down her bare arms and legs. But reading the dismissive, one-line greeting from her father fired her determination—today was the first day of the rest of her life.

A new Essie rose from the ashes. One who'd learned valuable lessons from the way she'd treated Ash. Yes, she'd hurt him and lost him—he'd already retreated behind the walls he'd constructed long ago, the defences she'd helped to refortify.

But Ash, and to some degree Ben, had taught her something. In loving Ash, she fully understood herself worthy of love in return. She wanted his love, even though she could survive without it. She had all the theory, and now the confidence in her ability to practise and live an authentic life. Not sit and wait for the scraps others tossed her way.

She took the annual cheque—her father's way

of appeasing his own demons for his life choices and one she'd resolutely rejected since her fifteenth birthday—and tore it in two. With the birthday ritual complete, she dropped both halves and the card into the bin, donned her sunglasses and left for the Tube station, her step lighter.

Half an hour later she waltzed into The Yard to find Ben and Ash drinking coffee together at the bar.

Her feet stalled for a brief second as Ash's eyes landed on her. She'd wronged him, hurt him in the worst way. He might not be able to love her in return, but she was done apologising for loving him.

'Good. You're both here. I need to speak to you.' Essie stood before them, clutching the straps of her backpack.

Two sets of wide, wary eyes followed her—one so like her own, her insides trembled—and what she'd come to say clogged in her throat. The other so blue, she imagined she could see inside Ash, to his deepest darkest fears. And maybe she could. Maybe she'd always been able to. But she couldn't see what she wanted to see.

She'd messed up, but she'd survive.

All humans shared the same basic longings— safety, love, acceptance. She deserved those things and so did Ash. But it was too late for him to find them with her. She'd ruined what tiny chance they'd had.

Essie turned her burning eyes away from Ash and focussed on her brother, her chin lifted. Slipping the backpack from her shoulder, she retrieved the letter she'd composed at six a.m. this morning after writing her latest blog post on the importance of self-love, self-acceptance and self-forgiveness, and handed it over to a puzzled Ben.

She cleared her throat. 'I'm handing in my notice.'

Ben took the envelope with a wince. Essie ploughed on—she needed to get all she wanted to say out, before emotion paralysed her vocal cords. Because she was done being needy. Done waiting for other people's approval. Done with scientific theory.

She would survive the practice and emerge improved, wiser, unstoppable.

Her bruised heart would heal eventually.

Essie cleared her throat. 'As we only had a verbal contract, I won't be working that notice, but you'll be fine without me.' Ash could wax lyrical on the ins and out of employment law as long as he liked. They wouldn't force her to stay. And Ben didn't really need her. His clubs were well-oiled machines. She suspected he'd offered her the job as some sort of olive branch, and she loved that he'd tried to make amends for their father.

'I know you only employed me because you somehow felt responsible for what Frank did. But there's no need. If you're short-staffed, I recommend promoting Josh to my position as manager, until you find someone permanent. He's way more qualified than I am anyway.'

She flicked her stare to Ash, her lungs on fire and pressure building behind her eyes so she was tempted to don the sunglasses. How long would it take him to replace her in his bed? Would he even bother? Perhaps he'd go back to his lonely one-night rule. She loved him enough to want more than that for him, even when, because of her foolish actions, it couldn't be her.

'Essie,' said Ben.

She held up her hand. She needed to say everything she'd come here to say. 'Going forward, I want us to have a real relationship. We have a chance to build a lasting bond, away from the usual influences of childhood sibling rivalry. I don't resent you for getting a phone before me or being allowed to stay up later and you never had to play dress-ups with me or read me dumb stories.'

He grinned, giving her the courage to continue.

'If you want to be a part of my life like I want to be a part of yours—' her breath caught, but she sucked in air through her nostrils, fighting the burn behind her eyes '—you'll meet me halfway.'

She shrugged, her whole body buzzing with renewed energy.

Ben nodded, his eyes sliding to Ash. 'Of course I want that.' He reached for her hand and squeezed her fingers. 'But what will you do without a job?'

She squeezed back. 'I have plenty to do. I want to put more time into promoting my blog to wider audiences, and I'm thinking of writing a book. It turns out I have something valuable to say about relationships. I'm a bit of an expert in the field, actually.' She winked at him. 'You know you're damned lucky I'm your sister, don't you?'

She swung her backpack onto her shoulder and offered a beaming Ben a small smile. She loved him. Always would. But her happiness was her responsibility—no more waiting around for someone else's acceptance or approval. No more settling.

And Ash…

Her eyes stung and she blinked away the burn.

Well, that was over. She'd hurt him, and he couldn't love her back. But she'd meant what she'd said to him last night.

Her vocal cords constricted, almost choking off her newfound bravery.

As if sensing the private moment, Ben muttered something about making an important phone call and disappeared.

Part of Essie wanted to follow him. But it was time to own her mistakes and her feelings.

His expression was closed off, wary. The last shred of hope inside her withered and died. 'I know I messed up. I'm truly sorry I hurt you and I hope one day you can forgive me.'

Her voice broke, but she smiled through the scalding heat behind her eyes. 'But more importantly, and I'm saying this because I love you and I want you to be happy, I hope one day you'll want more with someone. You deserve more.'

He swallowed, his jaw bunched. Her hand itched to touch him, to feel the silk of his hair or the scrape of his scruff. She dug her nails into her palm and looked down, her own vision swimming. 'I allowed what my father did to hold me back but I'm done with that. Don't let yours hold you back, Ash.'

With a final, slightly wobbly smile, she turned her back on the man she loved and made her way out into the sun of a new day.

'What did she say?' Ben joined Ash at the window, where he'd moved to stare after a retreating Essie.

He shrugged, his lungs too big for his chest as he grinned at his friend. 'She's magnificent, isn't she?'

Every nerve, every muscle, every impulse in him fired, urging him to chase after her. He'd missed her beautiful, ready smile, her effervescent personality and her dirty laughter over one of her own jokes. But he'd put paid to her trust with his bastard move last night. He had no intention of suing her. He'd been angry. He'd lashed out.

Asshole.

Now he had something his friend needed to hear. 'I love her.'

Ben swivelled to face him. 'Of course you do. Dickhead.' He thumped Ash's shoulder, making his point.

Ash sighed, a wistful smile tugging his mouth. He'd been blind long enough. 'I allowed my hang-ups to cloud my judgment. You don't need me to tell you she's the best thing that ever happened to me. To both of us.'

Ben nodded, still looking a little dazed by his sister's declarations. 'What are you going to do?'

Ash retraced his steps, his restless limbs unable

to stand still for a minute longer, and tossed a note on the bar to cover the coffees. 'I'm going to do what I should have done at the wedding. I'm going to fight for her.'

Ben nodded. 'You'd better not hurt my sister again.'

Ash shook his head, his mouth pulled to a grim line. 'I will. I'm a fuck-up. But she'll put me right.' He grinned. 'Just like she did you.'

Ben nodded, another incredulous smile tugging his mouth.

Ash released a long sigh. 'Now, I'm going to say the same thing to you. You'd better always be there for my woman when she needs you. You're the man of her family—time to step up.'

Eyes rounded, Ben nodded. Then he grinned. 'Looks like we both have some ground to make up.' He reached out his hand and Ash shook on it.

'Good luck,' they said in unison.

CHAPTER THIRTEEN

ASH STEPPED INSIDE the relative gloom of the stuffy university hall, his throat so dry he'd never be able to say what he'd come here to say. He rolled his shoulders, scanning the mingling crowds for her golden hair. He'd come to present the most important closing argument of his life. No time for nerves or hesitancy.

This was what he did.

He won.

Every negotiation.

How he'd managed to fool himself he could live without her astounded him. For an intelligent man, used to getting his own way, how had he blocked his own path for so long?

He gripped the bag containing the rain boots tighter, the smell of new rubber reminding him of what was at stake. Had he waited too long? Woken up to himself too late?

He spotted her and his heart jerked out of rhythm.

A stunningly dressed Essie, as he'd never seen her before, stood not ten feet away. She wore a fitted green dress that outlined every one of her perfect curves, matching green skyscraper heels and a light smattering of make-up, which accentuated her rosy complexion and bright eyes. Her hair was loose, styled in soft waves that made his clenched fingers itch, and a formal graduation gown completed the look.

Damn, he wanted to mess her up. To peel from her the smart, professional outfit and tangle her hair while he kissed her senseless until she believed what he had to say. Believed it down to her bones. Because he meant it and he'd waited too long to tell her.

Ben caught his eye as he strode towards the siblings, his steps determined.

Essie turned at the last moment, the laughter at whatever Ben had said sliding from her exquisite face. A bubble of stilted anticipation enclosed them as the conversations around them muted into background noise.

'What's with the wellies?' said Essie, eyeing his bag. He deserved the cold shoulder after giving her that notice of legal action. But that wasn't Essie's style.

Ash pressed his lips together. Now wasn't the time for laughter. But of course she would say the thing he least expected. So full of surprises, so refreshing, so unique. His Essie.

Don't get ahead of yourself, asshole.

'If you mean these—' he held up the rain boots '—a graduation present. Congratulations, Dr Newbold.'

She eyed the spade sticking up next to the boots in silence, keeping his worthless ass on tenterhooks.

He should have come here today with champagne and flowers and a fucking brass band. But he'd got what he'd told her from day one he'd wanted—her out of his life, him out of hers.

What an idiot.

Her magnificent bravery and heartfelt declaration yesterday had been the final slap he'd needed to wake up. Ash himself acted as the only barrier standing in the way of contentment. He'd done the hard part, breaking free of his old life, free of the poisonous relationship with his father. The rest, loving Essie, was easy.

Now all he had to do was grab hold of this wonderful woman, pray she'd walk alongside him and never let go. If she'd have him.

That remained to be seen. But if forced to do this in front of this room full of gowned academics like some sappy idiot from a romantic comedy movie, he would.

Ben cleared his throat. 'I'll uh…go find your mum and get us some champagne.' With a look that said 'don't fuck this up', his friend offered them privacy.

Ash gestured Essie to accompany him to the less crowded foyer. She obliged and he followed the sway of her gorgeous ass that was unfortunately obliterated by her billowing gown.

In a deserted corner, she turned her big blue eyes on him.

'I bluffed about the lawsuit. I was angry. I'm sorry.'

The longer she looked at him, wary and hesitant, the more his intestines knotted. 'I fucked up, too.' He held her stare, willing her to hear the earnest regret in his voice. He stepped closer, taking an indulgent second to register how fantastic she smelled, how he wanted to wake up tomorrow with her scent in his hair, on his sheets, and every morning after that.

She pointed at the shovel. 'You bought me a shovel? Are we burying a corpse?'

This time he couldn't hold in the laughter. He was messing this up. And she applied her usual quirky sense of humour to help him out.

His fingers twitched, desperate to reach out and cup her waist. To drag her closer. He eyed her full mouth, which was painted red. 'Someone once told me to consider my carbon footprint and I promised I'd plant a forest. Fun fact—did you know a flight from New York to London produces eighty-four tons of the greenhouse gas, carbon dioxide?'

She stared at him for so long, her features an unreadable mask, a countdown began in his head as if he waited for the gavel to fall.

'I know you're celebrating with your family, so I'll cut straight to my closing statement.' Not a flicker of her beautiful smile. Damn—his best lawyer humour... 'You were right. I allowed the poor way I'd dealt with my past to stand in the way of us, and I'd like you to consider taking me back.' Her lips parted a fraction.

'Now, before you send the jury out to consider, let me present my evidence.'

'Aren't you supposed to do that *before* you close?' She tilted her head.

Heat raced up his spine. She was magnificent. Keeping him on his toes, challenging him, calling him out on his bullshit. How had he been so blind for so long? How was he managing to keep his hands off her?

'Good point. The thing is, I've done a little research myself. I'm sure you know all about Sternberg's triangular theory of love?'

She shrugged, her colour heightening a fraction. 'I do.'

So far, so good.

'We definitely have the passion, or we did have, until I behaved like a douche and overreacted. We also have the intimacy down pat.' His hand cupped her waist, fingers flexing to draw her another millimetre into his space. 'Two out of three isn't bad, as the song goes.'

She didn't step away, her eyes lifting to stare him down. 'The thing is, Ash, I'm no longer willing to settle for two thirds of what I deserve.'

His groin stirred at her proximity. At her demanding her absolute dues. Fuck, if this went his way, he'd hold on tight and never let her go.

'You don't have to, because I came here today to tell you I'm completing the triangle.'

She raised one eyebrow. 'Commitment?'

He nodded, an unfettered smile taking over his face. 'I'm all in. I want you. Every second I've spent with you has been the best fun. And, unless I fuck it up, which I plan not to, I know there's more fun in our future.' He dropped the bag and reached for both her hands, holding them between their bodies. 'I love you, Essie. Is it too late?'

She stared.

The gavel clattered to the block, the harsh clap of the hardwood echoing inside his skull.

He'd blown it.

But then she jumped into his arms, her hands tugging his neck and her body pressed to his as she kissed the shock from him with the enthusiasm he'd grown to expect. This woman was incapable of half measures, one of the things he loved most about her. Her honesty. Her emotional availability. Her complete lack of artifice. What you saw was what you got. And he wanted it all.

With his arms banded around her waist, he hauled her feet from the floor, groaning into her mouth as he swung her in a circle and then lowered her and broke free.

'I messed up your lipstick.' He wiped a smudge from her chin.

'I don't care.' She laughed, smearing the rest of the colour from his lips with her fingertips. 'That was quite a statement, counsellor.'

He shrugged. 'Some things are worth fighting for. You are worth fighting for.'

He swooped on her again, his tongue delving into her mouth and his hand slipping beneath her ceremonial gown to cup her waist and press her close. She pulled back with a small sigh, her eyes slumberous with lust.

'Wanna go to a stuffy degree ceremony lunch? I guarantee it *won't* be fun.'

He nodded, warmth spreading from his chest to the tips of his fingers, which held her a little tighter.

'As long as I can peel you out of this later, Dr

Newbold.' He fingered the edge of the ceremonial gown. 'Or perhaps you could keep it on. That might be fun. Ever made love in a cap and gown?'

She laughed, shaking her head. 'Call me doctor again.' She writhed in his arms, waking up the parts of him inappropriate for the setting.

'Doctor.' He nuzzled her neck.

'Counsellor, I think you've just won your case.'

'No, I've won something better—you.'

They sealed the contract with a kiss.

Essie pushed the spade into the dirt and struck a rock. The field bordering a track of mature woodland on the Oxfordshire estate owned by Alex was marked out with rows of bagged tree saplings ready for planting. 'How many more do we have to plant before that delicious lunch you promised me?'

Ash laughed. 'Well, if you want to accompany me to New York for Christmas, you have to plant this whole forest.'

Essie pouted and attacked the rock in earnest. The quicker they planted the damn trees, the quicker she could get Ash naked. She glanced over at him dressed down in jeans and a T-shirt. As mouth-watering as ever. Who cared about greenhouse gases when Ash was around?

And he was hers. Her smile made her cheeks ache. She had two new men in her life. A fully committed brother and a proper boyfriend who was in love with her…

'Fun fact,' he said. 'Couples who play together, stay together.'

She picked up the inconveniently placed rock and tossed it to land at his feet.

He shot her a look that promised thrilling retribution.

She laughed, dropped her spade and went to him, wrapping her arms around his neck and tugging him down for a kiss. 'You totally made that up.'

He laughed. 'I did. But you're not the only one with a clever fact up her sleeve, Doctor.'

She sobered. 'Well, even if it is true, you'll be practising law again soon—not much time for playing or fun.'

He scooped her from the ground and she wrapped her legs around his waist, grateful she'd worn the cut-off shorts he could never resist as she felt the prod of his erection between her legs.

'There's always time for fun.' His lips brushed hers. 'But to be certain, ever experienced living with the man you love?'

She gasped and shook her head, which spun with his question as if he'd twirled her around in a circle.

'Good. Because I think we should move in together.'

Essie wriggled free, sliding down the length of his hard body. 'Seriously?'

He nodded, wicked light glinting in his eyes.

'But you live on the wrong side of London.'

He shook his head, holding her hips still and rubbing himself against her belly. 'I'm moving. New legal practice. New apartment. New girlfriend…'

She couldn't stop the grin that made her cheeks ache. He turned serious. 'Will you live with me—

somewhere we choose together?' He cupped her cheek, his fingers tangling in her hair.

She nodded, flying into his arms once more. After a kiss that turned heated enough she scoped the nearby woods for a potential spot to take things further, he placed her feet on the ground and wiped what was probably a smudge of dirt from her cheek.

Taking her hand, he tugged her towards the car. 'Come on. Turns out I'm starving.' He winked, promising more than a delicious three-course lunch.

'But what about the trees? I want to see New York at Christmastime. I've never experienced ice skating in Central Park or the Rockefeller Christmas tree.'

'I'll hire someone to plant the damn things for us.' He lengthened his stride, his steps more urgent now he'd made up his mind.

'Are we driving back to London?' She didn't think she'd be able to wait that long with the persistent buzz between her legs.

Car sex...?

'No—I've booked a room at the hotel. We're going to celebrate moving in together. I'm going to lick champagne from every part of your body.'

'I'm not sure I'll survive that experience.'

'You will. It will be fun.'

She nodded. It totally would.

* * * * *

NO STRINGS

CARA LOCKWOOD

MILLS & BOON

For PJ, my love and inspiration.

PROLOGUE

Saturday

HE STOOD BEFORE HER, the curve of his bare chest an invitation as he stood in the moonlit hotel suite overlooking the glass high-rises of downtown Chicago. She ran her finger down the firm slope of his well-defined muscles, amazed at their taut perfection. He gently slid the bra strap down off her shoulder, the wisp of his touch setting her skin on fire, and all she could think was: *I don't even know his name. I'm going to let this man do whatever he wants to me, and I have no idea what to even call him.*

She opened her mouth to ask, once more, but he covered her lips with his, and the question of the night evaporated in the heat of animal want. A moan escaped her, as he deftly undid the front clasp, setting her heavy breasts free. He dipped down, expertly flicking a tongue across one nipple, bringing it to attention. He then cupped the other in his strong hand, kneading it with intent.

His mouth is on me and I don't know what he does

for a living. I don't even know if he has a dog. Or hell, a wife. I met this man one hour ago. A simple text exchange from an app on my phone. And now I'm here, half naked...

"I—I've never done this before...a stranger, I mean," she murmured. He nibbled her nipple, the flick of teeth on the soft skin making her shiver. "This is... I mean, this is crazy. I don't usually do this."

He straightened, meeting her gaze with his unnervingly perfect hazel eyes. A lazy grin spread across his handsome face, warming up his squared-off jaw. "Even good girls should be bad, once in a while."

She was a good girl. She never did this kind of thing. She'd only ever had sex with two other men her whole life, and both of them after a minimum of three months of dating first, but something about him made her feel reckless. Wild.

"I just can't believe..." She wasn't even sure how she'd gotten here this fast, how she'd met a man and within an hour, was letting him see her everything. To put his hands and his mouth on her body. "I just... I don't know anything about you."

"You having second thoughts?" He paused, hazel eyes fixing her in a locked stare.

"No," she said. No, she wanted him. She did.

He pressed his hard, muscled chest against hers, dipping his face so close their noses nearly touched. "And all you need to know about me is this," he promised. She felt heat rise in her very core. He wanted her as much as she wanted him. And, God, did she want him. She'd wanted this the moment they'd met in the hotel bar an hour ago. She'd decided then in that split second to let him do what he wanted. She was willing.

"You can tell me whatever you want me to do to you. I want you to tell me." She sucked in a breath and her knees trembled slightly. She didn't have to be a good girl. Not with him. She could be bad. Very, very bad. She could do whatever she wanted. She could let him do…whatever he wanted.

She could feel her want, soaking the thin fabric of the lace, the last thin barrier between her and this rash act she was about to commit, this terrible, inconceivably bad thing. Part of her wanted to say no, but her body was in control now. Her body wanted this, wanted it badly, and she became simply an animal in heat, overcome by desire and thousands of years of instinct. For this night, she would give in to her basest desires. There was no turning back now. She was going to give her everything to a man she didn't know, to a perfect stranger. She was going to let him do things to her no man had before.

And she was going to like it.

CHAPTER ONE

The day before

EMMA ALLAIRE STARED at the newly downloaded *Nost* app on her phone and sighed. "You're sure I need to do this?" she asked her best friend, Sarah, once more as they sat together at their favorite brunch place in Lincoln Square, the mild, not quite fall air of mid-September gliding across the open patio as people meandered past them on the busy city sidewalk. *Nost,* short for No Strings, was the latest hookup app that all of her friends were talking about, a place to meet men for casual sex. The app's ominous black logo appeared on her phone and she double-tapped it.

"Em, just give it a shot, okay?" said her gorgeous redheaded friend with the perfect alabaster skin, the curves that didn't quit and the string of musician boyfriends who paraded in and out of her life. "You never know until you try."

"But *this* is what's wrong with us," Emma cried, holding up her phone, to show *Nost*'s loading page. It read, "No names. No strings. 100% fun." She pushed up her black-framed, librarian glasses and scowled at her phone. "How is *anyone* going to find true love *like this*?" She showed Sarah a picture of a shirtless man making a kissing face at a mirror. The app implored her to "swipe right for a good time" or "nope, swipe left."

"Honey, you know this isn't about true love. It's about getting off." Sarah's eyes gleamed.

Emma shrieked a laugh. "What are you *even talking* about?"

Sarah waved her fork in the air. "Wait, you do get off, don't you?"

Emma felt her face flush red. "Um… Yes. I do."

Just, you know, with only two guys. Ever. In her whole dating history, but Sarah didn't need to know that right now.

Sarah pushed up her sunglasses on her nose and leaned back, lifting her face to the fall sunshine coating the small patio of the restaurant. "Good. I thought for a second you were one of those poor souls who'd never had an orgasm."

Emma glanced around the restaurant, suddenly worried someone might overhear. Sarah just shook her head at her friend. "Orgasm!" she cried, louder, and a father of two glanced over at their table and frowned.

"Hush!" Emma commanded. Not that it would do any good. Sarah spoke her mind. Their server appeared then, placing delicious-looking plates of food in front of them. Sarah dug in, while Emma focused on the app.

"*This* is what is wrong with us. Anonymous one-nighters? I mean, you are seriously going to have sex with a man and all you know is his handle is…" Emma peered at her screen. "Hot4U?"

Sarah laughed a little. "Who cares about love when he's got abs like that?" she said, pointing to the man's six-pack.

"And enough tattoo ink on him to write *War and Peace*," Emma pointed out. "He's got *two* arm sleeve tattoos."

"You just have to fuck him, not marry him," Sarah said, rolling her eyes, as she forked a mouthful of spinach quiche into her mouth. "And bad boys are *very* good in bed. Live a little, Em. *Seriously.* You know you settle *too* fast for just about any guy who buys you a drink. Then you end up in a two-year relationship with them while they bore your friends to death."

Emma knew she was talking about Devin, her last boyfriend with the less-than-sparkling personality. He'd been the only other guy she'd seriously dated other than her high school boyfriend.

"Not *all* of my exes are that way."

"You need to *date around*. Hell, *sleep around*. Not just commit to the very first guy who shows up. You know I'm right." Sarah studied her friend.

Emma twirled a loose tendril of hair around her finger and sighed. She glanced down at her flowy, flowered peasant top and her modest jeans and tried to imagine herself meeting up with Mr. Tattoo and taking all her clothes off. She simply couldn't.

"I need romance," Emma declared. "There's no romance in this. This is what *men* want. It's not what women want."

Sarah snorted. "How do you know if you've never tried it?"

"I know that this is just one more way men are manipulating us into thinking that what *they* want is somehow *us* being liberated," said Emma, her women's studies major coming out in blazing good form. "This is just *Girls Gone Wild* in sex app form."

"Em, can you spare me the feminist rant until *after* I've finished my mimosa?" Sarah held up her champagne glass.

"No…this is what I *do* for a living." She wrote freelance stories about women's issues for a women's online magazine, and she had a small but loyal following. "And because clearly you're being manipulated by the patriarchy," Emma declared and grinned. She knew what she sounded like: a militant femi-Nazi. But honestly, she felt like she was the only one who could see it—the fact that the wage gap was still a thing. And that the US was the only industrialized nation not to offer paid maternity leave, and…now there was *Nost*. Like Tinder, but in its most extreme form. The app men didn't have to even *try* to get laid. She was all for the sexual revolution, but not when it meant that the advantage went entirely to men.

"This is just…this is just one more way men have tricked us into getting what *they* want. Sex and no commitment."

"Fine, so delete it," Sarah said, sighing, showing

her exasperation, as she finished off the last of her meal. Emma, who had already devoured her blueberry waffle, wondered, not for the first time, how she and Sarah, so total opposites, ever got along. Their random pairing as college roommates had set off an unlikely friendship: Sarah, the impulsive redhead, who never flinched at a dare, and Emma, the bookworm, who one day hoped to run for elected office. If she were honest with herself, finding Mr. Right ranked somewhere between growing her blog readership base and putting money in her IRA. Dating just didn't seem important at the moment—she was just twenty-eight. She had plenty of time. At least, that's what she told herself. After her last disastrous relationship, where her boyfriend, Devin, chose a new job in Seattle over her, she just wasn't too into the idea of putting herself out there again.

"Actually," Sarah said, sipping her mimosa. "You don't even *need* to delete it. Your profile will become invisible to the guys on your screen in forty-eight hours."

"What? Why?"

Sarah put down her fork, and looked exasperated. She flipped her dark red hair off one shoulder.

"Because the whole point of it is *not* to have a relationship longer than that. Every two days, you get a whole new slew of potential guys and the old ones can't find you. Every time, it's new, and the best part is, there's no awkward follow-up. You have sex and then—whoosh!—you disappear. It's ghosting, but the app does it for you. Everybody knows the score. Nobody gets hurt."

Emma put her head in her hands and groaned. "Are you kidding me?" She peeked at Sarah from her fingers. "The profiles become invisible?"

"That's the point," Sarah said. "Wham, bam, thank you, ma'am. Emphasis on the bamming part."

"Sarah! What about rapists? Serial killers?" Emma couldn't believe her friend was even seriously suggesting anonymous sex. Wasn't that beyond sketchy?

"The good ones already have a background check. See that little *v* next to 'Hot4U'? He uploaded a background check. No felonies. *Nost* verified him. So, you don't have to."

Emma blew bangs out of her eyes. "What about… STDs?"

"See that little *c* next to him?"

Emma nodded.

"That means he's been tested in the last month. He's clear."

"I guess they've thought of everything. You know, except real human intimacy."

"Ha. Ha. Very funny. Don't knock it till you try it." Sarah pointed at Emma with her fork.

"Seriously, though, how can you do…this?"

"I'm busy. I work sixty hours a week because those commercial buildings aren't going to sell themselves. And, yeah, it's kind of hot." She took a swig of her mimosa, finishing it, and glanced back at

Emma. "And, a one-night stand? I mean, who hasn't had one of those?"

Emma froze. *She* hadn't, actually. She could never imagine herself getting naked in front of a stranger. She'd only ever had sex with her high school boyfriend, whom she'd dated three years before they'd even had sex, and then her post-college boyfriend, Devin, whom she dated three months before they'd done the deed. How could someone just… jump into bed with a man they'd only just met? By the time she'd had sex with someone she was already emotionally invested, even in love. She couldn't imagine it any other way.

Sarah paused, glancing at her friend and read her expression. "Wait. You've…never?"

Emma felt on the spot, suddenly. Did that make her a prude? From the expression on Sarah's face, the answer was yes. "No. Never."

"Not even…college? I mean, everyone has one then." Sarah leaned forward, her shock evident.

"Not me." Emma took another sip of her mimosa.

"Well, then. You *have* to do this. You can't turn thirty without having *done this*." Sarah leaned forward. "Look, why don't we make a deal? You try it for forty-eight hours. Go on *one* drink date at least. You don't have to sleep with anybody. But can't you write about it? If it turns out to be so bad, rant about it online for your magazine."

"I don't *rant*," Emma corrected. "I discuss issues."

"Honey, you *rant*, but that's okay. It's one reason why I love you. You've got opinions and you're not afraid to share them." Sarah leaned forward and patted Emma's hand. "What have you got to lose? You either get laid *or* you get the subject of your next article. Win-win."

Sarah had a point there. And it had been a long time since Devin moved to Seattle.

"So what do I do?" Emma asked, holding up her phone.

"First, you get a better picture than that," Sarah declared, looking at Emma's profile and wrinkling her nose in disapproval. She swiped Emma's phone out of her hand and took her Elvis Costello glasses off in one quick swipe.

"I need those to see!"

"Not now you don't." Sarah clicked a few impromptu shots of Emma at the table.

"No! Don't... I..." Emma laughed a little, as Sarah clicked a few more before stopping.

Sarah swiped through them. "Yes, *that* one." She showed her friend the shot: Emma looking away, mid-laugh, blonde hair loose and cascading down one bare shoulder, her peasant top slipping ever so slightly downward revealing the curve of cleavage. "My shirt is practically falling off!" Emma protested.

"That's the point. News flash: Guys like boobs." Sarah rolled her eyes as she tapped on Emma's phone.

Emma sighed. "Sarah...this is just playing into all the stereotypes..."

"Don't go lecturing me on how you hate being a sex object. *This* is the picture you use. You look like you're fun...and you don't have a stick up your butt."

"I don't!" Emma cried, reaching for the phone. Sarah batted her hand away, typing up her profile. "And what are you doing?"

"Making sure you go through with this." Sarah tapped her screen a few more times, concentrating hard.

"You think all problems can be solved by getting laid."

"Can't they, though?" Sarah grinned, her green eyes sparkling with mischief.

Emma giggled and tried to take back her phone. Sarah ducked deftly. Emma gave up and reached for her coffee mug. "Sarah, come on."

"Fine." Sarah glanced at her friend, the dare unmistakable in her gaze. "It's not live until you hit that button."

Emma glanced at the screen and nearly choked, almost sloshing her coffee. "You called me 'Kitten'?" Inwardly, Emma groaned.

"The sex part is implied," Sarah said, signaling the waiter to refill her mimosa. Emma had a feeling she'd need another one, too. "Just hit the 'get laid' button, and you're good to go." Sarah grinned.

"A 'get laid' button? Seriously?" Emma hesitated. Was she really going to do it? This was so unlike her and yet... *It's just research. How bad could it be?*

"You don't like it, you can delete the app whenever you want," Sarah said. She studied her friend. "You're not scared are you?"

"Are you seriously peer pressuring me into this?"

"Whatever works." Sarah shrugged.

"Fine." Emma tapped the button, sending her profile live out into the universe, telling random strangers in the Chicagoland area she was willing and available. She wasn't sure quite how she felt about that.

"That's my girl," Sarah said, patting her hand. "See? That wasn't so bad."

"Now what?" Emma glanced at her phone, as if it would suddenly hold all the answers.

"Now you wait." Sarah took a big swig of her mimosa. "Don't worry. You probably won't even hear from anybody for hours—until tonight."

Emma glanced at her empty plate when her phone dinged. The *Nost* app lit up her screen with an incoming message.

"Did I say hours?" Sarah put down her champagne glass. "With your hot self, looks like *you* just had to wait a minute."

Emma's phone dinged once more. And then, a third time.

What have I gotten myself into?

Sarah grabbed her phone. She began scrolling through options. "Nope. No. *Oh, God...no.*" Sarah held up the phone and showed Emma a picture of a man trying to shove a foot-long hot dog in his mouth in one go. Emma wrinkled her nose. Who would want to have sex with...that?

"I feel like I've just wandered into an ugly bar, and I'm going to spend the next twenty-four hours being harassed."

"Maybe." Sarah flicked through a few more pic-

tures. "Oh my. Here's the man for you." She showed
Emma another one, this one of a man in a full Spi-
der-Man suit, his face covered.

Emma barked a laugh. "No, it's not. Look at his...
You know." She pointed to the picture's groin where
his very little bit was fully outlined for nearly all
to see.

"Ew!" Sarah cried and dissolved into giggles. "No
baby carrots for you!"

Sarah flicked through a few more. "Oh, this guy
is nice. Mr. X? Sounds...intriguing."

"Mr. X? Uh, no." Emma shook her head.

Sarah kept flipping. Then, she stopped on one.
"Ooh...he's cute." Sarah showed the screen to Emma
and showed a blond, blue-eyed thirty-something in
a suit.

"I guess so." Emma shrugged.

"Guess so? He's one hundred percent Christian
Grey. And even his name is cute... Happy Fun Time!
I am setting this up."

"Sarah!" Emma tried to grab her phone. "Don't!"

"You're on for tomorrow night, at the bar in the
Ritz-Carlton downtown."

Emma blew a strand of hair out of her face. "Why
did you do that?"

"Because I knew you wouldn't."

CHAPTER TWO

EMMA HAD SPENT twenty-four hours trying to figure out a way to cancel this date. But as Sarah had pointed out countless times, it was only a drink. If she didn't like Mr. Happy Fun Time, she could simply walk out of the bar and never talk to him again. Yet, the idea of meeting a man *just for sex*, well, she just didn't know if she'd be able to go through with it, even if she wanted to.

I'm just going to meet him. Have a drink. Then, tell him politely that maybe we could have more dates before we...uh...do it... IF we ever do it and that's a big if.

Emma would need about six dates before she'd even consider taking her clothes off. Maybe twelve. Emma realized with a start that she'd never even had sex with a man she wasn't almost or totally in love with already. When her friends were hooking up in college, she was tied to her high school boyfriend long-distance. Then after college, she began her relationship with Devin. That was before he took a job in Seattle and told her they ought to see other people six months ago.

Emma had thought they'd been headed for marriage, but turns out, she was just headed for…dating apps.

She stood before her closet studying the contents and wondering what on earth she was supposed to wear on this date that was almost, surely going nowhere.

"Hmmm," she muttered, as she pulled out a flowered sundress which screamed summer and wouldn't work for the cool September night she was expecting. Besides, it showed too much leg. *Don't want to give the wrong impression,* she thought. *Oh, wait, I already have, because this is NOST.*

No strings.

She sighed and pulled out a black turtleneck sweater. Maybe she ought to show up wearing this and baggy sweatpants and see whether or not she'd send the shallow Mr. Happy Fun Time running. She grinned to herself, but then decided against it. She put the sweater back in her closet and tried to dig around for something middle of the road. Emma lamented the fact that she was wasting so much mental energy on what she was going to wear on a date that she didn't even want to have in the first place. She ought to be outlining more chapters in that book she planned to write.

She glared at the closet, wishing it was her computer screen.

"I should cancel this date," she told her closet. "I should text him and cancel."

She whipped out her phone and pulled up the *Nost* app. Then Mr. Happy Fun Time's picture came up: blond, sophisticated suit, like a successful and rich businessman. Well, what could it hurt? Just because his picture looked like something she'd find on a corporate About Us page didn't mean that he was all that stuffy. Maybe he had a sense of humor. Maybe he'd be quick-witted. Maybe he'd just buy me drinks, she thought, as she remembered her less than stellar bank account balance that month. The freelance gigs had been a little less than hot and heavy these last few weeks, and she'd had to lean on credit cards more than she'd like.

I don't need men to buy me anything, she reminded herself. Just because her budget was tight didn't mean that she wasn't a fully functional independent woman. One more reason to cancel. She was already buying into the patriarchy—the idea that this guy in the suit should *buy her a drink.*

Of course, Sarah would say that casual sex proved her independence from men. Emma shook her head. Feminism was complicated. She glanced once more at her closet, grabbed a pair of jeans and one of her favorite off-the-shoulder sweaters and paired it with a pair of ankle boots, no heel. Emma stood five-seven, so she already knew she was better off assuming Mr. Happy Fun Time was shorter than her. Emma didn't care, but she knew men did. It had been her experience that men lied about their height. He said he was five-eleven, but that could mean anything.

She pulled on her outfit, dusted on some light

makeup and then checked out her reflection in the mirror. Even she could tell she looked tense, even when she plastered on a fake smile and tossed her blond hair over one shoulder.

This is just research, she told herself. She'd take mental notes and then have a hell of a story to pitch to her editor tomorrow.

She nodded at herself in the mirror, meeting her clear blue-eyed gaze. "One drink," she told herself. "An hour tops."

Emma sat at the upscale bar in the Ritz-Carlton bathed in the fading sunlight of early evening beaming down through the canopy of windows encasing the tastefully decorated lounge. She felt self-conscious as she nursed the Hendrick's and tonic she'd ordered from the bartender and kept checking her phone. Where *was* Mr. Happy Fun Time? He was seven minutes late was what he was. Emma glanced once more around the bar and saw three women chatting happily around a coffee table in the lounge, two men in business suits that were about ten years too old to be Mr. Happy Fun Time *and* both brunettes, and a tourist sitting in the corner in a leather armchair, wearing a St. Louis Cardinals jersey and looking more than a tad underdressed in the swanky bar with the white leather couches and the enclosed-window view of the impressive buildings in Chicago's Loop. She gazed out the window, across the way at the copper-colored windows of the Time Life office building across the street, and wondered how long she ought to stay before abandoning this futile exercise altogether.

Until I finish this drink, she promised herself, as she rattled the ice cubes around the cocktail glass and took another deep sip of the clear liquid. *No date and no story.* She couldn't help but feel a pang of disappointment. Not because she wanted casual sex, but because she had started to like the idea of writing a story about her first *Nost* date. Skewering it relentlessly. She'd already thought of about 500 words she'd like to cram in it about women's self-esteem and respecting yourself and a whole lecture she planned to give about the dangers of embracing casual sex. Feeling someone watching her, she glanced up and saw Cardinals Jersey staring. He had a matching baseball hat, too. Bold move wearing rival team paraphernalia in Chicago. She glanced away and focused on her phone. No messages, no *Sorry, I'm running late*, or anything. Figures. Not like one-night stand seekers cared about manners. Emma studied her drink. Three more sips, probably, and she'd leave.

A new man came to sit in the lounge and she glanced up, hopeful it was Mr. Happy Fun Time, but realized instantly he wasn't. He was much, *much* taller than five-eleven, probably at least six-two, and looked like a former wide receiver with broad shoulders, big hands and thick, muscled arms. He seemed to almost change the atmosphere of the lounge somehow, as everyone took notice of the dark-haired stranger who strode confidently to the bar. He slid

into an empty stool at the end of her row and signaled the bartender. That was a man, she thought, his
muscles evident even through the thick fabric of his
shirt. He was a smidgen older than her. Early thirties, maybe? He had a smooth olive complexion but
piercing, hazel eyes, not quite green, almost golden.

Wow, but the man had a body. Trim waist, thick
legs. He had to be a professional athlete, she thought.
Did she know him? Blackhawks? Cubs? Something.
Had to be. A body like that was made to be put to
work. That was a body that could make a million-
dollar contract, no doubt. Model? Maybe he was a
model. Or an action star. Someone from the cast of
Chicago Fire? Seemed like he had to be famous.

He glanced up for a second, and sent her the
smallest quirk of a smile, and that was when she
realized she was staring at him like an idiot. She
grabbed her phone and glanced down, wondering
if he realized she'd been mentally undressing him.
Emma felt a blush creep up the back of her neck. *I
must have sex on the brain,* she thought. *Look! Nost
is already working.*

He was handsome, she admitted to herself as she
tried not to openly stare. He had jet-black hair and
wore a button-down shirt tucked into dark washed
jeans. His arms looked muscled even through the
fabric of his shirt, and his stomach was flat and hard,
not a hint of unfit abs anywhere. He wore a watch on
his wrist that even from a distance looked expensive,
but no wedding ring, Emma noticed. The bartender

served him a top-shelf rye on the rocks. The man took a sip as he pulled out his phone.

This is why we have to use apps all the time, Emma lamented. *We don't see who's right in front of us.*

It reminded Emma of the time her mother asked her why she didn't just go out with her friends to meet someone. *This was why,* she inwardly groaned. All the best prospects kept their noses in their phones. Her own phone dinged with an incoming alert, and she grabbed it from the bar. Maybe it was Mr. Happy Fun Time.

She glanced at her phone and saw a message from *Nost* all right, but it hadn't come from Happy Fun Time. It had come from "Mr. X," the same profile that had popped up earlier yesterday. Emma saw a timer already going on the profile signaling how much time she had to reply. Emma also noticed he had both a *v* and *c* next to his name: verified and clear, she remembered. Good. That was good.

Just wanted to say hi, since you're in my neighborhood.

Neighborhood? Huh?

How did you know that? She typed quickly, glancing around, almost as if she'd find someone staring at her.

The maps feature? He offered.

Emma literally smacked her own forehead. Of course. The "who's closest to me on *Nost* right now" map. Or, as she liked to think about it, the *I have to*

*get laid right now and anybody will do, ANYBODY
in a one square mile area* feature. She glanced at the
map and saw the markers and realized about a dozen
Nost users were in the vicinity, hell, the very building
she was in. *But I'm in a hotel, so duh.* She tried to
figure out where Mr. X might be, but couldn't quite
make it out. There were so many little triangles, they
all overlapped in one big blob.

What does Mr. X stand for? she asked.

X factor. Of course. Besides—Tall Dark and Handsome was already taken.

She had to grin. Confidence was sexy. She took a
look at his picture. Wow. Mr. X only just scratched
the surface. Jet-black hair…amazing hazel eyes…
smooth complexion with just the hint of stubble on
his strong chin. He looked vaguely familiar. Why
did he look so familiar?

A new message popped up from Mr. X.

Want to grab a drink? You're right here. As in…liter-
ally…right here.

She felt the heavy weight of a stranger's gaze on
her. She glanced up and saw Mr. Must Be Famous
raising his glass in her direction. Mr. X…was *him.*
A shock of surprise and delight ran through her.
The gorgeous man next to her was on… *Nost.* Well,
maybe Sarah had been right. Maybe this wasn't such
a crazy idea after all.

He was even better looking than his profile picture, and his profile picture was darn near perfect. Mr. X flashed a bright white smile and Emma felt her stomach tighten. Would she join him for a drink? She was sorely tempted. Maybe she should. What did she have to lose?

Emma grabbed her drink and caught movement from the corner of her eye. She hoped it was Mr. X, but instead, she turned to see the tourist in the Cardinals getup standing right in front of her, blocking her path. He sent her a goofy, bent-toothed smile and she grabbed her phone.

"Hey." The tourist plopped down on the stool next to hers. He had some nerve, especially since he was decked out head to toe in her least favorite team of all time. Her family had been die-hard Cubs fans for as long as she could remember. She was sure if she lived in St. Louis, she'd have a closet full of Cardinals jerseys, but even she wouldn't be rude enough to wear one deep in enemy territory. Plus, he had to be…fiftyish? Her dad's age? Older? He certainly carried a lot of extra weight, too. And were those white sneakers he was wearing? And white socks. She felt a creep of revulsion down the small of her back. Ugh. Just…ugh.

"Uh…oh. Hi." Emma glanced up briefly and then tried to look for Mr. X, over his shoulder. Mr. X frowned, clearly annoyed by the interruption, but he calmly took a sip of his drink. Mentally, Emma sent him a *what's up with this dude?* vibe.

Emma didn't want to be rude, but…she really

didn't want to talk to the tourist. She knew that probably made her one of the snobby city folk her relatives were always complaining about, but sheesh. He was wearing a Cardinals baseball hat deep in Cubs territory. Plus, who wore a baseball cap to the Ritz-Carlton?

"Are you… Kitten?"

Emma froze. Her *Nost* name. "How did you…" She glanced once more at the man, who had a day's worth of stubble on his double chin. He looked like no picture she'd seen on the app. And she'd flipped through plenty.

"I'm Happy Fun Time."

Emma could feel all the blood drain out of her face. *This* guy, this older…much heavier-set guy, with the white tube socks, looked literally nothing like his picture because she realized he'd used a photo of someone else.

He grinned, showing crooked, yellowed teeth. And, she got the whiff of stale cigarette smoke. Ugh. If the Cardinals jersey wasn't enough of a deal breaker, this would be. For sure.

"You look *just* like your picture," he said, beaming, looking pleased.

That's because I'm actually in my picture, she wanted to say but didn't.

"So, I got us a nice hotel room…"

Emma's jaw dropped. "Here?" she squeaked, glancing at his worn sneakers. How could he afford a room at the Ritz-Carlton?

"Oh, God, no," he said, shaking his head. "Can't

afford here. There's a Motel 6, just off the express-way a little ways out of town. If we get in my car now…"

Emma suddenly had visions of duct tape and chlo-roform. She tried to get Mr. X's attention, but now he had his eyes on his phone. Argh. She wondered if he was scouting the room for other *Nost* possibilities.

"Look…you've gotten the wrong idea," she said, trying to be nice but firm. There was no way she was going anywhere with this guy. No way. He needed to leave. She needed to go to Mr. X. *That* was a *Nost* date she wouldn't mind.

But Mr. Happy Fun Time stood, and reached out to grasp her elbow. She tugged her arm away, just out of his reach. No way was he *touching* her.

"What's the problem, baby?" He moved closer to her and the acrid scent of burnt tobacco got stronger.

She actually leaned back away from him, fight-ing the urge to flat-out flee.

"Look, you seem nice, but I don't think there's a connection. I think…" *You are totally disgusting and you put up a bogus picture and there's no way I'm going to spend five minutes with you, much less an evening.*

Happy Fun Time frowned. "You said you wanted to meet." He acted as if that entitled him to see her naked.

"Yes, but…"

"So, what's your problem? You a tease?" His voice had an edge to it now, and suddenly she realized that he was much bigger and heavier than her. If he wanted, he could sling her over his shoulder and carry her out of here. Emma felt a tingle of dread in the pit of her stomach, that little instinct that told her *Careful. Something's off here.*

Emma glanced at the bartender, but he was at the other end getting drinks. The other patrons were busy with their own conversations. All except Mr. X, who studied her. Thank God. He was tuned into the situation once more. Would he do something? She met his gaze. He quirked an eyebrow, and she only thought one word: *help.*

At least someone might notice if this guy dragged her out by her hair.

Emma tried to flash Happy Fun Time a conciliatory smile. "I'm sorry," she said, though she wasn't the least bit sorry. "But, I just don't think there's a spark between us. It's just…uh, not going to work."

His frown deepened, and he stood there, seething, looming over her.

"Bitch." The word came out hard and cold and so low she almost wasn't sure if she heard it.

"I'm sorry?" Emma blinked fast. She wasn't used to open hostility.

"You heard me." The look in his eyes was flat, cold, devoid of all emotion. Now she knew something was really off. *Danger,* her instincts screamed. This man was dangerous. Still, she wasn't going to back down. And, had he called her a *bitch*? For what, for saying no?

Now anger flared in her chest. She slid off her bar stool and faced him.

"You need to go. Now." She might be half his size, but she wasn't about to let this guy push her around. No means no, and right now, she was saying *hell, no*.

He blinked at her, rage building in his cold blue eyes. Was he going to do something? Her heart thudded in her chest. What would she do if he did?

The whole bar seemed to go quiet, even though nobody else moved a finger to do anything. Emma felt suddenly that this man intended to hurt her, and he didn't care who was watching.

"I asked you to go," Emma told the man, voice lower this time, but still firm. *Be calm. Be firm. Don't let him know he's scaring the hell out of you.*

That's when the furious man before her grabbed her arm, hard. "I don't think so." He squeezed and she let out an unintended cry. Panic gripped her as she felt the darkness in him; her instincts were right. This man wanted to hurt her. She tried to wiggle out of his grasp.

"Let the lady go." Mr. X stood behind the man, his voice low but clear.

CHAPTER THREE

THE MAN WHIRLED, off guard. Her savior was about five full inches taller and far more in shape. The two men might weigh the same, but Happy Fun Time's weight came in fat, while Mr. X was pure working muscle. He could wipe the floor with him, and both men knew it. The now angry Happy Fun Time frowned, but backed up a step, releasing Emma's arm.

"We were just talking," he said, defensive.

"Didn't look like a very nice talk to me." Mr. X was all business, eyes serious, shoulders tense. Emma wouldn't want to be on the other end of that angry gaze. She glanced from one man to the other, her heart still thudding hard in her chest, her mind going a million miles a minute.

"You're not worth the trouble," her assailant said, and glared at her, eyes full of menace as he turned and walked quickly out of the lounge and past the lobby. Emma watched him go, feeling a sudden whoosh of relief as she exhaled the tension she'd been holding. That was so close.

"Wow…uh, thank you," she managed to say, grateful now for the backup. Her savior studied her with hazel eyes flecked with gold.

"You okay?" He reached out and touched her elbow, ever so softly. Emma rubbed her arms self-consciously. "I'm sorry I didn't come over sooner… I thought…well, I thought maybe you'd planned the date."

She sighed, still feeling her hands tremble with adrenaline and fear. "I had, but that's the last time I *ever* make a date with someone from *Nost.*"

Her rescuer cocked an eyebrow. "He's on *Nost?* What's his name?"

"Happy Fun Time."

Mr. X frowned. "Not so happy or fun."

"Agreed," she said. "Ugh. Why did I even *try* this? I knew it was a mistake." She sank her head in her hands.

"We're not all bad on *Nost*… Miss *Kitten.*" Mr. X grinned. "Come on, let me make up for that asshole. At least let me buy you a drink."

Emma felt shaken, and a drink was desperately what she needed. A drink, and a bit of time to stare at those golden eyes a bit longer. "Sure," she said, though her body felt wired—nerves, fear, all the *fight or flight* chemicals buzzing through her veins. Her heart still thumped in her ears and she felt shaky, but she gestured to the empty bar stool. Having his big body next to hers felt good right about now.

He slid onto the bar stool next to hers and she felt his presence, broad, next to her. The two buttons undone at his neck revealed smooth, bare skin. She was so thankful for him at that moment, she wanted to throw her arms around his neck and squeeze.

"What can I get you?" he asked her, and she felt the gravelly baritone in her stomach.

She felt the heat in her face intensify as her thoughts instantly went to naughty places. *What can't he get me?*

"Hendrick's and tonic," she managed to answer, suddenly feeling shy. What was wrong with her? She'd never felt this kind of instant attraction, the strong pull of basic, animal magnetism before. Sure, she'd found guys handsome, but this one…she could feel his strength, his pull. Every slight shift he made with his body she felt in hers, keenly aware of even the tiniest of movements. Mr. X signaled the bartender, his tanned and muscled forearm raised. He had solid hands. Strong hands. Big ones. Emma imagined what they'd feel like on her body and felt a current of electricity run down her spine. The entire effect just made her feel more rattled, more unsettled, yet in the best way possible.

This must be just adrenaline, she told herself. A dangerous experience, coupled with a handsome guy. *That's all.* It was just hormones and chemicals in her blood, making her aware of this man's every move.

The bartender brought the drink but she barely noticed. She was glancing at his flat stomach and the curve of his chest muscles beneath his shirt. What would the weight of him feel like on top of her?

"Are you okay?" he asked once more. He reached

out and grabbed her hands. She glanced up at him, shaken from her thoughts. "You're trembling," he said, voice low with concern, his eyes never leaving hers.

He squeezed both hands tightly. "That jerk is gone. He won't bother you again." Mr. X made it sound like a promise. "You're safe now."

Emma glanced down at his strong hands covering hers. Why did she feel anything but safe at that moment?

"Thank you," she said, her heart filling with gratitude. He raised his glass.

"To a better evening," he said and grinned.

"To a better evening," she echoed, and they clinked glasses.

Xavier Pena sipped at his drink and gazed at the beautiful blonde sitting next to him. Gorgeous, blue eyes, streaks of spun gold in her blond hair, her skin still tanned from the summer sun. From her thin frame and taut muscles, he would guess she worked out. Ran maybe? She had the body of a triathlete, someone who took her fitness seriously. Just like he did. All the men at the bar—single or attached— noticed this woman, tall, lithe, strong. He'd noticed her the second he'd walked into the bar, and when he'd pulled up *Nost,* was gleefully happy she'd had a profile.

Part of him was surprised to find her there at all. A woman as drop-dead gorgeous as this one shouldn't need an app to find a date. Or anonymous sex. Any man in this bar would be happy to oblige her, and yet…that was the beauty of *Nost*. Xavier remembered the hard grilling the investors had given him over the concept, especially because they thought women wouldn't want to participate.

"But women have the most to gain from this app," he'd told them. "It gives them a background check *and* allows them to shop for the best mate, without having to weed through suitors at a bar. Women are going to find out that this is exactly what they've been looking for."

It turned out, Xavier had been right. While men slightly edged out women on *Nost,* it wasn't by much.

Xavier sipped at his whiskey and watched the beautiful woman next to him. She'd begun to relax a little. He studied the curve of her bare shoulder, revealed by her off-the-shoulder navy blue sweater. He'd been more than glad to scare off Mr. St. Louis, a man who had no business being in the same room with this woman, much less talking to her. He shouldn't be anywhere near *Nost,* either, a fact he filed away for later. He'd created the app as a fun and *safe* place for women. That was why he'd written in all the background checks. Without the safety net, the app would be a playground for predators, which would be unacceptable. He made a mental note to bring up the user at the next board meeting. They might need to tweak some of their safety checks.

Now he focused on the woman before him. She was more than a pretty face. He suspected there was a lot going on behind those intelligent blue eyes.

He wondered if she felt the little current of *whatever this was* floating between them. The strong physical connection. The *I feel like we've met before* feeling. Xavier had only felt this once or twice before, once with his now ex-fiancée, Sasha.

The minute he thought about her he pushed memories of her away. They were too painful. They were the whole reason he and a group of his fraternity brothers had created *Nost* in the first place. The little app had exploded over the last few weeks, taking them from a bunch of largely unknown software engineers to being propositioned by Google and Facebook for potentially millions. Xavier had nearly the whole world at his feet, but all he wanted was a little companionship. *Temporary companionship,* he reminded himself. He thought of Sasha, her dark eyes and cocoa skin, the way she tilted her head back when she laughed, how much she reminded him of his own mother. His mother who died when he was a kid. Sasha used to have him wrapped around her little finger. That was...until he found out she betrayed him.

He didn't need more pain. Not now. Probably not ever.

Concentrate on the now. The future is too painful. That's why you live in the moment, he reminded himself.

"So...was that really your first date from *Nost?*" he asked her, which was his way of prying without prying. He got why anonymous sex wasn't for everybody. Newbies were a wild card. But he wasn't about putting pressure on anyone. You were in or out, as far as he was concerned.

He watched the color bleed into her cheeks. "Yep. Happy Fun Time was it. Just signed up yesterday… and not sure it's for me. My friend Sarah actually insisted I try it. But… I don't know. I'm a little skeptical. What's in it for women?"

"Oh, everything, actually," Xavier said, raising his glass to his lips. "You'd be surprised."

She quirked an eyebrow, clearly intrigued, as she set her own glass back on the bar, and played with the small black straw, pushing the slice of lime around her cup. "Casual sex was invented by men."

"I don't know about that. Women want just as many partners as men do, you know. It's just that society tells them they should be good girls. But that's all just a construct, really, something *men* want."

"You're saying men want women to have fewer partners," she challenged.

"Of course. Men want it both ways: they want to have sex with as many women as possible, but keep most women at home, under wraps. A fully realized sexual woman who isn't afraid to go after what she needs terrifies most men."

A small blush crept up her pale cheek, which Xavier found a little bit adorable.

Definite newbie. Xavier had more than a handful of women who claimed they'd never consider *Nost*, who suddenly wound up in his bed. And it wasn't just his imposing physique. He knew that anonymous sex could be freeing. If you let the concept in.

"I write for *Helena,* the women's online magazine?" He knew it and nodded. "I kind of thought this would all just be fodder for my next article."

"Ah, so you're going to tell your readers how terrible and sexist the whole thing is," he teased.

"N-no," she countered. "I mean, I was going to research it and…"

"But you'd made up your mind before you even tried it," he said, reading her like the open book she was.

"Maybe." She stirred her drink once more, focusing on the ice cubes there. "And Happy Fun Time didn't help."

"Don't let him be the poster child for your experience," Xavier said. "Believe me, he's the exception not the rule."

"So what do you do for a living?" she asked him, blue eyes intent on an answer. She was a seeker, a collector of facts, someone who wouldn't rest until she got all the information.

"Work in tech," he said, and shrugged. He glanced at the melting ice cubes in his glass.

"Where?"

"Here and there." He grinned. It was the truth. He'd worked at other companies before founding *Nost.* He'd had a lot of practice not revealing details about himself. He'd made that mistake in the past, letting on where he'd worked, and a woman found him through a Google search with only his first name and *Nost.* She stalked him, showing up at work, at his apartment, asking for a relationship he wasn't willing to give. He'd been up front with her, but after two nights with him…she'd fallen for him. It had been a whole mess, actually. Now he'd learned to be more careful. He knew exactly what to reveal—and what to keep secret. He had his rules.

"Tell me more about this article," he said, deftly changing the subject as he deflected interest away from him. "Am I changing your mind about *Nost*?"

She glanced up at him. "Not sure yet," she said. "I'm Emma, by the way."

"X," he replied, and she laughed a little. He never gave his name anymore. Not after the other woman found him.

"No, really."

"Seriously—that's what my friends call me." *Because Xavier is too much of a mouthful for most.* "But, also, no names, it just makes it simpler. On *Nost.*"

"So I should just call you Mr. X?" Emma giggled at the idea. "What are you, a comic book villain?"

Xavier leaned in closer and got a whiff of her perfume…white flowers? Something light and floral. "That depends. Do you like bad boys?"

Now Emma just threw her head back and laughed. The sound was all light and air—music to Xavier's ears. The only thing he loved more than making a woman laugh was making her come.

"No. Not usually. I'm the strictly nice guy type."

"How's that working out for you?" Xavier sloshed his whiskey around the ice cubes in his glass, still studying her perfect cheekbones, and the lovely tilt of her chin. He wanted to kiss the tiny dimple that lay there.

She self-consciously played with a strand of her hair, and glanced at him sideways. Her eyes sparkled just a little. She was flirting with him. He was one hundred percent sure.

"Not that great," she admitted. "All the nice guys I've dated ended up being…not so nice." She frowned, her full, pink lips falling into a pout that could drive most men wild. "My last boyfriend decided a promotion was more important than me. He took the job across the country without even talking to me about it first."

"Maybe you should just start with a bad boy and then you know what you're getting." Xavier flashed a grin and Emma laughed.

"Maybe," she conceded. "Why are you on *Nost*?"

Her eyes probed him for an answer. This was the journalist at work, he realized. He liked the fire in her, the curious intelligence in her blue gaze. She wasn't like the other women he'd met recently. This one thrived on information. Keeping it from her would be a challenge, but one he'd happily accept.

"I love women," he said. "Sex for me isn't about me, it's about them. I can't be satisfied…unless they are. There's nothing more beautiful…or more humbling than giving a woman pleasure." To him, this was absolute truth. Nothing satisfied him more than seeing a woman, head back, mouth open, lost in ecstasy. Knowing that he brought her there.

Emma shifted uncomfortably in her seat and rattled her drink. "But don't you want…more? Don't you want love and…a real relationship and all of it?"

"I used to want that. I had that," he said, feeling a wave of sadness that was stronger than he expected. "I was engaged last year. But…" He thought of Sasha, of finding the passionate text messages she'd sent to another man, of the photos she'd sent wearing the lingerie *he'd* bought her. Those images would be seared into his brain forever. "I found out she'd been sleeping with someone else. Actually, a lot of someones." He took a long sip of his whiskey, the alcohol leaving a distant burning sensation down his throat. "I'd never been so blindsided. So…heart-broken." He shrugged. "I guess I'm just not ready for any of that, anything more serious. Not right now. Maybe not ever."

"She did a number on you," Emma said, her blue eyes sad, empathy radiating from them.

He nodded and shrugged.

"What was her name?"

"Sasha," he said, almost at the level of a whisper. "I thought she was the one." He remembered her dark eyes, her throaty, sexy laugh. The fact that she'd been so free in bed, willing to try anything, game for whatever he asked. Turned out, he wasn't the only one she was free with.

"But she wasn't."

"No," he said, biting off the word, eager to stop talking about Sasha. "But what about you? Why *don't* you like the idea of *Nost*?"

Xavier moved closer, and their knees touched. Emma didn't move away. He took that as a good sign.

She swooped her long, shaggy blond bangs from her forehead. "It seems like it's just what men want. Not what women want. Women want commitment, they want relationships…"

"Yes, with the right man, but what about the freedom to indulge in a fantasy, to play with someone who's *not* the right man, but then walk away the next day? There's something *more* liberating in that for women than men." Now Xavier felt like he was right back in front of the venture capitalists, telling them why *Nost* was worth their time, and more importantly, their money. "Look, women choose. They always choose. We men? We're powerless over that. We wait for you to decide. The power's all yours."

Emma rested her chin on her elbow and cocked her head to one side. "You think?" She shifted a little, so that their knees and legs touched. They were side-by-side now, elbows almost touching on the bar.

"Sure. You decide who's fit enough, strong enough, alpha-male enough. Every decision women make about men is based on that immense responsibility—those thousands of years of you being the ones bearing the reproductive cost and the future of the species. That's a lot of responsibility. But how are you supposed to *know* who's right for you, who's the perfect man, if you *don't* play around? What if the man you always thought was perfect for you wasn't, because you'd never allowed yourself to date outside that very confining box?"

She sent him a lopsided smile. "You're saying I need to sleep around with bad boys to find a good one."

He was aware of the feel of her thigh against his, the heat coming from her. "You need to know what it is you want. How are you supposed to know that without experimenting a little?"

"But, it's all so impersonal… How are you supposed to find something real when it's all just fake?"

"Oh, it's far from fake," he said with a strong shake of his head. "People can often have their most authentic connections when they're with strangers. You don't have to worry about what the other person might think, or if you'll hurt their feelings or how you might be judged. You can be your *real* self because you aren't worried about the future. You're just living in the now."

"Is that right?" Emma still seemed a little skeptical.

"Sure," he said, taking another sip of his drink, which was now three-quarters gone. "For instance, you can tell me anything you want. You can be a hundred percent honest. We probably won't see each other again after this night."

"Okay…" Emma hesitated.

"So, in that spirit, say you do sleep with me tonight." Xavier leaned in closer.

Emma barked a laugh and ran a nervous hand through her hair. "Aren't you a little overconfident?"

"Maybe," he said, even though at this point, he thought she'd have to feel the pull between them, the magnetism that drew them together. "But, just indulge me in a little theoretical. Say we do fall into bed tonight. Say we go upstairs into this room." He pulled out a hotel key card and laid it flat on the bar. Emma glanced at it, intrigued. *Tread carefully,* he told himself. "Which, by the way, is completely and totally up to you. But if we did…what's the first thing you want me to do to you?"

CHAPTER FOUR

THE KEY CARD ON the bar *and* his question sent a thrill through Emma. What did she want him to do to her? Short answer: *Everything.*

She felt her throat go dry. She had a hard time concentrating when Mr. X leaned in so close to her. His strong chin, the unwavering golden-eyed gaze. The thick jet-black hair that she badly wanted to put her hands in. She glanced at the Ritz-Carlton key card on the bar. That was it. The key to a room upstairs where…where…she could indulge in…him. That squared-off, strong chin, the barely-there stubble, those full, sensual lips. All she could think about was how he'd taste if she kissed him, how those lips would feel on hers. The attraction felt palpable, as if it was a physical law of nature that couldn't be denied, like gravity. Emma realized the absurdity of this situation: that just minutes ago she'd dismissed Happy Fun Time in an instant, but X was different. Calm, collected, confident. Emma couldn't remember the last time she'd felt this kind of pull, this kind of attraction. It had been instantaneous the minute he'd walked into the bar. She'd been aware of him every second, every little move he made.

And the more she learned about him, the more intrigued she became. He had loved deeply before. She saw it in the hurt on his face. He was a complicated man, and as much as she hated to admit it, she loved complicated.

He studied her, waiting for her answer, and she felt the weight of his golden gaze. For the first time since signing up for this ridiculous app, she almost felt *tempted*. What would it be like to follow this man up to a room and…?

"If we went upstairs right now…" He leaned closer, so their elbows were now touching on the bar. "What's the first thing you'd want? This would be a night for you. So…?"

She stared at his full lips.

"A k-kiss?" she offered.

He let out a low chuckle, and she felt the reverberations in her toes. She loved how he laughed—almost like a sensual growl. "You're still behaving like you can't be one hundred percent honest with me. You can. You don't have to tell me the answers you think I want to hear." He studied her. "What did you want your last boyfriend to do…that he'd never do?"

Emma thought about her predictable, staid boyfriend, Devin. He'd never been interested in how she felt about sex. It was always quick, the same position, with him coming in about two minutes, just when she was starting to get warmed up. Emma blamed herself: she never complained about it, and they'd just got stuck in this terrible kind of rhythm. But she didn't know how to talk about it without hurting his feelings, so she didn't.

Now Mr. X was waiting for her answer. And why not be honest? After all, he was right: they probably would never meet again. Even if they didn't have sex tonight, what did she have to lose?

"He never let me…come first." As soon as the words were out of her mouth she felt a little bit lighter. Admitting that—the first time she'd admitted it to anyone—felt like a burden had been lifted. Like she'd finally let go of a dirty secret.

Mr. X stared at her. "He always came first?" He looked shocked, even bewildered as his dark eyebrows knitted together in confusion.

She nodded and took another drink of her gin and tonic, the second cocktail heading to her head with rapid speed. She felt pleasantly light-headed, but didn't know if that was the Hendrick's or Mr. X's eyes on her.

Her experience limited, Emma thought maybe that was how it went with most men: they'd do what they wanted first, and then if they had the energy left over, they'd handle the woman's needs.

"That's unacceptable." The finality of his tone sent another little thrill through her. "I'd make sure you came at least three times."

"Three times?" She nearly spit out her drink. "That's a lot."

"Not nearly enough." He grinned, and his bright

white smile in his tanned face seemed blinding. "But we'd have *all* night."

"All night?" Devin subscribed to the one and done philosophy. She doubted sex had ever lasted for her longer than about twenty minutes, and that was a marathon.

"And, of course, all positions. We have to find the one that's right for you." A teasing smile tugged at the corner of his full mouth.

Emma felt the blush inch its way up her neck. She wasn't even sure she *knew* all the positions. The thought was a bit naughty…and a bit thrilling. She was beginning to see the allure of anonymous sex. She wouldn't have to worry about what she looked like from certain vantage points, a concern that nearly always plagued her, or whether or not she ought to suck in her stomach. X was a stranger, and would remain a stranger, so why worry about… any of the normal things she worried about?

She ran her finger around the lip of her glass. "I'm beginning to see why women would want to fall into bed with you right when they meet you."

He leaned in, his voice barely a whisper. "Well, I can tell you this. If you do, you won't be disappointed." She felt the warmth of his breath on her ear and the delicious naughtiness of the whole situation delighted her. She liked flirting—scratch that—loved flirting with this man. She even found herself seriously considering his proposition.

"Somehow, I believe you."

"You should." His confident gaze never left her.

He slowly reached out and took her hand. He held it palm up, running a strong finger down her life line. "I like to start slowly. Explore you. Like so." His delicate, featherlike touch sent electric sparks darting upward. Goose bumps ran up her arm. "Every woman is different, and I'd spend a lot of time finding out how unique you are."

"Just how *many* women have you…" She figured probably hundreds. With eyes like that and a body that seemed ready for an underwear ad. She thought he probably got laid anytime he wanted it. Women lining up on *Nost* to have a drink date.

He cocked his head to one side, looking coy. "I've had my share."

Now he was so close to her that when she looked up, she almost felt like she could fall into his gaze, a pool of hazel with flecks of gold. So close to him, she inhaled his spicy sweet scent, like cinnamon with a hint of some woodsy aftershave. He looked good. Smelled good. *I wonder if he tastes good, too.*

The thought jolted her.

"I'm not usually so impulsive."

"Why not?" He wasn't being flippant, she could tell. He really wanted to know.

"I don't know. I guess I worry about what people will think." There, she'd said it. It was her dirty little secret: she cared about other people's opinions. She spent a great deal of time writing in her articles about how women need to believe in themselves and be independent, and yet, she feared the weight of judgment herself.

And was she falling into the trap of believing that women who sleep around, who have casual sex, were somehow less than the ones who were more particular? That little feminist thread would have her head spinning for days.

"No one has to know," Mr. X said simply, as if this answered everything.

"But what if I want to write about it?" she asked. And part of her did. This little drink date was bringing up all kinds of feelings in her: Was she wrong to assume casual sex just benefited men? Should she try to find out? Why did her gut tell her to lean forward right now and kiss this man she'd just met?

"Then, do. I promise to give you something worth writing about." He was so confident, so sure. And part of her knew he was telling the truth. She couldn't imagine sex with this man being anything other than amazing. She could almost feel the electricity zapping between them. He was so close now that if she leaned forward, even slightly, their lips would touch. She held eye contact, unable to break it, caught in a kind of trance. He inched forward and she felt in that instant, he was going to kiss her. Suddenly, she got cold feet. Was he going to kiss her right here at the bar? Was she ready for where that kiss might lead?

She pulled away, ever so slightly. He paused, studying her face. Then, he let her hand go and leaned back. He smiled at her, gently.

"I think I want… I don't know…a real connection," she admitted. This was true. She wanted the whole package: amazing sex *and* love, but what she wanted above all else was a true connection. Something that meant something. Could she get that in one night?

He nodded. "You're not ready," he declared as a statement of fact.

"I'm…" Was he right? She felt all sorts of hormones rushing through her body, nerves tingling along her arms and up the back of her legs. She wanted love, but would she take sex right now in this moment?

"It's okay." He squeezed her hand. "*Nost* isn't for everybody."

That almost sounded like a goodbye. Was he abandoning the chase?

"I make it a rule never to pressure women," he said and shrugged, as he finished the last bit of his drink in his glass and signaled the bartender for his tab. "This is something you want or you don't."

But…wait. I haven't decided. Not yet. Maybe I do want this. The inner admission shocked her.

He signed the check and tucked his credit card back into his expensive leather wallet. "Emma, you're an amazing and beautiful woman and it's been my pleasure sharing this time with you." He took her hand and kissed it, lingering a little over it, his lips soft and gentle.

She still felt shock. Was he leaving? Was this it? But she didn't want the night to end. She didn't want him to walk out of her life and never come back. This connection between them, it had to be real, didn't it? He had to feel it, too?

"Can I…call you?"

He slowly shook his head. "I think we want different things."

Did they? All she knew in that moment was that she didn't want him to leave.

He stood, showing again how tall he was as he towered over her, and then he leaned over and gently kissed her cheek. She felt the warmth of his soft lips pressed against her skin and her stomach tightened. *Don't go,* she willed him. *Don't.*

"Goodbye, Emma," he whispered in her hair.

CHAPTER FIVE

EMMA SAT THERE stunned as she watched Mr. X turn away from her. "Wait," she said, and snaked out and grabbed his arm. She felt the strong muscles of his biceps contract. Wow, they were thick. And strong. She wondered what they'd be like wrapped around her. He stopped, and turned.

"Yes?" The single word held a question, an unspoken dare.

"Maybe I am ready." The words came out in a low whisper.

Mr. X leaned closer to her, putting his body between her and his bar stool. "Maybe?" He quirked an eyebrow. "Maybe doesn't sound very definite."

She inhaled his spicy sweet scent, suddenly feeling light-headed. Still seated, she stared directly at his chest, his taut pecs outlined beneath this cotton shirt. She had to crane her neck to meet his gaze.

"I am. I am ready."

"You sure? This has to be your idea, not mine. You have to want this."

"I do. I do want this." She had the strong urge

to put her hands on his chest, feel the firm muscles there. His sensual mouth was so close to hers now that she tilted her head up and grabbed the front of his shirt. Before she realized fully what she was doing, she'd reached up and kissed his lips, ever so gently. The soft, gentle touch of her lips on his sent hormones buzzing through her brain. It was just a peck, but a sensual one, carrying the promise of more to come. Instantly, she felt herself grow hot and cold. He stood very still, as she pulled away once more, suddenly feeling like there were no other people at the bar.

Emma surprised even herself. Normally, she was never so forward, never so…aggressive. She'd never been the first to kiss a man at a bar like this. Yet, Mr. X made her want to do things that…she never had before.

Mr. X cocked his head to one side, studying her, the intensity of his gaze almost feeling like a heavy weight. She blinked fast.

"I see. Well, you have to trust me. Do you trust me?" He studied her, his expression serious, as he reached out, under the bar, and gently laid his hand on her hip, resting it there. The touch sent a current through her, a delicious current. Then, he moved his hand back to the waistband of her jeans and tucked a single finger down the small of her back. She gasped a little, as he ran his finger along the top edge of her lacy black thong, the gesture containing a promise for things to come.

She swallowed, hard, and nodded. He tugged hard

at her waistband and she felt the pressure between her legs. She let out a little gasp. "I—I do. I do trust you."

"Good. Let's go." He handed her the key card to the room. Her heart beat wildly. Was she going to do this? Going to go up with this man she *just* met, this gorgeous, handsome man with the golden eyes? She looked at him and saw more than just a handsome man: she felt a connection with him. He'd been brokenhearted, and she could almost feel that pain in him. She wanted to heal him, somehow, because it was as if they'd met before now. The connection, the pull, she felt to him was real. Not just lust. Something more.

"Okay." She slipped her hand in his and followed him as he led her out of the bar. Every fiber of her being stood at attention: she was going to soon be in this man's arms. This stranger's arms. Doing things she usually reserved for the twelfth date. She met the bartender's gaze as they passed. Did he know? Did all the people in the bar know? Emma felt a little thrill then. The thrill of doing something naughty, something risky, something…she never thought she'd do. She watched his broad shoulders moving a little bit ahead of her, as he led her to the elevators and pushed the up button. The elevators dinged, and Emma felt the sound in her belly. Was she doing this? Oh, God. She was going to do this.

The elevators slid open, and a bellhop, pushing a cart of luggage, stepped out.

"Excuse me, miss," he said, and he gave her a half

smile. Did he know, too? What she was about to do? She felt delicious guilt run through her. She almost felt that everyone knew. Mr. X squeezed her hand and she glanced up at him as they moved inside the empty elevator and he pushed the top button.

As soon as the elevator doors slid shut, he'd pulled her into his arms and covered her mouth with his. The pent-up attraction of the last hour exploded then as he devoured her mouth and she responded in kind, her mind overwhelmed with the taste of him. She opened her mouth then, letting him inside her, as their tongues met in a primal dance. She wanted him in every way, as she felt herself grow wet, the slickness in her thong warm as he put his hands on her hips and pulled her closer to him.

She felt him grow hard. Was that all him? Width and...all? Then, his hand reached down and un-hooked her jeans. Right here? In the...elevator? She sucked in a breath, and then his hand went down the front of her waistband, all the way to her slickness. She moaned in his mouth, as his gentle fingers ex-plored her, his palm cupped her through her open jeans and her hips moved, pushing her deeper into his hands.

She no longer cared about the elevator, or the cameras that might surely be here. Was some se-curity officer somewhere watching him claim her? She couldn't care less. She almost felt like she could come right there. Then, the elevator dinged, and his hand slid out of her thong, releasing the smell of her-self in the small space. He grinned at her, and pulled her down the empty, carpeted hallway to a corner room as she held her jeans together. He slipped the card into the door and it swung open, his lips once more finding hers as he backed her into the room. Once she broke free she had only a second to glance around at the huge suite: a master bedroom and separate living room, and windows with a spectacular view of the other skyscrapers along Chicago's lakefront. A single lamp was lit in the corner, giving off a golden light, and the crisp white linens on the bed were turned down, an offering to them both.

The door clicked shut behind them and now it was just her and Mr. X. It was then she realized she didn't really know his name, didn't know anything about him, and yet here she was, pants undone, alone with him in his hotel room, his fingers carrying her scent.

Could she really do this? He took off his own shirt, and she was amazed by his chest, chiseled with muscle. Her belly grew warmer. Then, he took a step toward her, wordlessly, and tugged at her sweater. She lifted her arms, unable to resist him and her top came off.

"I—I've never done this before…with a stranger, I mean," she murmured. He nibbled her nipple, the flick of teeth on the soft skin making her shiver. "This is… I mean, this is crazy. I don't usually do this."

He straightened. A lazy grin spread across his handsome face, warming up his squared off jaw. "Even good girls should be bad, once in a while."

She felt his hands on her jeans, gently tugging

them downward. He walked her a step backward and she sat on the edge of the bed, her jeans around her knees. He knelt and pulled them off, as he took in her bare skin. He laid kisses on her bare legs.

She was a good girl. She never did this kind of thing.

"I just can't believe…" She wasn't even sure how she'd gotten here this fast, how she'd met a man and within an hour, was letting him see her everything. To put his hands and his mouth on her body. "I just… I don't know anything about you."

"You having second thoughts?" He paused, hazel eyes fixing her in a locked stare.

"No," she said. No, she wanted him. She did.

He pressed his hard, muscled chest against hers, dipping his face so close their noses nearly touched. "And all you need to know about me is this," he promised. She felt heat rise in her very core. He wanted her as much as she wanted him. And, God, did she want him. She'd wanted this the moment they'd met in the hotel bar an hour ago. She'd decided then in that split second to let him do what he wanted. She was willing.

"You can tell me whatever you want me to do to you. I want you to tell me."

She sucked in a breath and her knees trembled slightly. She didn't have to be a good girl. Not with him. She could be bad. Very, very bad. She could do whatever she wanted. She could let him do…whatever he wanted.

"Are you ready for the night of your life?" he

growled in her ear, as he slipped his hand past the thin fabric of her lace thong, his fingers finding her soft center. "Well, well," he murmured, appreciative. "You're more than ready."

Then, he smiled at her, putting her at ease. He was so handsome, so warm. Did it matter what his name was? Or that she didn't know where he lived? Or... anything at all about him. He was a walking puzzle piece, and she wasn't sure where he fit. But the attraction between them was undeniable.

"You're beautiful," he said, as he pulled her closer to him, kissing her once more. She kissed him back, feeling the heat once more in her belly.

"So smooth," he said, as he grasped her knees, sliding his hands up the top of her thighs. Then he leaned over her and trailed a line of seductive kisses down the tops of her breasts making her shudder. He pressed his lips gently, almost reverently against her skin, as if worshipping every inch of her. She couldn't help it. She felt like a queen.

Then he moved backward, straightening. She leaned forward and touched his bare chest, so smooth, so...fit. He sucked in a breath as she leaned forward and gently laid a kiss between his brown nipples.

He groaned, throwing his own shirt to the ground while she explored the ridges of his abs. So tight, she thought, so... solid. He put his hands in her hair, and she glanced up at him. He knelt down, putting his hands on her knees once more.

"I'm going to make you come now." The promise

sent a thrill through her as the breath caught in her throat. He gently moved her knees apart, and she lay back on her elbows, his eyes never leaving hers. "I'm going to make you come again and again."

She believed him, as he laid a gentle kiss on the inside of her thigh. Then, suddenly, she knew what he intended. She wanted to tell him…wait… because going down…well, she felt self-conscious a little. What if she smelled? What if he didn't like how she tasted? And, Devin…well, Devin flat-out refused to do it.

He squeezed her inner thigh.

"I want to taste you," he said. "I want to worship you. Will you let me?"

His declaration sent a thrill through her. He didn't mind doing this. No, he *wanted* to do it. Worship her? Yes, please. She nodded, frozen by his determined gaze.

He moved upward, gently, teasing kisses leading a trail straight to her center. She arched her back, at once wanting and not wanting him to do what he promised—she suddenly felt self-conscious. Was her shower still good from earlier? Had the wax job she'd gotten still held? All those busy, insecure thoughts ran through her mind.

Then, he kissed her… there. Laid his lips on her most delicate part, his tongue flicking outward in a gentle exploration. The minute his tongue touched her, she felt white-hot molten heat roll through her.

"Oh," she moaned, her senses overtaken by his warmth. He held his tongue there, and the warm wet-

ness overtook her. He was... He was good at this.
She'd never had someone... so good at this. Instantly,
she felt her arousal grow, her want for him. The desire built as he worked, teasing her at first, gently,
with little flicks of his tongue.

He lifted his head a moment. "You taste so...
amazing," he murmured. "God, Emma," he groaned
as he pleasured her, lapping deeper into her center,
devouring her. He slipped a finger inside her, tickling
her, teasing her, caressing all those nerve endings inside. She'd never felt so wanted... so desired. Emma
arched her back, moved into his hungry mouth and
then suddenly she was on the edge of orgasm, every
muscle in her body tensed. This never happened so
quickly... Never... And then she was over the edge,
consumed by Mr. X's talented tongue, her body rip-
pling with pleasure as she cried out. The release took
them both by surprise. She glanced down at him.
This man whom she'd known just an hour, had just
given her one of the best orgasms of her life.

"You sure are talented, Mr. X," she breathed, as
her heart rate began to return to normal.

"Oh, you haven't seen anything yet," he promised.
She felt her body come to life once more. Hungry
again, as if this first climax was a simple appetizer,
something to curb her appetite which only seemed
to grow. He anticipated her every want, every need,
and his gentle touch set her skin on fire.

Now it was her turn. She sat up, and grabbed
his belt loop, tugging him closer. She unzipped his
pants and released him, closing her hands around

him, amazed at his size. She'd never seen one so… big. She worked him with both hands as he leaned into her touch, letting out a small moan, and then she leaned over and put the tip of him in her mouth, teasing him with her tongue and he clutched at her shoulders, his entire body tensing and she knew she had him, knew she was driving him as crazy as he'd driven her. The power made her light-headed, and she felt even bolder. She worked him deeper and he ran his hand down her back. He pulled her up then and kissed her with an open mouth, his tongue urgently meeting hers in a primitive dance. She felt all her baser instincts take over. This was pure lust, amazing, animal lust. She'd never wanted a man so badly as in this moment.

He pulled away from her in that moment. "What do you want, Emma?"

She felt dazed, off-center. "I want you to fuck me." The words came out low, hoarse. She'd never said that out loud to anyone before.

A knowing smile played at the corners of his mouth, as he reached out and gave her nipple a teasing little pinch. It sent a shiver of delight through her. "Are you sure?"

She nodded, once, mouth open, her whole body feeling like one quivering nerve.

He reached for a condom from his discarded jeans then and ripped the foil open easily. Then he was rolling it down his ample self, which stood ready to take her in the basest way possible.

CHAPTER SIX

FOR XAVIER, EVERY new woman was a gift, and yet, he couldn't remember feeling this kind of eagerness before. From the moment they met, he knew she'd be amazing, and here she was, beautifully naked in front of him, offering herself up in the most vulnerable way. He wanted her. Badly. He'd wanted her the moment he'd laid eyes on her at the bar, and now, here she was, giving herself to him. He'd always been a man to appreciate all kinds of women: short, tall, ample-chested, flat-chested, he enjoyed them all. But Emma was different somehow, just the best combination of curve and muscle, and her lean, lithe, perfectly proportioned body just screamed *playground*.

Her legs parted for him and he felt a ripple of desire as he teased her with just the head, running it around her wetness, as she lifted her pelvis up to meet him.

"Don't tease me," she cried, which made him want to tease her all the more, push her to the very edge of sanity. She spread her legs wider, willing him inside her, making him feel giddy. He pushed inside her a single centimeter and then withdrew.

"Oh!" she cried, grasping at him.

He teased her a bit further, maddeningly, as she clutched at his arms, frustration growing on her face.

"More," she cried, when he gave her just his full tip.

When she was almost at her wit's end, then he pushed into her tight center, a gasp escaping both their lips as he moved in on top of her, her warm, soft breasts pressing against him. He almost wanted to come right there, she felt so amazing. Was there anything better than this moment? This moment when he entered a woman for the first time? Xavier didn't know it.

"Is this what you wanted?" he murmured in her ear.

"Yes," she croaked, her voice dry. "Yes."

And he worked her harder, as her hips met his. He wanted to come at every moment. She was beyond delicious. Everything about her overwhelmed his senses. The smell of her. The taste of her. The feel of her. Xavier had been with many women in his life, and he appreciated them all, but Emma…. Emma just felt special. Not only was she gorgeous, but he'd never been with a woman so at odds with herself. In the bar, she'd been buttoned-up, conservative, even, he thought, on the verge of leaving, but once he'd gotten her into his hotel room, she'd turned into someone else: a woman overcome by desire and want, not caring about anything but satisfaction. Her passion ran deep, and the dichotomy thrilled him. He needed to have her in every way possible.

He withdrew, and turned her over so she was on her hands and knees in front of him, her amazing ass on display, her shell-pink lips exposed. He took her then from behind, enjoying her in the most primal of ways. He licked his finger then and reached around and touched her. She threw her head back and moaned, moving against him as he pushed deeper inside her. God, she was so tight. Amazingly tight. He feared he wouldn't be able to hold it, and then, she gave a hoarse shout as she came, tightening even more around him in spasms of pleasure. He grasped her hips then, thrusting slowly and deeply as she rode the waves of her climax. He loved making this woman come.

He withdrew and rolled her over, marveling at her flushed face. Her chest heaved as she tried to catch her breath. He dipped down and put a swollen pink nipple in his mouth. She groaned. He flicked his tongue, and she moaned again. He ran his teeth along her nipple and she shuddered beneath him. He went to the other nipple, running his teeth over the edge ever so softly.

"Oh, God," she murmured, her nipples standing at complete attention, as he nuzzled one breast. She watched him. "W-what is it that you'd want? To ask a stranger…"

Xavier smiled. There were so many things. So many things he'd asked women to do for him. But he knew exactly what he wanted her to do.

Xavier pulled her to the edge of the bed then, standing in front of her.

He entered her once more, this time with her flat on her back, knees up. She gasped as she took the full length of him.

"I want you to touch yourself," he said. "I want to watch you."

Emma hesitated ever so slightly, but then, as he watched, her hand snaked downward. Gently, she touched her self, delicately at first. Her eyes slid shut.

"No," he commanded. "Watch me, Emma. Watch me."

Her eyes flicked open and met his gaze. He saw her eyes widen as she brought herself closer to a third time, and he could feel her grow wetter. What he wanted was to watch her face as she came, that beautiful face. It was the most vulnerable a person could be, and he wanted to see it. Most women couldn't do it: most women looked away. Would Emma be able to hold eye contact?

He moved faster, deeper, never breaking eye contact. She held his, her blue eyes turning bluer as the redness crept up her cheek.

"That's it," he coaxed her. "Come for me."

Her blue eyes grew more urgent then with need, and as he thrust deeper, suddenly, her whole body tensed. Her toes curled beside him, and then, eyes never leaving his, she dissolved, the climax taking her past the edge, tumbling her into oblivion. Her eyes turned a brilliant blue as they held his, the most beautiful thing he'd ever seen in his life: the raw vulnerability of this beautiful woman as she came. Then, instantly, he poured himself inside her in a rush of nearly unbearable pleasure. She'd pulled it out of him, demanded it, and he'd given it to her.

They didn't get much sleep. Xavier didn't sleep at all, truth be told. He held this beautiful woman in his arms, cradling her naked against him beneath the thin cotton sheet of the hotel bed. He breathed in her scent: hints of earthiness and the fresh, bright smell of lavender shampoo in her hair. They'd ended the night in the shower, where he'd gently washed every amazing curve, the suds slipping down her taut body in all the right places. He'd worked up the lather, but she'd been the one to turn the tables on him. She'd gotten on her knees and taken him in her mouth, making him come one last mind-blowing time. Before that, they'd gone twice more that evening, trying out almost every position he could think of, as he worked hard to sate his growing desire for her. Normally, by now in a *Nost* tryst, he'd tire, begin to have his fill, start planning his getaway, but Emma was different. Every time she climaxed, every time she brought him over the edge, she seemed to grow more beautiful. Every time they joined together, the experience felt brand new, his exploration of her seemed never to grow dull. They fit together in a way that took him by surprise. They moved together like a couple who'd known each other for years: she seemed to anticipate his every want. Even now, as she lay sleeping against him, he felt his groin stirring. A full night and usually he was spent, drained, done for, but his body *still* wanted her in the most animalistic way. Was this what it meant to be a slave to passion?

Or...a slave to love?

Suddenly, he remembered something his father had told him: *No man can resist the woman he loves.* He shook the thought from his head. He hadn't thought about his father—or his troubled mother—for years. Why now?

Was it Emma? Had she somehow dredged up memories he thought long buried?

Was this more than sex? It felt like...more.

Emma just gave all of herself. Even now, as she slept pressed against him, she held nothing back. Most women were careful. Most women kept a part of themselves hidden away from him. Most women... No, nearly all women, couldn't look him in the eye when they came—perhaps too embarrassed, or too unwilling to show just how vulnerable they could be. Emma let herself be seen. She'd been so open and honest, she'd laid herself completely bare, and, somehow, that got to him. She'd given him a gift, a precious gift.

So that meant he'd fall in love?

He pressed his eyes shut. He wasn't going to fall for this woman. He couldn't. He thought of Sasha, of her dark, penetrating eyes and the curves that didn't quit. He'd been a slave to her, and she'd crushed his heart. Left him broken and helpless. He still remembered the gut-punch he'd felt the day he'd discovered the text messages, the half-naked pictures she'd sent to another man, the declaration of how she couldn't wait to have him inside her. Sasha had lived a double life, and the worst part was that he'd failed her. He'd failed to satisfy her. She'd gone elsewhere, looking for the pleasure he apparently couldn't give her. He'd known that their sex life had become a bit stale. He thought it was what naturally happened in a long-term relationship. They'd become too used to each other, too familiar, and he hadn't known they had to break out of that.

Sasha had…by seeking attention elsewhere.

The memories still hurt, like little razor blades through his mind. He wasn't even sure he *could* love another woman again, could leave himself so open to hurt. He'd built an emotional wall so thick and tall, he wasn't even sure how to get through it anymore. *Yet, she had,* a voice whispered in his mind. *She's made a crack in that wall.*

No. He'd have to fortify it again.

She murmured and snuggled into him, and his body responded as he cradled her against him. He wasn't sure he wanted this to end. Wasn't sure he wanted to say goodbye to her.

In another twelve hours, her profile will be hidden from me, a small, urgent voice told him. *But then, the decision will be made for me,* he thought. He felt both a smidgen of relief and a stab of panic but decided that it would be best to let the app take care of this for him. If he saw too much more of her, he would fall for her. Of this, he was certain, and then what? He knew what happened to all long-term relationships: the sex died, the desire died, and then came betrayal and heartbreak. It just wasn't feasible to keep the passion alive. He thought of Sasha. At this point, could he really blame her? She'd cheated first, but wouldn't he have eventually? Human beings need passion.

And there was nothing more passionate than sex with a stranger. Why ruin the amazing night they'd had by letting it get boring…predictable?

Xavier's phone jangled on the bedside table, announcing the alarm he'd set just two hours ago. He had a meeting at *Nost* to discuss new directions of the app, which member roll was growing bigger every day. He had to get to work. Emma shifted against him, rubbing her full breasts against his side. The feel of her soft nipples against his skin sent a ripple of tightness through his groin. He wanted her again… yet, he had no time. As it was, he might be late. He dropped a kiss on the top of her head and she murmured, sweetly, still sleepy. He slipped from the covers to get dressed.

As he moved quickly and quietly, he watched this beautiful creature in his bed, her golden hair spilled out over the pillow, her pink lips parted as she slept. The white curve of her shoulder just visible beneath the edge of the sheet. She lay deliciously naked beneath it, her skin almost calling to him. He wanted nothing more than to climb back into bed with her and taste her all over again. He wanted to feel her again, explore the very depths of her. See if they were as amazing on the repeat as they were the first time.

But he couldn't. His phone vibrated with incoming messages from his partner at *Nost*. He needed to get in the office.

He bent down and laid a gentle kiss on Emma's temple. She shifted but she fought with sleep, as it tugged her deeper downward. He wanted to stay here, watch her sleep, memorize every detail of her face. He wanted to keep this with him, this amazing night. He half wished she'd wake, but as he touched her golden hair, she dug in with a satisfied murmur. Even now, she was vulnerable and trusting: sleeping so deeply with him, a stranger. Emma simply didn't hold back. She put herself in his hands.

He felt the need to care for her. He reached down and pulled up the warmer blanket, tucking it over her bare shoulder. She let out a satisfied sigh. God, she was perfect.

Now's the time to leave, he thought. *When she's still perfect.*

Reluctantly, he turned to leave, grabbing his wallet and cell phone. On his way out, he saw the hotel pad and pen on the desk. On a whim, he scribbled a quick note and then smiled to himself.

They technically still had twelve hours on the *Nost* clock, he reminded himself. A lot could be done in twelve hours.

He opened the hotel room door and slipped out, careful to make sure the door shut quietly behind him.

CHAPTER SEVEN

A BURST OF chimes from her phone woke Emma with a start. The hotel room was dark, the light-canceling shades drawn, and for a second she was disoriented. Where was she? Then she realized she was naked beneath expensive thick cotton sheets. *Mr. X.* Memories of the night before flooded her mind and all the various ways they'd explored each other's bodies. Her neck grew hot just thinking of his strong hands on her body. That was by far the most amazing sex she'd ever had. Bar none. She sat up in bed and found it empty.

Where was he? The bathroom light was on, door ajar. She opened her mouth to call his name, but then remembered with shocking clarity that she didn't know it. Was she really going to shout out, "Mr. X?" to the room?

Oh, God. Had she really done this? Had she really fucked the brains out of a man and she *didn't even know his name*?

Sure, she knew women did this all the time. Sarah came to mind. This was probably her normal Tuesday night.

But Emma? Never. As in, not once. Not at a frat party, or a club, or a bar. She'd never taken a stranger into her bed. She thought of all the many ways they'd gotten to know each other last night. Not so strange anymore, she realized. Emma could practically sketch his amazingly fit body in her mind. She might not know his name, but she sure knew every other thing about him.

She studied the light from the bathroom. "Hello?" she called from the bed. No answer. Emma pulled the top sheet off the bed and padded over to the bathroom, finding it empty.

"Huh," she murmured out loud as she crossed the room to the curtained window. She flung back the curtain and sunlight poured in. Outside, the day had already begun, and far below the street was crowded with small cars and the sidewalks teemed with people on their way to work. The Loop bustled with energy and focus. She'd soon be among the throng, making her way to the L. She glanced at her phone. She had a half hour to shower and get dressed, then she'd need to head home and finish up that last article that her editor wanted today. Such was the life of a freelancer.

Emma turned, and that was when she saw the letter on the nightstand. She went to it, reading the precise, neat handwriting:

8 p.m. tonight. Meet you in the lobby.

A little thrill ran through her. He wanted to see her again? Was this something that happened with *Nost*? She thought it was purely for one-night stands.

But there was also no mistaking what Mr. X wanted. He wanted more sex. Tonight. *Here.*

She could feel a little tingle in her inner thigh. Yes, please. More of him, please.

Then she felt deliciously naughty. *I don't know the man's name. Nothing. And I'm coming back for more.*

She folded the note carefully and tucked it into her bag. Then, she bit her bottom lip. She really *ought* to know his name. Some detail about him. She searched her brain, but came up with nothing. He'd vaguely said something the night before about working in tech, but that could mean anything. She had no idea where he lived or worked. She did know that he came alive beneath her touch, that he loved it when she focused her tongue on the tip of his…

Suddenly, the room got hotter. Emma absently cupped her own breast through the sheet, remembering Mr. X doing the same thing the night before, remembering the feel of his teeth against her nipple. She felt a rush of heat then, and almost felt the urge to slip her hands beneath the sheet and touch herself.

She shook her head. What was happening to her? Just thinking of Mr. X sent her into a tailspin. She glanced at her phone. Emma needed to get ready. She retreated to the bathroom to find the shower where just hours ago, Mr. X had sudsed her down, washing every part of her in delicate, perfect circles. She turned on the pizza pan–sized shower head, and the room soon filled with steam. Mr. X was everywhere in this room, and her body felt like he'd claimed it. As she let the sheet fall down, she remembered ev-

erywhere he'd touched her, every little ripple of pleasure he'd sent through her body. Suddenly, it seemed
that the evening felt like years away. She wasn't sure
she could wait.

Xavier arrived at his corner office in the west Loop
in a four-story brownstone not far from the United
Center. Inside, the building was all gleaming new
tech company: open floor plan, stocked fridge, ping-
pong table in the glassed conference room that sat
in the middle of the office space on the raised first
floor. The open floor plan accommodated just four
offices: one for each of *Nost*'s partners. Everyone
else worked in glassed-in cubes. As it was a pet-
friendly office, dogs sat near various cubes, and a
big bowl of dog treats was laid at the front desk.
Xavier wanted to push for in-office day care, but so
far, only two employees had children, not enough to
make a program.

The staff of *Nost* was almost all young, hip and
attractive. It hadn't been on purpose, but the people
who'd showed up for the job interviews just fit that
bill. Pets were their priority, and kids seemed a long
way off. It made sense to Xavier. Not too many forty-
somethings with families would be looking to work
for a hookup dating site.

Xavier crossed the main office floor just in time
to get the knowing look from his assistant, Justin
Tanaka. Justin wore his usual uniform of colored
bow tie, slate-gray vest and skinny jeans. The color
of the vest and bow tie changed daily, but the gen-

eral outfit did not. He wore wingtips on his feet and his thick, jet-black hair in a precise cut.

"Well, well, *well*," Justin crooned as Xavier arrived, hopping up from his desk and following Xavier into his office. "Wearing the same clothes from yesterday?"

"Only you would notice that," Xavier grumbled as he put down his messenger bag. Justin, just twenty-four, was the best personal assistant: on time, organized, a hard worker. His only flaw was his nosiness, but Xavier didn't mind. Justin kept things lively, and he was instrumental in making sure *Nost* was LGBT friendly.

"Of course I would." Justin rolled his eyes and put a hand on his hip, jutting it out for emphasis.

Xavier laughed. "I know. You don't let the office forget it."

"Hey, if you've got it, flaunt it." Justin shrugged one shoulder, back to his normal, less theatrical self. "So…" Justin perched himself on Xavier's desk. "Tell me…who was the lucky *Nost* girl?"

"Emma," Xavier said, sitting at his computer and pulling up his email.

"Emma! I like that name. My cousin's named Emma. Let's see, that makes…" Justin mimed flipping through a binder. "Girl number 438."

"There haven't been that many," Xavier protested, glancing up from his keyboard.

"Oh, my bad. That's 437. Better watch out or you'll break my record."

Xavier eyed him. "Which is?"

Justin quirked an eyebrow. "You don't want to know."

Xavier laughed. "You're right. I *don't* want to know."

Justin crossed his arms across his vest. "All right, mister. Remember you've got the meeting with the board at eleven, and this evening, the development team wanted to know if you'd join them for their happy hour at seven."

"Can't do it," Xavier said, categorically, thinking about Emma and the lobby of the Ritz-Carlton. "I've got plans."

Justin quirked an eyebrow. "With Emma?" Xavier said nothing, but something in his face must've given the truth away, because Justin shrieked, "You are! You're going out with Emma *two* nights in a row?" He clicked his tongue to the roof of his mouth with disapproval. "You're dipping your wick in the same well! What will this do to our brand?!"

"Technically, *Nost* promotes the forty-eight-hour relationship," Xavier explained, as he typed in his email password. "And it hasn't been forty-eight hours yet."

Justin narrowed his eyes, doubtful. "Mmm-hmm. You sure you're not developing a thing for this girl?"

Xavier laughed. "No," he said, shaking his head. "You know I don't do that. It's the whole reason I founded this company."

The company his father told him was a mistake. "Love needs more than forty-eight hours," he told his son a year ago, before the last heart attack took him.

"Papi, this isn't about love," he told his father, who'd simply arched an eyebrow and replied, "Isn't everything about love?"

The damn romantic. More and more, memories of his father kept popping up lately. He wondered why. It had been a year since Xavier had put him in the ground at the graveyard next to his mother. A year he'd been an orphan, and he'd done pretty well by himself: had launched a wildly successful company. Had found comfort in the arms of many women... Maybe not 437. But a sizable number.

"There's a first time for everything." Justin's dark eyes gleamed. "You know the *only* constant in this world is change."

"Does that come with a free side of zen meditation?"

"If you'd like. Want me to pencil that in for you?"

Xavier laughed. "No thanks." He didn't need meditation or yoga. He just needed to see Emma one last time.

Justin gave him a knowing look as if he could read his mind. "Well, I'll leave you to it. And remember, no texting this girl Emma. You didn't get her phone number, did you?"

"No," Xavier replied.

"Good. Maybe there's hope for you, after all." Justin sauntered back to his desk.

Was there? Xavier wondered. Was he developing a thing for Emma? No, he told himself. Just one more night. One more night to scratch this little itch. One more night ought to do it. He'd never gone three nights before, never found a need to go beyond the forty-eight-hour rule. But, he admitted, he'd hardly ever come back for seconds either. Usually one night was plenty. One night and he'd felt satiated. But not with Emma. What made her different? He'd need to see her again to find out.

He pushed the little worry out of his brain. It didn't mean he was falling in love with her, did it? The sex was amazing, more than amazing, sizzling hot, but that didn't mean he needed to go pick out wedding bands. Plus, if he really wanted to cool things off, he ought to just start dating her. Propose. Like he did with Sasha. That would fix his want and hers—for good. They'd be a bored couple in no time.

He sat at his desk and logged in to his computer, pulling up the code for *Nost.* It was brilliantly simple, and yet teasingly complex. He loved it. It had been his baby and he still liked to tweak it. He remembered Happy Fun Time from last night and frowned. The man had violated pretty much *every Nost* behavior guideline at the bar last night. He pulled up the man's profile. Whose pictures was he using? Not his own. Xavier squinted. No way that male model was the same man he'd seen in the Cardinals hat the night before. And the little *c* and *v* next to his name… might not even be his real name. He might not be vetted at all. He remembered the way the man had talked to Emma the night before and his blood boiled just thinking about it.

With a few keystrokes, he turned up the Facebook profile, where Xavier saw the real Happy Fun

Time clearly had stolen his pictures. He'd stolen this man's identity, whoever he was, and was using it as a front on *Nost*.

Xavier clacked away on the keyboard and with a few commands, barred Happy Fun Time from the app. For good. Still, uneasiness lingered. The guy used a name that wasn't his, and he could do it again. He could slip into the roster of *Nost* under another stolen name at a later date. The thought irked Xavier. He wanted the app to be safe and to be fun, and it would be neither if assholes like Happy Fun Time found ways around *Nost*'s safety settings.

Xavier made a mental note to ask the security guys for a way around this. He worried Happy Fun Time wasn't the only one gaming the system. Still, he'd have to have the man's social security number in order to run the verified test. But plenty of identity thieves had numbers that weren't theirs. Xavier shot an email to his friend, a Chicago police detective, asking his advice.

Xavier focused on his computer once more. He had the information of every *Nost* user at his fingertips. Yes, the site was publicly anonymous, but on the back end, there was all kinds of personal information he could find. Names, addresses, phone numbers.

His fingers paused on his keyboard. Should he look up Emma's information?

He glanced outward through his walls of his glassed-in office at Justin's back as he worked. He shouldn't, he knew. It violated tons of ethics standards, but...

No. Xavier closed the window on his machine.

I shouldn't do it. Should I?

He tried to focus on work emails, but he kept being drawn back to the minimized box on his computer screen. The *Nost* app database.

Eventually, he could resist no more. The temptation was just too great. What could it really hurt?

With a few clicks of the mouse, he'd pulled up Emma's information. Emma Allaire, age twenty-eight, lived in Lincoln Square. Before he could stop himself, he'd searched her on social media, and found her Instagram account. Dozens of pictures rolled up for him, as she had her account public. As he scrolled through them: her with her friends, her with what looked like her mom, several of Emma at her favorite coffee shop on North Avenue… He felt a surge of guilt. He was snooping, stalking even. And what was he even doing? Not only was he invading her privacy, but he was doing the very thing he told himself would kill their attraction: he was trying to get to know her.

Yet, he gobbled up every new bit of information like a starving man. He'd never felt this way about any *Nost* girl before. After exploring their bodies, he'd been content to just let them go. But something about Emma was different. She intrigued him.

Was it her fire? Her determination to challenge him on his beliefs that a no-strings relationship was the best kind? Was it the way she'd stood up to Happy Fun Time at the bar? Or, was it the way she'd given herself to him so authentically, so honestly the night before. She'd let herself be vulnerable in a way no woman had before, not even Sasha.

He soon found her articles online and devoured them, one after another. Emma came across as thoughtful, razor-sharp and insightful. More liberal than he on most issues, he found, she was the kind of woman who wasn't afraid to put herself out there. To let others know how she really felt. Her writing mimicked her passion the night before. Emma was just herself—no pretense.

He found that amazingly refreshing.

So many of the women he'd been with were so concerned with pleasing him, with molding themselves into something they thought he'd like, rather than just being *them*. He made no apologies for who he was and always wanted a partner do the same.

Before he'd realized what he was doing, he'd spent the entire morning combing the internet for information on Emma.

But, he reasoned, it didn't mean anything. Did it?

CHAPTER EIGHT

EMMA THREW ON a sweater and headed out of her modest, one-bedroom Lincoln Square condo. She skipped down two flights and outside into the fresh fall air. The morning chill had lifted beneath the bright, warm haze of the midday sun, and the leaves on the trees were beginning to turn shades of red and gold. A cab rushed down her tree-lined street as she made her way for Armitage Street nearby. She wasn't sure if it was the beautiful fall day in the city or the fact she still felt like she was glowing from her amazing night with Mr. X, but everything just felt shinier…and brighter.

Emma turned the corner and saw the little diner where she'd planned to meet Sarah for lunch. She saw her pretty redheaded friend sitting at a booth near the window and waved to her as she slipped inside and almost skipped to the booth where Sarah sat. Sarah, wearing one of her striking business suits, stood and gave her friend a hug.

"You got laid," Sarah declared, the second Emma sat down.

"What? How do you know that?" Emma exclaimed.

"Because you're *literally* glowing. Radioactive glowing. So... Happy Fun Time was...happy?" Sarah sat, adjusting her expensive wool blazer. No doubt, she planned an afternoon of showing off business offices to corporate representatives.

Emma wrinkled her nose. "God no. He was horrible. Probably a date rapist. Maybe a serial killer."

"Oh, no." Sarah leaned forward. "Then don't tell me you hooked up with your ex, because so help me..." Sarah was no fan of Devin's. She'd once said he was about as exciting as watching someone else watch paint dry.

"No! He's in Seattle." Emma shook her head furiously even as the waitress sat down waters in front of them and a couple of laminated menus. "No, another *Nost* candidate. Mr. X."

"Ooh. Mr. X. Mysterious. I like it. Have a picture?" Emma pulled up Mr. X's profile on her phone and showed her friend. Sarah snatched the phone out of Emma's hand.

"No way." She peered at Mr. X's photograph. "I'm impressed." Sarah bit her pink lip. "Now, this is what I'm talking about." She handed Emma's phone back. "Now...on to a new one tonight?" she half joked as she picked up the menu.

"New one! No. I'm going to meet Mr. X again."

Sarah dropped the menu in her hands. "Emma. *No Strings.* No second dates!" Sarah shook her head. "Second dates just get...complicated."

Emma felt a little disappointment. "Why?"

Sarah shook her head. "Because. Then, you start to almost expect to see them. Best to just keep it at a single date. Trust me. Guys are the worst. You think they'll be able to cut things off easier than women, but sometimes, it's just the opposite."

"What do you mean?" The waitress returned and quickly took their orders. Sarah opted for a lightly dressed salad, and Emma, feeling famished from all her exercise the night before, chose a hamburger and fries.

"Just that. Last time I went on a second date, the guy online stalked me. Started leaving messages for me on Facebook. I had to eventually block him." Sarah took a sip of water and shrugged. "He actually said he wanted to marry me!"

"No way!" Emma shook her head. "I mean…what on earth did you do to him?"

"What didn't I do?" Sarah shrugged and laughed a little at her own joke. Her green eyes sparkled with mischief. "But he just couldn't keep up with me. He was just too vanilla. Sweet, but there's no way I would've wanted a long-term relationship with him."

"Well, I don't mind if Mr. X turns into…more." Emma thought of Mr. X's strong hands, his sexy hazel eyes, the way he seemed to *know* her, even though they hadn't known each other that long. She wouldn't mind that turning into a regular thing.

"No!" Sarah slapped her hand on the table. "Emma. We talked about this. You are just too quick to settle. That's what happened with Devin, remember?"

Emma nodded, reluctantly. "But Mr. X is *nothing* like Devin. They're polar opposites."

"From the picture you showed me, I believe that much is true, but still. The whole point of this little exercise is to show you how many fish there are in the sea."

The waitress appeared then with their lunches, setting the plates in front of the women. Emma dug into her fries like a woman who hadn't seen food in days.

Sarah quirked an eyebrow. "Well, I can see Mr. X worked up an appetite in you." Emma coughed.

"You have no idea," she said, between mouthfuls.

"Well, then. Tell me. All the juicy bits!" Sarah leaned in, eager.

Later that afternoon, Emma sat at her computer and stared at the cursor. What on earth was she going to write? Nearly all of her date with Mr. X was…uh, X-rated. At least, the good parts were. She couldn't imagine how her editor would even *go* for something so…graphic. After all, their online magazine was read mostly by working moms, not co-eds looking for the *hottest tips for spicing up the old blow-job*. She glanced at the handwritten note from Mr. X and felt a little shiver of anticipation. She'd see him again tonight.

She didn't even know his name!

All the things he'd done to her and she had no idea what his first name was. More than anything, she wanted to find out. Yet, as she pulled up Google to start her search, she had no idea how to start. "Amazing hazel eyes and abs that won't quit... Chicago?"

"Mr. X Chicago?"

Both of those searches pulled up beefcake photos and one news article about a TV pilot being shot in downtown.

Argh. She searched *Nost and Mr. X*, but just got his profile, which she realized with a start as she looked at the little wristwatch graphic in the corner, would disappear from her feed sometime this evening. A little prick of panic tickled the back of her neck. What if she never got his name? What if she never saw him again after tonight?

But there would be tonight, and then...she'd just ask him. Flat out. What's your name? Can I have your number?

Because I want to fuck you many, many more times.

The naughty thought popped into her head unbidden, shocking her. She sat for a few minutes, staring at the blinking cursor, but all she could think about was Mr. X's golden eyes on her while she came for him, the way he'd held her, as if keeping her under his spell. She'd never felt so exposed, yet, so protected at the same time. Maybe it was the thrill of being with a stranger. She could do things she never dared with someone she knew.

Emma knew she'd get no work done today. She opted instead to try to find an outfit for tonight. She rummaged through her drawers, but even the laciest of her lingerie seemed not sexy enough. She grabbed her bag and decided to head to the stores on Armitage. She was going to stop at the lingerie shop.

Emma stood anxiously in the lobby of the Ritz-Carlton, wondering if she'd arrived too early. It was ten until eight, ten full minutes before Mr. X had set the meeting date. The lobby was mostly empty, with just a couple of workers behind the desk and few patrons milling about. The elevators dinged occasionally, announcing the arrival of a new guest, and Emma found it hard not to glare at each one, hoping to see Mr. X's face. She wore a tight black dress, one she hadn't worn in years. It was stretchy and long-sleeved, and clung to her curves. Beneath the dress, she wore the most delicate laced thong she'd ever owned, a matching push-up bra, and actual thigh-high lacy tights, which she'd never worn her whole life. But the idea of Mr. X peeling them off her had made them a must-buy. She wore stiletto heels and carried a small clutch bag. She'd tied her blond hair up this time in a messy bun, with silver dangling earrings that skimmed her jawline when she moved her head. She felt…pretty. She also felt…very much like she wanted to get back up to that hotel room with Mr. X.

Her stomach fluttered with nerves. She'd never before shown up at a hotel lobby with the express intent of sex. She felt beyond naughty. She was being bad, wasn't she? Good girls didn't do this. A flutter of nerves cinched her stomach. A bellboy went by with a golden cart full of bags, maneuvering around the giant fountain; he nodded at her, an appreciative look on his face.

But all she wanted was Mr. X.

Okay, she told herself, *just breathe. When he comes in, ask for his name and his number first. Then...*

She felt someone looking at her and at that moment glanced up to see Mr. X walking toward her from the other side of the lobby, beyond the fountain. Their eyes locked and she froze. He looked amazing, even taller than she remembered, even more darkly handsome than his *Nost* photo. His jet-black hair was perfectly combed. He smiled slightly as he saw her, a knowing smile. She felt a shiver run down her spine. It was as if he could see straight through her dress, straight to her sexy new lingerie, and the fact that she was already feeling a slickness between her legs. Just looking at the man made her wet.

He wore a button-down shirt and a leather jacket that only made his shoulders look broader. He covered the distance between them in no time.

"You look amazing," he told her, hazel eyes bright as he took a long sweep of her outfit.

"I hoped you'd like it," she said, feeling suddenly self-conscious.

"Oh, I do," he said, slipping his hand around the back of her waist. She moved into him and he kissed her, lightly. She deepened the kiss, lacing her hands around the back of his neck. He tasted like cinnamon: gum he must've been chewing. His hands wandered down the back of her dress, his hands squeezing her hips and running down the length of her.

When they finally broke apart, Emma's heart thudded in her chest. The fire between them was unmistakable, the attraction palpable. Emma no longer cared about the bellhops, or the hotel workers behind the desk.

"I want you," Mr. X murmured, so softly only she could hear. She nodded slowly.

"I want you, too." Emma hesitated. "But…first… what's your name?"

Mr. X grinned. "You know my name."

"Mr. X isn't your full name."

Mr. X considered her. "You want to know my name?" She nodded once more. "Then, you have to do something for me."

Emma felt the nerves tighten in her stomach. "Yes?"

Mr. X chuckled, a deep growl in his throat. She bit her bottom lip, waiting. He glanced around the lobby and then leaned in, his lips near her ear. "See that bathroom over there? Why don't you go in. Slip out of that sexy underwear you're wearing and bring it back to me."

Emma's head shot from side to side, as she glanced around the lobby, her face growing hot at the mere suggestion. But suddenly she wanted to do it. She liked the idea, even. Him telling her what to do. Her doing it. Something felt naughty about it. Naughty but right.

"All right." She accepted the challenge with a nod.

She walked to the restroom, giving a quick glance over her shoulder. Mr. X leaned on the bar, watching every movement she made. She felt exhilarated then: he wanted her, just as much as she wanted him.

She pushed open the bathroom door to find one of the nicest bathrooms she'd ever seen: marble white countertops and gleaming floors. Real towels instead of paper ones, heavy oak doors that went all the way to the floor. The bathroom was empty and she slipped into the first stall. Her heart thudded in her chest as she raised the hem of her black dress. What was she doing? Was she really going to hand him her underwear? But then, she thought of the glint in his golden eyes, the spark of a challenge. She felt empowered suddenly as she whipped her thin, black lace thong off. Then she heard the bathroom door open and shoes clacking on the tile floor.

A soft knock came on her door. She jumped, startled.

"Ready for me?" Mr. X's smooth voice asked from the other side of the stall door. She whipped it open, shocked.

"What are you…" She didn't get to finish, before he'd swept in and was kissing her passionately, his hands on the hem of her dress. He yanked it upwards, revealing her bareness and her thigh-highs. He whistled, low.

"You are so fucking sexy," he murmured, as he leaned in and touched her, his fingers slipping into her wetness. She moaned and so did he as he worked her most tender spot. He bent down and kissed her, slipping his tongue into her mouth as his expert fingers brought her to the brink. She couldn't believe this was happening—a bathroom? The thought flittered across her mind. She'd never in a million years thought of having sex here…but now, with Mr. X's hands on her, all rational thought disappeared.

He flipped her around then in the oversized stall so that her hands were up on the wall, her dress pushed up to her waist, her legs trembling and inner thighs slick with wet. She heard him unzip, and the condom package rip open and then he was taking her from behind, filling her up with every inch of himself, and she gasped, louder than she intended, as her hands pressed against the slick tiled wall.

"I want you to come for me," he growled in her ear.

"I…" Could she? Her whole body felt like it was on fire, her whole self wanted him in a way she'd never wanted anyone.

"I want you to touch yourself," he commanded, in a voice that left no room for argument. She was hyperaware that at any moment, someone could walk in, someone could hear them.

"Touch yourself," he demanded again, and then she did, her hand snaking downward, finding her sweet center. This was what she wanted. Pure, unadulterated lust, taken by a man who couldn't wait to get her in a bed. Couldn't wait to even get her fully undressed.

She pushed against her own hand, as he delved deeper and harder in her. She could feel the tension

build. Oh, God, could she. Not caring about who
might come in or who might hear them, she let go,
toppling over the edge in a furious, urgent climax.
She let out a shout, even as he, too, came inside her
with a hard thrust. He collapsed against her, breathing hard.

"You are…so fucking perfect," he growled in her
ear, as if even he couldn't believe it. "What are you
doing to me?"

Her legs felt like jelly, and she didn't even know
if she could move just yet. He withdrew, discarded
the condom and zipped up, then kissed her neck as
she pulled down the hem of her skirt. One thigh-high
was now down around her knee.

"I'll keep these," he promised, tucking her G-
string in his pocket. Then, he kissed the back of her
neck once more.

"You promised your name," she said.

"Xavier," he said and slipped out of the stall.

"Xavier… What?" she asked, staying behind to
straighten out her thigh-highs. She'd never had such
an amazing orgasm so fast in a public space before.
She felt light-headed and overcome, her knees literally wobbled as she stood up. The storm of passion had left her spent and panting, unsure of what
to do next. Her head spun. The last time she'd even
done anything so…public was in her college dorm
study lounge.

"Xavier?" she called once more, but heard no response. She came out of the stall to find the rest-

room empty. Was he outside? She smoothed her now mussed hair as she rushed out.

The lobby, however, was empty.

Xavier was nowhere to be found.

CHAPTER NINE

XAVIER JUMPED INTO a waiting cab as his heart beat rapidly in his chest. He could still smell her on him, on his clothes, and his veins still buzzed with arousal and yearning for her. She ought to be in his arms right now. Hell, he ought to have taken her upstairs to a new room and taken her eight more times. But he couldn't. He was getting pulled in, as if Emma were quicksand. He'd felt that urge for more grow in him just when he thought it ought to be abating. He wanted to spend the night with her again and wake up with her in his arms, and he couldn't do that. He knew what it would mean if he did. He was falling for this girl. As he came he'd almost said, *I love you*.

Never before had he felt such swift emotions, not during sex, and certainly not with what amounted to a stranger. The last time he'd felt so consumed had been Sasha. And he had no intention of making that mistake again.

Leaving her now was the best thing he could do for them both. He'd thought that he could get her out of his system by having one last night with her, but now, he realized, she was like a highly addictive drug: the more times he went back, the more he'd need her. And he couldn't do that. He wasn't ready. Sasha had torn out his heart and he vowed never to let another woman get that close to him again.

His phone pinged, the *Nost* app alerting him to the fact that her profile was officially disappearing from his app in less than fifteen minutes. There was nothing he could do to prolong the inevitable. He'd been the one to engineer it, after all, and despite his partners wanting a fail-safe, a way of extending time, he'd been bullheaded about that feature.

"Can't close the deal in forty-eight? Then you start over," he'd said. And eventually he'd gotten everyone to agree with him. "You want a longer relationship than that? Then head to Bumble."

The board had eventually agreed. They couldn't be the "looking for love" app when they were strictly about no-strings. It was the way to set themselves apart in an already crowded market. But now, Xavier doubted himself. Had he done the right thing?

Still, he had her number. He had a way to contact her. He knew where she worked.

Can't do it, he told himself. *The sex was amazing, but that's all it was.* The words rang hollow even in his own head. He knew he was lying to himself, and yet, he stubbornly refused to admit it.

Instead, he decided to hit the gym. That's where he went to work out his frustrations and maybe after an hour or two lifting weights his mind would be clearer and he'd get his mind off Emma's gorgeous, lean body and the way she gave herself so freely, came so deeply. He'd never had a woman offer up so much of herself to him so willingly, and he wondered if that included her heart as well. Would she love him as passionately as she fucked him? Thoughts of love unnerved him. What was he doing? He'd decided long ago that love was toxic. Why would he want that now?

He felt the urge to pull up Emma's Facebook, but then stopped himself. What was he doing? Becoming some creepy tech stalker? No. He needed to pull himself together. Emma was amazing, and their time together had been outstanding. But the *Nost* clock had less than one minute left.

Then, a message lit up his screen.

Where are you? she wrote to him on *Nost*. I...

Then, the app reset, her profile disappeared and the rest of the message was lost.

Emma watched her phone reconfigure *Nost*. Mr. X was suddenly gone from the app, and there was no way to find him, no way to continue the message.

"Damn it," she cursed as she sank into a leather couch near the fountain in the hotel lobby. What was she supposed to do now? She'd searched the bar, the lobby, and had even walked out to the street, but had found no sign of Mr. X. Xavier. That's all she knew about the man. She had no idea where he lived, how old he was, or what he did for a living other than the vague "work in the tech sector" explanation he'd given her.

Emma could feel a delicious soreness creeping in between her legs. Just moments ago Xavier had filled her up in the most intimate way possible, and now he was gone forever, a ghost, a stranger she might never see again. She couldn't understand why he'd left so quickly, why he'd bolted. Had she offended him in some way? Had she done something wrong?

Why had he left in such a hurry? She needed to know. She wanted to know. She had to see him again.

Maybe he was a wanted man, she wondered. It would explain a lot, and yet, Emma wouldn't believe Xavier was a felon. He'd told her about his fiancée betraying him and breaking his heart, but she'd never met a man so clearly petrified of commitment. She'd heard of toxic bachelors, but this was ridiculous. Emma glanced up at the lobby desk manned by a hotel clerk, a young man in his twenties. Emma got up and walked toward him. Maybe she could get answers.

"Hello." The clerk greeted her with a friendly smile. "May I help you, miss?"

"I was wondering if you could tell me if Xavier booked a room tonight. He had one last night. We were in room…" Emma stopped. What room were they in? 12…something. 1209? 1208? She racked her brain. She knew it was the twelfth floor, but why couldn't she remember? Granted, she'd been a little busy when Xavier had swept her inside to notice much about the golden numbers on the door. He'd had his mouth on hers, a memory that made her shiver with delight remembering his soft, determined tongue as it gently probed her. She felt her face flush. "Uh, a big suite. On the 12th floor. Maybe 1209?"

The clerk now studied her with suspicion. "There are *several* suites on the twelfth floor. Your name, miss?"

"Uh, Emma Allaire. But the room wasn't in my name. It was under Xavier's."

"Xavier...?" The clerk paused, waiting for the last name. But Emma didn't know it. That's what she needed to find out.

"Yes, Xavier."

"Xavier...*what*? His last name, please?"

Emma bit her lip. She realized she was going to get zero information from this clerk. She was sure this hotel had all kinds of privacy rules, and now that she thought about it, it was probably insane to just go asking about hotel guests. Besides, what was she supposed to tell this man? She'd had sex *multiple* times with a man and she didn't even know his last name? In fact, she could still feel the wetness of her own come between her legs from him taking in her their very restroom just a hundred feet away.

Emma glanced at the young clerk. No, he wouldn't understand.

"Never mind. I'll just call him." She held up her phone as if somehow Xavier's number might magically appear on her screen. Emma hustled away from the lobby counter, her face red with embarrassment. Even with a first name, she knew next to nothing about the man who'd made her come harder than anyone ever. Of course, now she knew his first name.

Maybe she could find something on Google or Facebook? Maybe if she went home and tried, she might.

Emma rushed out to the dark Chicago night and hailed the first cab she saw, hoping that once she got home she might still be able to find the mystery man.

The next morning, after a few hours Googling "Xavier" and "tech" Emma came up with absolutely nothing. "Xavier" and "Chicago" yielded thousands of entries, none of whom seemed to fit Mr. X, though she discovered a local Xavier College, an apartment building and one restaurant. None of which were connected to Mr. X in any discernible way.

"This is so frustrating," Emma complained out loud as she set her coffee mug down on her desk with a little extra force. This was the digital age, after all, where all information was supposed to be a single Google search away. She'd never been in a position where a few clicks of the mouse wouldn't open up someone's whole identity.

Emma shook her head, scouring her memory for any little detail she could've missed about Mr. X, anything else she might type into Facebook, Instagram or Google. She couldn't think of any. The man had been deliberately vague about all the details of his life. She didn't know where he lived, worked, his last name, or even where he'd grown up. Then again, they hadn't spent a whole helluva lot of time talking, either, she remembered, a blush creeping up her cheeks.

I shouldn't even be doing this, Emma thought.

The man left me in the Ritz-Carlton bathroom, half naked! Clearly, all he wanted was sex.

Not that she could blame him. The sex was freakin' amazing. The sex enough would be fine, yet, Emma couldn't shake the feeling there could be more than just physical attraction between them. She believed that amazing sex only happened with some kind of authentic emotional connection. They might be near strangers, but they had that connection. Somehow.

And he walked away from it.

She ought to be angry, but instead, she just felt mystified. Why had he bolted? Her mind went a thousand different directions: maybe she'd offended him somehow. Maybe he was really just using her and could *only* stand to be in her presence for the frantic minutes it took for sex?

But that didn't make any sense to her. He never let on he felt annoyed by her. *The first night, he'd held her all night long.*

No. It was almost as if he was fighting himself a little last night, but she couldn't say why.

Emma knew Xavier had been hurt, *knew* he wasn't looking for any commitment and he'd made it abundantly clear that he was only interested in knowing her for forty-eight hours. She ought to just face facts: he'd disappeared forever.

The thought suddenly depressed her. How could he walk away from something so…amazing? Surely, she wasn't the only one who felt like the sex was… well, white-hot. Surely he didn't have that kind of connection with every girl he met? Emma knew she'd never experienced sex like that her whole life.

She almost heard Sarah whispering, "You need to get laid more."

Emma sighed. Maybe it was that she'd only had a handful of boyfriends, all of them…well, on the boring side. She brushed away the thought. Why would Xavier be in such a hurry to leave?

Left on autopilot, her mind went to darker corners. Was he secretly married? His wife could have been *waiting outside in their car* while he came into the lobby of the hotel. Her palms grew clammy at the thought.

Emma typed in *Nost* and *married men* and about a dozen articles popped up on her screen. The headlines screamed at her: *Nost a Playground for Adulterers*…and *No Strings Doesn't Always Mean Single*…

Emma pored through the articles. Looks like *Nost* did have a cheater problem, with several spurned spouses—men and women—complaining about finding the app on the phone of their husband or wife. Could Xavier be one of them? It made sense: he was steadfastly attached to the "no contact" rule and guarded his last name with CIA-level dedication. Hell, his first name might not even be real.

She banged the edge of her desk in frustration. What was she supposed to do now?

Emma picked up her phone and noticed that her screen now included all new *Nost* men, none of whom were Mr. X. A search again found nothing, and there was no way to message him any longer.

She put her phone down. Emma stared at her computer for a beat and then pulled up a new Word document. Maybe if she couldn't find him, she could write about him. She began typing out her story about *Nost*. She worked on it furiously for the next couple of hours. She called it:

Mr. X, where are you?

When she'd poured out her emotions, doubts and fears onto the page, she sent off the draft to her editor and let out a breath. She had no idea if her article, written as PG as possible, was too risqué for the women's blog, but she was willing to take that chance. She crossed her fingers that somehow her little message in a bottle would make it to Xavier.

CHAPTER TEN

FOR THE REST of the week, Xavier felt…empty and alone. The feeling that he'd been making a huge mistake walking away from Emma at the Ritz-Carlton hadn't faded, and had only grown in its intensity. Rather than fade from his memory, Emma just loomed larger and larger, until almost every waking thought was of her. Her lips, her amazing curves, the softness of her skin. The way she simply *gave* herself to him, the completely vulnerable way she let him pleasure her. The out-of-this-world look on her face when she came for him.

Emma. What are you doing to me? He wondered, as he sat in his townhome in the west Loop, just blocks from his office. From his second-story bedroom window, he watched a couple walking together, hand-in-hand, down Jackson Boulevard, swinging their arms, happy as they laughed together beneath the unseasonably warm September sunshine on a bright Saturday afternoon. He envied their happiness, but he also felt it was all fake somehow. He knew that no matter how happy they seemed, beneath the surface trouble could be brewing. After all, Sasha held his hand, kissed him, even took him to bed while seeking the affection of another man.

Sure, all relationships started out filled with passion, but eventually they all petered out, under the weight of routine and familiarity. Or, they become something worse. Something harder. Like his parents' troubled relationship. He shook his head. No way was he going to become like his father, a slave to love.

He and Sasha had ripped their clothes off the night they met, but then a year later, beneath ratty old T-shirts and dozens of nights in the same bed, they had grown tired of one another, bored. Sex had become mechanical, predictable. No wonder she'd looked outside their relationship for satisfaction. He couldn't blame her. The passion that had once lit their relationship had fled.

Xavier pulled up his *Nost* profile on his phone but barely even looked at it. This was not like him at all. Normally, he was already on to his next challenge, his next anonymous rendezvous. The last year since Sasha had been a blur of bodies for the most part. He knew on some level it wasn't the healthiest way to get over his ex, but it sure was the most fun. Instead of browsing through the new candidates on his phone, he headed to the laptop in his study and once more pulled up Emma's profile. She'd been active in the last twenty-four hours, he saw, sending a little pang of jealousy through him. Had she already gotten over him? Was she trolling for new mates as he sat here at his computer?

His fingers froze on the keyboard. Would he snoop to find out? No. He shouldn't. That broke every privacy rule *Nost* had.

Get a hold of yourself, Xavier said. *What are you doing?*

He decided to Google her once more. That was safer than digging through her *Nost* profile—safer and not opening him or *Nost* up to a lawsuit, either, he mused. With a few quick clicks he discovered Emma had posted a new article for *Helena.* About *him.*

Interest piqued, he scanned the article.

Where is Mr. X? I never thought I'd ever use an app like Nost, or like it, but...

Xavier scanned the article, eating up every word. She enjoyed every minute of being with him, she said, enjoyed the freedom, the intimacy, the immediate connection. He knew they'd connected, but seeing it written in black and white delighted him. The way she described him was godlike. He grinned to himself. He hadn't even used *all* his best tricks. He still had some in reserve for...

When? When would he ever see her again? Their time was up. Forty-eight hours. That was his rule, but...

He glanced at her small profile picture that hovered above her article. Cornflower-blue eyes, lush blond hair, amazing pink lips. He remembered her small, pink nipples, the way they puckered beneath the caress of his tongue. Remembered below her waist, her delicate pink folds. He wanted to taste her again, make her arch her back and squirm with pleasure, see that amazing look in her eyes when she let the whole world go and embraced the climax he gave her.

He just wanted her.

He glanced once more at the end of the article.

Mr. X, if you're out there, find me at the Brew Coffee House. North Avenue. Four p.m. Saturday.

Xavier glanced at his watch. He had an hour to make it. If he really wanted to leave Emma in his past, stick to his rules, he'd let her wait. But he also felt desire growing inside him, a white-hot burn. She was asking for him. Could he really refuse?

By the time the fourth awkward, pimpled and over-weight guy stumbled up to her and claimed to be *Mr. X* at the Brew Coffee House, Emma was beginning to think her idea to call out Mr. X publicly had backfired.

"You're not Mr. X," she told the twenty-some-thing, acne-prone gamer who stood before her wearing a *Game of Thrones* T-shirt. He shuffled his massive feet.

"No, but I totally am!" he insisted, pushing up his flat-brimmed baseball cap to reveal unwashed, greasy hair beneath.

"You're not," she said, shaking her head. He didn't fight too much harder, and eventually shrugged and left. The cup of coffee she'd gotten half an hour ago now sat empty and she wondered how much longer she ought to keep this up. Mr. X clearly wasn't coming. He might not have even seen her article, and even if he did, might have chosen to ignore it. After all, he had the forty-eight-hour rule. No strings. No attachments.

But Emma wasn't asking to marry him. Just… explore him. A little longer. She just wasn't ready to let him go yet. He'd become a craving, more than that, an addiction. Something she didn't just *want,* she *needed.* The idea of going back to her boring, vanilla boyfriend sex life just felt horrible. She didn't want to do that. She wanted Mr. X.

Emma scribbled down a few notes on a notepad about *Game of Thrones* guy and figured that at least this would give her enough material for another article. Her *Helena* editor had *loved* the *Nost* piece, and no wonder, it was the top trending article on the blog and already had thousands of shares on social media. The article was blowing up, and Emma thought that was in no small part because more and more users were intrigued by *Nost,* and she was the good-girl-next-door who'd tried it and liked it. The story almost sold itself.

But then there was the thorny problem of Mr. X. Was he married? At least thirty percent of *Helena*'s readers thought so, if the comments on the post were any indication. *Keep moving, honey. He's married,* wrote one. Or, *Available men don't disappear like that. He probably has a wife and kids in the 'burbs,* wrote another. One woman had simply written *TOXIC BACHELOR* in the comments section and another wrote *escaped felon?* And he might be all these things. Or none of them.

Yet, deep inside, Emma just felt he wasn't. He was a man who'd been hurt by love, betrayed by the one woman tasked with loving him above all others, and this was his way of dealing with it. She took what he said at face value. She knew she might not be able to change him, and probably couldn't. He'd flat-out told her he wasn't able to have a real relationship. Yet she couldn't shake the feeling that they belonged together. How many couples fit together so well? The sex wasn't just sex. At least not to her.

She might not be able to change him, she figured, but she just wanted to know him better. That's all.

She glanced around the near empty coffeehouse and sighed. This was a bust. An absolute bust. What a waste of time! Emma let out a long sigh as she gathered up her things, her flowered peasant top sliding down, revealing one bare shoulder. She wore a flouncy skirt and sandals, knowing that the warmth of this rare mild autumn afternoon would soon be traded for the chill of October. The summer seemed to be having one last hooray in September, but she knew the cold winds off Lake Michigan would arrive soon and they'd all settle in to coats and gloves for the rest of the season. She stood, about to leave, when a dark shadow fell over her table.

She glanced up to see Mr. X, wearing a simple dark T-shirt and cargo shorts. The T-shirt left nothing about his muscular chest to the imagination, and as she pulled her gaze away from his impressive muscles, she locked eyes with the man she'd been searching for for days.

"Xavier," she breathed, her heart thudding in her chest. "Where did you come from?"

"The door," he said smoothly and grinned. "Am I late?"

"Yes…er, n-no. Sit." Emma slumped back in her chair, feeling part shocked and part giddy. *He'd come. She'd called on him and he'd come.* "You… saw my story."

Xavier gave a single head nod, his golden hazel eyes never leaving hers as he slipped gracefully into the seat, all lean muscle, all stealth. "I especially enjoyed the part about…our kiss, but we did more than that."

"I—it had to be PG," she explained. How else to talk about how *Helena* wasn't the kind of magazine that published explicit sex.

"I liked our x-rated parts the best." Xavier flashed white teeth beneath his tanned face. The man was gorgeous, a dark-haired god. Emma forgot how much she felt the charismatic pull to him, and realized that she hadn't been crazy about letting this man do what he would with her—the electricity, the connection between them, couldn't be denied.

Xavier leaned forward. "Maybe we ought to retreat to the bathroom?" He let the offer hang there, and Emma's mind went straight back to the Ritz-Carlton, where he'd taken her, panting, inside the stall. She'd never done anything like that her whole life, yet as soon as he mentioned it, her whole body tingled in anticipation. Then she remembered—The Brew didn't have bathrooms.

"No bathrooms here," she said, of the tiny little coffeehouse with only a couple of tables. The counter took up one whole wall of the establishment, and then windows and the door were on the opposite. The bathroom, if there was one, was for employees only.

"That's a shame." Xavier's hand snaked out under the table and rested on her knee, and she could feel the heat and the heaviness of his hand through the thin fabric. He then moved his hand beneath her skirt, his hand touching the bare skin of her inner thigh. She sucked in a breath. Here, in the middle of a public shop, he had his hand up her skirt. He stroked her inner thigh, inching ever higher. Emma's heart beat harder as Xavier's index finger reached the fabric of her panties. He gently laid pressure through the thin fabric, a temptation, a promise.

Emma had never wished for a bathroom so much in her life. She could feel her insides turning to warm mush, her arousal growing as his finger gently probed her through the fabric, which, she thought, had to be drenched. A patron came in through the front door then and Xavier withdrew his hand, and Emma felt its cold absence. Now her body was abuzz with a million wants, and the man who could fulfill them leaned back in his chair across the table and took a sip of coffee, calm as ever.

"Are you married?" Emma blurted, suddenly.

Xavier nearly spit out his coffee. "No."

"In a relationship? Pregnant girlfriend at home?"

"No! Of course not. I'm on *Nost*." He acted as if the idea was preposterous.

"I read about married men...and women...seeking...fun on *Nost*. It's a perfect cover, right? No names, no strings, no way of your spouse finding out you're cheating." Emma's voice was rising and she worked hard to keep it down. *Keep calm.*

"Well, that's unfortunate that some are not who they say they are." Xavier frowned. "I'm sure that's not what *Nost* intended. In fact, I think it says something about that in the user agreement."

Emma waved her hands, not caring about the fine print of *Nost*. "Why did you run out on me?" This was the hardest question, and she wasn't even sure she wanted to know the answer. "At the Ritz-Carlton?"

Xavier studied her a moment. "I was scared," he finally admitted, shifting uncomfortably in his chair and not meeting her gaze.

"Scared?" Emma didn't understand.

"I...want more from you. More than forty-eight hours."

Emma's heart leaped. "That's exactly what I want." She leaned forward and grabbed both his hands with hers. "Why don't we do that? Here... Here's my phone number." She frantically scribbled on the pad of paper, gave him her name and phone number. "You can give me yours, and we can start there." He stared at the paper on the table. But instead of looking excited, he looked...sad.

"Emma, if we continue on, this relationship won't last," he said.

She felt as if he'd struck her, the pain, the disappointment sliced through her. Did he not like her as much as she liked him after all? "What do you mean?"

He squeezed her hand and studied her hand linked in his. "It'll grow old. All relationships do. It'll get comfortable. Predictable. Or worse, volatile." He spoke as if the words left a bitter taste in his mouth. "And then, regardless, boring or volatile, you or I... will stray. That's what happens."

"Not to *all* relationships," Emma protested.

"To all the ones I've had," he said, and she saw the fresh pain of his fiancée's betrayal on his face.

"But you can't assume all women are like...her." She wasn't Sasha. How could she prove it? "I'm not the kind of woman to cheat."

Xavier laughed, a bitter, hollow sound. "Emma, all people can cheat, given the right circumstances. People aren't like penguins. We don't mate for life. People get bored, they get tired, they get frustrated. I'm not so sure it's possible to have a healthy, monogamous relationship."

Emma sighed in frustration. None of what he told her was exactly new. Hadn't he admitted after they first met that that's why he liked *Nost* so much? Why was she surprised to find a commitment-phobic man on *Nost*? Yet she just couldn't give up on the connection they had. She wasn't ready to walk away yet.

"But don't you want to explore...this?" She gestured between the two of them with her free hand. "You can't have this—what I'm feeling—with just anyone."

That made Xavier pause and think. Right then she knew he felt more than he was saying. He felt their strong bond, too. This was more than just white-hot sex, more than just two people wildly attracted to one another. Something real lay beneath, something that felt like they'd met before. Emma didn't believe in reincarnation, but if she did, she'd swear they'd met in a previous life.

"This…is real," Emma said, squeezing his hand tighter.

"If you knew me, if you *really* knew me, then all of this…this chemistry…would disappear." Xavier sounded so sure.

"How can you be so sure? I mean, it might. You're right. There's a risk it could. But what if it didn't?" Emma shifted her legs beneath the table and her knee touched his. She could feel the electric current of want flow between them and as he leaned in, she knew he felt it, too.

"Want to go for a walk?" he asked her.

CHAPTER ELEVEN

EMMA WALKED BESIDE Xavier down the crowded street of North Avenue, strangers passing them, seemingly unaware of the current running between the couple. The late-afternoon air had turned cooler, as the sun dipped below the horizon, setting a blue tint to everything. Night was coming, but it wasn't quite here yet. The slight breeze ruffled the changing leaves as a few yellow ones fell at their feet. Emma could almost feel it: a force field of desire, a pull between them. He was the earth and she was the moon, attached by gravity, an invisible force, aware of every little move he made.

As they walked, he slipped his hand over hers, possessive, a promise.

"I already knew about you, Emma Allaire," Xavier said suddenly.

"What do you mean?" she asked, thinking about the paper she'd scribbled in the coffee shop. The paper that Xavier hadn't taken. She'd folded it and tucked it in her bag.

"I searched you on Google," he admitted. "You

told me the magazine where you worked, so it wasn't hard to find you. Your Facebook page is set to public, by the way. Did you intend that?"

Emma felt hot suddenly. He'd searched for her? Just as she'd searched for him. Then, of course, he had to: after all, he'd found her at the coffee shop, hadn't he? Read the article she wrote? But the fact that he was admitting to wanting to know more about her, admitting to not being satisfied with them being perfect strangers, linked only in carnal knowledge, went against his life philosophy, didn't it? Maybe she was getting to him, tearing down the walls he'd built to protect himself, to keep her out.

"You broke your own rules, then." Emma felt strangely smug in pointing that out.

Xavier gave her a sidelong glance, his eyes looking almost golden in the autumn sunlight. "Yes," he admitted. "You intrigued me."

"You intrigued me, too. I searched you as well. But you gave me nothing to go on."

Xavier chuckled, low in his throat. "I know."

"Give me one detail. Just one."

The two passed a narrow alleyway between two brownstones. Xavier pulled her into it and around the corner, protected by a Dumpster on one side and a brick wall partition on the other. "Kiss me first," he demanded, voice low, a gravelly whisper.

Her lips parted, and all she could do was nod her head. Xavier swooped down, claiming her mouth, and suddenly the heat flared between them, their mouths and tongues wrapped together in an ancient

mating dance of want and desire. God, she wanted
him, the passion flaring, her need growing as he
delved into her mouth again and again. They devoured each other, the passion like none she'd ever
experienced. Was it because she knew that he could
disappear from her life at any moment? Was it because he *was* a stranger? A man who stubbornly refused to open himself up to her? To give her a detail
as small as his last name? Could it be that he was a
blank canvas, someone she could project everything
on to, the perfect man?

She didn't know. All she knew in that moment
was that her body became a melted puddle of want,
that in that moment, passion made her a slave. She'd
do whatever he asked, whenever he asked it in that
second. She'd long forgotten about the people passing by just around the corner on the sidewalk, or the
fact that in the alley, even in the darkening dusk,
they could still be seen by a row of condo windows.
She didn't care who saw them. All she wanted was
more of his mouth and his hands, as they roamed her
body. She might not know his name, but she knew
his hands, the sure way they possessed her, stroked
her, made her beg for more. Emma suddenly didn't
care that she was in public, in the darkening dusk,
partially hidden and yet still visible. All she cared
about was getting more of Xavier, of not wanting
this moment to end.

"I want you. Here," Xavier growled in her ear,
and then his hands were inside the thin lace of her

thong, feeling how much she wanted him, too. "I want you now."

All thoughts of caution fled her mind. She was just a pulsating nerve of want, nothing more. She'd never done anything like this before: in public, barely covered by the darkening light. Yet, she wanted him just as much as he wanted her. She pushed her own thong off her hips and it dropped to the ground. She felt the coolness of the night air slide between her thighs. She felt exposed, but it only added to her desire, her want. She was ready. Suddenly, Xavier lifted her, pressing her against the brick wall of the alley, taking her with his whole self. She gasped with shock and pleasure, instinctively wrapping her legs around his waist as he pushed inside her, his eyes meeting hers, the want in them as strong as her own. Emma took him all, feeling reckless, feeling how deliciously wrong this was: a stranger, an alley, herself, exposed to anyone who happened by, doing the thing good girls never did. Good girls never did this with strangers, in public. Yet, here she was, spreading her legs eagerly, letting him in, ready for him; the combination of adrenaline and want sent her instantly over the edge, as she hit a ragged climax, swallowing the shout of pleasure in her throat.

Xavier came as well, in a last urgent and shuddering thrust before quickly withdrawing.

"I want a detail," she murmured to him in the dark, grabbing a fistful of his shirt. "I want to know your last name."

"If you knew that, you wouldn't have come for

me so hard," he warned, voice low as he zipped up. "You wouldn't have let me take you here."

"You promised a detail," she pressed. "For a kiss. And I gave you more than a kiss." She was still panting as Xavier glanced back and forth, looking for witnesses. Then he leaned forward and whispered the digits of a phone number in her ear. He kissed her hard and left her wanting more.

Emma memorized the digits, repeating them in her head long after they'd gone separate ways from the alley. She watched as Xavier moved down the crowded public sidewalk. She was spent and sore, feeling like she might be standing on the edge of a precipice with no way down. Should she follow him? She felt weak-kneed and spent. Had she just fucked him in public? In full view of the condo window across the alley? She'd no idea if someone had seen, and she hurried on her way down the block and back to the safety of her own condo, so quickly she'd abandoned her thong on the concrete ground. She wondered what on earth had come over her. But then she knew what had: Xavier. His hands, his steady hazel eyes, his jet-black hair. The way he fit inside her perfectly, seemed to hit every nerve ending in her body all at once.

Was he right? Was the chemistry between them just because were strangers? Emma didn't feel this with the men she saw on the sidewalk, or on the train, or passing her in the aisle of the grocery store. Being strangers didn't automatically mean chemistry.

She stuck resolutely to her belief that she and Xavier shared something: a past life, a spiritual connection, *something* that made the sex so amazingly mind-blowing, that made her want him so badly that she took off her thong in an alley for him, let him inside her in the darkening dusk.

Would the sex be as wild, be as amazing, if they were a couple? Sleeping over in each other's beds, knowing the ins and outs of each other's routines? She thought about her past boyfriends, about knowing all the little details: the sound of their snores, their favorite Thai takeout dishes, their childhood stories. Had that made the sex…boring as well? Predictable?

The more sex she had with Xavier, the more… unpredictable, hotter, it got. She'd never in a million years guess she'd let him take her against a brick wall outside, just a few feet from a bustling city street, yet she had. She'd wanted it as much as he had. Was that because she didn't know him? Would knowing him make her too shy, too embarrassed to do those things?

Emma wondered. Still, it didn't stop her from immediately typing in the phone number he'd given her to try to find its owner. Every site she tried came up with a dead end. The number, whatever it was, wasn't registered to anyone. A burner phone? Maybe.

She decided to text it and find out.

I want to know your last name, she texted.

Well, hello to you, kitten, Xavier wrote back almost instantly, as if he'd been waiting for her. I enjoyed you today. Did you enjoy me?

Yes, she typed, her fingers trembling slightly as she remembered the passion with which he took her just a half hour ago.

I love the way you feel. You were made for me.

And you for me, she typed. I've never done that before. Outside. In public.

I know, he wrote, as if he could read her mind. But, that's what can happen between two strangers. No inhibitions.

You're not a stranger to me, she said. I know what you like. How you come. Your body. She knew how he came, the look on his face of pure release. She knew the little shuddering movement he made when he was done, a little hiccup unique to him, and the rush of air from his lungs when he did. That made them less than strangers. She knew he never came before she did, she knew he was always determined to please her first. She knew his touch drove her wild.

You already know too much.

I want to know more, she furiously typed back.

And then, Mr. X went quiet. No more texts. Emma stared at her phone, wondering where he'd gone. To work? She had no idea where he even worked. There were dozens of tech companies, and he'd been deliberately vague. Home to his wife?

He'd said he wasn't married. She believed him, and yet…he seemed so extremely commitment-phobic for a man who'd only lost a fiancée. Sure, that was traumatic, but this felt so…extreme. Emma wondered about that. Was there an extreme form of commitment phobia? Was it a *condition*? She ran a quick Google search.

"Relationship anxiety," she read aloud, skimming a few psychology articles. "…in its most extreme forms means a person is afraid to make a real commitment to another. This can be caused by the end of a relationship they didn't see coming, or, in some cases, childhood trauma."

Emma paused then. Childhood trauma? Could this be it?

She skimmed further. Most often, she read, sufferers of extreme commitment phobia failed to have secure bonding with one or both parents, or they might have been hurt by someone they trusted, a relative or caregiver. "Sometimes," she read, "those with the severest cases of relationship anxiety often show conflicting signs: they might be passionate one minute, and aloof the next."

Emma nodded her head with conviction. That was Xavier in a nutshell.

"To cure relationship anxiety, the sufferer often needs to confront his or her past and understand that those traumas might not be repeated in the present," she read aloud. She wondered if it would be that easy? She shut off her computer. Was she really going to diagnose his psychological failings by Google? Wasn't she projecting her own thoughts and worries *onto* him? That's what happened when she didn't know him. All she could do was guess.

I want to see you. Dinner tonight? She tried.

Emma stared at her screen but saw nothing. No reply. Had she lost him? Was he just in an aloof phase? Still, she couldn't shake the feeling that her fishing line had gone slack and he'd cut bait.

Xavier stared at his burner phone, the one he only used for *Nost,* at Emma's invitation. Every fiber of his body wanted to say yes, wanted to see her again, smell her lavender shampoo once more, feel her again: soft, wet and willing. But the very need that rose in his chest scared him. He hadn't felt this needy since growing up as a child, alone in his room, his father desperately trying to talk his mother down from one of her rages. Later, of course, he'd know it was that she was bipolar, but that would only come after. He buried those memories of his mother so very deeply that he wondered why he thought of her now. She'd died when he was just nine. His memories of her seemed vague at best, though he knew that sometimes she was vibrant, energized, unstoppable, the brightest star in the room, not caring who she burnt, and other times, she wouldn't leave her bed for days at a time. Papi remained loyal to her her whole life, and when he questioned why, his father told him, *you can't choose who you love.* The old romantic. Look what it had gotten him: a troubled marriage, the early death of his wife, almost a whole lifetime living without her.

He shook the thought away. He could choose *not* to love, couldn't he? He shut off his burner phone and tucked it into his pocket, vowing not to look at it for the rest of the week.

CHAPTER TWELVE

EMMA TOOK A deep swig of her gin and tonic as she sat at the crowded bar in the heart of Wrigleyville. Outside, the sidewalks were thick with bar hoppers, and the air was chilled with coming fall. The Cubs had long since finished their game at nearby Wrigley Field, though the revelers hung on, still celebrating the first post-season victory.

"You need to let him go," Sarah advised, as she took a sip of her vodka soda. She wore her red hair up in a messy bun, and a slinky sweater, skinny jeans and open-toed ankle boots that showed off a new cherry-red pedicure. "He's been AWOL for a week, he probably gave you a burner number and, anyway, he's not responding… I mean, the writing is on the wall."

"But…we *had* something," Emma protested, staring moodily into her glass. She'd barely paid attention to her outfit: a slouchy sweater that kept sliding off one shoulder and black leggings. She wore her hair loose and naturally dried, the natural waves showing through. The vibe around them was boisterous and loud, but Emma just felt isolated and alone. Despite being surrounded by attractive men, she only wanted to think about Xavier.

"You mean you *had* amazing sex," Sarah corrected, thumping her glass down on the bar for emphasis. "And you never know, it could've gone south when you found out he still lives in his mom's basement and spends his off time smoking weed."

"He doesn't do that!"

"How do you know?" Sarah arched an eyebrow and Emma sighed. She didn't know, not really. She didn't know the man's last name, much less where he lived.

"It's driving me insane. You can find *anything* out about *anybody* these days just on your phone!" Emma waved her smartphone in the air. "But he's a black box. It's just not right."

"Maybe it's better this way," Sarah cautioned as she took another small sip of her drink. "Maybe he's bad news. Gang-banger?"

"No!" Emma exclaimed.

"Okay, white-collar felon." Sarah took a little sip of her vodka soda, shaking it so the ice cubes clinked against the side of the glass.

Emma shook her head. "He's just…troubled."

"Mental issues?"

"Commitment issues. Relationship anxiety."

Sarah shoved her shoulder. "Have you been Google diagnosing again?"

Emma gave a guilty shrug.

"You know that stuff is dangerous!" Sarah cried,

putting her glass down on the bar. "By the time you were on the outs with Devin, you were convinced he had a borderline personality." Sarah rolled her eyes.

"He does!" Emma exclaimed.

Sarah heaved a frustrated sigh. "You need to close WebMD, and start facing facts. Mr. X is gone, but that's okay. He wasn't the staying type."

Emma remembered how quickly he'd left her the last two times they'd been together. He'd been in such a rush to leave her he'd barely said goodbye. Staying was absolutely not his strong suit.

"And he's gone radio silent for a week. It's done, sweetie. I know you want there to be something there, but there's just not." Sarah gave Emma's shoulders a reassuring squeeze. "Doesn't mean you can't find someone else."

Emma stared morosely at her drink. She didn't want someone else. She wanted Xavier. "What if he got into a car accident…? What if he really does want to contact me, but…"

Sarah let out a long, frustrated sigh. "Honey, that isn't what happened. This is *Nost*. No strings, remember? That's what you signed on for!"

"I know, but…"

"You just need to shift gears a little. Quit focusing on one man. What you need is a distraction. Give me your phone," Sarah demanded, holding her palm up.

"Why?"

"Just…gimme." Sarah opened and closed her hand impatiently. Reluctantly, Emma set her phone in her friend's hand. In seconds, Sarah had pulled up *Nost* and all active members within a half-mile radius.

"No, no, no!" Emma cried, reaching out and trying to grab her phone back, but Sarah held it just out of reach.

"This is for your own good," Sarah said, sending out a few winks to nearby suitors. She glanced up around the bar, looking hopeful.

"I don't want to meet anyone else!"

"You might not *want* to, but you *need* to." Sarah typed a message to one member Emma couldn't even see.

"Who are you messaging? What…"

"Just trust me," Sarah exclaimed as she grinned into the phone.

"Let me *see*." Emma reached out and tugged on Sarah's arm.

"I'm just saying hi to a few nearby possibilities." She peered at the screen. "Oh, my, there are like *dozens!*"

Given that they were in a sports bar surrounded by guys, that didn't surprise Emma in the least. "Show me."

Eventually, Sarah pulled up a few profiles. "See? He's not so bad."

Emma looked at the blond guy who was slim but not fit, kind of cute but no Xavier. She saw his hazel eyes in her mind, his jet-black hair, the look on his face when he pulled her in for a kiss… Then, she felt herself dissolve a little. How could he walk away from that? From *them*?

Sarah showed her another. "Hey, you got a new message from Good Lookin' Good Times. He looks kind of familiar. Did we message him?"

"What?" Emma glanced down at the screen, her Xavier revelry broken. That's when she saw the fake profile picture that Happy Fun Time had used, the man who'd been so nasty to her at the Ritz-Carlton bar.

"That's Happy Fun Time!" Emma exclaimed, swiping the photo so it got bigger. "I mean, that's not *him,* him, but it's the fake photo he used. Trust me, he looks nothing like that *GQ* model." She studied the map on the phone. "It says he's *right* near us, too."

Emma glanced around hurriedly. Then, seconds later, she saw a telltale Cardinals cap in the back corner of the bar, by the pool tables.

"Oh, God! There he is! Cardinals hat?" Emma told Sarah, trying to covertly side nod with her head.

"The old guy? Seriously overweight?" Sarah wrinkled her nose. "That is false advertising."

"I know." Emma stirred her drink. "Don't stare," she admonished, suddenly fearful the man would see them. He must know they were nearby. He'd messaged her, but maybe there was a chance he hadn't seen them yet. The bar was crowded, and Emma cringed, using the men behind her as a shield.

"And who in their right mind wears a St. Louis hat to a Cubs game?"

"He's a jerk, so who knows?" Emma shrugged, remembering the vile way he'd clutched at her elbow, the coldness of his voice when he'd hissed *bitch* in her face.

"He's the guy that grabbed you, right?" Sarah's frown deepened. "Let's report him," she suggested, quickly clicking on the "report user" button, and she tapped in their complaint. She made sure to write *false advertising* in all caps, as well as *belligerent* and *rude* and *assault.*

"Maybe we should go," Emma suggested, suddenly feeling uncomfortable. She didn't want the man to find them.

"Fine. I got this round." Sarah slapped down a few bills in the small shot glass that held their bill, and then they made their way through the thick crowd to the exit.

They were barely out the door when behind them, someone shouted, "Hey, Kitten!"

Emma froze, for a second, wondering if it was Mr. X.

But, when she turned, she found the average-looking blond with two of his friends. "Kitten, you're even prettier in person. We were going in to Barleycorn." He nodded at the big Irish pub near them. "Buy you and your friend a drink?"

Sarah gave Emma nudge.

"Okay," Emma reluctantly agreed.

Xavier sat at his laptop at home, poring over a bug in the *Nost* code that some of his engineers couldn't figure out. He'd spent the week burying himself in work, trying to stave off thoughts of Emma: what she was doing, what she was wearing, who she might be with. He'd resolutely refused to answer her query about dinner, and yet, he worried that she might be giving up on *him.* After all, he'd never responded, but she hadn't followed up, either. Her question sat on his phone, almost like a dare, a challenge. So far, he'd resisted caving, but he could feel his fingers itching to respond. Itching to set a time and place.

Only work could keep him from doing that. He had to throw himself into work and hope that eventually he'd forget about Emma.

You don't forget about the woman you love, his father had told him. He hated that his father's voice seemed to be in his head constantly. *I don't love her, Papi,* he wanted to say, *I don't even know her.*

Yet, why did he suddenly understand why his father kept coming back to his erratic mother? Why else would he suffer so much?

Emma doesn't seem like suffering, though, an inner voice of reason said. *Emma is passionate, vulnerable, whole. She's not Mama. Or Sasha.*

Sasha. The moment she betrayed him, Xavier saw his mother all over again: the woman who burned so brightly, she burned everyone around her, too. He might have been young, just eight, but he remembered the nights his father would go out looking for his mother, the worried look on Xavier's aunt's face as she tried to reassure him that everything was fine. He knew everything wasn't fine.

Xavier blinked away the memory of the frightened little boy. He was a man now, a man in charge of his own destiny. And he wasn't going to be weak like his father.

In fact, he'd prove it. He pulled up the *Nost* app on his phone. Beautiful women smiled back at him from his inbox. Yet, even as he pored through the pictures, all he could do was compare each and every one of them to Emma. They all came up wanting. Why couldn't he get her out of his mind? Why couldn't he put aside thoughts of her? He would find a way to rid himself of this desire, of this *weakness*. He wouldn't be his father. He forced himself to message a gorgeous brunette and a beautiful twenty-something. He needed a palate cleanser, that's all, he reasoned. The second he had another woman, he'd forget all about Emma. Wouldn't he? He put his phone down and turned his attention back to his screen.

As he typed on his computer, he saw a notice coming into his inbox. He'd signed on to be copied on all complaints registered at *Nost*. He opened the message, and that's when he saw Emma's account flick before his eyes. She was active again? was his first thought. A flame of jealousy rose up in his chest. Was she, right now, in the arms of another man?

The thought of her flirting…or kissing…another man, made him shift uncomfortably in his office chair. He didn't like that idea. Not one bit.

Then he read her complaint, and as soon as he pulled up the profile picture of the guy, he knew it was the same man who'd hassled her at the bar. He'd put up the exact same fake photo of himself, and

the description she'd typed of him—down to the St.
Louis Cardinals baseball cap—all rang a bell. *Dammit,* the asshole had slipped into the system again.

This time, Xavier dug deeper. He pulled up the
man's fake profile, but, unlike other profiles, he'd
actually put in a local phone number. After being
booted from the system multiple times, he'd be
locked out, unless he used a number that worked,
a number he could confirm by text. This could be
Xavier's break. He used reverse look-up online for
the number, and found it registered to a Jimmy Keith.
Could it be that easy? Was Jimmy Keith the man?
Or would it be another dead end?

Xavier ran a few more searches on him, and
landed on a social media page, which confirmed it:
this was the guy who'd bullied Emma at the bar. He
had only a handful of Facebook friends, but was born
and raised in St. Louis. Xavier went a step further
and ran the man's name through a criminal background check. Results instantly popped up: trespassing, public intoxication—and then Xavier saw
something that made the room spin. He had pleaded
guilty to sexual assault ten years ago in St. Louis.
Another Google search pulled up local newspaper
articles about it. He was sentenced to eight years,
but was paroled early.

This piece of shit had managed to get into *Nost*
at least twice and was right now in it again, preying
on unsuspecting women.

This asshole had grabbed Emma's arm at the bar.

Xavier felt his blood boil as he called his friend,

the Chicago detective. He didn't know if there was anything that could be done, but he sure as hell would find out. He got voice mail and left a message. He pulled up some of Emma's messages and realized the ex-con had tried to message Emma again, this time under his new profile. Xavier wished he could pull up her location, but even he couldn't do that from the code in his office. He'd need a new profile on *Nost*, and fast, in order to find her and even then, that might take too long.

But he had to warn her, he thought. If Emma was anywhere near this man, he had to find her. The man was dangerous.

CHAPTER THIRTEEN

EMMA SAT WITH the friendly, but a little bit bland, guys who'd bought drinks for them. She was pretty sure two of them were interested in Sarah, but one—the blond with the average build—was absolutely fixated on her. He kept finding reasons to touch her, which Emma wasn't so sure she liked. He seemed nice enough. Casey, who lived around the corner in an apartment he shared with the two friends he was with, was working a low-level accounting job, but hoping for advancement. They were exactly the same age, but somehow that just didn't feel quite right. His friends kept trying to order Jäger shots, which just made Emma's stomach turn. Clearly, these fellas hadn't left the college binge-drinking scene behind just yet. The way they slammed beers made Emma think about frat parties and keg stands. She sighed. She missed Mr. X: his sophistication, the way he seemed…beyond all the immaturity.

Except for the fact that Mr. X wouldn't even give you his real name, a voice in her head reminded her. At least Casey here gave his full name right off the bat. And she knew so much about him already in the first five minutes: Boston College grad, licensed accountant, loved college football and camping. Wanted to take her sometime, he said, to Starved Rock, his favorite local campground. Emma tried to muster up some interest, but just failed. He was nice enough, but just dull.

Then, she wondered if it was because she knew too much about him. Had Mr. X been right? Did knowledge make a person...boring?

"One time when we were camping..." Casey continued, happy to steer the conversation, as Emma nodded and smiled weakly. As Casey spoke, relating some tale about raccoons getting into his cooler and stealing a beer, Emma tried to block out his voice. She studied his blue eyes, his average, but somewhat cute face, and wondered: Would she have sex with this man in an alley at dusk? In a public restroom at a fancy hotel?

Inwardly, she shook her head. It didn't matter if she knew everything about him or nothing, she decided. Casey just didn't light that spark in her.

Mr. X was different. Special, somehow. He had to know that.

"And then we found that he'd somehow *popped the top of the can.* Can you believe that? Raccoons, man...they are smarter than you think."

Casey finished his story and Emma laughed politely. She glanced at Sarah and couldn't tell whether or not she enjoyed the attention of Casey's friends. Would she be up for bailing? Now? Sarah flipped

her red hair off one shoulder. Looked like she might
be flirting with one of them…or hell, both, for all
Emma knew.

"Well, this guy needs to go drain the snake,"
Casey said, getting up from his bar stool. Emma
flinched a little at the vernacular. Did he have to
say it *that* way?

Emma just nodded and Casey sauntered into the
crowd, looking for the men's room. Emma felt her
phone buzz in her pocket and she tugged it out of
her jacket. She glanced at the face and saw a text
from Mr. X.

Where are you?

She felt a ripple of anticipation run through her.
He hadn't contacted her for a week! Emma thought
Sarah had been right—he'd been done and it was
time to face facts: that whatever they had was just a
temporary thing. But, here, on her phone, was proof
that Mr. X hadn't walked away. Not just yet, anyway.
And he hadn't been in a car accident, either. No, here
he was on her phone.

Emma felt such relief, such joy, that he'd contacted her, she immediately started typing a reply.
I'm drinking at…

Then she paused. He'd kept her at bay for a whole
week. Kept her wondering, kept her hanging. She had
every reason to be angry at him, she reasoned. She
thought she might never see him again! He *let* her
think that. Besides, if she let him in, if she invited

him out, they'd just end up with steamy, amazing sex, and then he'd probably just disappear again. Is that what she wanted? No, she decided. Not this time.

Why do you want to know? she responded, instead.

I need to see you, he typed, almost instantly.

Her heart sang a bit. He needed to see her! *Probably just for a quick hookup,* that little voice in her head said. And then, another quickly replied, *And what's wrong with that?* She felt her thighs tingle. He knew how to satisfy her, that was for sure. The sex would be amazing, even if it was of the wham, bam, thank-you, ma'am variety. She wanted that, but she also wanted to know his full name. And he owed her that much. This time, she wouldn't let him arrive, seduce her with his amazing charisma and expert hands. No, this time, she'd get what she needed *before* she saw him.

On one condition, she typed.

Emma, please. Just tell me where you are! That guy—the one who harassed you at the bar the night we met—I know he's trying to message you. He's dangerous, so do not meet him anywhere!

Emma read Xavier's message and frowned. How did he know the man was messaging her? Did he know the Cardinals hat guy? Emma already knew he was dangerous from her run-in with him at the Ritz-Carlton, but what did Xavier mean?

I just saw him but I don't think he saw me, Emma texted back. How did you know he messaged me?

Turn off your Nost location finder, he told her once more. He could find you.

Emma felt a chill run down her spine. Quickly, she hit "location-off" on her app.

Where are you? Xavier asked once more, ignoring her inquiry.

First you have to tell me your first AND last name. Now let him try to worm his way out of this one. At least she'd make him work for it.

She stared at her phone and saw he was typing. His answer popped up on her screen:

Xavier Pena. Where are you?

She felt a surge of satisfaction. There. She knew his name now, and he wouldn't be able to disappear so quickly from her life. Not now.

Casey had returned from the bar but she only barely looked up from her phone as she tapped out her response: John Barleycorn.

Stay there, he responded. I'm on my way.

Emma felt a surge of excitement. He was coming out! She was going to see him—the elusive Mr. X. Now she knew his name, as well. *Xavier Pena.* She itched to Google him, but Casey was in front of her once more.

"So, tell me about *you*," Casey said. "I've been talking this whole time. What's a gorgeous girl like you doing on *Nost*? You could have any guy at this bar with a snap of your fingers."

She squirmed at the compliment and felt a bit of guilt. After all, she was not going home with Casey tonight, not if Mr. X, Xavier, was on his way. *Xavier Pena.* The name suited him. And she'd be Googling him at the first available opportunity. She glanced at the door of the bar and saw the revolving doors swing around. Was Xavier here already?

But then, she saw the telltale red baseball brim. *Cardinals hat.* He was back. Had he found her before she turned off her location finder on *Nost*?

Emma crouched down, trying to use Casey as a shield. "Everything okay?" he asked her.

"Uh, just someone I don't want to see," Emma said. Casey turned to look at the front of the bar. Emma took the opportunity to reach out and grab Sarah's elbow and tug her close. "Cardinals Hat is here," Emma whispered in her friend's ear. Sarah craned her neck and saw the man working his way through the crowd. Suddenly, the man lifted his head and through the crowd, managed to make eye contact with Emma. She wanted to look away, but she found herself frozen, unable to move. The man's lip curled up in a cruel smile of recognition. Emma knew in that minute that he had been looking for her, and that his intentions were anything but good. She felt a cold chill run down her spine, all of her instincts telling her to get away from that man.

"Who is that guy?" Casey asked.

"An asshole," Sarah responded. "Don't worry. We'll make sure he doesn't come near you."

Emma was thankful for the offer, and yet, despite her presence and the dozens of other people in the bar, she still felt vulnerable, exposed.

"Want another round?" Casey asked her suddenly, but all Emma wanted to do was to get out of the bar, away from the man who now took up a position leaning against a column in her direct line of sight. He wasn't coming up to her, and she guessed she ought to be grateful for that, but the way he just stood across the bar, staring at her, made her even more uncomfortable. She just wanted to get out of his line of sight. She couldn't shake the feeling that in his mind, he was plotting terrible things to do to her. She knew that sounded crazy, but she felt that he might become violent and that if he caught her alone she might be in serious danger.

Then Xavier came through the doors. She saw him first, and then their eyes met. Emma felt relief and more seeing his handsome self, clad in a simple black T-shirt, windbreaker and jeans, looking dark and dangerous as his tall and imposing figure cut through the crowd. Emma nodded to her left, toward her stalker, and Xavier saw him at the same time.

"Jimmy!" he shouted, which got the man's attention. He turned, saw Xavier, and then suddenly bolted for the back, shoving bar-goers out of his way. He pushed one woman to the ground who fell hard, spilling her drink on a group of guys standing next to her.

"Hey!" one of them cried, and then Cardinals Hat had more than one pursuer, as the girl's boyfriend gave chase.

Stymied by the thick crowd, Xavier couldn't catch Jimmy. Emma watched as the man disappeared through the back. Xavier followed and Emma, worried about him, bolted for the back as well.

"Where are you…" she heard the blond shout after her, but she was already gone, worried about Xavier. She wiggled through the crowd, and before she knew it, found herself at the back kitchen, where Xavier had stopped by an open alleyway door.

"He's gone," he told her, running his hands through his thick hair. "I went out there, and… I don't know, he's just gone."

Emma felt a bit of relief. Xavier was safe, the jerk was gone.

Xavier turned, looking at her with a pained expression. "Emma, that man…he's got a sexual assault conviction on his record."

"He…what?" Emma tried to process that information. "But he was certified with a background check." The noise from the clang of pots and pans in the kitchen and the low rumble of music from the bar made it so Emma had to raise her voice.

Xavier shook his head. "He got past the safeguards somehow, but I'm going to figure out how and stop him. Put in more security. Something. I'm working on it, but, Emma, I'm sorry."

She wasn't sure she'd heard right over the noise in the bar.

"Why are you sorry? And what do you mean, 'working on it'?" Now Emma was beyond confused. What was he talking about?

Xavier hung his head. He glanced around as if he wasn't sure how to break bad news. Then he caught her eye once more, his own eyes fixed on hers, deliberate and serious.

"You'll find out with your first Google search, anyway." He sighed, shaking his head. "I built *Nost*. I own it."

CHAPTER FOURTEEN

EMMA FELT LIKE the earth suddenly tilted beneath her feet and she had trouble steadying herself.

"You *own Nost*?" A million confused questions raced through her mind, none of them good. Had he gamed the system? Had this somehow been just an elaborate joke?

Xavier nodded his head once.

"You use your *own* app to pick up girls?"

A flash of guilt crossed his face. "What kind of hypocrite would I be if I made the app but didn't use it?" Xavier was trying to be lighthearted, to joke, but Emma found nothing about this to be funny.

Somehow, it just seemed all wrong that he was using his own app, his own program, to find women, but Emma couldn't say why. Maybe it was because he'd be able to game the system (he created it, so he'd have to know how to take advantage, right?) or maybe it was because his commitment phobia went far, far deeper than she ever realized.

"You *created Nost*." She just couldn't get over the fact that the man she was falling for had relationship anxiety so deep that he built a company around it. There might never be a cure for him. All of her hopes about them *being something more* felt like they disintegrated in that moment. *Poof,* up in fantasy fairy-tale smoke.

"Yes." Xavier moved closer and she backed away until she was flat against the wall in the corridor between the kitchen and the bathroom. "I told you up front that no strings was what I wanted."

Yes, he had. He'd been more than up front about that. So why did it bother her so much that he owned *Nost*?

It was because he was here and he knew the man in the Cardinals hat would be here. He also knew the man was messaging her. But how?

"How did you know that man would be here tonight?" She pointed toward the back door where the jerk had fled.

Now Xavier looked uncomfortable. He rubbed the back of his neck. "I looked at your account," he admitted.

"You can see the messages?" Now Emma felt shocked. He could hack her account? She felt a jumble of emotions all at once. She took a deep breath. The fact that he cared enough to dig around to find out about her proved her whole point that there was more between them than he ever admitted. Yet, another part of her felt unsteady, uneasy.

Xavier wouldn't meet her eyes. "Yes," he admitted. "And since you sent a complaint about him, I followed up. I just wanted to make sure you were safe, and I had a bad feeling about that guy so I checked into him. That's when I saw he had a criminal history. That's when I knew I had to warn you."

Emma blinked fast. That was so much information but she could only focus on one thing.

"*You* looked in my account."

First, she felt flattered. He was trying to protect her. Trying to make sure someone followed up on her complaint. Ensuring that she was safe. That felt good.

At the same time, however, she didn't like being in the dark and she felt duped. He'd taken pains to make sure she knew nothing about him, when he knew... everything...down to her billing address and credit card number. "I thought you said knowing things about me would make the sex dull."

Xavier had the decency to look guilty. He raised his hands in surrender. "I'm sorry, Em. I shouldn't have done that, and I know it. I just... I wanted to make sure you were safe and..."

"And you wanted to find out where I lived. Were you just going to pop by sometime? Here I was *not even knowing your name*, and you knew everything about me!" The unfairness of it stung. Also, the mistrust. Did he not trust her to know even the littlest thing about him? Yet, he'd gone and found out everything about her. Without her knowing about it.

Xavier shifted uncertainly on one foot. "Wait," he said, reaching out for her, but she dodged his advance.

"I think you should go home, Xavier," she said, moving away from him. Emma decided she'd go

back to Sarah, back to Casey and his friend. Casey
might be bland, but he didn't sneak around and find
out where she lived behind her back, all while telling her information killed a relationship.

"Emma, please. Let me explain."

"Explain what?" Emma whirled, feeling anger
build up in her. "How you lied to me? How you mis-
led me?"

"Let's talk about this."

Emma just felt hurt, betrayed and angry. She
didn't want to talk about it. She wanted to go home.
"I thought you were honest with me. I thought that's
what you said, that strangers could be honest. Be authentic with one another. But you weren't that. You
weren't that at all."

That was what hurt the most. Not that he'd
snooped, but that he'd kept secrets.

"Emma, if I'd told you the first date that I owned
Nost, we wouldn't have gotten this far," he said.

"How do you know that?" Emma fired back. "I
was honest with you, but you lied to me."

"I just didn't tell you the whole truth," Xavier said,
trying to defend himself, raising his voice higher.

"Same thing," she said. "You know what I think?
I think this is all about power for you. You want to be
the one with all of it. This isn't about love or heartbreak or anything else, it's about you calling all the
shots. But that's not how real love works." Emma felt
the truth of the words as she said them, understanding for the first time that she'd truly been a pawn
in his game. "You told me information would kill

the passion in a relationship. Well? You know what, you're right. Knowing this about you. It does kill it."

"Emma!" Xavier exclaimed, pain on his face as if she'd hit him. She felt a flicker of guilt then, but she couldn't let it in. She knew she was right.

"You wanted no strings, right? Well, you got your wish," she said. "There's nothing holding us together." Then she left him.

Xavier watched her go, feeling his gut wrench with guilt and loss. Even worse, he found that she marched right back to her friends, including the decent-looking, but decidedly unremarkable guy who offered her a beer. He felt jealousy well in him, and felt a strong desire to go over there and tell the man to get lost. Who was that? Some other guy on *Nost*, no doubt. The idea of her with another man made his blood boil. *But what claim do I have on her? Everything she told me is true. I lied. I betrayed her trust.*

I was just trying to protect her.

Or was he just trying to keep the balance in the relationship unequal? Was he trying to be the one with all the information? Did he like keeping her in the dark? She accused him of just wanting to keep all the power, and maybe she'd been right. Sure, Sasha had hurt him, more than hurt him, nearly killed him with heartbreak, and maybe he thought the way he'd never let that happen again was just to be sure that he held all the cards. She'd seen right through him, and it scared him to his core.

That was why he'd not revealed who he was at

the start. That was why he'd kept all his cards close to his vest.

Yet, the attraction between them was real. Even now, he wanted to sweep Emma off her feet and kiss the life out of her. Even angry, he'd never seen a woman look so beautiful. Her blue eyes flashed fire when they glanced at him, and he wanted to do whatever it took to earn her forgiveness. Did trying to save her from a sexual predator count at all? Would it have been better if he'd just let her take her chances?

Xavier shoved his hands deep in his coat pockets. Should he go after her? Explain himself? He badly wanted to. Then his phone rang. His police detective friend, Ian, was on the line.

"X!" he cried. "It's been too long, buddy." The two of them had gone to school together on the South Side, but now they ran in slightly different circles.

"I know, man, sorry about that. It's been busy."

"Getting all that tail," Ian said.

"Right. That." There was only one bit of tail Xavier wanted at that moment, and she wasn't speaking to him.

"So you got a perp that is getting into your site, huh?" Ian cut right to the chase.

"Anything you can do to help me get him out?" Xavier said. "He's been hassling a…user." The noise in the bar almost made it too hard to hear his friend. Xavier decided to step into the alley to finish the conversation. Getting Cardinals Hat out of his system, and hopefully in jail, was his priority at the moment.

"How bad?" Ian asked, and Xavier filled him in on what had happened so far. Ian made a disappointed sound. "I don't think anything he's done is technically against the law, *but* send me the guy's full name. If he hasn't checked in with his parole officer in a while, that could be enough to lift him, and if you really think he's up to no good, maybe I could get one of my guys to check in on him. See if there's anything to find."

"Could you?" Xavier said, feeling suddenly hopeful.

"Anything for you, X. You know that." Xavier felt suddenly grateful to have such loyal friends.

"Thanks, man."

Something that sounded like a police scanner went off. "We'll have to grab a beer sometime, but right now, I gotta run. City's on fire, as usual."

"Okay, Ian. Thanks, man."

Ian clicked off and Xavier returned to the bar, determined to go find Emma and explain the situation. But when he turned the corner, he found Emma and her friends were already gone.

CHAPTER FIFTEEN

EMMA WENT HOME—alone, after breaking the news to Casey that she wouldn't be his next *Nost* fling. Casey had tried to persuade her, but Emma was in no mood. They'd parted ways as she ducked into her own cab and headed home. Sarah, for her part, had called it an evening early as well, without taking anyone home. The whole mood had turned bleak the second Emma found out Xavier had lied to her. Well, not lied, exactly. Omitted the truth. Still, what an omission.

Emma sat on her bed in the tiny one-bedroom condo and glanced out her window, which overlooked Welles Park. Normally the pretty view of the full trees and big metal gazebo comforted her, but today she just felt isolated and alone. The leaves in the park had turned red and brown in the cool fall night, visible beneath the park's streetlights. Emma sighed, and kicked off her ankle boots, opting to close her shades and then put on a pair of her comfiest flannel pajama bottoms. Emma swept her blond hair up in a messy bun, and grabbed her laptop as she sank into the ruffled pillows on her bed. She felt a storm of different emotions: anger, hurt, but also confusion. She opened up a Word document and did what she always did when she felt this lost: she started to write.

Turns out, the creator of Nost, Xavier Pena, uses it as his own personal playground to pick up unsuspecting women...

Then her fingers froze on the keyboard. Was that fair? Was she being too hard on Xavier? Objectively, what was wrong with the creator of *Nost* using it himself?

He has an unfair advantage for one, and for another, he can secretly look up profile information. The part of her that was still bubbling over with indignation wouldn't be easily appeased.

That was reprehensible, yes, there wasn't a way around that.

Yet, another part of her argued that he wouldn't have stalked her if he hadn't cared. *Why else would he come find me? Warn me about Jimmy?*

Emma stared at the blinking cursor on her computer screen and bit her lip. Was she angry? Sad? Yes, but she wasn't willing to let it all go. Not yet. She'd told Xavier they were done, but in her heart, she knew that wasn't true. And, as much as she hated it, she wasn't done thinking about Xavier.

As if she could conjure him up with just her thoughts, her phone rang. Xavier's number popped up. Surprised, she sent it to voice mail. Then, seconds later, a local number she didn't recognize called. Who was that?

"Hello?"

"It's me. Xavier."

Surprised, she was almost speechless. "You have two phones?"

"The first number... it belongs to a burner phone."

The words hit Emma like a fist. He hadn't trusted her enough to even give her his real number!

"Unbelievable," she murmured.

"Emma... I just want to talk to you. Can we talk? Can I try to explain?"

The sound of his voice still sent reverberations through her stomach. Despite all her best intentions to remain distant and cold, the sound of his voice melted away most of her anger. As she struggled with her feelings, he took that as his opening.

"I'm sorry," he continued, his deep baritone like honey in her ears. Why did even his voice have this effect on her? Why couldn't she just shut off her feelings for him? "I just wanted you to know that. I'm sorry." That was a start, she thought. "I should've told you, but God. This is impossible on the phone. Can I see you?"

Emma glanced down at her flannel PJs. "Uh, no. I don't think that's a good idea."

"I'm on your doorstep. If you want me to go, I will. Just say the word."

In a rush, Emma flew to her living room window and peeked through the curtains. Xavier took a step back and waved up at her. Of course he knew where she lived, she thought. He'd searched through all her *Nost* account information. She felt a renewed surge of anger. How dare he?

"I don't know. Seems like you already know so much about me. You're a stranger, so why would I invite you up?" She watched him on the sidewalk. He looked dejected, in his windbreaker and jeans, his perfectly coifed dark hair seeming to absorb the streetlamp light. He was so tall and imposing in person, and even looking down at him from the third floor, she could see the breadth of his shoulders, see how his big palm dwarfed the cell phone in his hand.

"Emma, I'll tell you whatever you want to know. I swear. Ask me anything."

"Tell me one thing nobody knows about you."

Xavier began to pace on the sidewalk. "What do you mean?"

"A secret. Tell me that, and I'll let you up." She watched him fidget. "Make it a good one."

Xavier bit his lip and let out a long sigh. "Fine." He let out a long breath. "My mom was bipolar. She was institutionalized, too, for a bit when I was young. Only my dad knew about that. I never told anyone. Not even Sasha."

Emma felt blindsided by the sudden revelation. His mother had been bipolar? She realized they had more in common than he thought. Her father suffered from severe depression all his life…and nearly killed himself over it.

"Because of Mom's illness…well, let's just say she had a hard time being faithful to my dad. Not that that stopped him from loving her until the day she died."

"Oh, Xavier," she said, her heart breaking for him. She knew what kind of damage could be wrought between two people who tried to love each other despite their biggest obstacles. Her parents had failed, as her mom made the hard choice to leave her dad when he stopped seeking treatment for his depression.

Xavier glanced up, a pleading look on his face. "Now, will you let me in? Please? It's starting to rain."

Emma glanced at the sidewalk near him and saw it was suddenly dotted with raindrops. He spread his free arm wide.

"Please, Emma. I just want to talk."

Emma considered the request and felt like she couldn't turn him away. Despite feeling betrayed, she still wanted to know more about the man. She couldn't help herself.

She left the window and punched the buzzer, opening the door downstairs. Emma listened to his heavy footsteps on the stairs and then suddenly he was standing at her front door. She'd forgotten at that very moment she was wearing her least sexy pajamas until she looked down. *No matter,* she thought. *Tonight, I'm not getting naked. Not this time. Not before I get some answers.*

Xavier swooped in for a hug but Emma stopped him with her hand.

"You said you wanted to talk," she said, proud of

herself for holding him at bay. "That's what we're going to do."

Surprised, Xavier took a step away from her and nodded as he slipped into her living room. "You're right," he agreed. "We should talk."

Emma crossed her arms over her flannel pajama top. "I'm listening."

Xavier sat down on her small leather love seat. "I screwed up, Emma. I know I did. I'm sorry I didn't tell you sooner. What can I do to make it up to you?"

Emma sat down on the small blue chair adjacent to the couch. She didn't trust herself to sit next to him. He already felt too big for her small living room, his long legs nearly bumping against her glass coffee table.

"Tell me about your childhood."

"I don't see how that's relevant." She could see how he took on a defensive stance, his shoulders tensing. He was a walking vault, she thought, a locked door.

"I want to know about you. And you owe me details. That's how you'll make it up to me." Emma crossed her arms across her chest.

Xavier nodded, seeming to get her message: she wanted information and she wanted it now.

"I grew up on the South Side, where most people I knew either grew up to join the police or to join a gang—there really weren't many other options. My dad worked his whole life as a plumber, a decent job, and he was faithful to my mother every day he lived, but..." Xavier shook his head. "She'd go manic sometimes, and when she did that, she was just this unstoppable bundle of energy…and then she'd go out, and sometimes, I don't know why, she just went home with other men. It crushed my father, and I vowed, no matter what, I wouldn't be him."

Emma felt like she began to understand Xavier better. "And then came Sasha."

Xavier nodded. "I was never the get-married type, but I just fell for Sasha hard. I guess she reminded me of my mother in a good way. She wasn't bipolar, wasn't manic, but she had the same kind of charisma, the same energy, I guess. Turns out, they had more in common than I thought. Sasha also cheated when she got bored."

Emma reached out her hand and Xavier took it. She suddenly saw Xavier as he must have felt when he discovered Sasha's infidelity—a scared boy brought right back to when his own mother had done the same to his father. Emma didn't know that. Her mom led a mostly boring life, raising her and her brother in a modest house in the suburbs. They still went home monthly for dinner at Mom's house. Dad moved to California years ago, and they didn't see him much. None of her boyfriends had ever cheated on her—that she knew of. Though, if anything, she'd been tortured with neglect, like with Devin, who'd lost interest the second they'd moved in together.

"Everyone cheats when they get tired of a relationship," Xavier continued.

"I wouldn't." Emma shook her head firmly.

"How do you know?" Xavier cocked his head

to one side, doubtful. "Everyone can cheat. Everyone has the capacity to cheat. It's not something you plan, I don't think. It's something…well, you have the need, the resentment builds, and then you find yourself in a stranger's bed."

Emma hesitated. Was that true?

"Ask yourself—if you'd met me in a bar when you were still with Devin… Would you have really turned me down?" A confident smile curved his lips upward. She tried to imagine her life with Devin, if he hadn't taken the job that took him out of state, if she hadn't realized how easy it was to let him go.

"I don't know," she answered honestly. She met his golden gaze and then glanced away, but then studied his thick, strong hands. The hands that she knew could bring her so much pleasure. She shivered. "Maybe," she admitted.

"I know I wouldn't be able to resist you," he said and she felt a growing heat in her belly. He let out a long sigh. "And what if all relationships end that way? All of mine have. Either I've tired of the woman, or the woman has tired of me."

"But…" Frustration welled in Emma. "You can't say for sure *all* relationships are like that. Look, I know many that fail. My parents, for instance."

"What happened with them?" Xavier leaned forward.

"My dad suffered serious depression. He was always switching out meds, but nothing seemed to work. He tried once to kill himself."

"Oh, Emma." Xavier reached out for her hand. She let him take it.

"One day, Dad just decided he'd had enough of the drugs and the therapists, and he just quit. He always said the drugs made him feel like he was sleep-walking through life, and he didn't want to do that anymore, and Mom, well… Mom decided she couldn't handle it anymore. She left him and took us with her."

"I see." Xavier seemed to process this a bit. "So you understand what I mean. Love doesn't last. Your parents were just smart and admitted it earlier than most. Who do you know that's been in a marriage twenty-five years and can't keep their hands off each other?"

Emma thought a second. Aunts and uncles and neighbors flitting through her mind, all couples that seemed decidedly tepid in their affection at best. "I can't, I guess."

"See?" Xavier looked sad. "I don't even know if monogamy is a reasonable goal. For anyone."

Emma felt disappointment strike her fast and hard. She might not be wanting to get married this second, but could Xavier truly feel this way? Was he really so determined never to be faithful?

"It's no accident that *Nost* is so successful. I'm not the only one who feels this way," he said. "I'm not alone. I made *Nost* because it seemed safe, it seemed like a way to ensure that nobody got close enough to hurt me again. I did it to protect myself, because if I fell for Sasha, I could fall for someone else, and I didn't want to be that vulnerable ever again." Xavier stared at the floor, unable to meet her gaze. Emma saw how vulnerable he was, how open. He looked up then, his golden eyes full of sadness…and something more, guilt. Then it clicked for Emma.

"There wasn't anything wrong with you walking away from Sasha. I know you must feel guilty about that."

Xavier's head snapped up, defensiveness in his posture. "Why do you say that?"

"Because of your father. Your father showed you a model of *always* staying with the person you love, no matter how bad it gets. And you must've felt like maybe…maybe you weren't strong enough to stay with Sasha. But that's not right at all. You stood up for your needs, and that's healthy. That's important. It actually makes you strong, not weak."

"I…" Xavier just stared at her, speechless. "How did you know that? I don't think I've ever really known that. But… You're right. My father, he always seemed so perfect in love, so patient. I'm not that patient. Never was."

"And that's okay. Don't you see?" She squeezed his hand tighter. "Not every relationship is a life sentence. Some don't work out and that's okay, too."

Xavier studied their hands, intertwined. "You make it sound so easy."

"It can be," she urged him.

Xavier leaned forward and gently took her hand in his. "I never thought I'd even consider love again, but you make me wonder. You got past the wall I built, and it was a pretty amazing wall. A hundred feet high, made of steel."

Emma felt her heart surge a little. She had? But did she want that? Xavier was damaged, possibly beyond repair.

"But you don't believe in monogamy."

"That's right." He nodded.

"You think all relationships die."

"Yes."

"So…what are you asking me?" Emma didn't know if she could give him what she wanted. Or that he could give her what she needed.

"I want…to get to know you." The words seemed almost to stick in his throat. "When I'm not with you, I'm thinking about you all the time. I'm Googling you. Hacking the *Nost* database to find out even the smallest detail about you. You intrigue me, Emma Allaire. Even now, wearing that plaid flannel, no makeup on… All I want to do is strip you naked and make you come."

Emma felt warmth creep into her cheeks. All of that was so flattering…and yet, he never wanted a real relationship. He said as much.

"But I thought you didn't want a relationship," she said. "You were so sure."

"I'm not sure I do, and that's just me being honest," Xavier said. "But if I did want one, I'd want one with you."

Xavier moved slowly closer to her, leaned in so their knees touched. Emma felt a spark even through her flannel bottoms. Why did the proximity of this man do such things to her? She knew she ought to keep her guard up and yet, all she wanted to do right then was lean forward and put her mouth on his.

"Be honest with me, Emma. Do you even know what you want? You had experience before me, but that experience…well…" He grinned. "You've had boyfriends who've never pleasured you the way I have."

This was a true statement.

"Do you want to explore this chemistry? You and I both know this doesn't come along every day. Do you really want to end it?" That had been *her* argument, and now he'd co-opted it. Xavier was now firmly in her personal space. She could smell his scent: something spicy and sweet. No, she didn't want to end it. Not really. That had been a lie.

He leaned forward and whispered in her ear, "Say the word, and I'll go."

"I—I don't want you to go." Her voice was a low croak.

"Then, come here." His voice left no room for argument as he patted his own lap. She slid off her chair and went to him, her body seeming to have a mind of its own. She straddled him on her sofa, distantly realizing her curtains beyond were slightly parted. *This is more privacy than an alley,* she reasoned, but somehow, with Xavier, she still felt on display. It was the way he looked at her, drinking her in.

He tackled the buttons of her pajama top one by one, each one releasing a bit more skin, as she stared at him. Now that she knew more about him, about his difficult childhood, all she wanted to do was comfort him, make it better, heal those old wounds. Knowing more about him made her fiercely protective, too. *I want to fix you,* she thought in her head, as he slid her top free. Naked beneath, she arched her back a bit, her nipples puckering in the cool air of her condo. He murmured his appreciation as he rubbed one nipple with his finger, and cupped the other breast with his hand.

"You're beautiful," he said, studying her body. "Simple perfection."

His gentle touch sent ripples of pleasure through her body as she leaned into his touch. She could feel his lap stiffen in anticipation, and she ground into him as she bent down and claimed his mouth with hers. The fireworks began then, passion exploding in her mind with urgent want. Knowing him made the kiss even *more* intense, she thought, as she anticipated every move his mouth made. She knew him on a deeper level and that made the passion even stronger. Couldn't he feel that, she wondered? Couldn't he feel how well their mouths fit together?

Xavier broke free. "I want you," he murmured.

"I want you, too," she replied, a low whisper in her throat.

Then Xavier stood, lifting her in his arms, as if she weighed nothing. He carried her to her bedroom, where he laid her gently on her bed and kissed her once more, their tongues melting together in a desperate heat. Here, with his weight on her chest, she felt like she'd known him for years. He anticipated her every want, his hands driving her wild. He seemed to know exactly how she wanted to be touched, as if he could see right into her mind. She let him take her to the places she knew he would, leading her right to the edge.

Xavier devoured Emma's body. He couldn't get enough of her, her perfectly puckered pink nipples, the way she moaned in such delight as he touched her. Her body was an instrument he'd never get tired of playing, and as he explored her curves, he realized with a shock that he'd never felt this way about anyone before. Was it her amazing pheromones? She smelled delicious, and tasted even better. He'd had many women, but something about her just instantly made him hard. His desire and need for her thrilled him and frightened him all at once. If he needed her this badly, what would happen when he lost her?

He tried to push the worry from his mind, even as he slipped inside her, feeling her tense around him, hugging him so deliciously tight. She wrapped her bare legs around his waist and he thought he might come then and there. Amazing. Just absolutely amazing. Mind-blowing, even. Could he allow himself the risk of wanting her? Did he even have a choice?

She pulled him deeper inside her, and he knew he wouldn't be able to last much longer. He needed to fill her, needed to make her his.

CHAPTER SIXTEEN

XAVIER CAME AWAKE the next morning to the smell of pancakes filling the small apartment. He rolled over and found Emma's side of the bed empty, and heard the clatter in the kitchen that was his lover making him breakfast. He fell back into his pillow, inhaling the sweet scent, feeling strangely satisfied. Perhaps it was because he'd spent the night exploring Emma's body. God, he just never got tired of the woman. Could it be that they shared a passion that wouldn't wane?

He sat up on his elbows. He still wasn't convinced. He wasn't like his father. He didn't believe that love came to stay. He believed that love came and went, on its own accord, on a timetable known to no one. He was playing with fire with Emma, and he knew it. He shouldn't have spent the night, shouldn't have indulged in all that sex. He felt warm and comfortable, and that was dangerous. He grabbed his phone off the dresser and glanced at the face of it. No urgent messages from work, so he had that flexibility. He noticed the *Nost* app told him he had ten messages waiting for him, but for once, he didn't feel the urge to check them. He remembered, distantly, messaging a few women last night before he discovered that Emma might be in trouble. Now that urge to see another woman faded into the background. He had all the woman he wanted, right here. Of course, that was what troubled him. He still felt uneasy about his growing need for Emma. The lazy Sunday stretched out before him and all he wanted to do was spend it with Emma. Preferably naked.

He rolled from bed, pulled up his boxers and his jeans and walked into the living room. He saw Emma, blond hair messy, wearing an oversized sweatshirt and nothing else, and he wanted to spend the day with her. Hell, the month. Maybe longer.

"Morning, sexy," Emma called from the kitchen, her eyes flicking appreciatively down his bare chest. "You hungry?"

"Starved." He grinned as he set his phone on the breakfast bar. "We worked up an appetite."

"You bet we did." Emma sent him a knowing glance and her delicate features made his groin tighten. God, she was beautiful. What had he done to deserve such a beautiful woman? He wanted to drop at her feet and worship her…with his tongue, he thought, a wry smile spreading across his face. He closed the distance between them and swept her into his arms, dipping his head so he could kiss her lips. Her lips were so willing, so soft, that he wasn't sure if he could control himself long enough to eat breakfast.

Emma fed him a bite of pancake.

"Mmm, delicious," he said, appreciative, as she flipped the last pancake onto a nearby plate. He grabbed the syrup from the table and the bowl of berries she'd washed and headed to her breakfast bar.

"I'll get a separate plate," she offered, but he waved her off.

"Let's share one," he said.

She giggled and then took the tall stack of pancakes to the bar. The coffeemaker dinged, announcing a new full pot of coffee. "Do you want coffee?" she asked him. "Do you even…drink coffee?"

"I do. Black," he said.

"Oh, too strong for me," she said, grinning, as she poured her own cup and added a hefty serving of milk so that the cup was almost beige and three big spoonfuls of sugar. "I like it sweet." He found, with surprise, that he liked that little detail. Now he knew how she took her coffee. Wasn't that something every long-term couple knew? Usually those kinds of details made him nervous, but suddenly, he was glad to store that bit away. Remember it for later. He wondered what would be her favorite order from Starbucks. He found himself wanting to know more about her, that no detail seemed too small. *What was happening to me?*

"Syrup?" he asked her, and she nodded.

"Yes, please. As much as you can handle. Sweet tooth, can you tell?" She grinned at him. He doused the stack in syrup and then took a hunk of the stack and offered it to her. She leaned in and took the bite, as he watched her perfectly pink lips wrap around the fork.

"Mmmmmm," she murmured, closing her eyes. "Delicious."

"Not as delicious as you," he said and grabbed a bite for himself. "What's your favorite meal of the day?"

"Breakfast, by far," she answered immediately.

"Have you been to Dawn? The new restaurant in the west Loop?"

Emma shook her head.

"I have to take you there," he said. "You're going to love it. They have this amazing banana walnut French toast." Xavier found himself eager to take her to his new favorite brunch place, as soon as possible…maybe even next weekend. The fact that he was already making plans in his head with Emma for the following week should've caused him more anxiety, but instead it all just felt right. He'd take Emma out next Sunday, because he'd see her that whole weekend. He'd make sure of it.

"I'd love to go." She took another bite of pancake and he felt buoyant, upbeat.

"What do you want to do today?" he asked her. "Go out? Stay in?" He pushed his knee against hers.

"Anything you want to do," she said. "I've got no plans."

"Let's play it by ear."

Soon enough, the two polished off their plate of pancakes, Xavier feeling happily full. Usually, he watched his carb and sugar intake. You couldn't get cut muscles on a diet of junk, but even he had his splurge days. Today would be one of them, he decided. He went into the bedroom to grab his shirt, the air in the apartment suddenly feeling chilly.

He helped Emma clean up the dishes and then he joined her on the couch. She flicked on the TV and he joined her, as the political shows came on.

"I always watch," Emma said, nodding to the roundtable commentators on the screen. "I like to know what's going on."

"Me, too," Xavier said, surprised to find someone else who was interested in politics. Usually, reality TV took a front seat and news a backseat. *Everything I learn about her just makes me love her more.* The thought shocked even him. Was he really thinking about *love*?

They settled in to watch the show and Emma curled up next to him, and the feel of her cuddled under his arm made everything feel right in the world. She pulled up a soft throw and tucked it around them. They just fit together, like they were made for each other. Their passion was amazing, that was true, and yet, here, in this tender moment, Xavier felt content as well. Could they really have both passion and tenderness? Was that even possible? Normally, Xavier felt restless when he sat with a woman—he usually only felt at home when the clothes were off—but here, snuggled in together on a couch beneath a blanket, he felt like there was nowhere else he wanted to be. The restlessness in him evaporated. He could see himself here, on her couch, with her in his arms, watching TV for endless weekends to come.

Was he really settling in? Was he really considering a serious relationship?

Something about Emma just made the whole idea seem not just possible, but inevitable. They fit together in a way he'd never fit with another woman. Could he take the chance that maybe he'd been wrong about relationships? Emma snuggled into him and he felt happy. How could he *not* take the chance? He wanted this: Emma in his arms, naked and wild on Saturday night, and then tender and cuddly Sunday morning. Maybe he could have both. Maybe he should try.

During a commercial break, Emma shifted a bit against him, and Xavier stretched, too.

"Nature's calling," he said, hating to break their warm embrace. "I'll be right back."

Emma watched Xavier dip into the adjacent bathroom and sighed. She could get used to that amazing hunk of man walking around her apartment. She hadn't realized how small it was before she saw his broad shoulders in it, seemingly taking up all the available space. She didn't mind, though. He was tall and imposing, and, oh, so strong. She thought back to how he'd picked her up the night before and carted her off to the bedroom, and she could feel the tingle of the memory in her toes. She still wasn't sure how she felt about his relationship anxiety, the way he seemed so skittish about commitment. She told herself she wasn't exactly looking for a ring on her finger either at the moment, but since she'd never had a casual one-night stand, she didn't know exactly how to do casual. All she knew at that moment was that Xavier made her knees weak, and she wanted more of him. Much more.

She knew how he took his coffee, and that he liked watching news shows, just like she did. They had so much in common, and yet there was so much she still didn't know about him.

Emma snuggled up on the couch with the blanket just as his phone sitting on the coffee table dinged. She recognized the sound: it was an incoming message from *Nost*. Emma glanced up at the closed bathroom door. Should she snoop? No. She knew she shouldn't. That was wrong. And yet… She couldn't fight the thirst for curiosity about this man. She wanted to know everything about him. Curiosity overcame her at that very moment. She pushed down the blanket and glanced at the phone, which was still lit with the new message.

Hey sexy. Let's get naked tonight.

The message sent a chill through her. A pit formed in her stomach. Now, unable to contain herself, she grabbed the phone and touched the message and his *Nost* app came up. The message was from a gorgeous brunette who wasn't afraid to use a string bikini shot as her profile picture. She was all cleavage and amazingly flat stomach, a little hoop through her belly button. She was blowing a kiss to the camera. Emma couldn't help herself then. She swiped through other messages. Xavier had dozens, and that was just in the last twenty-four hours. He'd also reached out to a few on his own just last night. *Last night.* Right before he texted her, he'd texted three other girls. With the clear intent to meet them. Emma bit her lip.

The betrayal hit her hard. Had he only reached out to her because the others hadn't responded quickly enough?

She felt the pit in her stomach grow bigger. Jealousy flared in her, taut and ugly, and yet she knew logically she had no reason to be jealous. He'd been up front with her, hadn't he? He'd told her he had no intention of being monogamous. He was the *founder* of *Nost*. Why wouldn't he still be using the app? Yet, all the gorgeous women, some even younger than her, made her feel nauseous suddenly. This was what Xavier's life was like: a phone full of beautiful women ready to take their clothes off for him, and he was only too happy to oblige them. She thought of her face in the roster, just one more in a never-ending list of conquests.

The room spun. *I can't do this,* Emma thought, panic in her throat. *I just can't.*

"Emma? What are you doing?" Xavier had come out of the bathroom and stood hesitantly outside the door.

Emma was caught, his phone in her hand. And she felt awash with another wave of new emotions: shame, guilt, embarrassment. She'd been caught snooping. Yet, now, she couldn't unsee what she saw. She wished she'd never looked at his phone. It was one thing to imagine him with other women. It was another thing to see their faces.

"I think you should go," Emma said, handing him his phone and wrapping the blanket tightly around her.

Confusion flickered across his face. "Emma… what?" Xavier took the phone reluctantly. He glanced down and saw the *Nost* app open. "Emma, you can't be mad about this. You know I'm not looking for anything exclusive. I thought… I mean, we talked about this."

"I know we did," Emma said, nodding, biting her lip to fight back the tears that threatened to spill. *I was just one woman among so many. He never cared about me. He isn't capable of caring about any one woman.* "I thought I could do it, but I can't."

Xavier moved forward, ready to join her on the couch. Emma, in a panic, stood, dropping the blanket on the floor.

"No," she said, shaking her head and wrapping her arms around herself. "I thought I could do casual. I just can't. I can't. The idea of you being with me and then all those other women…" She stared at his phone. "It makes me sick to my stomach. I thought I could do breezy and cool, but you know what? That's just not me."

Xavier stood, sadness stooping his shoulders. "You shouldn't have looked on my phone."

"I know." Emma hugged herself even tighter,

wishing she could take back the last five minutes, wishing she'd played it differently. But, then again, didn't she *need* to know?

"Why did you?"

"Because…because… I want to know. Everything about you. I guess."

"Now you know." Xavier glanced at the *Nost* app and frowned. "But I told you…this is who I am. I can't do commitment. I can barely even do more than a one-night stand. I told you."

"I know you did." Emma bit her lip, the tears forming a lump in her throat. He had been honest with her. It's not like he'd tried to hide his proclivities. "I thought I could do this. Imagining you with another woman…it hurts."

Now is the time for you to tell me that you'll change, Emma thought. *Now's the time to tell me that those women don't mean anything to you, that you're ready to take a chance on us.*

But when she looked up at him, Xavier stared at her helplessly. He seemed unable to give her what she wanted.

The two stood in silence for a moment, the weight of the impasse building an invisible wall between them.

Emma took a deep breath and tried to muster the courage to ask him the question she needed to ask, but was suddenly afraid of his answer.

"Would you have slept with one of those women last night if we hadn't met?"

Xavier glanced at the floor. "Yes," he admitted.

The admission hit her hard. It almost felt like a physical blow to her stomach, a deep jab. She took a step backward. She had no right to feel this hurt. He'd told her what he wanted, told her who he was, and yet, she couldn't deny the pain, the hurt, of realizing she was just a cog in a wheel, one more body among dozens.

Why couldn't she be enough? It was the question that bounced around her head, and made her feel small and insignificant.

"Would you ever not do that? Would you ever consider quitting *Nost*?"

Xavier ran a hand through his thick, jet-black hair. "Emma, I told you—"

"Yes, yes, I know. You're afraid of love. Of risking anything. You'd rather…" Emma bit back her words. She couldn't say them out loud. *You'd rather sleep with a new woman every day.*

Xavier took another step closer. "You knew this about me, Emma. I told you the very first day." Xavier reached up to hold her, but Emma jumped back.

"I know you did." She didn't want him touching her. Didn't want to melt back into his embrace and have all logic fly out the window. She didn't want to turn a blind eye to this, to pretend it was all okay with her. Because it wasn't.

"You seemed to be willing to try…" Xavier paused, seeming to have trouble putting a label on whatever it was they were trying.

He was right. She had been willing last night to

invite him into her bed. He'd not made any promises, really. He hadn't even said he wanted a relationship, exactly, only that he'd been drawn to her, intrigued by her. That had been enough last night for her to wiggle out of her panties, but now in the gray light of morning, with his phone dinging with incoming messages from strange women, it just didn't seem enough.

"I guess I was wrong." Emma couldn't look him in the eye. She wanted him to tell her that those other women didn't mean anything, that he could quit them anytime he wanted to, but the longer he stood there without saying those words, the more she came to be convinced that they mattered to him more than she did. "If you can't… I mean, if you have to keep seeing other women while you see me, then I can't do this."

"Emma." Xavier let out a long breath. "I just… don't know if I can do that."

"Would you even try, though? That's what I want to know." Emma met his eyes and saw the conflicting emotions there, and the conflict within him hurt her even more. Why didn't she mean enough to him to even say he'd *try*? She knew what they had was special, so why didn't he?

"Emma, what are you asking me to do? Not see anyone else?"

Emma nodded.

His phone dinged with another incoming message from *Nost*, another woman looking to have sex with him.

"Would you tell her, that one, right now, that you're not interested?" Emma pointed to his phone. He looked at it and then back at her. He hesitated too long. Now, whatever he said, she thought, might be a lie. "You need to go."

"Emma, come on. Let's talk about this."

Emma shook her head, the tears threatening to spill, and the last thing she wanted was for him to see her cry.

"Now," she said, marching to the door and opening it. Now would be the time for Xavier to tell her he'd try. That he didn't care about the women on his phone, that all he ever wanted was her. But, instead, he just grabbed his jacket and wallet from the chair in her living room and headed out. She didn't know what hurt more: the fact that he'd probably go right on out and meet one of his *Nost* conquests or that he left without a single backward glance.

CHAPTER SEVENTEEN

XAVIER SAT ON the Brown Line train, which would take him to the Loop, which would mean a quick walk to his condo. The cityscape rushed by outside, a blur of brownstone buildings out his window on the elevated train tracks, as they weaved through buildings toward the Fullerton stop. He thought of the look of hurt and betrayal on Emma's face and her eyes glassy with unshed tears as he left her apartment and couldn't help but feel a pang of guilt. Yet, why was he the one feeling guilty? He'd been honest about who he was. He didn't try to hide or lie about anything, and she still ended up hurt anyway.

He shook his head as he stared out the train's window. He should've known the very night he met her that this was a mistake. He knew she'd never done this before, had even been reluctant about trying it, and so he ought to have known she couldn't handle it. Xavier sat down and scrolled through his *Nost* app. It was probably for the best. She'd ended what he couldn't, and it would've just led to disaster anyway. Relationships didn't work. *Just ask Sasha.*

The train rattled to a stop and a few passengers got off. Then a sexy blonde got on. She wore knee-high black boots with stiletto heels, skintight leggings and a short black leather jacket. Xavier couldn't help but notice her as she slid down into a seat across from him on the train. She wore heavy smoky makeup and looked like she was headed out somewhere, even though it was only midafternoon. She made eye contact with him, her blue eyes serious in a look that told Xavier she was at minimum not disinterested. He hadn't shaved, and wore his clothes from last night, but there was no mistaking the fact that she'd noticed him. Then she dug out her phone. Seconds later, his own dinged with an incoming message.

He picked it out of his pocket and saw that the slinky blonde across from him had just sent him a message on *Nost*.

What's a fine man like you doing on the Brown Line? She'd written.

When he glanced up, there was no mistaking the look on her face: desire, interest, a decided invitation. *It has to be a sign,* he thought, a sign that he should try to forget Emma as soon as possible. Xavier smiled at the woman, and she grinned back.

Well, well, well. The universe just delivered a sign that he couldn't ignore.

Emma met Sarah that afternoon for a late lunch in Lincoln Square. The small Greek restaurant was half-full, despite the odd hour, though outside the weather had turned decidedly colder and the gray sky matched Emma's gloomy mood. Fall had arrived, and Emma sat at the table wearing an oversized scarf around her neck, still fighting off the chill outside despite having been inside for fifteen minutes. Then again, she felt like she hadn't been able to get warm since Xavier left her place that morning. She wondered if she'd ever see him again.

Emma had told Sarah the whole story, ending with Xavier's abrupt departure.

"It's all my fault," Sarah said. "I never should've turned you on to *Nost*. I knew you couldn't handle it."

"Exactly! This *is* all your fault," Emma moaned, but she didn't mean it, not really. "No, it's not, Sarah. You were just trying to get me laid."

"Well, at least you were successful there."

Emma sighed and rolled her eyes. "Too successful, actually. He was *so* good, though. In bed. He said it was because we were strangers, but do you buy that?"

Sarah considered this a moment, her fork paused over the salad she'd ordered. "Maybe. Sometimes. Rarely, actually. I mean, stranger sex can be great but it's always going to be on the surface. Like simply scratching an itch." Sarah took a bite of salad and nibbled. "Look, I love a good one-night stand, but nothing beats really knowing a person. The best orgasms happen after you drop the L-bomb."

Emma raised a skeptical eyebrow. "You've told someone you've loved them? When?"

"College." Sarah shrugged and pushed the salad

around on her plate. "Since then, I haven't found anybody else worthy."

Emma laughed. The hamburger that sat before her was largely untouched. She'd thought she wanted comfort food, but now, faced with it, she'd lost her appetite. She worried it had everything to do with Xavier. "Still, the queen of *Nost* believes in love."

"Sure I do. It's what we all want, isn't it?"

Emma picked up a French fry and chewed on it absently. "All of us except Xavier."

Sarah shook her head as she took a sip of her water. "I still can't believe the guy *started* the app. I mean, he must be a bizillionaire."

"Who knows? I don't even know where he lives." Or much else about him either. Except how he takes his coffee, and *the way he sounds when he comes*. The dirty thought popped into her head unbidden. Damn that man. Every time she thought of him, she felt a little tingle down the back of her legs.

"Oh, that would be easy to find with property records. I could look that up for you in a second."

Emma nibbled on another fry, chewing thoughtfully. "I'm almost tempted."

"It would only be mildly stalkerish," Sarah said.

Emma shook her head. "No. Not going to do it. He's a toxic bachelor, he admits it. Why would I want to get involved in that?"

"Because you already are," Sarah pointed out. "I can tell this is bothering you. Hitting you hard."

"I know!" Emma sank her head into her hands. "But why? We've only had sex a couple of times, and… I mean, I knew what I was getting into… But…"

"He's got a magic penis. Made of crack?"

Emma barked a laugh. "Kind of."

"Makes you do things you'd never do, and now you're addicted." Sarah wiped her mouth with her napkin, sounding as if she'd run into a crack penis before.

Emma nodded. "But I just *can't* do this casual thing. I tried, but the second I saw those other messages on his phone…"

"You felt like shit," Sarah finished as Emma sighed.

"Exactly. You should have seen him, Sarah. He was all, 'I told you about this.' He's never going to change. I can see it on his face. All those articles I read about commitment-phobes said the only cure is them *wanting* to change. Nothing else will help. And he doesn't want to."

Sarah gave a half shrug. "Leopards and spots. But I'll tell you one thing. If he doesn't realize how amazing you are, then let him go."

Emma felt weighed down and sad. She still didn't understand how such a quick relationship could affect her so deeply. She even had trouble explaining it to her best friend, but it all had to do with a feeling that their connection meant more, that somehow it was special, even if Xavier refused to see it.

"I don't know if it'll be that easy."

Sarah reached out and patted her friend's hand. "Well, I'm proud of you. You stuck to your bound-

aries, you know? You didn't cave. Casual isn't what
you want, and so you kicked him out of your place.
I don't know if I would've been able to do that."

"Oh, sure you would."

Sarah shrugged. "Nah. You're so good at not taking shit from people. Love that you're not afraid to
ask for what you want."

Emma smiled weakly at her friend. "Except that
Xavier's not going to give it to me."

"Who knows?" Sarah said, waving her fork in the
air. "He might come around yet. You're an amazing
woman, and if he doesn't see that, *he's* the fool. I
don't care how good-looking or rich he is."

"I hope you're right." Emma couldn't shake the
sinking feeling that no matter what, Xavier wouldn't
change. He'd warned her, after all. She remembered
the look of resignation as he left her apartment earlier that morning. He was stuck in his ways and not
about to change, for her or anyone else.

The waiter came with the bill and Sarah snatched
it out of his hand. "I'm getting this," she said. "Least
I can do since I caused all this drama."

Emma laughed. "I agree with that. You are totally
paying for this," she joked.

Back at her condo, Emma started working on a new
story for her editor, but no matter how she tried to
write a follow-up to her first Mr. X story, she just
couldn't seem to finish this one. With a jolt, she realized that part of the reason she had trouble writing
was that writing about it made it all final, somehow,

and she wasn't ready for that. Emma abandoned her Word document, with only two paragraphs written and a blinking cursor silently admonishing her that she'd need at least 800 more words to sell her editor. Instead, she pulled up a browser and typed *Xavier Pena* into Google.

Dozens of articles popped up about him being a tech prodigy, a cutting-edge app developer whose future was bright. Tinder had offered to buy him out, and reportedly at a hefty multimillion-dollar payout, though he'd yet to accept their offer or any-one else's. Sarah was right about his bank account at least. Xavier's social media accounts came up then and she clicked on them, finding them strangely bare of personal information. She expected to see an ac-count full of selfies with beautiful, willing fans, but instead, she found hardly anything posted by the *Nost* creator. His accounts, Instagram and Facebook were thin, with hardly any posts, and those that were there largely centered around *Nost* milestones and his dad, though a quick look through Instagram found a picture of a funeral, a snapshot of his father's pic-ture in front of a ring of memorial flowers. His fa-ther died a year ago.

He hadn't mentioned that.

She dug deeper to find an obituary to find out why he'd died. She read the small notice:

Henri Pena died of a heart attack. His wife, Gena, died eighteen years before. She struggled with bipo-lar disorder. Pena never remarried, citing Gena as the love of his life. He is survived by a son, Xavier...

Emma stared at the article online. Xavier lost his father a year ago. Then he lost his fiancé. The emotional trauma went much deeper than she realized.

Not exactly going to convince him that trying love again is a good idea.

Emma sighed. No wonder he didn't want to risk a relationship. She stared at Xavier's picture, wondering how she could convince him to try, and yet she knew it was out of her hands. He had to decide to risk his heart and his future. There was nothing she could do.

Emma pulled up her Word document once more and began typing.

The mystery woman from the subway train led Xavier by the hand to the steps of her apartment building and with a quick punch of numbers on a keypad, buzzed them both inside. On the stairwell, she turned and pressed her body against his, so that he felt the fullness of her breasts, even through her leather jacket, and even without kissing him, she reached up and gently massaged his groin, a bold, aggressive move that would normally have him standing at attention inside of a minute. But for some reason her touch felt clumsy and awkward, and he was keenly aware of her too-red lipstick. Everything about her was just…wrong. Not that she wasn't gorgeous—the woman could have any man she wanted, especially with that body—but there was something about her that was just lacking.

Xavier realized it was because she wasn't Emma.

Every time he looked at this mystery woman all he could think was: *her nose isn't as cute as Emma's. Her hands are bigger than Emma's. Her butt's almost too skinny. Not like Emma's.* No matter how hard he tried, he couldn't shut his brain off. She went on working him with her hand, but she was quickly finding him unresponsive. Would he not even be able to get hard?

That had never happened to Xavier before. Not once. *This woman before you is gorgeous. What's your problem?* A voice shouted in his head. But he knew exactly what his problem was: Emma.

"Kiss me," she murmured, flicking her hair back, too-red lips parted. Xavier didn't want to. That was the worst part. This woman was willing and sexy and he…didn't want to kiss her. Yet, he dipped his head and kissed her anyway. She slipped her tongue in his mouth, and ground against him. Every move she made just made him less turned on. Because she wasn't Emma.

When you fall in love, other women, they just aren't as beautiful, his father had told him. Xavier never believed him. Now, he wasn't so sure. He thought he'd loved Sasha, but he'd always been able to look at other women, appreciate them. Now, here with this woman from the train, objectively gorgeous, he couldn't even appreciate how sexy she was.

"Come on," the woman said, taking his hand and leading him down to the basement apartment—her apartment. Part of him wanted to flee. What was he doing here? He should go find Emma. Apologize, try to convince her that he'd been wrong.

Had he? Was he really going to turn Nost off? What would his co-workers say, what would the investors say? The headline: *Founder finds true love on No Strings website* didn't seem like it would exactly reel in users.

He followed the woman down the stairs and into her apartment as the door shut behind them. Yet, was he really going to do this? He glanced around at the woman's mismatched furniture, the clutter of junk mail choking the coffee table, an empty pizza box sitting on the kitchen counter. The apartment was nothing like Emma's carefully designed place, where every piece of furniture seemed made for the space, where she had her pots and pans neatly hanging from a rack above her sink. He could relax there all day. But here? No. Here would be a quick and dirty fuck and then he'd never see this apartment again. Or this woman. And he'd never know her name, either.

Normally, the idea of that turned him on, made him so hard he could feel the blood pulsating to his very tip, but that was before Emma. The thought of Emma made him want to go be with her. Made him want to see if she could rouse him where this woman couldn't.

Now would be the time that Xavier would normally pounce, where he'd work his magic on a stranger, but instead, he just stood in her living room feeling uncertain.

"What you say we get our freak on, Mr. X?" she

said, and her words jarred him back to reality. She grabbed his crotch once more, but it didn't respond to her touch. The strange woman didn't seem to care. She knelt before him and began to unzip his pants.

"How about I suck on you awhile?"

The idea of this woman doing that…well, he just knew it wouldn't work. Knew he wouldn't get hard.

"Wait," he said, stopping her. He couldn't believe he was doing this. He'd never turned down an offer like this before. Had he gone mad?

No, he could almost hear his father say. *No, you're just falling in love. Love is its own kind of madness.*

"Mr. X? Something wrong, sugar?" she asked him, as he pulled away from her. She pulled herself to her feet.

"I just… I'm sorry. I can't do this." He ran a hand through his hair while the woman just stared at him.

"Newbie, huh?" She crossed her arms across her chest, every move now skeptical. Apparently, she'd run into reluctant men on *Nost* before. That surprised Xavier. He hadn't realized men would be reticent. Not with a woman as gorgeous as this one in front of him. "Or married?" She quirked an eyebrow.

"Newbie," he lied. New to love, though, so it wasn't all a lie. He zipped his pants and backed out of her apartment, glancing back once at the disapproving look on the train girl's face. "It's not you," he said.

"Oh, hell, honey, I *know* it's not me." She sat on her sofa and crossed her fit legs, showing a flash of inner thigh. She shook her head as if to say, *you're missing out,* and part of him knew he was. Even as Xavier left, gently shutting the apartment door behind him, he still couldn't believe he was doing this. He never thought he'd ever feel about a woman the way he felt about Emma. Sure, he'd loved Sasha, but if a gorgeous woman had been on her knees offering him a little piece of heaven, he seriously doubted he'd be able to resist. Emma was different. Emma consumed his thoughts, made him want to be a better man. That was it, really. He'd need to try to be the man Emma deserved.

He flagged down the nearest cab.

All he wanted to do now was find Emma.

CHAPTER EIGHTEEN

ON HER WAY home from lunch, Emma made a few stops including the corner grocery store where she grabbed a few essentials for the week. Her hands laden with a couple of bags, she still felt a heavy weight on her shoulders as she thought about Xavier. She didn't know why he'd gotten to her so much, but then she knew why: she'd fallen for him. It was that simple. Sarah was right. He did have a magic penis, but he had more than that. She just felt she *got* him on a deeper level. She understood what it was like to grow up with two very dysfunctional parents as they tried to navigate the ups and downs of serious issues. As much as she wanted to make it just about the sex, it wasn't. If her own mother had stayed with her chronically depressed father she might have turned out just like Xavier: feeling that no matter what, love was a life sentence.

No wonder he was so riddled with relationship anxiety, unable to commit on the most basic level. But maybe she ought to let him go. After all, he didn't seem all that willing to change his ways. She remembered the expression on his face when she asked him about ever quitting *Nost*. His answer was plain to see: never. He was probably, right at that moment, texting another woman, figuring out a time to meet. Then she'd only know him as Mr. X. The thought sent a spike of jealousy into her brain, like an icicle, cold and unyielding. She hated that feeling.

The cold fall wind sliced through her thin utility jacket as she walked down the leaf-laden street near her condo. The sidewalk was surprisingly empty for a Sunday afternoon, and Emma figured the gloom and dark clouds above that threatened rain kept everyone inside. She felt a cold drop on her cheek and hurried her pace, hoping to make it to her condo before the rain hit.

Her phone dinged with the telltale sound announcing an incoming message from *Nost,* and she paused on the street. She'd forgotten she'd even had the app running at all, and made a mental note to delete it. After all, what was the point in being on it? She'd proven to herself that casual wasn't what she wanted, and the idea of floating around in the universe that Xavier created felt too painful suddenly.

She shifted the bags in her arms so that her right held them both, and then fished her phone out of her pocket.

Her heart lifted a bit. Maybe Xavier had texted her? Maybe he'd changed his mind? But why would he use *Nost*? He had her number.

Then she pulled up the message, from a handle she didn't recognize: *Cuming4U.*

Ugh, how cheesy, she thought, as she flipped open the message. She nearly stopped in her tracks. *Cuming4U* had the photo of the man in the Cardinals hat. He wasn't even trying to hide behind a fake photo anymore. *Here he was.* She clicked the link to read the full message.

Those bags look heavy. Want some help?

Goose bumps stood up on the back of her neck. Frantically, she glanced around her. Where was he? All she saw was a younger woman walking her dog across the street, and only one other couple walking away from her ahead on the sidewalk, hand in hand. No cars pulled by on the small side street, either. Where was he? She glanced at nearby condo windows, but saw no one. Still, she could almost feel his eyes on her, watching every move she made. Her own condo was more than a block away. Was he following her? How had he even found her? Was it just luck…or something more sinister?

She fumbled with her phone, trying to turn off her location setting, but even as she did so, she knew it was too late. In her haste, she dropped one of her grocery bags and an apple rolled out.

"Dammit," she cursed, stooping to pick up her groceries.

Another message from *Nost* dinged.

Love it when you bend over.

Now she just wanted to quit the app. She wanted him out of her phone, out of her life. She picked up the apple, shoved it into her bag and whipped the reusable tote over her shoulder. Another message followed.

Better watch it, or the apple isn't the only thing that's going to get bruised.

In a panic, Emma deleted the entire app off her phone. Her heart thudded in her chest as she frantically scanned her surroundings. Now it was just the woman walking the dog, who'd gone halfway down the block. The couple had turned at the corner, and the street was empty save for a few parked cars. Where was he? How was he watching her? She quickened her pace to her apartment, wondering what she should do: Call the police? They might laugh at her. What would she say? A mean guy is texting me? Claiming to be watching me?

Yet, the hairs on her forearms stood straight up. She knew with certainty that the man was nearby somewhere, and she knew he planned to hurt her. She remembered Xavier saying the man had a record, a history of assaulting women. She didn't know what to do, so she called Xavier. The phone rang once before he picked it up.

"Emma. I'm so glad you called, I…"

"Xavier. He's here. The guy who wore the Cardinals hat. Somehow he found me, but I don't know how. He's been messaging me and I think he's watching me. Can you talk to me while I get to my apartment? I'm just a half block away now."

"Emma, you need to call 911. Now." Xavier sounded panicked. "Get inside your apartment as fast as you can. I'm coming to you now. I'll be there as fast as I can."

Her heart thudded even faster as she threw a quick glance behind her. Still no sign of the man, but she knew he was watching her. She could feel it.

"Are you sure?"

"More than sure. Hang up. Now. Call 911."

"Okay," she agreed, suddenly even more afraid than she was before. She'd never heard Xavier sound so rattled. The fact that she wasn't overreacting to the situation didn't make her feel any better. Reluctantly, she hung up. Emma quickened her pace so that she was almost jogging as she headed to the stoop of her three-flat, which she could see. It was just about fifteen feet away. Emma fumbled with her phone, dialing *9-1-1*. She was about to hit send when she felt someone come up behind her. Then came the rough hand that slapped her arm and her phone went flying. She whirled in time to see the man she'd dreaded. He wasn't wearing his Cardinals hat now, but she'd recognize the cold glint of his gaze anywhere.

"Where you going so fast, Kitten?" he said, voice low and full of menace.

Xavier's heart leapt to his throat as he began his full-on sprint from the Brown Line L stop near Emma's condo. He'd already dialed his Chicago detective friend, Ian, who happened to be on duty not far away.

"I'll be there in five minutes," Ian said, and he could hear the whir of the siren of his unmarked police car in the background as he flicked it on.

"I'll be there in two," Xavier said, kicking it up a notch as he ran even faster, his arms pumping, his heart beating wildly in his chest.

Please let her be okay, he prayed. *If that asshole so much as touches her, I'm going to kill him,* he vowed as he skidded to the corner of Emma's street. All he had to do was turn and her condo was the third on the left. *Got to get there.* Every cell in his body worked frantically to propel him forward. He rounded the corner and saw what he most feared: Jimmy grabbing Emma. She was struggling against him, her tote bags full of groceries scattered on the deserted sidewalk. She was no match for his massive strength as he dragged her toward a nearby alley, his thick hand wrapped around her throat. She couldn't scream, could barely breathe. Xavier's blood ran cold.

"Jimmy!" Xavier shouted. "Stop!"

The man's massive head snapped up, as he focused on Xavier. He frowned, even as his grip on Emma's throat loosened and she screamed, frantically clutching at the man's massive forearm. Jimmy hesitated, obviously not wanting to let go of his victim, but after taking in Xavier's size and his speed, he must have thought better of holding on. Instead, he shoved Emma hard to the ground. She fell with her arms outstretched, but hit the ground hard on her palms and knees. Jimmy took off back down the street but his heavy frame meant he couldn't run that fast. Distantly, Xavier heard the siren of his detective friend. Thank God.

"Emma! You okay?" Xavier cried, stopping to help her up.

"Fine... I'm fine," she croaked, gently rubbing her neck. "Fine."

Xavier glanced up at Jimmy, who'd only made it about ten feet, but he clicked the remote on his key chain, opening up a car across the street. He was going to get away. That would not happen. Could not happen.

"I'll be right back," Xavier promised and sprinted to his feet, running as fast as his legs would carry him, taking the quickest route to Jimmy, who was in the middle of the street, just feet from his car door, when Xavier slammed into him and laid him flat on the ground. They fell in a tumble of limbs, and Xavier heard Jimmy's face hit the asphalt with a sickening crack. His nose maybe? But then the two men had tumbled to the ground, and Jimmy managed to pop up, arms swinging.

"You're going to regret that," he promised, wiping blood from his nose.

"I think you're going to be the one with regrets," Xavier promised. The sky opened up then and the rain came down, but Xavier hardly noticed. He was fixated on the large man in front of him. Not in shape, but heavy, and sometimes weight mattered more than muscle in a close fight.

Xavier had taken boxing lessons, so wasn't entirely out of his element. Plus, the man was going to be slower and tire easily. He jabbed and Xavier danced out of the way. Then Xavier swung, his right hook connecting at the man's chin, sending him backward. Jimmy lunged forward once more, but Xavier landed a hard blow to the man's stomach which sank him to his knees. A hard jab to the cheek toppled him then, even as the unmarked police car skidded to a stop in front of the men, lights flashing. Ian popped out of the driver's side, gun drawn.

"Hold it right there, asshole," he called to Jimmy. "Hands where I can see them."

Jimmy held his hands up, away from his bleeding face. Xavier backed away, hands up as well.

"Well, geez, X, looks like you didn't need me after all." Ian grinned. "Looks like you coulda handled this perp just fine."

"You better take him, Ian. 'Cause if you left him with me, I'd kill him."

Ian grabbed handcuffs from his back pocket. "Don't blame you," he agreed as he went about working Jimmy into a sitting position and handcuffing his wrists behind his back. "Jimmy, looks like you violated parole about eight ways to Sunday. You're going back for a long time."

"Fuck you," the man growled as he spat blood on the asphalt.

"Gotta love my job," Ian said. He glanced over Xavier's shoulder. "She okay?"

Xavier turned, to see Emma standing on the side-walk, tears streaming down her face.

"I'll make sure she is," Xavier promised as he crossed the street and swooped her up in his arms. Tears flowed down her cheeks.

"I thought you… I just worried. Thank God you're okay," she cried, squeezing him hard.

"Me? I'm fine. I could handle ten of that jerk. No problem." Xavier squeezed her to his chest. "It's okay. He's going away for awhile, too. You don't have to be scared."

They watched together as Ian put him in his un-marked squad car. "Bring her down to the station for her statement, okay, X?" he called as he ducked into the driver's seat.

"Will do." Xavier kissed the top of Emma's head. "You going to be okay with that?"

She nodded into his chest.

Xavier drank the stale coffee at the police station as he sat beside Emma and listened to her recount the horror of the afternoon. With every new detail, he felt like he ought to have hit Jimmy one more time. The guy got off easy. Xavier held Emma's hand the entire time, squeezing it to let her know she wasn't alone and that he was there.

All he kept thinking was: *What if I'd stayed with the sexy woman from the train?* If he'd done that, if he'd indulged, then what would have happened to Emma? Just the knowledge of how quickly things could've turned, how him *not* being there for her could've been such a disaster, made him feel sick with guilt. Yes, he'd made it on time. But he almost hadn't. And that was because of his stupid pursuit of…what? A pretty woman? Empty sex? Hadn't he been trying to fill the void inside him for more than a year with just sex with strangers?

He hadn't realized just how meaningless that life had been until he met Emma, until he felt the promise of something more. Now he realized that contentment couldn't be found in avoiding feelings. He'd just have to risk getting hurt, or not measuring up, or whatever love would ask of him, because he didn't want to live with the alternative: with Emma out of his life. When he thought about how Emma could've been hurt, all because he been too stubborn or too scared to admit that Emma was right, he wanted to hit himself. They did have a connection, a strong one, and he wasn't going to walk away from that.

The female officer across the desk finished taking her notes.

"Thanks for helping us," she told Emma. "I'll let you know if we need any more from you, but I think we're done for today. You have a ride home?" She glanced at Xavier.

"Yes," Xavier said. "I'll make sure she gets home."

She glanced at him, looking grateful, and as he sat there, holding her hand, he realized for the first time about what his dad meant when he'd said, *Love isn't something you choose. It chooses you.* He realized then that he didn't want to live a life without Emma. He didn't want her on her own, walking down sidewalks by herself with people like Jimmy out there. He wanted to be there for her, in every way possible. For the first time, he started to think that love wasn't a prison, it was a gift. His father hadn't been a slave to his mother, he'd signed up to protect her, no matter how hard that task would be.

Xavier held Emma's hand as they walked out of the police station.

It wasn't far from her condo, so they opted to walk. The sun had set and the air had turned colder. The street lamps were bright, but even so, Xavier worried about her. He studied her profile, wondering if she was still scared, if she felt at all uneasy.

"Are you okay? Walking in the dark, I mean?" He squeezed her hand.

"With you? Of course. I saw your right hook," she teased, and he laughed a little. "Where did you learn to fight like that?"

"Boxing classes." He shrugged.

"Is your hand okay?" she asked him. He glanced down at his bruised knuckles. The split on his second knuckle had already begun to scab over. "I'm fine," he said, hardly feeling the pain anymore.

"Thank you, by the way," she said. "I didn't get a chance to thank you before. But you saved me. Thank you."

"Don't thank me." He glanced down at the sidewalk, looking at the dark, wet leaves. The rain had come and gone, but the sidewalks still glistened beneath the streetlights. "I should've been here with you. If I had stayed, none of this would've happened."

"I asked you to give up too much. I realize that now," she said. "But, it was worth a try. I thought… maybe." They neared her condo now and Xavier felt her tense as they walked past the very alley where Jimmy had hidden in wait. He felt furious and helpless all at the same time as he ushered her past that spot. Thank goodness he'd gotten there in time.

"I don't think I want to go home," Emma said and slowed. "I just… I'm not sure I can sleep there."

Xavier pulled her into his arms. "Come to my place, then. Stay the night. Hell, stay as long as you want."

"You'd let me?"

"I wouldn't have it otherwise," he said, and then flagged down a cab that happened to be headed down her street.

They slipped inside the cab and Xavier held Emma's hand tightly, realizing this was the first time he'd ever let a woman into his condo since Sasha. He'd had his share of one-night stands, but they all happened in hotel rooms or their places…or…he thought, thinking of the white-hot sex with Emma behind a condo building, right outside. But he didn't feel anxious at all. He wanted Emma to see his place, wanted to invite her into his space and help her feel safe. It was the least he could do.

As they pulled up to his townhome in the west Loop, he paid the cab and then ushered her inside his brownstone. She stood in his foyer, eyes taking in his big staircase, his oversized living room and the granite island in his new kitchen.

"Wow," she said. "This is…beautiful." She noticed the pictures on his mantel above his wood-burning fireplace. The one old picture of his parents sat there, in the brown hues of the early 1980s.

"They look so happy," she said, studying the picture.

"Most of the time they weren't," he said, truthfully. "But sometimes, they were." He stood behind his couch, watching her. "That picture was taken before I was born. In fact, she was already pregnant with me at the time that was taken."

"Really?" Emma picked up the picture and studied it. Seeing her looking at the picture made him feel...understood somehow, though he couldn't figure out why.

"Are you hungry? Can I get you something to eat?" He asked her. "Maybe a drink? Some wine?"

"Is that what you tell all the girls you bring back here?" Emma joked, but the joke fell a little flat. There was too much jealousy in her voice.

"I don't invite anyone here."

Emma glanced up sharply.

"Not since Sasha," he said. "Wine?"

She nodded. He went to the kitchen and pulled out an expensive Pinot from his wine rack. She stood, uncertainly, as he popped the cork and poured two glasses. She rubbed her arms and stood awkwardly in the center of his living room. "Maybe coming here...it was a mistake."

He froze, midpour. "What do you mean?"

Emma frowned. "Maybe I should go."

CHAPTER NINETEEN

EMMA SUDDENLY FELT CLAUSTROPHOBIC. Being with Xavier at his home, she felt closer to him than she ever had before. Plus, she still felt rattled about what nearly happened. Her fingers tingled still, the echoes of adrenaline. All she wanted was to be warm and safe, and yet nothing about Xavier felt like either. Not when he seemed so dead set against a relationship with her.

"I don't want you to go," he said, putting a glass of wine in front of her on the light granite countertop. She studied the wine.

"I'm so thankful that you saved me, but being here, near you, it's hard." It felt even harder to admit. *I care about you,* she wanted to shout. *Hell, I'm falling in love with you.* Being close to him but knowing that he wouldn't be faithful felt like a knife slicing through her heart. She was almost tempted to readjust her standards, try to work around his lack of commitment, but she knew, in the end, she couldn't. She wanted a man who'd love only her. She'd tried no commitment, but it just wasn't for her. She wanted more.

"Is it?" Xavier put down his own wineglass and moved closer to her. "Is it hard to be close to me?"

Emma felt her resolve melting now that Xavier was close enough to touch. She wanted to put her hands on his strong, flat chest, wanted to touch him. Even after everything she'd been through that evening, even with the aftershocks of adrenaline still thrumming in her veins, she felt the pull to him, the irresistible tug.

"I think we should talk," Xavier said. Emma glanced up into his hazel eyes, studying her in the low light of the dimmed kitchen. She swallowed, almost fearful of what he'd say.

"You don't have to explain." *I've heard enough,* is what Emma wanted to say. *I know all about you, about your limits.*

"I want to, though. After I left your place this morning, I…" He paused and took a sip of his wine. "I met a girl. On a train. I went back to her place."

Stricken, Emma froze, her hands clutching the edge of the granite countertop, suddenly feeling like it was the only thing holding her up. She imagined a beautiful woman leading Xavier into her bedroom, a scene probably repeated dozens of times, if not hundreds. She felt so unwanted then, so lacking. They'd had sex just the night before and then the very next day…he needed someone new? Of course women would fawn over him. *Look* at him, and yet, the fact that he accepted her invitation just made her feel a cold, base rejection.

"What then?" Emma's voice was low, barely a

whisper. She'd asked the question, but she was almost positive she didn't want to hear the answer. She didn't want to hear about how he'd pleasured this woman, given her the best comes of her life, how he'd then come himself. Maybe in her mouth. Maybe inside her.

"All I could do was think of you," he admitted, eyes solemn as they met hers. "She wanted me, wanted to do things to me, but all I could do was think of you."

While you were fucking another woman, Emma thought bitterly.

"Did you make her come?"

He shook his head. "No," he said. "We only kissed. When I kissed her, I knew that she couldn't give me what I wanted. No one could give me what I wanted. No one except…" Xavier put down his wineglass and walked around the kitchen counter, now standing right next to her, so close, she could almost hear him breathing. "You. I want you, Emma Allaire."

She breathed in deeply, the spicy sweet smell of him, and felt a burst of hope light in her chest. "What are you telling me?"

He turned her to face him, and gently stroked her cheek.

"I'm falling in love with you. Actually, I'm in love with you already, Emma."

The words came as a shock, a surprise, like a bucket of cold water. What was he saying? Could it be true?

"You were right about me," he said, as he tucked a strand of blond hair behind her ear, his touch gentle, loving. "I was afraid I could never measure up to my father. To his dedication. I always thought it was because I didn't want to be weak, but I know he wasn't weak. Being faithful to my mother, that took real courage. Standing by her when she was sick, that wasn't weakness. It was strength."

"You don't have to be him. What he did for your mother, few could do." Emma couldn't break eye contact. She felt the warmth of Xavier's golden hazel eyes, the power in them, the magnetic pull.

"I probably can't be as strong as my father was, but I was afraid to even try," he said. "And when I think about how my fear hurt you…it makes me sick. Emma, if I'd stayed with that woman from the train, what could have happened to you? I could have really lost you."

Emma shuddered at the memory of Jimmy's rough hands on her, his big paw around her throat as he dragged her to a shadowy alley. The worst part had been the flat coldness of his eyes, the complete lack of humanity in them as he'd grabbed her. She swallowed, hard, and Xavier pulled Emma into his arms, squeezing her tightly.

"I want to make sure nothing bad ever happens to you, ever again," he promised, a murmur into her hair. She clung to him, hoping that was true, as a million emotions flooded her at once. "If you'll let me, I want to be your man. Your *only* man."

Emma pulled away and craned her neck to see

Xavier's face, her heart tinged with doubt. This man who'd been so committed to casual sex, she just couldn't imagine him giving it all up. "Are you sure? But what about the boredom of relationships and how it makes people cheat."

"I think it does for most people," he said. "But you and I know we're not most people."

Xavier dipped down and laid a sensual kiss on her lips, a small gesture that sent a current of want down Emma's spine.

He broke the kiss. "You'll quit *Nost*?" Emma asked, still feeling dazed by Xavier's reversal. Could this be true? Could he really want to commit to her? Leave casual sex with strangers behind?

"I'm going to do more than quit *Nost*," Xavier promised. "I'm going to take it completely offline."

"But your business!" Emma cried.

Xavier shook his head. "I can make a new app," he said. "I don't want *Nost* up and running if a sexual predator like Jimmy can take advantage of it. I don't want a single woman terrorized like you were because of something I made. I'm taking it down and not putting it back up until I can either fix it or replace it with something better."

Emma realized Xavier was one hundred percent serious. "But just because one guy…"

"No," Xavier said, sounding emphatic. "I can't take the risk that anyone else will be hurt."

Emma nodded. She felt so proud of him suddenly, so full of love for this man. "But what about sex with strangers? I mean, won't you miss it?"

"Not if I get to have sex with you," he said, pulling her closer. "You are the best thing that's ever happened to me, Emma Allaire."

"I don't know what to say," she admitted.

"Say you'll be mine," Xavier murmured in her ear.

"Yes, *yes*, always," she said before he claimed her mouth once more.

EPILOGUE

One year later

XAVIER SAT AT the bar alone, drinking his scotch, when a beautiful redhead approached him, wearing a tight black miniskirt and a low-cut halter top. She was just his type: athletic, leggy, gorgeous smile.

"This seat taken?" she asked, smoky eyes never leaving him, as she signaled the bartender. She ordered a Hendrick's and tonic, as Xavier took in the curve of her long legs and the strappy stilettos she wore that just screamed sex. Look at those amazing muscles in her calves, and her small, round ass. Probably tight enough to bounce a quarter off of, he thought. She gave him a small, *come hither* smile, everything about her posture screaming, *I want to play.* The bartender set the drink down and she lifted it in her delicate hand. Her pink pouty lips took their first sip of her drink and Xavier imagined them wrapped around his cock. His groin grew hard then.

They sipped their drinks, neither one looking at the other, each one all too aware of the other.

Then the redhead leaned over. "I don't usually do this," she said to him. "But do you want to fuck?" She licked her lips to show the invitation was serious.

"Emma—" He stopped. He'd almost ruined their game, calling her by name. She was quick to intervene, shushing him with a single flick of her fingertip.

"No names, remember?"

"Right. I forgot." Emma had outdone herself this time, Xavier thought. The makeup, the wig…she looked like a different person. It thrilled him, the naughty game they played.

Emma slipped her hand in her purse and then retrieved a key card for a hotel room somewhere above them. She slapped it on the bar.

"Let's go upstairs," she murmured, voice low. "I've got a room."

"I don't usually do this," Xavier said, getting into the role, looking uneasy as he unbuttoned the top collar of his shirt.

"There's a first time for everything," she said. "That card is for you. I'll be waiting for you upstairs."

Emma slid off the stool, giving her red wig a pat with one hand, as she swayed her hips on her way to the elevator. Xavier would take her hard there, like he would a stranger, reliving the thrill of it all. He thought of the last year, of how he'd had Emma in so many ways, the hours they'd spent cuddling, getting to know one another, and now…the role play. They both worked together to find creative new ways to keep their sex sizzling. She truly was the perfect woman for him. He couldn't imagine sharing his life with another.

He slapped cash on the bar for the bartender and then slipped off his stool. Eager to join his "new" lover.

"You're a lucky man," the bartender told him, having overheard it all.

"You have no idea," Xavier said as he snatched the key card off the bar.

* * * * *